# Looking for
# *Ginseng*

Looking For Ginseng

Copyright © 2017 by B. S. Todd.

Printed in the United States of America

Editing by Teri@editingfairy.com
Book Formatting by Derek Murphy@Creativindie.com
Bookcover image@pixabay.com

Paperback ISBN: 978-0-9991169-1-3
Ebook ISBN: 978-0-9991169-0-6

Library of Congress Control Number: 2017909426

First Edition: 2017

10 9 8 7 6 5 4 3 2 1

# Looking for

# Ginseng

## A Cloverly Wolves Novel

# B. S. TODD

# One

*Jesse*

*Does this road ever end?*

Jesse leaned against the shoulder strap as the comforting rhythm of country music played softly on the radio. The four-hour drive would have been the perfect opportunity for sightseeing, but once the sun set, everything became one big mass of darkness, a sight she didn't care to observe.

Pulling herself out of the seatbelt, she lay across the bench seat and adjusted her body to a more comfortable position. The large box truck wasn't the easiest place to catch a few zees, but after packing boxes all day, she was more than exhausted. As the truck continued down the highway, her breathing eventually regulated and she drifted off to sleep. It wasn't until she heard a door slam that her eyes shot open and she realized the truck had stopped moving.

The cool night air and pervasive smell of gasoline filled the cab, causing her breath to hitch and her eyes to water. "Where are we?" The first thing out of her mouth was a simple enough question. Too bad her dad wasn't there to give her the answer.

Startled by the silence, she bolted upright in the seat and her legs bumped against the cat carrier that occupied most of the passenger side floorboard. "Sorry, Moose," she whispered as she leaned forward, looking up through the windshield. The single incandescent bulb from the overhead lamppost lit the area between the gas pump and truck, but did little to ease her mind. *You're at a gas station; relax.* But that couldn't stop the goosebumps from prickling her arms as she scanned the gravel lot.

Jesse looked past the pump to the small cinderblock building, cast in shadows from the towering trees that surrounded it. She noticed the interior light first, and then her dad, who was standing at the counter, waiting for the cashier to shuffle in behind the register. The cashier nodded and placed the money in the till before looking out the window—his green eyes flashed in the darkness.

She jerked back, pressing her body against the seat and turning her head to avoid eye contact. *That was creepy,* she thought, staring across the highway. She scanned the tree line as shadows danced with the swaying branches and wrapped her arms around her body to ward off a shiver. *And this is better?*

Hidden behind a thin layer of clouds, the moon dimly lit the area as the burning stare from unseen eyes crept over her. She sucked in a breath. *Stop it! There's no one there!* Even so, she quickly reached over and pushed the door lock down before rolling the window up.

"Welcome to Cloverly," the cashier said as he followed her dad out the door, drawing her attention back to the building.

"Thank you. It's good to be home," her dad replied, pulling open the driver's door.

Daring a glance towards the stranger, Jesse couldn't see his eyes for the shadow that fell across his face. *See? It's just your imagination,* she thought as an orange glow highlighted his features. He flicked the cigarette through the air, and it hit the ground in a shower of red sparks. "What an idiot," she mumbled as her dad slid into the seat beside her and started the truck.

Sparing one last glance over her shoulder as the truck turned onto the highway, the man was no longer in sight.

"What are you looking for?" Dr. Williams asked as he reached over and adjusted the volume on the radio.

"Nothing, I just never noticed that gas station before."

"That's because it's not usually open this late at night."

"How late is it?" she asked as they passed the *Welcome to Cloverly* sign.

"Midnight."


Morning came early as Jesse stretched out on the mattress and yawned. After multiple dreams of green eyes chasing her through the woods, she was glad when daylight crept between the curtains. She looked up at the black, spiral staircase that led to a small roof hatch in the center of the ceiling. That was something she would definitely check out as soon as she found the time.

Rubbing the sleep from her eyes, she rolled over to confront the sea of haphazardly stacked boxes and bags. *I'm really here.* She smiled as she crawled off the mattress, slowly making her way around the cluttered room to the window bench that overlooked the tree line.

"Here kitty, kitty," she called out as the gray tabby pattered his way between the stacks of boxes. "What do you think of your new home, Moose?" She picked up the cat and giggled when he nudged her chin. "I agree; I think you will love it here."

Moose sat on the bench while she opened the box nearest the window and pulled out a pair of white shorts and a pink paisley top. Excited to start her day, she changed her clothes and twisted her curly, black hair into a messy bun. It probably wasn't the prettiest sight, but it would do. She then slipped on her sneakers and walked out the door.

"A beautiful day this is going to be," Jesse sang out of tune while walking into the kitchen and hugging her grandmother. The smell of coffee and cinnamon drifted in the air, causing her stomach to rumble.

"Good morning, sunshine." Her grandmother patted her arm and reached for a cup in the overhead cupboard. "I didn't expect you up so early. Did you sleep well?" Gramma asked, handing Jesse the cup of coffee she had just poured.

She wasn't about to tell her grandmother she had only gotten a few hours' sleep, due to the anxiety from the night before. Her grandmother would more than likely offer her a room on the second floor, and she preferred the attic bedroom. "I was too excited to sleep. I have so much to do, and with it being my first full day as a resident of Cloverly, I don't want to miss a single second." She leaned against the counter, sipping her coffee gratefully while her grandmother busied herself about the kitchen. "I left Lori a message; she and Megan should be here soon."

"I'm surprised they weren't here last night." Her grandmother pulled another cup from the cupboard.

"They probably would've been, but I didn't tell them I was coming. I wanted it to be a surprise," she said with a glance around the kitchen. The large farmhouse sink and white-windowed cabinets dated the room, along with the old, daisy-shaped clock that hung on the wall above the round top refrigerator. She smiled and placed her cup in the sink and pushed away from the counter. "Gramma, if you need me, I'll be out on the front porch."

Jesse moseyed through the house, reveling in the warmth of family memories that lingered inside the rooms as she made her way to the front door. She stepped out onto the porch where hanging ferns cast soft shadows on the white clapboard siding in the early morning light. She loved everything about the old farmhouse, but especially the tall windows and wrap-around porch. Some of her happiest memories occurred right there on that porch.

A horn sounded in the distance and she glanced down the road. Growing up in a large city, the neighborhood in Cloverly was the polar opposite of what Jesse was used to. Quiet and somewhat secluded, Cloverly was a small town bordered by farmland, forest, and a low-lying river toward the west. To her, however, it was sheer paradise.

The warmth of the sun greeted her as she walked off the porch and followed the sidewalk to the edge of the woods that ran alongside her house. Her mind drifted back to the gas station when she reached into the bristly branches of a huge tree. Slowly withdrawing her hand, she allowed the soft pine needles to slip through her fingers. *See? There's nothing to be afraid of.*

Sunlight filtered through the branches as she stepped past the tree line and the woods around her came to life. Birdsongs drifted overhead and a lone squirrel jumped from branch to branch, making her wonder what other animals lived there. Jesse loved all animals, but most of all, her cat. Soft meows drifted down from the window and she stepped out from beneath the trees and glanced up to where Moose was pacing back and forth, his fur rubbing against the window screen.

"Moose, get out of that window!" Jesse yelled as a familiar voice called out from the street and she looked back over her shoulder. Chestnut-brown hair, mingled with a pair of arms waved frantically out the car's window and she instantly knew it was Lori. Squealing with delight, she raced down the steps, forgetting about Moose as Megan pulled the little, red car over to the curb.

As quickly as Lori could throw open the passenger door and jump out, Jesse caught her in a fierce hug. "Look at you; you look great!" She stepped back for a better view and Megan joined them in a group hug.

Jesse smiled, thinking back to the day they met. They had been best friends since she was ten years old after meeting on the sidewalk in front of Lori's house, two doors down. She was roller-skating that day when she noticed Lori and Megan playing at the corner house. After introducing herself, she handed her skates to Lori, and sat down on the concrete porch to play dolls with Megan. Lori spent the rest of the afternoon skating up and down the sidewalk as Jesse and Megan waved, smiling happily each time she passed. Later that evening, she invited the girls to supper, and over pizza and soda pop, the three girls sealed their friendship.

"What time did you get in? It had to be late because I didn't get your message until this morning. And I brought you a nightlight," Lori said through a yawn.

"After midnight. We haven't had time to unpack everything yet, so I was hoping I could get some help from my two favorite people. And there are fresh cinnamon rolls in the kitchen if you're hungry." Jesse grinned as they followed her up the driveway to the opened box truck that was parked beside the house. Bribing them with food was a brilliant idea because they would do just about anything for her grandmother's homemade cinnamon rolls.

The muddled expression on Lori's face when she noticed the mountain of boxes in the back of the truck made Jesse laugh. "Surely you didn't pack all this for a two-month stay," Lori said.

"Surprise!" Jesse said, throwing her hands in the air. "You're looking at the newest resident of Cloverly."

"You're kidding! You moved here?" Megan twisted her hips and danced around, a clear indication of how thrilled she was. Then she frowned when Lori grabbed her by the shoulders, halting her steps.

"This is a geriatric neighborhood. Do you mind?" Lori grumbled as Megan fell into a fit of giggles and Jesse pulled her from her grasp.

"I'm sorry. I should have told you sooner, but I wanted to surprise you. Dad's replacing Dr. Sanders at the end of the month."

"If you think that will get you off the hook, you are so wrong. I'm mad at you! You said you were going to spend the summer with us and when you didn't call, I thought you changed your mind and went to D.C. instead," Lori pouted.

"I did go to D.C. for two weeks, which is why I'm so late getting here. Mom wasn't happy that I wasn't spending the summer with her, but with Joey in Little League, she knew that most of their time would be occupied with him, so she caved," Jesse said as she repeatedly jabbed Lori with her elbow until she smiled.

Unable to contain her excitement any longer, Lori swatted her away and laughed as Megan bounced on her toes, causing her strawberry-blonde curls to flop around her head. "She's like a little jack-in-the-box. When she gets wound-up, she pops."

"I'm excited, okay? So back off, and pull that stick out of your butt," Megan retorted as she climbed into the back of the truck.

"I'm excited she's here too, but this is *Cloverly*. Who in their right mind moves to a small town like this intentionally?"

"Well, I don't care why you moved here," Megan said, passing boxes down from the truck. "I'm just glad you're here." She jumped to the ground and Jesse grinned as they followed the sassy blonde into the house. Standing every bit of five feet tall, Megan was probably the strongest of the three.

"There're my girls," Gramma said, holding open the front door. "If you're hungry, I have breakfast and coffee in the kitchen."

"Thank you, it smells wonderful." Megan kicked up

her knee to readjust the large box she was holding.

Jesse shifted her boxes to one arm and scooped Moose up off the floor. "What are you doing down here?" She nuzzled the gray feline before introducing him. "Lori, Megan, I'd like you to meet Moose."

"Wow, Moose, you're a big boy. The name's fitting." Lori reached out but quickly pulled her hand back when Moose growled. "Somebody needs catnip."

"Ha! That makes two of you. Ignore her, Moose, she's being ugly today," Megan said as she walked past, but apparently, Moose wasn't impressed. He reached out and snagged the sleeve of her shirt.

"Moose! Where are your manners?" Jesse scolded when he wedged his head beneath her arm. "I'm sorry; he's never done that before. He didn't scratch you, did he?"

"No, but he killed my sleeve." Megan laughed. "But don't be too hard on him. Most cats keep their distance because I'm more of a dog person, and I think they can sense it," she said before following Lori to the attic bedroom.

"You've got to be kidding me." Lori placed her box on the floor. "Is there really a room here, because I don't see one?" She looked back as Megan and Jesse walked into the room.

"Well I'm hoping to bring order to the chaos," Jesse said, placing Moose on the floor, along with her boxes. "We were in a hurry to unload as much as we could last night, so some of these boxes belong to Dad. But with my two besties helping out, I'm sure we'll have this room shipshape before nightfall." Jesse flashed a smile before merrily heading back down the stairs.

# Two

## Jesse

Trudging the heavy boxes up two flights of stairs became a chore all its own as the unpacking continued late into the afternoon. Jesse laughed while sorting through a box of sewing supplies and Lori and Megan giggled and goofed off—making Jesse's jaws ache from the entertainment they offered. "I really do appreciate your help," she said between bursts of giggles.

"Are you kidding? You couldn't keep us away if you tried." Lori chucked a purple teddy bear across the room and Jesse snatched it out of the air as her dad peeked around the door with a grin on his face.

"Cowards," Jesse said when Lori and Megan ducked behind the boxes, laughing.

"Anyone hungry? I brought pizza," Dr. Williams said, stepping into the doorway of what used to be his childhood bedroom.

"I'm starving," Jesse exaggerated as she tossed the teddy bear over the boxes, causing Megan to screech. She grinned and Lori's head popped up when she lifted the top of the pizza box, fanning the smell of pepperoni into the room. That was all it took to coax Lori out, and Jesse winked up at her dad. "So what do you think?" Jesse asked, trying not to laugh while watching Lori carry the pizza over to the mattress that lay on the floor in the corner of the room.

Dr. Williams chuckled when Lori bit into a large slice of pizza and moaned. He swore she had a tapeworm, considering how thin she was and the amount of food she could eat. "I think you have more boxes than I do." He stepped further into the room.

"Don't kid yourself. Some of these belong to you and you know it." Jesse handed him a small box.

"This is the thanks I get for bringing pizza?" Dr. Williams waved as Megan moved out from behind the boxes, her face turning red as her sneakers. She waved back.

"Yes and there's more where that came from," Jesse warned.

"Stack them by the door and I'll get them later." He handed her a six-pack of sodas and sauntered out of the room.

"Thanks, Dad," she called out before joining Lori and Megan on the mattress.

"I still can't believe you moved here," Megan said, lying back and rubbing her belly.

"By the time we get those boxes emptied, you'll believe it," Lori groused, shoving the last bite of pizza into her mouth.

"Yeah, but I figured Jesse would be on her way to college and we would never see her again." Rolling over onto her side, Megan propped up on her elbow and pooched out her bottom lip.

"As if. I love you guys, and I love Cloverly too, which is why I'm going to let life lead me for a while. Who knows what opportunities await me here?"

"You're delusional if you honestly think there are any opportunities here," Lori sarcastically replied. "This place isn't even on the map."

"I don't care." Jesse had always wanted to live in Cloverly, and now that she could, she intended to make the best of it. "What about you, Megan?"

"I told you last year what I wanted to do. And I'm still willing to share a space with you if you're interested?"

Jesse and Megan had talked in great depth about opening a business, which was why Jesse had worked so hard over the past year to build her inventory. She didn't expect to get rich, but with proms, weddings, and a limited number of stores to shop at, she hoped to sell a few of her designs locally. "It sounds great, but I need to get settled in first." Jesse walked over to the window and the afternoon breeze carried the smell of honeysuckle into the room. As she stared out the window, Megan squealed and Jesse practically jumped out of her skin.

"Do you know what this means? You're finally gonna meet Brian!" Megan clapped excitedly.

"Not if I have a heart attack first," Jesse complained, causing Lori to snicker.

"No, seriously." Megan pulled back the curtain at the front window. "I think you two would make a cute couple."

"Aren't you getting a little ahead of yourself there, sweet pea?" Lori chuckled, glancing between the two.

"But he's cute," Megan insisted as the curtain fell back into place. "His name is Brian Edwards and he lives right across the street."

"Ducks are cute. You have to give me more than that," Jesse said, pushing the curtain to the side. The glare from the afternoon sun was bright as it reflected off the windows of the split-level house across the street. The house itself had a unique look with brick at the bottom and vinyl siding at the top, but it didn't quite fit the neighborhood. Her eyes followed the roof line to the privacy fence that surrounded the backyard. From what she could see, large sliding glass doors opened up to a patio at the side of the house, and further out in the yard stood two large trees. She tittered as the curtain fell back into place. "So what's wrong with him?"

"Nothing, he's a fireman... and you know what they say about firemen." Lori grinned. Finally, her smutty best friend had arrived and she laughed when Megan rolled her eyes.

"You're vulgar. That's all I'm saying." Megan lifted her hand and snubbed Lori. "Brian spends his summers at Camp Semiway. He's a counselor there. Well, he used to be until this year. With his new job, he only has two weeks that he can volunteer now."

"Then what's the catch? I mean If he's all that, why is he still single?" Jesse looked back toward the window as Megan opened another box.

"I promise he's dated plenty of girls. He just hasn't found the right girl for him." Megan winked.

"If he's as great as you say, why aren't you dating

him?"

"Yuck! That would be like dating my brother," Megan gagged.

"You mean like Randy? Despite what Megan says, the only reason she doesn't have a boyfriend is because she won't give Randy the time of day." Lori wrinkled her nose when Megan stuck out her tongue.

"That's not true. I did go out with him, twice, but he's not my type."

"He rides a motorcycle for Pete's sake! How can he *not* be your type?"

"Maybe I don't like motorcycles," Megan said, trying to keep a straight face.

"Randy wags after her like a lovesick pup. I think she likes playing hard to get."

"Excuse me, but *love* is not a word in Randy's vocabulary. Love could bite him on the butt and he'd think he had fleas. Nope, love is definitely not a word he knows," Megan countered.

"See what I mean? She thinks he's a flirt, but I think it's his playful personality." Lori snubbed her nose.

"Wait a minute. Are we talking about the spindly, little, dark-haired pest that chased us around the neighborhood with frogs?" Jesse asked.

"That's him all right, but these days, he's not the one doing the chasing. He's all grown up and hot to boot." Lori faked a swoon.

"Well, if Randy's so hot, what does that make Brian?" Jesse asked, but Lori and Megan ignored her.

"Where would you like the bed? Pick a spot. You are not sleeping on the floor for a second night. This place could have spiders crawling everywhere," Lori said, changing the subject. The disgusted look on Jesse's face made her laugh. "Well, it's true! This house is like Civil War-old." She lifted the iron headboard away from the wall and rolled it across the floor.

Jesse scowled at the mattress as if that would do any good. She never considered the threat of spiders when she went to bed the night before and she shivered. "Umm, I think the bed would look good closer to the window, but not against the wall," she quickly added. "About here, I think." Jesse put her arms out, showing Lori the spot she had chosen, but as she gauged the distance from the wall to the bed, a movement out the window caught her eye.

"Holy moly!" Jesse marveled at the shirtless hunk in the neighboring yard. He stood tall next to his car with well-defined muscles and enough skin showing to turn her PG-rated thoughts to R.

Lori leaned over and pulled back the curtain. "That, my dear, is Jack, your new, hot-as-hell backyard neighbor. He's one fine-looking man. Most definitely drool worthy, but seriously stuck-up."

"Please, you would drool over any man not wearing a shirt," Jesse joked, leaning closer to the screen.

"What can I say? It's been a hobby of mine since I was fourteen." The flick of her brow was expected and Jesse rolled her eyes. Only Lori could say something like that and make it the truth.

"Let me see." Megan hurried across the room and ducked under Jesse's arm.

"Do you know him?" Jesse asked, looking down.

"No, not really. But I've seen him going into the bookstore. And he's not stuck-up."

"How would you know if you've never talked to

him?"

Jack looked toward the house before turning back to his car. "Oh crap! Do you think he heard us?" Megan dropped to the floor and peeked over the windowsill, despite the snickers from the other two.

"Doubtful." Jesse laughed.

"Hey, Megan, I dare you to flash him," Lori urged and Megan's face turned a deep shade of red. "It's a great conversation starter."

"I don't think so," Megan stomped back across the room.

"I was only kidding, but I do think you should talk to him." Lori nudged Jesse. "She has a secret crush on the guy; she just won't admit it."

"I'll pass. I have enough going on as it is, and he would be nothing more than a temporary distraction." Megan dismissed him with a wave of her hand.

"Oh, please. I could use more distractions like him in my life. You know, all work and no play will find you sitting home on a Saturday night. You need to walk on the wild side and live a little," Lori said, turning back to the bed.

By the time evening rolled around, the mountain of boxes that once stood in the center of the room were emptied and crushed down, with only a handful left to unpack. "Jesse, how do you want the fabric arranged on the shelves?" Megan looked down into yet another box of cloth.

"It doesn't matter. I'll organize everything when I have more time." Jesse yawned and carefully placed Moose on the window bench. "I can't believe how different this room looks."

The room had taken shape over the course of the day after all the dusting, sorting, stacking, stashing, and unpacking. The musty blue curtains were happily replaced by pink lace, which matched the pink and purple quilt Lori draped over the bed. And although the white walls were somewhat boring, the new material Megan was stacking on the floor-to-ceiling bookshelf added plenty of color to the room. "Thanks again for helping me. I couldn't have done this without you guys," Jesse said as a low growl resonated around the room and Moose bristled in the window.

"It's not because of me this time," Megan chuckled.

Jesse sat down on the bench and peered out the window as the cat growls turned into a hiss and then Moose bolted under the bed. Unable to shake off the spidery chill that crawled up her spine, she rubbed her arms. "Shut off the light," she whispered to Megan. Unprepared for the darkness that instantly engulfed her, she froze. "Lori, I thought you brought a nightlight?"

"I did. It's still in Megan's car." Lori inched her way toward the bench, bumping into the last of the boxes along the way. She cursed under her breath as she locked arms with Jesse and the two huddled at the window.

"Do you hear that?" Megan whispered while walking over to join them.

"No," Lori said.

"How can you not hear that?" Megan whispered again. She knelt down beside Jesse. "There's something moving through the trees. It's getting closer."

"Shh," Jesse replied. But as branches snapped below, she fell backward, knocking Lori to the floor before both rolled away from the window.

"What the hell?" Lori squawked while scooting up against the staircase.

"I don't know." Jesse shuddered.

"It was probably a deer," Megan said. Walking across the room, she flipped on the overhead light.

"Or a wolf," Lori countered, hugging her knees to her chest.

"I could be wrong, but I don't think we have wolves in this area," Jesse said, reassured by her knowledge of the local wildlife. She grabbed the side of the window seat and pulled herself up off the floor.

"Not according to the local legend," Lori mumbled. "Do we have bears? I'm pretty sure we have bears."

"No, it wasn't a bear. It was probably a deer." Jesse laughed, although she wasn't totally convinced herself.

"You say that now, Miss I'm-scared-of-the-dark, but I've read the stories, and I, for one, am glad I don't live next to the tree line." Lori smirked.

"So I guess that rules out you spending the night?"

"You got that right,"

"Sorry, but I can't stay either. I have to rise with the roosters, which means I should be getting home," Megan chimed in.

Two hours later, Jesse plumped her pillow and crawled into bed while adoring her new bedroom. Happily snuggled beneath the quilt, enjoying the cool night breeze sweeping through the window screen, she pulled back the curtain as headlights lit up the backyard. Expecting to see her sexy new neighbor when the lights shut off, her anticipation fueled her smile.

# Three

*Jesse*

"Gramma, why didn't you wake me this morning?" Jesse asked as the smell of freshly mown grass teased her nose, a true sign summer was just around the corner.

"With all the unpacking you girls did last night, I figured you needed the extra sleep," Gramma said as she stepped toward the doorway of what looked like an old wooden outhouse. Her flower-print gardening gloves clashed with the long-sleeved, plaid blouse she wore and her black plastic kneepads bunched up the light blue denim around her knees.

"You know how much I love working in the garden," Jesse said, glancing into the rustic, little shed, which was wide enough for a push mower and a few garden tools, but had seen better days. It leaned slightly to the left, causing the wood door to hang ajar; and if it weren't for the large holly bush at the back corner, it would have probably fallen down.

"I remember quite well." Gramma chuckled and Jesse grinned.

"In my defense, I'd never seen a baby snake before. I thought it was an earthworm." She glanced over at the pink rambling rose bush on the far side of the yard where she released "Frieda," the principal reason she never ventured back to pick the flowers. She shuddered.

"Yes, you were a delightful, little sprite back in the day." Gramma grabbed a straw hat off the rusty hook beside the door and slapped it against her hip before placing it on her head.

Jesse's jaw dropped. "There could be spiders in that hat!"

"Only if they survived the slap."

The idea of spiders crawling down her neck made Jesse's scalp prickle. "I'm here to work. Just tell me what you need me to do." Jesse followed her grandmother to the garden as a slight breeze lifted her hair. Wearing denim shorts that exposed the length of her legs and a light lavender tank top that complemented her complexion, she was ready to dazzle the daylights out of the dark-haired stud in the adjacent yard. She glanced down at the white, open-toed sandals that did little to keep her feet dry and groaned when the moisture seeped between her toes. It was not something she was expecting and she looked back towards the cabin, glad Jack wasn't outside to witness the green, furry feet she sported.

It took Jesse a couple of hours to rake out the tilled garden while her grandmother pulled the remaining weeds. "So that's your secret," Jesse said as she leaned the rake against the scroll-top fence separating the yards. She looked down at the soft blister that had formed between her thumb and index finger. She should have worn gloves but unlike her grandmother, she wasn't taking any chances with spiders.

"Calcium is good for tomato plants." Gramma lightly packed the crushed eggshells around the young plants.

As the sun rose in the noonday sky, Jesse lifted the hair off her neck and a stream of sweat trailed down her back. "Gramma, you need to cool off. I'll clean up the mess," Jesse said, noticing the flush on her grandmother's face. She helped her off the ground and waited until she was inside the house before gathering up all the tools. Once she had everything put away, she placed wire cages over the tomato plants and walked over to sit down beneath the large oak tree in the far corner of the backyard.

The shady cold made her shiver and Jesse looked over her shoulder, noticing the footpath that led into the pine-scented forest. With a quick glance towards the house, she stood up and inched her way behind the tree, chewing her lip as she studied the path.

Over the years, her grandmother had frequently warned her against going into the woods, but she was an adult now, almost eighteen, and perfectly capable of self-survival. Surely a few steps ventured in wouldn't hurt, and her grandmother would never have to know.

Grinning, she hurried along the path as sunlight streamed between the branches. Comforted by the light, she eventually stepped off the trail as a blue-tailed lizard zipped down the side of a maple tree and beneath the canopy of a poison ivy vine. Mindlessly scratching her arm, she continued walking deeper into the woods, where despite her isolation, she felt safe.

Moisture tickled her nose as she looked down at the large, flat stones resting on the bottom of a narrow creek bed. She kicked off her sandals and jumped into the shallow water and an icy tremor ripped through her body. Once the initial chill had passed, she stomped and splashed around, laughing at herself for acting like a child. Finally, when her feet were sufficiently clean, she shook off the last drops of water and slipped on her shoes.

The cushiony pine needles beneath her feet caught her attention and she froze. The area was quiet, eerily beautiful, and she glanced up at the thick canopy that blocked out the sun, making it somewhat dark. "This is just great." She stepped back onto the path, suddenly unsure of which way to go.

Twigs snapped in the distance, and she peered through the trees as her heart jumped up to her throat. She listened closely but nothing moved. No birds fluttered, and even the breeze had died down. She swallowed hard as she reached into her pocket and realized her cellphone was charging on the nightstand. Another twig snapped, shattering the silence, and she stumbled back against a tree.

"Who's there?" her voice cracked and her body trembled. "Is somebody there?" Jesse stared into the shadows, her imagination darkening the area even more. *You had to take a walk, didn't you?* She knew better than to enter the woods, and now she would have to explain her lame-brained adventure to her grandmother. That is, assuming she lived to tell the tale.

She darted about, searching for something to use as a
weapon, and spotted a large stick half hidden beneath a
vine. Grabbing hold of the stick, her body fell forward, but
the stick didn't move. "A tree root!" She stood up and
angrily kicked the root, sending her sandal flying into the
underbrush. Hopping on one foot, she quickly retrieved
the sandal and slipped it back on. With images of wolves
and bears flashing through her mind, she wrapped her
arms around her waist as sweat beaded across her
forehead.

"That was entertaining." The deep, sultry, voice
caught her offguard, and she spun around as her hand
landed on her chest. Greeted by beautiful, sapphire-blue
eyes, Jack was easily six feet tall with sooty, black hair
that was damp with sweat. She glanced down at the shirt
draped over his shoulder and drew in a calming breath.
*Great! Now he thinks you're staring at his chest.* Her eyes
swiftly descended to the shorts hanging low on his hips.
*Don't look down!* She quickly looked back up, her face
burning beneath a blush. The amused grin on his face only
deepened her blush, and if she could have found a rock
large enough to crawl under, she would have. *Damn! You
got caught ogling a complete stranger.*

"Jack, you scared me." she said, stumbling over the
root she had foolishly kicked.

He offered his hand to steady her and led her back to
the path. "How do you know my name? Have we met
before?" His brow creased as he released her hand.

Tucking a strand of hair behind her ear, a distraction
to keep from looking at the streams of sweat trailing
down his chest, she cleared her throat. "Um, I saw you out
my bedroom window yesterday. Lori and Megan were

helping me unpack. Do you know them?" She rambled on and wrung her hands mindlessly. She wasn't about to tell him they had been drooling over him; but judging by the smirk on his face, he probably already knew. Looking down at her feet, she was glad she chose to stop at the creek.

"So you're my neighbor?" he asked, pulling the shirt off his shoulder and slipping it over his head.

"Yes." She paused as his muscles flexed and scandalous thoughts flashed through her mind. "I'm Jesse," she said as his shirt fell into place.

"It's nice to meet you, Jesse. But I have to ask, what brings you to the woods all alone?"

"Nothing important. Just checking out the scenery, looking for ginseng, and I got a little side-tracked." She smiled sheepishly, trying to hide how nervous and lost she felt, while lying through her teeth. He was absolutely gorgeous. Perhaps she sensed a bit of attitude beneath the surface, but he was definitely not stuck-up.

Jack grinned. "You know, it's illegal to harvest ginseng this time of year."

"I wasn't really looking for ginseng," she admitted, after he just caught her in a lie. "But I did find some poison ivy. Actually, I was on my way home." *Mental note-call Lori ASAP!*

"Well, I'm going that way. If you don't mind, I'll walk with you."

"Good. I was afraid I wouldn't get out of here before dark, and this is no place I want to be when the sun goes down." Jesse talked like it was insignificant, but she sensed he could tell she was quite a bit shaken.

"Being out here in the dark and alone is not a good

idea. But you know, this path runs uphill, so if you're ever lost, all you have to do is close your eyes and take a few steps in one direction. If your body leans forward, you're going uphill. If it leans backward, you're going downhill."

"But we're not on a hill," Jesse argued as she scanned the area.

"We *are* on a hill. It has a very slight incline, and you can't always see it, but if you close your eyes, you can feel your body leaning automatically with it. It gets steeper further on up the path."

Jesse closed her eyes and took a few steps. Letting her body lean slightly, she opened her eyes. "That's uphill." She pointed victoriously as if she had just done something remarkable.

"Right, and you want to go downhill if you want to go home."

"That's good to know, but my hiking days are over. As it is, I'll probably have nightmares over this for a week."

"If you think this is bad, imagine it at night. The woods can be a very dangerous place."

"You sound like you speak from experience?" The ominous warning played in her head as she walked down the path beside him.

"Yeah, you could say that." He shrugged.

.

# Four

*Jack*

The tinkling of wind chimes greeted Jack and Jesse as they stepped out of the woods and into the shade of the oak tree. Jack grinned when Jesse ducked around a low-hanging wind chime, only to bump into one himself. He rubbed his head and reached up to quiet the offending chime as his eyes drifted from branch to branch.

"Sorry, my grandmother collects them."

Shaking his head as he walked over and leaned against the fence post, Jack was hoping Jesse wasn't in any hurry to go inside. She seemed oddly out of place when he first met her in the woods but after letting her guard down, she was fun to talk to, especially when she became flustered and red-faced. Her kicking at the tree root turned out to be the highlight of his day, until her shoe flew off. That was hilarious! And still funny when he thought about it, so he struggled to keep the grin off his face until he heard the soft patter of sneakers and his mood shifted. He knew it was Tracy without ever looking over his shoulder, but when she eventually disappeared down the road, he turned back to Jesse. "So where are you from?"

"Indianapolis," Jesse replied. "How about you?"

Glancing over his shoulder although Tracy was no longer in sight, he knew that didn't mean she wasn't lurking nearby. "I grew up across the river in Kinsley." Jack tilted his head as the faint crunching of dried leaves caught his attention. He turned, waiting for the fiery redhead to join them.

"Jack, I've been searching everywhere for you." Tracy cut across the edge of the woods and hurried over to where he stood. "And you must be our new neighbor. Hi, I'm Tracy."

The smile on her face adequately concealed the wolf within although her green eyes flashed with envy. The reason she acted that way towards other females remained a mystery to him. It wasn't like she had just crawled out of the dog patch. She was uniquely stunning in her own right, but as the black-haired beauty stood before her, it soon became clear that Tracy considered Jesse a threat.

"Is that your hair or is it a weave? It's really pretty, but I'm not sure the color suits your complexion." Tracy smiled smugly.

With narrowed eyes, Jack watched Tracy lightly pull a strand of Jesse's waist-length hair through her fingers. He knew the claws could come out at any moment, and he was ready to intervene if needed, but, if only for Tracy's sake, he hoped it wouldn't come to that.

"It's not a weave." The smirk on Jesse's face revealed

exactly what she thought about Tracy's observation, and she didn't flinch beneath the subsequent scrutinizing stare. Jesse was a few inches shorter than Tracy, but she didn't seem intimidated or envious as most girls might have felt.

Jack crossed his arms over his chest as the two girls continued to talk. Clearly, Tracy was jealous and that meant only one thing: she would be a pain in the ass for the next several days; ergo, they would all have to listen to her rant and rave. He glanced over at Jesse's house and the kitchen curtain fell into place. Uncomfortable as the target of spying eyes, he cleared his throat and turned back to the conversation. "It's been lovely talking to you ladies, but I need to get into the shower."

"I have a better idea. Let's go skinny-dippin' in the lake," Tracy suggested, leaning her body forward as if Jack were a magnet pulling her in.

"Thanks, but I'd rather not." He longed to continue his conversation with Jesse, to learn more about her, but obviously, that would have to wait.

"Oh, well, you can make it up to me tonight. Jesse, it was nice meeting you." Tracy ran her hand up Jack's arm and over his shoulder before she sauntered off across the yard.

Jack frowned at the confrontation he anticipated once he was back at his cabin. But if he didn't deal with Tracy before she left, her next encounter with Jesse might not be as friendly. He huffed out a breath. "Guess I should go too. Maybe we can talk later," Jack suggested, walking backward across the yard.

"Sounds good." Jesse smiled.

Tracy was waiting in the kitchen as he expected when he walked in the back door. "Really, Jack? I can't believe you're hanging out with that female," Tracy spat out once the door closed behind him.

Jack scowled, moving over to the sink and grabbing the bar of soap off the windowsill. Turning on the faucet, he wet the soap beneath the water and bubbly suds dripped from his hands. "I wasn't hanging out with her and even if I were, it's none of your business. So adjust your attitude."

"My attitude is fine. You need to remember: you're part of a pack, and as such, we stick together."

"No, Tracy, you need to stop interfering in matters that don't concern you. Pack or otherwise." Jack shut off the faucet and reached for a hand towel. "So again, adjust your damn attitude and mind your own business." He tossed the towel onto the counter and turned toward the living room, but stopped when Tracy grabbed his upper arm.

"I'm not trying to get in your business. I'm looking out for the pack's best interest, unlike you."

Jack jerked his arm away. "The pack's best interest? Since when does this pack matter to you? You have absolutely no desire to fit in with us."

"She's human, and humans always screw things up. You, of all people, should already know that." As her head bobbed, her earrings jingled, and the copper spikes touched her shoulders.

"You do not want to go there." His eyes flared. Trying to push back the memories of years gone by, memories that haunted his dreams, Jack struggled to control his anger. "I am the alpha here. So unless you are

29

challenging me, I suggest you do exactly as you're told." A harsh growl echoed through the room and she lowered her eyes.

"It wasn't a challenge. I was just saying they don't understand our kind. They always lead to trouble." She took a step back.

"You need to stop blaming humans for what happened to your grandfather. They did nothing to deserve his wrath."

"If they had done what they were told, he would still be..." Tracy's face paled as her voice trailed off.

"The alpha? Your grandfather was ruthless and cruel, so he got what he deserved. The pack lost a lot of good members because he was so power-hungry. So stop trying to defend someone that doesn't deserve my spit!" Jack stomped out of the room with Tracy following a few steps behind.

"That's not what I meant."

"It's exactly what you meant! And I'm not going to stand here and listen to you glorify an alpha that killed a female just for protecting her own." He opened the front door and stepped to the side, motioning Tracy forward. "This conversation is *over.*"

Tracy's shoulders slumped as she tromped across the yard, but Jack was long past the point of caring. Who the hell did she think she was? Trying to preach to him about pack politics? He waited until her foot hit the asphalt before slamming the door. Being an Alpha-in-Training, he expected he would have to play the alpha card from time to time, but he never thought it would be owing to Tracy's jealousy.

***

30

Honeysuckle and pine lingered in the air as Jack leaned back in the swing and closed his eyes. Still reeling from the pissing match Tracy started the day before, he could only imagine how the summer would be. He drew in a deep breath, willing his mind to settle. After a night of restless sleep, he was exhausted and within minutes, he drifted off to sleep.

"Looks like you had a rough night."

Jack opened his eyes to the enormous shadow looming overhead. "Whoa, I didn't hear you come up."

Tucker, a mountain wolf, was easily the largest male of the pack. With his tall stature and burly build, he dwarfed the Cloverly wolves into a pack of coyotes. "Damn, you look like hell." He took a seat on the edge of the porch and leaned back against the post as the swing came to a stop. "Tracy knows there's a new female in the area," Tucker said.

"Based on her history, she probably knows a lot of things." Resting his elbows on his knees, he looked up to see if the post would hold as the massive male leaned heavily against it.

"I was talking about the other night. On our way home from Sallee's, she picked up the scent at the tree line. She should be a scout. She sure has the nose for it."

"Well, her nose also tends to get her into trouble," Jack said. "She saw me talking to the neighbor, and afterwards—"

"You pissed her off."

"I always do. It's a gift I have, one that only Tracy seems to appreciate." Jack laughed to hide his frustration.

"Well, it sounds like she handled it pretty well, all

things considered."

"Not hardly. She's probably at home now, plotting ways to take over my position in the pack, assuming she knows what's best for us." Jack ran his hand over his hair, then stretched his arms overhead and yawned.

"Your position in the pack is not what she wants." Tucker flicked his brows. "By the way, are we still on for Sallee's tonight?"

"No. I think it would be safer if we went to the lake. You know how unpredictable Tracy can be when she's in one of her moods. I don't trust her." Jack lowered his arms and leaned back in the swing to watch Tucker pulling his long, brown dreads into a ponytail.

"It doesn't matter to me one way or the other," Tucker said as Whitney and Mason cut across the yard, joining them on the front porch.

"Why are we running at the lake?" Mason asked, his brows drawn down.

"Tracy," Jack replied curtly, as if he expected his beta to already know.

"What did she do this time?" Whitney asked.

"She met Jack's neighbor," Tucker chuckled.

"That can't be good. I remember the last time she showed her ass." It was clear Mason was troubled by the news when he rubbed his hand over his jaw.

"Well, in her defense, it was the first time she had come face to face with a group of females that weren't wolves," Whitney said.

"Maybe so, but growling didn't help her cause." Mason looked down the road as Whitney pushed up off the porch.

"I'll go talk to her and see what I can do," Whitney

interjected and Jack chuckled when she rolled her eyes. Unlike Tracy, Whitney wasn't the jealous type, having found her mate in Mason three years ago. As she walked across the yard, her long, black ponytail swished from side to side.

"You're a lucky man," Jack said, nudging Mason.

# Five

## Jesse

Jesse hurried down the street as Steve and Lori walked out her front door. It had been two years since she last saw him, and although he still wore the same spiked hairstyle, he had grown out of the gawky-boy stage and looked pretty frickin' fabulous. She skipped up the sidewalk and took a seat on the edge of the porch, grinning when he winked. *What a charmer.*

"It's almost dark, are you sure you don't need a ride?" Steve dangled his keys in front of Lori's face, but instead of grabbing for the keys, she pulled him down to her level and whispered in his ear.

Jesse's suspicions grew when Steve glanced her way before strutting down the sidewalk as he ran his fingers through his brown hair. With a grin, he climbed into the driver's seat of the patina-brown pickup and closed the door. "If you ever decide to dump him, let me know. I'll take your sloppy seconds."

She laughed and jumped off the porch to avoid Lori's swat. "That will teach you to whisper about me."

Lori smirked and joined Jesse on the sidewalk as the remaining daylight faded into a deep, royal blue. "So how's small town life treating you?" she asked, waving when Steve drove off.

"I love it. There's something about this place... it feels like home." Jesse hopped back and forth across the sidewalk. "Step on a crack, break your mama's back."

"Speaking of your mama, is she still working for the DOJ?"

"Oh yeah. It's her dream job." Jesse chuckled.

"That's so cool. Before long, she'll be president and I can brag that I'm the best friend of the first daughter. That's like badass royalty shit there."

"Well, it's not like she hasn't mentioned it once or twice. But I have to admit it would be cool to visit the White House."

"Like mother, like daughter?" Lori lifted a brow.

"Definitely not. I don't think I could handle the stress."

The two girls turned onto Main Street as the streetlights blinked on. The traffic was little more than a dozen cars since the town was settling in for the evening. Other than a horn honking and a few whistles from a passing truck, it was fairly quiet for a Friday night.

"Welcome to the nightlife," Lori said as they crossed the street, their sandals slapping against the blacktop.

"Oh, look, I didn't know Cloverly had a flower shop."

Jesse ran over and peered through the window of Brid's Flower Pot.

"Oh good Lord! Could you be any more girlish?" Lori rolled her eyes. "Maybe you should add *florist* to your list of career options."

"Maybe I should." Jesse pouted as Lori dragged her down the street. Giving the little shop one last glance over her shoulder, she swore she could smell every blossom in the building. Jesse loved flowers as much as Lori loved books, but becoming a florist had never even crossed her mind. *Who knows what other opportunities might pop up?*

"Where would you like to sit, bar stool or booth?" Lori asked as they passed by the bookstore and wove their way through the concrete tables that were set on the sidewalk in front of the cafe.

"Let's sit by the window," Jesse said as the overhead bell chimed, announcing their arrival.

Entering the cafe was like stepping back into an era of poodle skirts and skating waiters. The restaurant had been there since the fifties, and nothing about it had changed. The red vinyl stools with chrome accents lined the counter and matching upholstered booths hugged the walls. Decorated with tin signs advertising everything from chocolate malts to patty melts, it was truly a classic. Jesse waved when she spotted Megan in her teal and white uniform. She was adorable with her springy curls bouncing around her head and a little apron tied neatly at her waist. Too bad they didn't wear poodle skirts anymore. If anyone could pull off the look, it would have been Megan.

"I'm so glad you all stopped by. What can I get for

you? It's on the house," Megan offered, setting two glasses of ice water on the table before pulling the order pad out of her pocket.

"I'll have a sweet tea and she'll take a chocolate shake." Jesse looked over at Lori and she nodded.

"Well, that's easy enough. I'll be back in a jiffy." Megan smiled, tucking the order pad into her apron before heading back to the counter.

"I still can't believe you were in the woods with Jack after the other night. You're either crazy or you like to live dangerously." Lori took a napkin from the dispenser and spat out her gum.

"Not so loud. Gramma thinks I was at the edge of the woods. If she found out I lied, she would threaten me with a switch. You know how she was always warning us about going into the woods," Jesse whispered across the table.

"You're almost eighteen; I think you're a little too old for the switch now."

"Are you kidding? Dad still treats me like I'm fourteen."

"Yeah? Mom still treats me like I'm fourteen, too, but I'm young at heart."

"You mean immature." Jesse simpered.

"Whatever. You're just trying to change the subject. I still think you were staring at his ass."

"I was not! I was staring at his swagger," Jesse argued. After meeting Jack in the woods, as soon as she was back in her room, she called Lori, giving her all the details of their encounter. Right down to his swagger, and Lori practically swooned over the phone.

"Here you go, ladies," Megan said, interrupting their

hushed conversation as she set their drinks on the table and handed each of them a straw. "By the way, Jack does have a nice swagger."

"Shh," Jesse hissed, narrowing her eyes when Lori started to laugh. "Lori, you promised not to say anything."

"I didn't. Scouts' honor." Lori crossed her heart and flashed a peace sign.

"It's not my fault you all don't know how to whisper." Megan laughed as she pushed Lori's hand down.

"I did whisper!" Jesse insisted as Lori knocked on the window to get Steve's attention.

"That's what they all say." Megan tittered. "If you need anything else, whisper."

Jesse stared slack-jawed as the little eavesdropper hurried back to the counter. "There's no way she heard us."

"It's Megan. She hears everything," Lori said, drawing Jesse's attention to the window.

Steve's truck was parked at the curb, so Jesse assumed he was entering the cafe when the doorbell chimed. But hearing the commotion behind her, she glanced over her shoulder at the horde of girls gathered in the doorway, Steve was merely standing in the mix. *Someone's in trouble*, she thought and turned back to Lori. "Where did they come from?"

"Must've crawled out of the gutter," Lori sneered.

Jesse snickered at the sour look on Lori's face. Trouble brewed for Steve if he didn't play his cards right, and she couldn't help feeling a teensy bit sorry for the guy.

"Talk about a red carpet welcome," Steve said as he slid into the seat next to Lori, who ignored him. "Come on, don't be like that. You know anytime Randy comes to town, he causes a stir." Jesse sipped her tea as Steve tried to smooth things over but Lori wasn't having any of it.

"Whatever. It screams desperate."

"It's harmless. They just want his autograph or something."

"Shh, here he comes." Lori snarled when Randy approached the booth. "Glad you could join us."

Jesse's shot a questioning glance across the table before she turned to greet their guest.

"Well, I would've been here sooner had I known we were having company," Randy said aiming his smile at Jesse. His smoky voice and stormy eyes caused her breath to hitch.

Kicking Lori under the table seemed like a good idea, but her conniving best friend ignored her as she attempted to hide her grin. Jesse smiled and looked back at Randy, who was taller than Steve, *and when the heck did he muscle up?* Dressed in a black t-shirt and bleach-spotted jeans, his "bad boy" vibe demanded attention from every girl in the diner, and they eagerly gave it, including Jesse. She bit her lip when she noticed the silver cross dangling from his ear; and if he removed his shirt, she suspected there would be a fine-looking tattoo somewhere on his body. Her face flushed with his stare, but geez Louise! He was smoking. "Do I know you?" Jesse asked once she found her voice.

"You will before the night is over." Randy slid to the middle of the bench seat, caging her against the window. With a sexy-as-hell grin, he whispered into her ear, "I'll cook you dinner if you'll cook me breakfast." The stubble on his jaw grazed her cheek, and she sucked in a breath as her eyes widened at the proposition.

Unable to muster a snappy comeback, she gazed as he pushed back his shoulder-length black hair, causing a spark of excitement to zing through her body. He was extremely good-looking, and nothing like the spindly, little pest she remembered.

She smiled.

He winked.

*Crap! Caught ogling a guy again.*

Lori snickered as Jesse lowered her head, letting her hair shield her face. It was bad enough she had embarrassed herself by gawking, but Lori wasn't helping matters. She looked up through her hair and Lori snorted. Struggling to keep the grin off her face, she turned back to Randy. "You're bad news. You know that, right?"

"Yeah, and now you do." Randy nudged her with his leg. Crazy images rushed through her brain, causing her heartbeat to thunder in her ears and she was surprised the others couldn't hear it. Why Megan wasn't interested in him she hadn't a clue, but she didn't care. He was sitting next to her, and she was eating up the view.

"What can I get for you all?" Megan asked from the end of the table.

"Nothing, we can't stay long," Steve replied and Jesse looked over at Megan.

"I'm not hard to please. I'll take whatever you wanna give me." Randy tapped his knuckles against the table while flashing a grin.

"You are such a flirt." Jesse bumped him with her shoulder and laughed.

"Does that mean you're fixing me breakfast?" he asked, bumping her back.

"Not at all." She grinned and Megan rolled her eyes as she walked away. Their conversation continued with Randy pulling out all the stops. Not only did he offer to cook dinner, but he also mentioned something about dessert and handcuffs, all of which sent Jesse's mind reeling. Distracted by his charming personality, she didn't hear Lori asking Steve about wolves in the area.

"Let me guess. You've been reading folklore again," Randy said. The quick change of subject threw Jesse for a loop and she glanced suspiciously between the three.

"I wasn't reading anything. We heard something running through the woods over by Jesse's house the other night."

"It was probably just a deer," Steve answered. Putting his arm over the back of the booth, he twirled a strand of Lori's hair between his fingers. "You know, it could've been some of the local teenagers. They used to hang out at Sallee's from time to time, and they would have to pass by Jesse's house to get there."

"What is Sallee's?" Jesse asked.

"Nothing you'd be interested in," Lori replied.

"Why would she not be interested? It's the coolest thing we have going in this one-horse town." Steve turned to Jesse. "Sallee's Rock is a large boulder in the center of a clearing, about two miles into the woods, and the only way to get there is by hiking in. The Sallee family owns most of the land running along the south side of town and has for generations. According to legend, the great, great, grandfather of Old Man Sallee won the property in a poker game many years ago. Being new to the area, the Sallee family had planned to homestead until..." He paused and a wicked grin curled his lips before adding,

"Sightings of large animals, or beasts, depending on who's telling the story, have been told over the years. Some claim it was wolves, others swear it was black panthers, and some insist the hillbilly beast traveled from the east looking for its mate. All of which, I think, were the staggering effects of too much moonshine. Anyway, the property was never developed and the majority of the Sallee clan moved on to the neighboring county, but not before leaving Old Man Sallee the property. Of course, nowadays most people consider it nothing more than folklore, but you can bet your s'mores, it's still told around campfires today."

"That's frickin' cool. We need to go there," Jesse replied as the color drained from Lori's face.

"We have to work this weekend but if you want, we can go Sunday afternoon. Who knows? We might get lucky and find some tracks," Steve suggested as Lori glared across the table.

"Aren't you forgetting about the switch?" Lori asked.

"No. I'll tell Gramma we're looking for ginseng. It worked the first time."

"It worked the first time," Lori mouthed before sticking out her tongue.

Jesse laughed and looked over at Randy. "You're coming too, aren't you?"

"Depends. Does the invitation include dinner?" Randy jumped out of her reach, causing everyone to look their way.

"And with that, we have to go or we'll be late. Do you need a ride?" Steve asked as Lori latched onto his arm.

"What do you think?" She rolled her eyes.

"Come on, Jess, you can ride with me." Randy grabbed

her hand and pulled her from the booth.

Jesse suppressed a smile when Lori giggled as they followed Randy out the door. Caught staring at his butt, she would blame it on her best friend. Anytime she and Lori were together, her thoughts landed straight in the gutter. She rolled her lip as Randy straddled the motorcycle parked in front of Steve's truck. With his help, she settled behind him and he waited for her to fasten the helmet before pulling onto the road. Her grip tightened around his waist.

She enjoyed the feel of his body as he steered the motorcycle around the corner, and didn't notice him pulling over in front of her house until he shut off the bike. Heat blossomed in her cheeks when he looked back over his shoulder and grinned. He offered his hand and helped her off the bike and she removed the helmet. Walking up to the house, she was happy to hear his footsteps behind her. *What a shameful little hussy you've become!* She sucked in her cheeks to suppress the giggle.

Randy stopped at the bottom step and ran his fingers through his hair, pausing as if he wanted to say something. A mischievous gleam sparkled in his eyes as he rested one hand on the back of his neck. "I'm glad you moved to Cloverly."

"You gave me a ride home just to say that?" She playfully nudged him with her elbow and took a seat on the third step. The porch light stretched their shadows down the sidewalk, and she quickly ran her fingers through her hair, trying to detangle the wind-blown mess.

"Not exactly," Randy said, taking a seat beside her. He rested his elbows on his knees and flipped his keys back and forth against his hand. "Are you dating anyone?"

"No." Jesse pulled her hair around to the side, temporarily hiding her face. She was excited to have captured his attention but wasn't sure she could handle his fan base. He amply filled out his tall, lanky frame with the right amount of muscle and mass, and even she found it hard not to stare.

"Wanna go out sometime?" he asked, flashing his playboy smile.

"Maybe. I'll think about it," she said with a side glance.

"It's not like I'm asking you to marry me. It's just a date." He bumped her shoulder.

"No, I guess you didn't." Jesse laughed nervously and tossed her hair over her shoulder as he grabbed her hand and pulled her to her feet—her hand landing on his chest.

"I'd better get going before I decide to ditch work. And just so you know, I have no problem ditching work." The porch light reflected in his eyes and she could almost see him laughing.

"Well, as exciting as that sounds, I have to wash my hair tonight."

"Do you need help? I've mastered the technique. Lather... rinse... repeat." Randy's voice was dangerously sexy as his words brushed across her cheek and Jesse closed her eyes. His proximity made her dizzy and she braced herself for the intimate contact of his kiss. But when she opened her eyes, the smirk she saw on his face ignited the heat in her cheeks.

"I uh, think I'm good." Confused as to why he didn't kiss her, she cleared her throat.

"Well, if you change your mind, you know where to find me." Randy winked and let go of her hand as he backed down the sidewalk.

*What a tease!* Jesse watched as he strutted back to his motorcycle. Admiring the snug fitting jeans that showcased his long legs, she stood there until he was out of sight. Maybe it wouldn't hurt to go out with him. She placed her hand on her chest to cushion the blow of rejection. *Don't get all giddy. He's a player, and clearly not that into you.* Even so, a small part of her wanted to experience his kiss.

# Six

*Jack*

Relieved to be back at the cabin after giving Tucker a ride to the local parts store, Jack was both amused and annoyed. He wasn't sure who was more wound up about the new neighbor, Tracy or Tucker. Tucker was riding in the passenger seat when they passed Jesse standing with her hands pressed against the window of the flower shop. Seeing Jesse's long hair blowing in the wind, Tucker roared his approval as if he'd never seen a female before. She was nice to look at, he admitted, but Tucker's enthusiasm went off the charts.

"The female we saw, she's your neighbor?" Tucker asked, shutting the car door.

"Yeah, that's Jesse," Jack answered dismissively before he and Tucker headed down the road toward the ditch.

"So what's she like?"

"She seems nice enough. Like any other female, I

guess." Jack jumped the ditch and ran along the narrow path, Tucker trailing at his heels. "And for a human, she's not bad-looking," he said over his shoulder—a quiet chuckle poised on his lips.

"Not bad looking? Are you blind? If her front view is anything like the rear view, I'd say she's stunning."

"Well, when you put it like that, I guess she is stunning." Jack laughed and dropped back so Tucker could take the lead as they ran deeper into the woods.

Scanning the area as the others joined them at the tree line; Jack knew it wasn't really necessary. Very few people ventured that far into the woods. Probably due to the *No Hunting* and *No Fishing* signs posted on various trees, rather than Mr. Sallee's jovial personality. Being a loner with a constant frown on his face, most people thought Old Man Sal was always grumpy when in reality, he was quite nice. Jack glanced across the lake. It was a safe place to let loose, unlike Hunter's Ridge, which the county owned. As the moonlight shone down, it cast a soft glow over the area, and he glanced toward the sky.

"It's about time you got here," Tracy said and Jack frowned. There was only one person that could ruin a perfect night and unfortunately, she was standing ten feet in front of him with her hands on her hips. "Dare I ask what took so long?" Tracy aimed her glare at Tucker, but Jack knew it was meant for him.

"Sorry, we were briefly distracted by Jesse," Tucker said as Whitney elbowed him and crinkled her brows, giving him a silent scolding.

"Why does that not surprise me?" Tracy kicked off her shoes, pretending to ignore Jack, but he glimpsed her watching him from the corner of her eye.

"Maybe because you're not blind," Tucker joked, pulling his shirt over his head and tossing it over a tree branch. He winked at Jack.

"Don't poke the bear," Whitney warned. Apparently, the first scolding didn't discourage Tucker, and Jack chuckled, knowing the second wouldn't either.

"What? I'm just stating the obvious." Tucker raised his hands in mock surrender.

"So when are you bringing her home to meet the family?" Mason asked. He knew as well as Jack that Tucker could not be chastised into silence, you had to embarrass him.

"That's not likely to happen." Tucker kneeled down and untied his shoes.

"Well, I wouldn't say that. Remember? I was with you," Jack said, refusing to give Tucker an easy out. He also didn't want to add more fuel to Tracy's pissy disposition but seeing how his cousin was really into Jesse, it was something he couldn't pass up.

"What I remember is you not wanting to pull over." Tucker glanced up.

"We didn't have time." Amused by the rosy tint highlighting Tucker's cheeks, Jack chuckled.

"I don't know why we have to run so far out," Tracy interrupted. "Why can't we just go to the boulders? You act as if you're afraid Jesse will be there." She turned her glare on Jack.

And there it was. Tracy was obviously still pissed about Jesse, or maybe it was because Tucker had shown so much interest in her. "Pack safety," Jack said although he didn't expect her to understand what that meant.

"Pack safety, my ass! If you were worried about our

safety, you wouldn't be hanging around with her." Tracy yanked her shirt over her head, causing her earrings to clang as they dropped down onto her shoulders.

"Would you do us all a favor and stop being so damn territorial?" Jack kicked off his shoes, a low rumble building in his chest.

"Me territorial? I don't think so! If I were territorial, I'd hike my leg up and piss on you." Tracy batted her lashes and smiled innocently.

"We're wasting moonlight," Jack said as he ducked beneath a tree. Not willing to give her anymore of his time, he quickly undressed and phased, followed by Whitney and Mason.

"Come on, Trace, let's go have some fun. Or better yet, run off some of that pent-up anger." Tucker laughed when she flipped him the bird.

The air was cool as their wolves raced past the lake and followed the banks of the river. It wasn't often they ran in that direction but it was a nice change of scenery and it provided Jack the chance of seeing the work being done on the new cabins. After arriving at the construction site, he stopped while the others continued to run. There were three cabins under construction, all larger than the ones he and the others currently lived in. The largest of the three, overlooking the river, would be his as soon as he finished his training.

Sitting down on a mound of dirt, Jack stared across the river, searching for his dad's house and a bout of loneliness consumed him.

Ben Cooper was the alpha of the Green River Region, and he lived across the river with the Kinsley pack. Jack was his only son and in training to become the alpha of the Cloverly pack, with Mason as his beta. Expanding the pack to nearby cities was what Ben had wanted to do since first becoming the alpha; and now, after years of planning, it was finally starting to take shape. By training others to oversee smaller packs in the region, he hoped he could discourage larger packs from moving into their territory.

Jack missed the Kinsley pack, although he loved living in Cloverly. Plus, being with a smaller pack gave him more time to ponder his life and think about his future. What would he do once he became an alpha? Raising a family with his mate was out of the question, considering he didn't have a mate. Still, he believed everything happened for a reason, and although he was training to be an alpha, he didn't think that was the sole purpose for him being there.

He stood and stretched his legs as Whitney and Mason raced between the cabins. Seeing them together stirred thoughts of a mate for his own wolf, but he abandoned that idea years ago. He shook off the despairing fog that settled around him, and headed back into the woods.

His wolf raced beneath low-hanging branches and rounded the lake within minutes. When he slowed to a stop, he cocked his head, listening to the clinking which grew louder. Surely, Tracy didn't think she could sneak up on anyone wearing those gaudy earrings. He loped over to the tree line and phased, then quickly pulled on his pants.

Tracy's earrings flapped behind her head as she sprinted around the water's edge. Wearing dangling earrings was a distraction to the wolf, which was why most females wore stud earrings or nothing at all. Of course, Tracy wasn't like the others, and always refused to remove her earrings. She said something about feeling naked, which Jack couldn't figure out.

Jack glanced down at the alpha shield hanging around his neck. It wasn't something he would normally wear, if it were not required. Once he completed the training, he could ditch the necklace for a more permanent shield in the form of a tattoo. He slipped on his shoes and looked up just as Tracy phased.

The moonlight washed over her body as she seductively walked his way. "It's still early; we could go somewhere private," she whispered, resting her hand on his chest.

With thoughts of a mate still lingering with his wolf, Jack tried to imagine settling down and starting his own family. He closed his eyes as a sad smile tugged at his lips. *Would his mate look like Lizzy, with long, curly, blonde hair and the sweetest smile? Would she have brown eyes, green eyes, or blue to match his?* He swallowed down the pain that tore at his heart. *Could a person die from loneliness?* He had often considered it a possibility. *Female* and *mate* resounded in his head as Tracy's hand moved to the back of his neck, pulling him forward. The light touch of her lips caused his wolf to stir. *This is not your mate!* His eyes shot open, and he pushed her away.

"Jack, you know you want me. I can smell your desire."

"I desire a female; that's true, but not you." He didn't want to hurt her feelings, but it wasn't in him to lie, either.

"Is Jesse the female you desire? The little human who couldn't find her way through the scary woods? Is that what you crave, a helpless human female?" The sneer in Tracy's voice had Jack clenching his jaw and he grabbed his shirt off the ground and walked away. He could ignore the intentional jab at Jesse, but if she thought she could lay a guilt trip on him, she was deadly mistaken.

He had just stepped out of the woods and was crossing the yard when he heard the howl. Tracy's wolf raced past him in a blur and he silently cursed. He glanced up at Jesse's bedroom window, but the curtains were closed and the light was off. Hopefully, she was a sound sleeper.

Running down Cabin Run Road while in wolf form wasn't ordinarily a big deal. Little traffic traveled the road, and the pine trees offered plenty of shelter if they needed to take cover. A time or two, they had even phased at Jack's cabin without worrying about the neighboring house. Jesse's grandmother was usually asleep by the time they headed out to the woods, but with Jesse staying there, things had changed. She had a clear view of his yard and they needed to be careful, but apparently, no one thought to warn Tracy.

Waiting for Tracy to run past, if she got within his reach, Jack would grab her by the scruff. "Tracy," he hissed as she darted out from the shadows and back into the woods. He glanced up at Jesse's window, surprised to see her standing there.

"Jack, I'm coming down. Wait," Jesse whisper-hollered before the curtain fell back into place.

*What the hell was she doing standing in the window practically naked?* Normally, Jack would have appreciated the view, but not with Tracy so nearby. "Dammit," he growled and dropped his shirt as he raced across the backyard. The small fence wasn't difficult to jump, but as he landed on the other side, his foot caught on a tomato cage and he tumbled to the ground. He rolled over and kicked at the cage that entangled his foot. Losing a shoe in the battle, he jumped to his feet and ran up on the porch just as Jesse opened the back door.

"What's going on?" she whispered, pushing open the screen door.

Jack stepped into the doorway, hiding his foot behind his leg as the door shut against it. Determined to block her view of the yard, he leaned in and she blushed, standing mere inches from his bare chest. "I was chasing off a stray," he said in a low, sultry voice.

"But... I uh... I thought I heard a howl." Jesse fumbled her words.

"Yeah, that's what dogs do." Jack grinned at seeing the flustered look on her face. She wanted to question him more, but hearing the creak of an upstairs door, she lifted her eyes to the ceiling. Jack knew it was Jesse's dad by the sound of weighty footsteps on the wooden floor. "I'd better go before your dad finds me here. We wouldn't want him to get the wrong idea." The words rolled off his tongue and he licked his bottom lip when she turned and stared at his mouth. He could have kissed her senseless in that moment, but that would only validate Tracy's claim. "See you tomorrow." His words held a promise he knew he wouldn't keep. He was attracted to Jesse, any male would have been, but without a bond between them, his wolf could never be satisfied. Backing out onto the porch, he quietly shut the screen door as Jesse shut the back door. Hearing the chain lock slide into place, he released a heavy breath before jogging across the yard. He stopped long enough to place the tomato cage back over the plant and grab his shoe off the ground before stepping over the fence.

Focusing his attention back on Tracy, her being jealous of another female did not justify running through the neighbor's backyard in wolf form. His jaw ticked as he waited for the pack to return from their run.

Whitney and Mason walked up the street holding hands, followed by Tracy and Tucker. When he saw Tracy laughing as if nothing had happened, he stormed off the porch and grabbed her by the arm. "Why the hell were you running through the neighborhood? Were you intentionally trying to expose us? Because that's exactly what you did." He had every right to send her back to Kinsley, and at the rate she was going, it would probably happen sooner than later.

"Oh, I exposed something all right, but it wasn't the pack. Go ahead and tell them how you were sucking face with Jesse. I saw her in the window. You must have really enjoyed the view, you ran to her house fast enough," Tracy spat out in response.

"I didn't have time to enjoy the view. I was too busy trying to stop Jesse from coming outside and seeing your wolf-ass running through her yard!" The small pack was his to control, and it was damn time that he did so. "Don't push me, Tracy. I'm not my dad. I will gladly send you packing if you ever pull a stunt like that again. Do you understand?" The growl that resonated from him demanded submission, and all eyes lowered. "Tucker, take Tracy home and make sure she stays there."

"I don't need a babysitter. I'm not a two-year-old," Tracy huffed and kicked a rock across the street.

"Then stop acting like it," Jack scolded. He knew sending Tucker with her was his best option. His cousin could handle Tracy better than anyone, and he would defuse the situation as soon as they arrived at her cabin.

Tucker grinned at the scowl on Tracy's face. "Well, haven't you made a fine mess of things? Come on, I'll tuck you in."

"Shut the hell up!" Tracy grumbled below her breath as she stomped off and Tucker snickered behind her.

"I'm sorry, Jack. It's my fault. I thought she was calmed down," Whitney said, placing a hand on his shoulder. Whitney was always ready to take the blame in order to keep the peace, but even she couldn't help Tracy.

"No, it's not your fault. No one is at fault here except Tracy. She doesn't own me and she will never be my mate, but for some reason, she can't seem to get that through her head."

"At some point, Tracy will have to be responsible for her actions," Mason said, watching the door to Tracy's cabin close. "She's annoying and conniving, just like her uncle."

"I know. I thought if she moved away from him, she would change, but I guess not. I like living on this side of the river and I'm not willing to give it up because of her, are you?"

"No," Mason said. "We're here to support whatever you decide." Jack knew Mason would never give up his lifestyle for Tracy. He made that clear a long time ago.

Jack sat on the porch as Mason and Whitney headed back down the road. He was angry he had to play the alpha card, again, but felt he had no other choice. His dad would be pissed if he found out what Tracy did. He just hoped he made the right decision by giving her another chance.

# Seven

*Jack*

It was late Sunday afternoon when Mason stepped past Jack and slipped into the driver's seat. "You know, I could get used to this," Mason said, referring to the fact that Tracy hadn't disturbed them the entire weekend.

"Yeah, it's been pretty quiet." Jack's voice echoed from beneath the fender-well. He snatched the towel from his back pocket and sat back on the tire, wiping his hands as Mason pulled the door shut, just in time for him to catch sight of Jesse going into the woods.

"Was that the neighbor?" Mason asked, gazing in the side-door mirror.

"Yeah, her and Lori, I think. But why would they be going into the woods this late in the afternoon?" Jack glanced up at the sky and then back at Mason. "What are you smirking about?"

"I think you know why she's gone into the woods.

Tracy wasn't jealous for nothing." Mason quirked an eyebrow, then pushed opened the car door and got out.

"Whatever. Tracy's delusional," Jack said, getting to his feet. Grabbing his shirt off the car hood, he slipped it over his head and pushed the door shut.

"Maybe so, but you should be glad Tracy showed up when she did. If it weren't for her, you and the Jesse girl would probably be engaged by now." Mason threw his head back and laughed.

"Oh, yeah, that was likely to happen. I was blinded by her beauty." His best friend didn't often get the chance to rag him about a female, but when the opportunity so generously presented itself, Mason didn't miss a beat.

"And she was blinded by your wolfish charm," Mason teased. "It doesn't take much to get the attention of a female, and you did practically save her life." His last statement was a bit exaggerated, but Jack laughed nonetheless.

"Well, if I intended to save anyone, it might as well be her. Have you met her yet?" Jack asked, rubbing his knuckles over his chin. He wondered what reason Jesse had for going into the woods so late in the evening. Had he not warned her about avoiding the woods after dark? Not wanting to scare her at the time, he didn't mention the two black bears that passed through their territory a few months back, but clearly, he should have.

"I'm still waiting for you to give me the run-down. Based on Tucker's description, she's quite the looker."

Jack grinned when Mason looked down the road, knowing full well what was going through his mind. Growing up together, they were notorious for getting into mischief, an old habit neither of them had outgrown. "I bet they're going to Sallee's," Jack said, tossing the towel to the ground. The statement was more of a suggestion, and he waited to see if Mason picked up on the hint.

"I bet we could beat them there," Mason said with a glint in his eyes.

"By five minutes?"

"Ten," Mason challenged.

Since Tucker had been scouting the woods for the past two summers, he managed to carve out narrow trails that led to different locations, and Sallee's Rock was one of them. With the ditch being the safest place to enter the woods without being seen, it wasn't long before the others started using that path on a daily basis, instead of the trail beside the oak tree. Jack and Mason raced down the road and crossed over the ditch, in front of Tucker's cabin. Running along the path, a run they had made many times over the past two summers, it didn't take long for them to arrive at the boulders. Standing back at a distance, they waited.

"There, coming out of the woods." Mason pointed and the two quickly settled beneath the cover of a large pine tree. The low-hanging branches and thick pine needles made the area beneath the tree dark, rendering them undetectable by human eyes.

The pack had spent months searching the woods for hideaways such as the pine tree. It worked perfectly as a quick escape from prying eyes, as well as a place to stash spare clothing. Jack looked up at the black plastic bag tied to the tree trunk. "This is a good spot. There's no way they'll see us here," he whispered as a tall, slender male stepped into the clearing, followed by a petite blonde, who quickly disappeared behind the boulders. "What the heck was that?"

"I think *that* was a she, and she seemed pretty excited to be here," Mason said.

Waiting for the little speedster to make a lap around the boulders, their attention was drawn back to the trail. "That's Lori in the front. She lives a few houses down from Jesse, on the corner."

"Well, if that's Jesse behind her, everything Tracy's done suddenly makes sense." Mason bounced his brows.

"Nothing about Tracy makes sense." Jack turned his attention back to the group and listened in on their conversation.

"It's not funny, Steve," Lori said, reaching for his watch. "If we get stuck out here after dark, you're in big trouble." She glanced at the sky.

"You really aren't comfortable here, are you?" Steve asked as he draped his arm over her shoulders.

"No. There's something out here and I have no desire to meet up with it even if it is just a deer. They have antlers, and I don't want to end up as a shish kabob."

"Food," Mason mouthed and rubbed his stomach. Jack tried not to laugh at the pained expression on Mason's face, but since skipping lunch, the mention of food had both their stomachs rumbling in protest.

"This place is beautiful," Jesse said, stepping out from behind Lori. Hidden in the center of the woods was a huge, oval-shaped boulder that jutted out from the ground with smaller boulders stacked, forming what looked like steps leading to the top. Nudging Lori with her elbow, Jesse grinned and pointed towards the boulder. "I want to see the view from up there."

Jesse rambled on, but Lori didn't seem as enthusiastic.

Seeing how she stayed so close to Steve, it was apparent he knew the area. "As soon as they get to the boulders, we'll sneak out," Jack said, relieved. Thankfully, Jesse was smart enough to heed his warning, so there was no reason for them to stay.

"Come on, Megan," Jesse called out. "We're going up."

"I'll be there in a minute," Megan yelled back. She casually skipped out from behind the boulders, unaware she was being watched. She wore a blue tank-top and a pair of carpenter jeans, and seemed rather comfortable there, unlike Lori.

"What the hell?" Mason froze as Megan came to a sudden stop, her eyes landing on their darkened hideout.

Jack stilled at the thought of being seen, but when his eyes met Megan's, something familiar flashed in his memory causing a warm sensation to flow through his body, and he stumbled back against the tree. "This is not good." A fleeting smile lifted the corners of her lips, and he acknowledged her with a nod.

"How did she see us?" Mason asked when he looked over at Jack.

"She didn't." But as Megan darted around like a honeybee in a field of wildflowers, Jack knew it was a lie. Narrowing his eyes, he studied her as she kicked in the dirt, causing a yellow haze to swirl at her feet—she sneezed.

"What is she doing now?" Mason asked.

"I'm not sure, but whatever it is, she's determined." Jack stepped away from the tree to get a better view. Megan didn't seem fazed by them being there, so he wasn't totally convinced she had actually seen them. He frowned as sweat beaded across his forehead, and wiped it away before Mason noticed. The bond that formed between Megan and him was not something he expected, but seeing her shake off a shiver, it became quite clear it was affecting her.

"What is this, a party?" Mason quipped and Jack turned just in time to witness a dark-haired male racing across the clearing who grabbed Megan around the waist, lifting her to his shoulder.

"Put me down, Randy!" Megan screamed while beating against his back.

Jack bristled as a low growl rumbled to the surface. The urge to defend Megan was strong, and he pushed through the pine branches, his eyes locked on the threat.

"What are you doing? You can't go out there," Mason said in an earnest attempt to stop him.

"Wait here." Jack stepped around his beta, confident Jesse wouldn't think anything of him being there and at the moment, he really didn't care. Undaunted that he could be outnumbered, he knew at the first sign of trouble, Mason would be at his side. He hurried across the clearing as Randy laughed and dropped Megan onto her feet. Jack didn't think the male was trying to hurt her, but if he didn't confront him, his wolf would.

"Come on, Megan. I was just playing," Randy said. Within three strides, Jack was standing in front of him with his hand fisted in his shirt.

"Don't touch her again," Jack warned as he shoved Randy away but he quickly rebounded and pushed himself up in Jack's face.

"I wouldn't suggest you do that again."

Usually, the flare of Jack's eyes would be enough to make any human retreat, but either Randy hadn't noticed, or he was too cocky to care. "Don't push your luck," Jack said, drawing back as Megan pushed between them and grabbed his arm.

"It's not like I was attacking you. You need to chill the hell out; and tell your damn bodyguard to back the hell off!"

In one swift motion, Jack pushed Megan behind him and she smacked his arm away. She was tiny compared to the two males, but apparently, unafraid of either. "I don't need a bodyguard," Megan shouted as Randy spat on the ground and stomped away.

Randy disappeared into the woods and Jack turned back to Megan. With her fists clenched at her sides, she glared down at her feet. Unable to keep the grin off his face, he chuckled low, which prompted the little firecracker to explode.

"I don't need you to defend me either," she hissed and fire lit up her eyes.

Jack threw his hands up, surrendering to the fierce, little blonde. "Sorry, I didn't mean to upset you." Searching her eyes, something called to his wolf, something familiar that was buried deep beneath the mysterious green globes.

"Don't play up to me," Megan said before her face turned a deep shade of red. "I know who you are, and if this was an attempt to impress Jesse, you failed. Even she would frown at knowing you were spying on her."

He flinched at her accusations, but she wasn't totally off base. Jack was spying, but at no point was he there to impress Jesse. *She's confused. She's fighting the bond.* The thought echoed in his head as the battle to make sense of the situation distracted him from the scolding Megan swiftly unleashed. He frowned. *Maybe the bond is different for a human. If not, she hates you.* Snapping back to reality, a part of him wanted to pull Megan into his arms and never let her go, while the other part wanted to tuck tail and run.

"—so go crawl back under your tree! We don't need you to play hero today," Megan said as tears filled her eyes.

"What? I'm not here for Jesse," Jack tried to explain but Megan wasn't interested in what he had to say as she turned and ran to the boulders, not giving him a chance to plead his case. He looked up, meeting Jesse's glare. Not sure what he did to piss her off, he scowled and looked back at Megan. He was confused at how his actions had been turned around, making him the bad guy. It had to be his wolf that rendered him so forceful, but that's what his wolf was for— protection. *Pick your battles.* And with that, he turned and walked away.

Mason stepped out from beneath the tree and met Jack on the trail. "I don't know who she was, but she sure cut loose on you. That was harsh."

"I don't get it. What is it with me and females? Every time I turn around, I'm pissing one of them off. I thought it was just a Tracy thing."

"Don't try to understand it. Just roll with it. It's a lot less painful." Mason chuckled.

Jack glanced over his shoulder as they headed back toward the ditch. Hearing Megan and her friends running across the clearing, it was safe to assume they would be out of the woods before the sun set.

Leaving Megan without explaining the bond wasn't the smartest thing he had ever done, but considering how angry she was, it was his only option. She needed to calm down before he sprang the news on her if he expected her to give him a chance. He looked over at Mason and grinned. "I have a bond with Megan."

"And you didn't tell her?" Worry creased Mason's forehead as he stared up the path.

"What was I supposed to do? You saw how she reacted. Do you really think she would have listened? She believes the only reason I was there was to impress Jesse."

"Good point, but are you sure it's a bond? Until you've experienced it, you have no idea how it will affect you. And I say this with the utmost respect... are you sure it's not gas?" Mason laughed and ducked away from the arm that shot towards him.

"Is that what you told Whitney?"

"No, no, no. I was just messing with your mind."

"Uh-huh, I'm sure. Maybe I should ask her." Jack laughed and bumped Mason's shoulder.

"Well, for the record, the bond I share with Whitney is the best thing that ever happened to me. So if you're considering breaking yours, think about it before you do anything rash. It's there for a reason."

"Okay, Dad. I promise not to do anything without prior approval," Jack said. "I just don't understand what I did to piss her off. She was furious with Randy, yet she took it out on me."

"Maybe it's a human thing. They can be irrational."

"I guess, but trying to spin that to my wolf wouldn't work. I had no choice but to confront him." Jack replayed the events in his head. "There was something about her eyes. I'm not sure what it was; but standing next to her was like standing next to Whitney."

"If she were a wolf, don't you think we would have known? She didn't have the scent so I highly doubt she is," Mason said, jumping over a log.

"Yeah, probably."

# Eight

*Tracy*

Gritting her teeth, Tracy paced back and forth like a caged animal. Wound-up with nowhere to go, the short distance between her bedroom and the front door wasn't enough space to satisfy her wolf but what choice did she have? After arguing with Jack, she kept a low profile, and sitting in her cabin alone wasn't helping her realize the error of her ways. She also feared that if the regional alpha found out what she did, she would be back to pack grounds and that's not the place she wanted to be. *If Jack would stay true to his nature, Jesse would cease to be an issue.* The thought of them together roiled her stomach, and she gagged. *That's as nasty as a wolf with mange.*

In order to set things right with Jack, she had to swallow her pride and apologize; maybe then he would see her as a worthy mate. "I am worthy!" she said before stomping across the room. She had been training to become an alpha female since she was four years old, way before Jack ever considered being an alpha male, but being the alpha's son had its own perks.

She marched into the bedroom and yanked the closet door open, her foul mood getting the better of her. As the door bounced off the wall, the mirror rattled, and her breath caught in her throat. Seven years of bad luck wasn't something she dared to toy with, but thankfully, the mirror didn't crack.

Getting back to the task at hand, she sorted through her clothes, looking for something to change into. A simple olive green shirt and a pair of cut-off shorts weren't exactly her style. She would have preferred something a little more daring, but was trying to tone it down a bit, if only for the day. She quickly changed and slipped on her running shoes before standing in front of the full-length mirror for one last inspection. Raking her fingers through the waves in her hair, she liked what she saw as she twisted from side to side. *I could be the girl next door... well, almost.*

Creaking hinges caused her to scowl, and she walked over to the bedroom door and glanced towards the kitchen. "What are you doing here, Travis?" she asked when her uncle peeked around the corner.

"Are you alone?"

"Do I look like I'm alone?" Tracy didn't mean to sound snappy, but then again, it was her uncle who had an uncanny way of bringing out the worst in her.

"Aren't you a little ray of sunshine? What crawled up your ass?" Travis asked, looking around as if he expected to find someone else there. She rolled her eyes.

"Enough with the family bonding, what do you

want?" she said, trailing him into the living room. He always seemed to show up at the wrong time, but anytime he showed up was wrong in her opinion.

"I stopped by to see how things were going. I talked the alpha into letting me install the plumbing in the new cabins, so there will be no questions as to why I'm on this side of the river. Since you moved here, I can't keep an eye on you and we're running out of time." His eyes darted around the room. "This is a nice place. Just don't get too comfortable and forget why you came here."

Tracy plodded over and flopped down on the sofa, annoyed by his comment. "I'm not in the mood for this right now." She flipped her hand in a contemptuous manner. Entertaining him wasn't something she cared to do at the moment, and the sooner he left, the better.

"Excuse me! I call the shots here, not you! And based on your attitude, one would assume you struck out with Jack."

"I did no such thing. You don't know what's going on around here, so don't assume." Tracy made a mental note to spray sanitizer as soon as he left. She didn't need his scent lingering as a reminder of why she was there. Truth be told, she only agreed to move to Cloverly to get away from him; Jack was just a bonus.

"Listen, sweetheart, I've worked too damn hard to get you where you are and I have no intentions of letting you screw things up now. So tell me, how are things going with you and Jack?"

"Oh, you know... my love life is wonderful. I'm sitting here waiting for my knight in shining armor as we speak."

"That bad? You told me you had things under control but obviously not! I just saw him and Mason crossing the ditch. I don't think your knight is going to rescue you anytime soon." He walked over to the front window and pulled back the curtain.

Travis was tall and stocky with dusty brown hair and a full beard that covered the scars along his jawline. He wasn't friendly, and most of the other pack members kept their distance. Not because they considered him a threat, they just didn't trust him, which amused Tracy because she didn't trust him either. Pushing the chair back against the wall, he sat down across from her and she cringed, bracing herself for the lecture that was due to follow.

"Word's out Jack will complete his training within the year. If you're going to be his mate, you need to make your move *now*. We have to stop the alpha before he splits the region. If not, there is no way we can take back the pack."

"I know. I'm going to apologize, but I can't if I'm stuck here entertaining you."

"What are you apologizing for?"

"Nothing, just a misunderstanding."

"As in human? Don't tell me you are now friends with them? That is not allowed," he growled.

"Stop being ridiculous, you know me better than that." She fluttered her lashes. "They're trouble, I know. You've preached it for years."

Travis rubbed his beard. "Our family name is at stake here so don't screw this up." He pushed up from the chair and Tracy glared at him, but he ignored her and walked out of the room.

"Shut up and shave," she mumbled as the back door slammed behind him. Despite what he thought, she had no intention of failing. Jack would be her mate soon enough, making her the alpha female, and rightfully so.

She walked out the door and inhaled a calming breath. "Be convincing," she told herself as she stepped off the porch, heading down the road to Jack's cabin. *About the other day...* the apology played in her head as she walked across the street. With a bit of luck, maybe it would sound sincere enough to get back into Jack's good graces, or at least, she hoped so. Seeing his car in the driveway gave her the courage to face him, even if it were just an act.

She straightened her shirt and rubbed down her hair as she walked across the yard. Calling out to Jack, she stepped around to the driver's side of the car and snarled when she noticed the wheel lying on the ground. She hated that wheel, along with the entire car for that matter. Competing with other females for Jack's attention was one thing; she could easily threaten any of them. But how could she intimidate a car? She grinned and ran her hand over the shiny black surface. *A sledgehammer.* The thought was perfect, but considering Jack loved the car more than himself, that probably wouldn't gain her any favors.

Jack wasn't the type to go off and leave a mess, like tools scattered around, unless... She looked down the road and tapped her fingernail against her lip as a plan formed in her head.

Tracy knew she'd have to make up time in order to catch them, so she raced across the backyard towards the oak tree. She didn't know where the two males were headed, but at least she wouldn't run into them if they decided to turn back.

She skittered up the trail as quietly as her adrenaline-infused body would allow. Excited she might actually beat them at their own game, she grinned. *Oh yeah. I got this.* She knew the area well, better than most, considering all the time she spent scouting with Tucker. As she ran along the path, she wasn't expecting anyone to be in the woods that late in the afternoon, but upon rounding a bend, she screeched.

"Whoa!" Randy said, throwing his hands up to catch her as she barreled forward, knocking him to the ground. "Where's the fire, gorgeous?"

"What? Who are you?" Tracy's long, red hair fell over his chest as she lifted her head, clearly bewildered. Feeling the heat slithering up her neck, she didn't embarrass easily but there she lay on top of a complete stranger. Thankfully, the others weren't around to witness her fall. They would've had a field day with all the snide remarks they could make at her expense.

"For starters, I'm Randy, and I could be wrong, but I believe you just ran me down. But an apology isn't necessary. You can run me down anytime," he said, his hands gripping her waist.

Her wolf perked-up and Tracy jumped to her feet and backed away. *Oh hell*, she thought as Randy rolled over and propped up on his elbow, his gaze raking slowly down her body.

"Damn it, girl, you got it going on," Randy said, clearly enjoying her utter discomfort.

"Shut up!" she snarled. She didn't know who he was but seeing him cocked up on his elbow, and the thin line of dark hair that disappeared beneath the waist of his jeans—she fidgeted. *He's human. He's beneath you. He's trouble, always trouble. But damn!* Feeling both excited and aggravated, she smirked at his grin.

"Controlling... I like it." He chuckled when she placed her hands on her hips and glared.

Unable to look away, she shifted on her feet. Something about him drew her in, and she extended her hand. "Get up," she said hatefully. Irked by his laid-back manner, she wanted to slap him as she pulled him off the ground but the feel of his callus-covered hand around hers sent warning tremors through her body.

"I already am," he said, invading her personal space.

With her hand splayed over his chest, his muscles flexed beneath her touch, and a stifling heat pooled low in her belly. He smelled of woods, soap and sweat, a lethal combination all its own and she wanted to push him away, but instead, her traitorous body leaned forward. As she searched his steel-blue eyes, her breath hitched, and she instantly knew she was in trouble. The pull towards him was strong, a bond or lust? She wasn't sure. He was human, and she could never be bonded with a human, so it had to be lust. She shuddered and pushed him away. "What are you, some kind of—"

"Perve," he finished for her, "It takes one to know one."

For a split second, Tracy was taken aback by his comment. She believed him to be a player, a tomcat, a horn-dog even, but at no point did she consider him a perve. She glanced up at the mischief that sparked in his eyes. His wicked sense of humor amused her, and as hard as she tried, she couldn't keep from grinning. "I'm Tracy. Do you live around here?" She had to admit: for a human, he was delicious, and her wolf started drooling.

"Yeah, I live just outside of town," he said, shoving his

hands into his pockets. "So what's your hurry?"

*I was looking for Jack, but now that I found you, my wolf likes you better.* She blushed at the thought. "No hurry. I needed to run off some steam." Ignoring her wolf as a soft growl rumbled in her chest, she cleared her throat to disguise the sound. She needed to run and get away from him, but her head couldn't command her feet, so she stood there in a drool-induced haze.

"Well, I'm glad you ran into me, but I hate to think this all ends here," he said, rocking back on his heels.

"Who says it has to end here?" Tracy frowned and cocked her head to the side. It was getting late, and she could hear voices in the distance, which couldn't be good. *He's human. He's trouble, always trouble.* But with his closeness, she also felt a sense of protection. "Did you have something in mind?" Her wolf had a few suggestions of its own, but she was quick to push those out of her head.

"Yeah, but we need to get out of here first," Randy said, holding out his hand.

Tracy wasn't sure where he was leading her, but to see his smile, she would follow him to the moon. *Trouble, always trouble.* The annoying voice taunted her, but the soft growl that rumbled in her chest spurred her on. When they walked out of the woods, she glanced back at Jack's cabin before they followed the tree line to the street.

"Here we are," Randy said, dropping her hand. Standing beside the large black motorcycle, Tracy grinned when he pulled a key from his pocket. "Wanna go for a ride?" he asked before gripping the handlebars and mounting the bike.

"Hell yeah!" Tracy exclaimed as the large, black beast

roared to life. Uttering a low growl of approval that couldn't be heard over the rumble of the motor, she took the helmet he offered. She glanced back towards the oak tree and seated herself behind him as all thoughts of Jack vanished. Warning bells sounded as she placed the helmet on her head, but she didn't care. Just once, she wanted to do something for herself, which, at that moment, was riding on the back of his motorcycle.

"Hang on!" he yelled over his shoulder.

Snugly planted behind him, Tracy placed her hands on his sides, but when the bike moved forward, she slid her hands around his waist. Her wolf was excited by the way his body moved with the bike, and she drew in a sharp breath. As they turned onto Main Street, the bike accelerated, and she squealed, practically wetting her pants. It was crazy, a death wish, and so *her*. She squealed again. *Trouble always trouble.* She growled at the persistent voice. How would she explain it if she were caught? Would she even try? Travis would be pissed, no doubt, but she was willing to risk it. For the first time in her life, her wolf was content, and she was over the moon.

With her chin resting on his shoulder, they continued down the highway, and she wanted to remember every detail and every minute of the ride. From the white lines that zipped past, keeping rhythm with her heartbeat, to the security she felt tucked safely behind him as her body melded with his. And if it weren't for the thought of falling off the bike at highway speeds, she would throw her arms out and fly! It was the most amazing experience of her life, an experience she would never forget.

Too soon the ride ended when Randy turned onto a narrow dirt road that curved behind a church, past a small cemetery before stopping in front of a large, weathered barn. As he pushed the kickstand down, he put out his hand to steady her and she stepped off the bike.

"That was incredible." Tracy laughed, raising her hands to her chest and trying to catch her breath. Her first ride on a motorcycle made her legs shake and her heart race. She was hooked.

"Have you ever been on a motorcycle before?" Randy asked as he observed the excitement dancing in her eyes. He took the helmet and placed it on the seat.

"No, but I loved it. Could you teach me to ride?" Tracy adored the freedom she felt as they flew down the highway. She didn't understand guys and cars, but she understood the whole wind-in-your-hair thing. "Please, please, please. I'll beg if I have to."

"Wow. Most girls are happy just riding." He flicked his brows and she blushed. He had no idea the images he sparked in her mind, and she wasn't about to tell him. Her wolf, on the other hand, was anticipating an all-out belly rub. She chuckled as he led her over to a rickety, old wagon parked in front of the open barn doors. Unsure of what he had planned, she gasped when he grabbed her by the waist and set her on the edge of the wagon.

"So, if I teach you how to ride, what do I get?" Randy asked as he jumped up beside her and poked her in the ribs.

Tracy swatted his hand away and giggled while gazing at Randy. What would she give him? She sucked in her lower lip and looked around the area. With a cornfield to the right and woods to the left, she was certain no one would know she was there. "Anything you want." She really didn't expect him to teach her how to ride the motorcycle, but if he were willing, she would not refuse the offer. Unlike Jack, Randy was attracted to her, and as much as she didn't want to admit it, she was equally attracted to him.

"Anything could mean just about everything." Randy flashed a smile and she smiled back, or at least, she thought she did. Who knew at that point?

"Anything." Her voice was wispy and she leaned against his shoulder. His scent drifted around her and she practically purred in his ear. *Trouble, always trouble.*

"So when did you want to start?" Randy asked, his breath sweeping across her cheek.

"Can we start tomorrow? I'll meet you around noon at the park." Tracy would have loved nothing more than to have stayed there and forget the world around her existed, but she needed time to clear her thoughts. He was messing with her mind, which was messing with her wolf, and that was something no male had ever done before. *He's our mate,* her wolf insisted, but she wouldn't allow herself to go there. It would be too dangerous, not only for him but for her.

"Tomorrow's good. I'll meet you around three," he said before jumping down from the wagon and wedging his body between her knees. "Or better yet, I could tie you to the wagon and keep you here." He grinned.

"What a smooth talker. I bet you sweep all the females off their feet with that line." She giggled, again. "Three it is."

"Where do you live?" he asked as he lowered her to the ground.

"Down by the river on Cabin Run, but it's not a good idea for you to take me home. My uncle is extremely over-protective," Tracy said, trying to come up with an excuse to keep him away from the cabins. "He has a rule against motorcycles. He thinks they're dangerous."

"Oh, hell, the bike is harmless. Me on the other hand, I don't follow anybody's rules," Randy said as they walked back toward the motorcycle. Handing her the helmet, he straddled the bike. "Just because you live in a small town doesn't mean you should let your guard down. This world is full of crazies, and I'm sure there are a few here in Cloverly as well. Get behind me. I'm taking you home, like it or not."

Tracy smiled. Never in her life had anyone ever worried about her or her safety. He was human, and they only cared about themselves, or so she was always told. But it was late, and the chance of Travis being at the cabin wasn't likely, so against her better judgment, she agreed to the ride. "Fine, but as soon as you drop me off, you have to leave."

"Well, that sucks. I was hoping we could neck on the porch."

# Nine

*Jesse*

Jesse rolled over and glared at the ringing phone on the bedside table. It was morning, based on the chirping outside her window, and the thought of throwing the phone at the unruly birds seemed like a reasonable thing to do. Instead, she closed her eyes and answered Lori's call. "It's eight-thirty, I'm sleeping," she grumbled before the phone slipped out of her hand, landing on the carpet next to her bed. Rolling back over, she shielded her eyes from the sunlight that sneaked through the curtains. A minute later, or so she thought, her head bounced against the mattress as the pillow slid out from beneath it.

"Wake up!" Lori said, swatting her with the pillow.

"It's Saturday; don't you ever sleep in?" Jesse asked, staring daggers at her ex-best friend. As the curtains swayed in the breeze, the blinding light entered the room, and she hid her eyes behind her hand. "Go away!" After spending the entire week working with her dad, moving furniture, painting, and organizing his office, like it or not, she was going back to sleep.

"Fine, I'll bring Brian over here. But do you really want him to see you in that ratty, old shirt and zebra-striped underwear?"

Jesse lay there with her eyes closed as Lori bounced on the edge of the bed, causing the mattress springs to squeak. Relaxed with the movement and thinking about Brian as his name echoed in her head, Jesse's eyes shot open and she suddenly shrieked. She sprang off the bed, kicking out her legs, trying to escape the white linen monster that clung to her feet as she reached over and grabbed Lori's arm. "Help!" she snorted before falling to the floor, "Brian's home!"

"Duh, ya think?" Lori laughed. "Aren't you a comical one early in the morning?" She pulled loose the sheet that was twisted around Jesse's legs, and tossed it on the bed. "Steve said they would be here around ten-thirty, and since I can't perform miracles... it's all on you, babe. You have less than an hour."

"I can't perfect this in an hour," Jesse whined, falling back on the bed.

"And Rome wasn't built in a day, I know, but do your best."

Jesse tromped over to the walk-in closet, and yanked open the door. Grabbing a soft-yellow tank-top and a pair of white shorts off the shelf, she flashed Lori a dirty look as she entered the bathroom. "Back off my underwear," she grumbled, slamming the door. She would never admit it, but she was excited to meet Brian. After the way Lori and Megan refused to describe him, she figured he had to

fall somewhere between Randy and Steve. And considering Brian was Steve's best friend, that in itself spoke volumes. Steve was a dreamboat, so wouldn't Brian be the same? No matter what, she wouldn't get her hopes up because she was looking for Mister Right, and so far, he was nonexistent.

"Hurry up," Lori said through the door. "We don't have all day."

"Yah, uh no," Jesse said with a toothbrush shoved in her mouth. Spitting out the toothpaste, she snarled her lip. She didn't like rushing through her morning routine, but if she refused, Lori would have probably kicked the door down and dragged her out in her underwear. She washed her face and grinned at her reflection. Her nightshirt wasn't as bad as Lori remarked. It was white and worn, which probably made it a little see-through, and a tad bit on the short side, but she never imagined she'd be entertaining anyone that morning. She pulled the shirt over her head and tossed it into the laundry basket beneath the sink as Lori banged on the door.

"Would you come on?"

"I'm trying to get dressed. Could you give me three minutes?" Jesse fastened her shorts and slipped the shirt over her head before opening the door.

"I gave you twenty-two, now let's go."

Jesse ignored her and turned back to the mirror to finish her routine. She grabbed a brush and ran it through her hair before walking into the bedroom. Sitting down on the bed, she applied sunscreen to her face, arms and legs and then slipped on her sandals. Snubbing Lori who was standing propped against the door frame, she hurried over to the mirror hanging on the closet door. Satisfied with her appearance, she turned and grinned. "So where is Prince Charming?"

"Never mind him. I smell bacon and I'm hungry." Lori took off down the stairs without looking back.

Sitting at the kitchen table, Jesse watched Lori neatly stack bacon and tomatoes on the two slices of toast she pulled from the toaster. It smelled delicious, but food was definitely out of the question for her.

"I can't believe you're not eating. You're starving me to death." Lori took a large bite of her sandwich and moaned. "This is better than sex."

Jesse jumped from her chair and ran over to the sink as coffee spewed from her nose. She squeezed her eyes shut and coughed while groping for a dish towel. "I cannot believe you just said that." Her voice was raspy as she glared back at Lori.

"Hey, I just wanted you to know what you were missing." Lori took another bite.

"I'm too frickin' nervous to eat, and you're not helping. I have no idea what I'm getting myself into, thanks to you and Megan." Jesse sat back down at the table. "Is there anything else you would like to say before I finish my coffee?"

"Nope, I'm good. You're the one acting like I'm leading you to slaughter. I promise you will survive this." Lori placed her plate in the sink. "It's just Brian, and he doesn't bite. I don't think."

Rolling her eyes, Jesse looked down at the cup which she pushed back on the table. "Come on, I'm ready to get this over with." If her morning were any indication of how the day would go, she was doomed.

B . S . T O D D

Jesse followed Lori across the porch and down the steps when a basketball bounced against the pavement and Steve yelled. Afraid of looking like a giddy school girl, she focused her attention on the ground. It was far safer for her, at least until her heart calmed. Finally, mustering up enough courage to take a quick peek, the wind gusted, wrapping her in a layer of thick curls. She wanted to die right there on the spot but she struggled to contain her long, black tresses, and bumped into Lori while gathering her hair over her shoulder. "Why did you stop? Good Lord, could this day get any more embarrassing?" Following Lori's line of sight, queasiness churned her stomach. "I can't do this," Jesse whispered, sneaking another peek at Brian. "You should have told me he was..."

"We told you he was a fireman, what did you expect?"

"I didn't expect him to be so, so... Thor-ish. I'm definitely not his type."

"What are you talking about?"

"Lori, look at me! Guys like him have skinny chicks hanging off their arms, and in case you haven't noticed, I'm not a skinny chick."

"Oh, I've noticed and so have all the guys in Cloverly. And I agree you're not built like a stick, but you are the next best thing to a goddess." Lori grinned when Brian walked across the street. He was wearing a red Camp Semiway t-shirt and faded jeans. "Hey, Brian," Lori said, pushing Jesse out in front of her. "This is Jesse, my best friend."

"Steve told me I had a new neighbor. It's nice to meet you," Brian said.

"Yeah? Well, I've heard a lot about you too," Jesse said. *Great! Now he knows you've been talking about him.*

*Good job there, sister.* Brian looked exactly like she thought he would, *times one thousand.* Ripped with muscles, he could have just stepped off the cover of a bodybuilding magazine for all she knew. Tall, with golden blonde hair and hazel eyes, he wasn't the type of guy she normally dated. Not that she wouldn't have wanted to, but because he would never have been interested in her. She had curves in all the right places, but in a world where thinness ruled, she was a scant eight.

"Hey, guys, we have a few hours before we have to be at Megan's, so I was thinking we could hang out at Sallee's," Steve suggested while tossing the basketball across the street.

"Whatever you all want to do is fine with me," Jesse replied. Hanging out at the boulders sounded like the perfect day to her. If only Lori would agree.

"Come on, Lori. It's early. We have plenty of time," Steve said, slipping his arms around her waist and whispering in her ear. Jesse pursed her lips when Lori giggled. They were up to something, and she was confident that something involved her.

"Okay, let's go," Lori said a little too quickly. Her eagerness was a giant, red flag flapping in the wind, which only confirmed she and Steve were up to no-good.

After their first hiking adventure, Jesse knew the path would be clear, so she sat down on the step and quickly adjusted the straps on her sandals while Lori and Steve made a beeline around the house. "I'm ready," she said and Brian pulled her to her feet.

"So how do you like Cloverly?" he asked as they hurried around the house to catch up with Lori and Steve, who were nowhere in sight.

"I love it." Glancing down, she sucked in her cheeks to keep from grinning like a fool. She wasn't sure what just happened over the course of two minutes, but Brian was still holding her hand. Following him into the woods, Lori's laughter could be heard in the distance and she mentally rolled her eyes. "I hope you know the way because I've only been to Sallee's once."

"It's not hard to find, just stay on the main trail," he said. The walk didn't seem to take as long, which she credited to Brian. His casual conversation and the way he smiled managed to dissipate all the awkwardness she felt earlier and she relaxed.

"Well, look who decided to join us," Steve said and Lori grinned.

Assuming they had jogged to the clearing in order to embarrass her, Jesse snubbed her nose when she walked past the dynamic duo. They may have thought they were pulling a fast one on her, but she had them pegged from the start.

"Where do you want to sit?" Brian asked once they were standing in front of the boulders.

"Up there," Jesse said while quickly braiding her hair down one side. Climbing up the boulders, she was excited to spend the afternoon with Brian if only to learn more about him. That was until her ankle twisted and her foot slipped out of her shoe.

"Are you okay?" Brian pulled her against his side to steady her.

*Kill me now.* Jesse slipped her foot back into the sandal and knew her complexion couldn't hide the blush infusing her cheeks. How many more times would she humiliate herself before she spontaneously combusted?

She scowled and flinched at their subsequent snickers, knowing she was their entertainment for the day. Pulling away from Brian, she continued the climb until she was firmly seated on the top of the boulder.

As the day wore on, Jesse talked about her childhood, growing up in Indy, and her summer visits to her grandmother's. She even accused Brian of hiding from her during those visits. He chuckled and she giggled. He was easy to talk to and listening to him chatter on about Camp Semiway made her want to break out a tent and go camping.

"Come on, lovebirds, we need to go or we'll be late for the party!" Lori yelled.

"On our way," Brian said. Helping Jesse to her feet, her foot slipped and she squealed. Scissor-splits were something flexible cheerleaders in high school attempted, and now she gave it a try. Hiding her face in her hands, it became very clear the universe wasn't on her side.

"Are you all right?" Lori laughed as Jesse's legs splayed out across the stone.

"I didn't realize you were so flexible!" Steve laughed.

"Hush, Steve. You have no idea what I've been through today," Jesse said as the blush moved up her neck.

Brian pressed his lips together to keep from laughing as he lifted Jesse off the rock. "Let me go first," he said. Climbing down the boulder with Jesse hanging on his arm, he finally cracked a grin.

Jesse had composed herself long enough to get to the ground, but when she looked up at Brian, she lost it. "Thank you," she said between snorts, which caused more laughter to boom around the clearing. "It's not funny, guys!" But it was funny, and as hard as she tried not to laugh, she couldn't contain it.

"What do we have here?"

Jesse startled and the four quickly turned to see to whom the voice behind them belonged. Wearing a pair of low-rise, denim shorts and a green, polka-dot bikini top, Tracy was definitely not suitably dressed for an outing in the woods. Stunned by the swanky redhead, Jesse opened her mouth to say something but soon decided against it. It was none of Tracy's business what they were doing there, at least, as far as she was concerned.

"Hi, I'm Steve." Taking a step forward, Steve smiled and his eyes dropped down to the green dotted top while Jesse cringed.

"It's nice to meet you, Steve. I'm Tracy."

A sudden urge to barf settled over Jesse when Tracy flipped her hair over her shoulder and flashed a toothpaste smile. She had to admit, the girl knew how to get a guy's attention, as proven by the goofy grin Steve wore. Unable to hold back any longer, she rolled her eyes. Steve was like a bluegill chomping at an empty hook, and since Tracy managed to snag him within a minute of joining their group, it was a little telling. She looked over at Brian but Lori was the one who caught her eye. Steve didn't have a problem with the feisty intruder, but the flip side of the coin wasn't as shiny. Jesse sucked in a breath and waited for Lori to intervene. *Three... two... one...*

"I'm Lori. Steve's girlfriend." Lori wedged herself between them, and Jesse smiled when she crossed her arms over her chest, sending a clear signal to the fiery vixen, but Tracy just smirked and looked down her nose.

Unfazed by the yappy, little brunette, Tracy winked at Steve and his chuckle landed him an elbow to the stomach. The poor guy didn't realize he was caught between a tiger and a wildcat but as Tracy stepped back, Jesse scowled. Playing the catch-and-release game, Steve was already history and Tracy turned from him, setting her sights on Brian.

"What's your name, handsome?"

"I'm Brian. It's a pleasure to meet you," he said as he offered his hand. Playing her touchy-feely routine, Tracy seductively smiled and slid her hand into his. Jesse shuddered.

"Oh, the pleasure is *all mine*," Tracy said.

Jesse glowered as she looked up at the towering two. Three inches was the height difference between Brian and Tracy, making Jesse's five-foot-seven seem insignificant. "Tracy!" Jesse snapped. Her eyes scanned down Tracy's scantily clad body and stopped at their connected hands. Tracy could have made burlap look hot, but at the moment, Jesse wasn't impressed.

"Jesse, I didn't recognize you without the curtain. I see you're taking full advantage of the testosterone in the area." Tracy chuckled when Brian pulled his hand from hers.

"What are you talking about?" Jesse asked with a slight sneer.

"Saturday morning. Three a.m. Your window," Tracy replied as the color drained from Jesse's face. Leaning down, she whispered, "This is the only warning you get. Keep to your own."

The hissing whisper and the flare of Tracy's eyes caught Jesse offguard, and she stumbled back against Brian. She wasn't a violent person, but being bullied was something she refused to tolerate. "I hardly think you own

Jack, but if I'm wrong, maybe you should invest in a leash," she said while regaining her footing and resting her hands on her hips. She didn't really consider Tracy a threat, yet something in her eyes said otherwise.

"Tracy!" A commanding voice boomed from behind them, and Jesse stiffened as Jack stepped around Brian and walked over to the cringing redhead. With his arms crossed over his chest, he looked quite intimidating before a silent conversation passed between them. But Jesse still didn't believe they were a couple. Jack reminded her more of a scolding big brother, rather than a jealous boyfriend.

"Ben's waiting for you," Jack said. Judging by the frown on his face, Jack wasn't thrilled to be there, or maybe he wasn't thrilled with Tracy being there. Either way, it looked like Tracy had pissed off the wrong person and Jesse found it slightly amusing. *So not his girlfriend.*

"But I didn't..." Tracy paused when she realized everyone was watching her.

"I didn't say you did." Jack's brow creased in warning.

Tracy huffed and stomped into the woods as Jesse struggled to keep the smile off her face. It wasn't the nicest way to respond, but it served her right for acting like a pain-in-the-butt.

"Sorry for the intrusion," Jack said, and just as fast as he appeared, he was gone.

"I take it that was Tracy?" Lori glanced over at Jesse and pulled a face. "Let's get out of here or Megan will think we're not coming."

# *Ten*

## *Jack*

Jack kept pace behind Tracy as they made their way
through the woods. When the alpha showed up
unannounced, he volunteered to go get her, knowing she
would be at the boulders. What he wasn't expecting to
find was Jesse and her friends there as well. As soon as he
walked out of the woods, he heard Jesse telling Tracy to
*get a leash*. For what purpose, he didn't know, but seeing
the sneer on Tracy's face suggested the conversation was
about to get heated. Interrupting them as he stepped
around the large male, he could feel the tension in the air
and if he read Jesse right, she was pissed.

Scolding Tracy in front of them probably wasn't the
best way to handle the situation, but he needed to shut her
down before she could do any real damage, and using the
alpha was the perfect solution.

Tracy kept her head down as she stalked across the

yard. With her arms wrapped around her body, she peeked up at the door. Jack could tell she was nervous and wondering what the meeting was about, but he didn't know himself. She paused for just a moment before dropping her arms down. Lifting her chin, she straightened her shoulders as she shoved her hands into her back pockets.

"Are you ready?" Jack asked as he walked across the front porch.

"No," she whispered. Tracy inhaled a shaky breath and blinked back tears. The worried look on her face told Jack exactly what was going through her mind.

"It's not what you think," he said, giving her a minute to pull herself together. Jack felt guilty for allowing Tracy to believe she was in trouble with the alpha. Although he hadn't come out and said she was, he knew she would assume so. He opened the door and motioned for her to enter.

"I'm sorry, Alpha Cooper. I didn't know you were coming today," Tracy said as she entered the cabin.

"No need to apologize, it's an unscheduled meeting," Ben replied.

She smiled half-heartedly as she hurried across the room and found a seat next to Whitney on the couch.

Once Jack was seated, Ben stood in front of the group. He was strong and intimidating. Not because of his size or attitude, but because he wasn't afraid to step up and take control of a situation that would benefit the pack. He wasn't the type to throw around his authority and never expected the others to do anything he wouldn't do himself. He was honest and fair and went out of his way to make everyone feel important, whether they deserved it or not.

"I stopped by to talk about the living arrangements, but first, I have a package for... Tucker Wilson," he read. Handing Tucker the stuffed envelope, he waited for him to take his seat. "I spoke with the elders and we agreed you all have represented the pack well here in Cloverly. So along with Jack and Mason, if any of you want to stay past the summer, you are welcome to do so. That is, as long as there aren't any problems," Ben added. "We still have a lot of work to do, but I hope by the time winter sets in, there will be at least three others joining you. You have plenty of time to decide, just let me know your answers by the end of August."

"I would like to stay," Whitney said as she squeezed Mason's hand.

"That goes without saying." Ben chuckled.

"I would like to stay. If I can." Tracy looked over at Jack and he nodded.

"I'm staying," Tucker said.

"Well, it wouldn't be the same without you." Ben laughed. "But if there is ever a problem, I will put you back with the pack. This is not a game. We will continue to show respect to our neighbors and community leaders by living alongside them peacefully. That being said, enjoy the rest of your summer and if there's anything you need, let me know and I'll have it waiting for you at the next pack meeting."

Jack waited for the others to exit through the back door, eager to celebrate their new residential status. "Do you have a minute?" He nodded in the direction of the front door.

"Sure," Ben said and Jack followed him out to the

porch.

"So you finally gave him the package," Jack remarked as they headed across the yard and down the road.

"Yeah, I wanted to give him plenty of time to weigh his options. I know he'll want to go back to the Blue Ridge Pack and discuss it with his dad. But I've already talked to the alpha and since I am his mate's younger brother, she owes me for all the times she beat me up when we were little."

"You don't have to worry about Tucker. He already made it clear he wants to stay, and I know he will make a great alpha." Jack cut across the yard to Tucker's cabin.

Ben sat down on the edge of the porch as Jack continued to pace the yard. "So are you going to tell me what's on your mind? I know you didn't walk all the way down here just to talk about Tucker."

Jack ran his hand through his hair and blew out a breath. "I have a bond with Megan."

"That's a relief! I thought this conversation would be about Tracy." Ben looked up, and still Jack paced. "So having a bond with Megan is your problem? That doesn't seem like a problem to me."

"She's a human, I think. I saw her at Sallee's Rock with her friends. I screwed up and tried to defend her, which pissed her off," Jack said, shoving his hands into his pockets.

"Why would defending her make her mad?"

"She thought I was trying to impress Jesse."

"Were you?"

"No! Jesse probably mentioned me walking her home, and when I saw Megan at the boulders, I guess she thought I was there for Jesse. I only went there because it was late and I wasn't sure they'd find their way out of the woods before dark. I wasn't planning to confront them. Mason and I stayed hidden, but when Megan came around the boulders, she saw us."

"And that's when the bond formed?" Ben looked across the road to the ditch.

"Yes. And when Randy came out, I had no choice but to confront him and that's when Megan got upset. At first, she wouldn't look at me, but when she did, her eyes flared like a wolf's. Do you know of any other wolves in this area?"

"If she were a wolf, you would have picked up her scent."

"I don't know. Something about it was off," Jack said.

The alpha grinned. "Congratulations!"

"You don't mind she's human? I mean, I know we have humans in the pack, but you're the Regional Alpha, and I'm going to be an alpha. I don't want any negative attention to fall on you because of me."

"No, I don't mind at all. I think it's great. Humans are just as important as wolves in my eyes. Her being a human only solidifies that we're our own pack and everyone is welcome. You should talk to Dr. Stevens. His mate is human. I'm sure he could answer all your questions."

"This just wasn't what I expected. I never, not in a million years, thought..." Jack closed his eyes and his jaw twitched.

"I know it's hard to let go, but I think it's time you face the facts, son. Lizzy isn't coming back." The alpha stood and placed his hand on Jack's shoulder. "You have to move on. It will probably be one of the hardest things you ever do, but it is time."

"I guess..." Jack's mind traveled back to the promise he had made years ago. "*What you're feeling is not a bond. You're too young. You're grieving,*" the elders told him. But as he grew older, time didn't erase the feelings that simmered in his heart. "*Why did you leave!*" he *screamed and fell to his knees. "I don't want this, I never wanted this." Staring at the moonless sky, his heart shattered. Where did you go? Where are you now?* The unanswered questions settled in the back of his mind, tormenting him. As her memory faded, he struggled to contain the heart-wrenching loneliness that bore deep into his soul. He was just past puberty, not old enough to feel the sorrow that burned in his heart, yet there it was. "*Lizzy, I know you're out there and I will find you. I promise.*"

It had been sixteen years, a century ago, and the idea of moving on without Lizzy was something he tried not to think about. But he also knew his dad was right and he had to give Megan a chance.

"When you get everything sorted out, I'd like to meet the female that has my boy so stressed and confused," Ben said, bringing Jack away from his thoughts.

"Good luck. After the way she brushed me off, I'm beginning to wonder if the bond has any effect on her at all," Jack said as they headed back down the road.

"Don't worry, you have plenty of time. The bond won't disappear unless you deny it, but it will weaken if neither of you pursues it."

"I guess it's a good thing, considering I know absolutely nothing about her or where she lives."

"I wouldn't worry too much. Fate has a way of

working things out," his father said. "Not trying to change the subject, but I'm interested in how the training is going?"

"Good, I guess. Sometimes I wonder if I'm really cut out for this alpha business. I'm not sure I can control my own life, let alone, a whole pack."

"Well, I have to admit. When you first picked Mason to be your beta, I wasn't sure it was a good idea. You two, together, I remember the days." Ben grinned and Jack laughed.

"We were a handful, but hey, we grew up. Somewhat."

"It's the somewhat that had me worried. Seriously, though, you both are doing a wonderful job. And it only proves sometimes the Regional Alpha can be wrong."

"Well, we won't hold it against you," Jack teased. "Mason may be my beta, but there are times when he comes off as an alpha. I guess that's why we work so well together. The lines get a little blurred at times, but in the end, we get the job done. Plus, being my best friend, he's not afraid to straighten me out when he thinks I need it."

"That's good to know. It's hard to find a good beta who's easy to work with and being your best friend makes it that much easier. So what about Whitney and Tracy?"

"Honestly? I think Tracy should train as a scout. She and Tucker are always out running. She's a strong female, and she feels more at home in the woods than anywhere else. Whitney likes to stay closer to the pack. She's as strong as Tracy but better with the pack in general. She's like the mother hen of the group, but don't tell her I said that," Jack replied as they crossed the yard.

"It's up to you. Someday they will be major players in

the pack, so place them where you feel the need."

"Alpha Cooper, can you stay for dinner? Mason's grilling steaks," Whitney asked as she walked around the house to meet them.

"I would love to," Ben said, following her to the backyard. Observing the small group, he turned to Jack. "I think you have a good pack here."

"Yeah, it gets a little hairy at times." Jack laughed. He did have a good pack, even though he had to contend with Tracy.

# Eleven

*Jesse*

Jesse glanced up at the large, plantation-style house that sat atop the hill. It was huge, twice the size of her grandmother's and probably just as old. The painted white bricks, large columns and an upstairs balcony fueled her imagination and she could picture debutantes gathered on the front lawn for a Sunday brunch. She grinned when Megan squealed and bounced out of one of the doors.

"I didn't think you'd ever get home," Megan said, wrapping her arms around Brian's waist. Their closeness was instantly evident by the smile on her face, which made Jesse smile.

"I wasn't gone that long." He laughed and hugged her back.

"Two weeks is a long time, considering I was so excited for you to meet Jesse. Isn't she great?"

Brian winked.

Grading a guy as a potential boyfriend was something

Jesse had always done until her last boyfriend disaster. But based on the defective Grade-A-Guy scale, Brian was making straight As.

"About that," he teased. "How is it she's been visiting her grandmother every summer and I'm just now hearing about it?" He tickled Megan's side, and she squealed as Jesse walked around the front of the Jeep and followed them up the drive.

"You all know where the changing rooms are; help yourselves!" Megan said as Lori and Steve walked up the drive, joining them. "Mom ordered pizza that will be delivered in an hour. I hope you're hungry."

Before Lori could comment, Jesse grabbed her by the arm and led her around to the back of the house. "Come on. I want to get into the pool before the guys do," she whispered as she pulled Lori into the changing room. Setting her bag on the small wooden bench beneath the window, she kicked off her shoes.

"What's the hurry? The pool's not going anywhere." Lori pulled her swimsuit out of her bag and glanced up. "You like Brian." Her silly grin and the flick of her brow made Jesse groan.

"I just want to get in the pool before they do, okay?" Truth be told, she was hoping to submerge herself from the neck down if only to hide her *not-quite-bikini-ready* body. Stepping into the first stall, Jesse undressed and tossed her clothes over the dividing wall.

"Don't be shy, Jesse. Everyone's already seen you in a bathing suit. Well, everyone except Brian."

Jesse chose to ignore the snickers from the neighboring stall as she tugged on the one-piece swimsuit. Once everything was securely in place, she fastened the strap at the back of her neck and pushed open the door. Glancing out the window, she watched Brian and Steve racing across the concrete patio before jumping into the pool and splashing Megan off her float.

"Damn, girl! You need to anchor that float 'cause you don't have enough weight to keep yourself top-side!" Steve laughed and grabbed the runaway float.

Jesse couldn't hear Megan's response, but seeing the wicked grin that flashed across her face as she slapped her arm down in the water, drenching Steve, she sensed payback was on the menu. "Hurry up, or I'm going without you," she called over her shoulder and Lori walked out of the stall.

"Wait! I need to secure the girls." Holding the bikini straps behind her back, she turned. "Where's yours?"

Jesse wanted to wear her new pink bikini, but since meeting Brian, her confidence had faltered. He was amazing, she was mediocre; and nothing like the girls she expected he normally dated. "I couldn't find it," Jesse lied.

"I have an extra one you can borrow."

"Yeah, right. Your bikini would fit like a thong and pasties."

"Well, if you got it, flaunt it." Lori turned and pushed out her chest. "These babies could rock a pair of pasties." She snorted.

"As if," Jesse said with a fluttering eye roll.

"What? Just because I'm small town doesn't mean I live in a cave. Free the nip and all that good shit!" Lori cheered.

"Would you just go get us a float before I change my mind?" Jesse laughed and pushed her out the door before drawing in a calming breath.

"Come out of the cave, Jesse!" Lori yelled.

*Dear Lord give me strength.* As Jesse walked out of the changing room, all eyes landed on her and she wanted to wring Lori's neck. She crossed her arms over her belly as her face heated and prayed the multi-colored design of the fabric hid her flaws. She sucked in her stomach and narrowed her eyes when Lori offered her a pink float. "Now you're giving me the float?"

"It's something to hide behind until Brian stops gawking."

Not trusting Lori, Jesse squeezed the side of the float to see if it held air. Although it felt firm, that didn't mean there wasn't a pinhole and as soon as she got into the water, she would sink like a rock. "Thanks, but I'll pass."

"But it's your favorite color." Lori laughed.

"Not today. I've got my eye on the blue float in the middle of the pool. Last one in!" The coolness of the water diminished the heat that filled her body as she swam out to the center of the pool, where Brian was sitting. "Do you have room for one more?" she asked, holding onto the edge of his float and looking up through wet lashes. Ordinarily, she wouldn't have been so bold, but channeling her inner Lori, what the heck? It was a ballsy move, and the look on Lori's face was priceless.

Brian lifted her up on the float and pulled her back against his chest before whispering into her ear. "Paisley's my new favorite color."

Jesse grinned and whispered back, "Paisley's not a color."

"Well, it should be because it complements your skin beautifully." She shivered as Brian's voice rumbled through her hair and Lori smirked her approval.

The idea of sharing a float with Brian worked out well for her, and Jesse quickly relaxed in his arms. As the conversation turned to his new job, if he intended to impress her, it worked. She peeked through her lashes when Megan's mother walked across the patio and placed a stack of pizza boxes on the poolside table. Mrs. Smith was a pretty brunette. Tall, with sharp features, she reminded Jesse of her own mother. She cut a glance toward Megan when she yelled, "Thanks, Mom." Megan's short frame and soft features must have come from her father's side of the family.

As the sun dipped below the horizon, the pool lights came on, casting a soft, rippled glow across the water. Jesse pulled away from Brian and sat up on the float. "Wow, this is amazing." Different sized globes were, nestled in the landscape, lighting the concrete walk and casting romantic shadows around the pool. "Now I see why you spend so much time out here."

"It's my thinking spot. I only swim when I have company," Megan said.

"Well, it must work for everyone because I've been thinking about what happened today. It's obvious I've been out of the loop, but where did Tracy come from?" Brian asked.

Megan filled him in on everything that went on while he was away at camp. And for someone who claimed to not know Jack, she sure knew a lot about the *Cabin Crew*, a name Jack and his friends had been tagged with. "I work at the cafe. I hear all the town gossip," Megan said as if she could read Jesse's mind.

"That's true. Anything going on is news at the café, and long before it hits the press," Lori said as she swished her hand through the water, taking her float closer to Megan's. "Psst, is there any juicy gossip you'd like to share?"

"Depends on what you call juicy. I do know that a certain redhead has been seen on the back of a motorcycle." Megan grinned and slipped off her float.

Jesse's jaw dropped. Based on what she knew about Randy and Tracy, he was on cloud nine and she was threatening to beat up every girl in Cloverly.

"He's a flirt. He loves the girls," Megan said while climbing out of the pool.

"One might say the same about her, based on the way she was acting at the boulders." Jesse's brain hurt the longer she thought about it. The snarky redhead was determined to put her in her place, and lucky for her, Jack just happened by. It was obvious he wasn't her boyfriend, which meant she was using Randy to make him jealous.

"Please tell me it's not so. He must be blind," Lori said, pushing herself up on the side of the pool.

"No, I think he sees what most guys see when Ms. Skimpy Britches is around," Jesse said. "Which explains why he's not here tonight." Following Lori out of the water, she glanced over at Steve. He and Lori had dated for years, so his reaction to Tracy at the boulders was a little disturbing. *Typical guy*, she thought, but if she were Lori, he wouldn't have gotten off so easily.

"Just between us, we need to do something about them. Randy may be a flirt, but he deserves better, and Tracy's not someone I want in my inner circle of friends," Lori whispered.

"Yeah, but like Megan said, he loves the girls. I give them a week," Jesse said as Brian tossed the last float out of the pool.

"There's nothing wrong with having a backup plan just in case. You're pretty stacked. You could give her a run for her money." Lori shimmied her chest as Brian climbed out of the pool.

"Sorry, I'm not into love triangles," Jesse whispered. At most, Tracy would play Randy at his own game in an attempt to make Jack jealous, and when that backfired, she would kick him to the curb. But with his fan base, he probably wouldn't notice she was gone. She followed Brian over to the patio table and took the seat he offered. *A+ for manners.*

The rectangular table was large enough to seat their group of five comfortably. With Megan sitting at one end, she and Brian sat on one side, and Steve and Lori sat on the other. Lori scarfed down her pizza while Megan rubbed lotion on her legs. Steve and Brian were discussing the Little League teams they expected to see at the World Series while Jesse pondered the empty seat at the far end of the table. Maybe she and Lori could sway Megan into giving Randy another chance, but that really wouldn't have been fair to Megan. She was a sweetheart, and Tracy was a brute. Jesse looked over at Megan, noticing the dark circles under her eyes.

"You look tired."

"Lack of sleep."

"Why didn't you tell us? We could have come over on another day," Brian said and Jesse nodded in agreement.

"Which is exactly why I didn't tell you." Megan squeezed more lotion onto her hand.

"Oh! That reminds me. I've got something I want to show you. I'll be right back," Lori said, getting up from the table. Within minutes, she walked out of the changing room, waving a piece of paper in the air. Taking a seat on Steve's lap, she unfolded the paper and placed it in front of Megan.

"Untold Secret Splits the Town," Megan read. "Am I supposed to know what that means?" She looked over at Lori.

"Have you ever heard of a town secret? I mean, you do work at the gossip mill." Lori leaned in on her elbows.

"All small towns have secrets," Steve said.

"So you know what this article is about then?"

"No." Steve shook his head. "But you show me a small town that doesn't have a secret, and I'll show you a town that doesn't exist."

Lori waved him off and continued. "Based on this article, there *is* a secret and shortly after the town formed, something happened. Half the town wanted to expose it, the other half didn't. It doesn't say what the secret was, but it was bad enough to warrant a write-up in the local paper. I found several articles like this, but none of them go into any detail."

"Where did you find them?" Brian asked.

"I was sorting through old library books for the book sale, and they fell out."

"Well, even if there was a secret, it doesn't pertain to Cloverly now. I mean, if something happened right after the town was established, there couldn't have been more than a handful of people that knew about it. So through all the generations, it's probably been forgotten," Brian reasoned.

"Not only that. Cloverly has some very unusual people with imaginations to match. Look at Old Man

Sallee," Megan added.

"It sounds reasonable, but I don't know as much about the town, not like you all do," Jesse said, glancing across the table at Lori.

"Are you thinking what I'm thinking?" Lori asked.

"We've got some digging to do." Jesse grinned.

"It's a total waste of time. That whole folklore bit gets rather tiring after a while," Brian said, reaching for another slice of pizza.

"I doubt the folklore surrounding Sallee's Rock has anything to do with a town secret. Everyone has known about that nonsense forever," Lori said.

"It still sounds like a waste of time to me."

Jesse was willing to bet Brian knew more about the secret than he was admitting, but if they could figure it out, how cool would that be? "Well, from an outsider, its sounds intriguing."

# Twelve

## Jack

Jack leaned against the porch post as the sky darkened to a deep indigo blue. The muggy evening air promised storms by midnight, yet there wasn't a cloud in the sky.

"Now what?" Mason asked once the coast was cleared of lingering ears.

"I don't know what you're talking about," Jack said. After the unscheduled meeting, the pack fired up the grill to celebrate their permanent living arrangements. Everyone pitched in and did their part: from packing firewood, to flipping steaks, to chopping up a salad. Even the alpha got down to business and sliced various kinds of fruit for their dessert. It was a good meal and a great way to wind down, but now that everyone had left, Jack was ready to turn his focus on Megan. He grinned when Mason stepped past him off the porch.

"You know what I'm talking about. I can see the gears

turning in your head."

"It's a good thing I like you or I'd be demanding you show more respect to the Alpha-in-Training," Jack said with a smirk. Pushing off the post, he stared down at his best friend. The two had known each other all their lives. Growing up in a small pack, they shared a brotherly bond and a knack for causing chaos in their younger years.

"Considering I'm your beta, I'm not that impressed. But I know you better than you know yourself, so again I ask, Alpha-in-Training, now what?" Mason returned the smirk.

"You're just itchin' to cause trouble. You do realize if Whitney asks it's your fault." Jack stepped off the porch and Mason fell in beside him as they cut across the yard.

"In my defense, if we're going to be living here, shouldn't we at least get to know the town?"

"It sounds convincing but do you think Whitney will buy it?"

"I sure hope so. If not, I'll be living with you." Mason coughed and then coughed again. "Daaamn. I swallowed a bug," he sputtered, his voice raspy as he tried to clear his throat.

Jack bent forward, laughing as Mason hacked on the side of the road. "Was it good?"

"Crunchy, cream-filled." Mason beat on his chest and then wiped his eyes. "Tastes like bacon."

"That's gross," Jack said as they continued down the road.

"You asked." Mason coughed again.

"It was a yes or no question. But bacon? I used to love bacon."

"Don't tell me the big, bad wolf has a weak stomach."

"I'm not listening." Jack ignored him as they turned onto Main Street, and Mason sniffed the air before scanning the area. He knew Mason was an excellent tracker from training alongside him when they were younger. Both excelled to the top of their class, were very competitive, and always challenged each other. "So what are the chances we'll find Megan?"

"I'd say pretty darn good,"

Tracking Megan should have been an easy task but lavender seemed to be a popular fragrance amongst the locals. "Is it just me or does everything in this town smell like lavender?"

"All I smell is gas." Mason covered his nose as they passed the corner station and the streetlights buzzed overhead. For two adult males, their footsteps were silent as they continued on their mission. "I smell lavender now but we are walking against the wind and there's a lavender farm at the edge of town."

"Where?" Jack peered down the road. Shoving his hands into his pockets, he stepped off the curb and crossed the side street. He didn't realize there was a lavender farm near the city although, upon thinking back, he did remember Tucker mentioning it.

"Just keep walking. You can't see it from the highway, but I saw it the other night when Whitney and I were out running." Passing the movie theater, the smell of buttered popcorn filled the air. "I see lights at the bookstore. Did you know Sonya was thinking about selling?"

"Yeah, but she didn't seem too happy about it." Jack looked up as the light went out.

"Well, you only wait so long before you give up and move on."

Jack knew all about moving on. It wasn't something he wanted, nor recommended, but it was time. He always thought one day he and Lizzy would be together, but the elders kept insisting it was impossible for them to share a bond at such a young age. Maybe they had been right all along and he was mourning the loss of his childhood crush. But believing that was a different story.

Crossing Main Street, the lavender sprigs displayed in the window of the flower shop caught Jack's eye. It was clear the residents of Cloverly were supporting the local farm, as evidenced by all the lavender products being sold around town. "Which side of the street should we be on?"

"It doesn't matter. We can cross back at the cafe and cut through the park."

Passing the bookstore, Jack noticed the cafe's neon sign reflecting off a large black motorcycle that was parked at the curb. "That's a nice bike," he said, eyeing it as he passed. A low growl rumbled in his chest but unlike his wolf, he could appreciate the machine for what it was: sweet! "Wonder who it belongs to?"

"Probably some badass biker dude," Mason said, looking through the window as they passed the cafe.

Female laughter disrupted the otherwise quiet night and Jack looked back as Randy walked out the door. Fending off a group of girls, he started the bike and took off down the road. Something about the bike troubled him. *You're jealous because Megan defended him.* That much was true but there was something more recent he couldn't quite put his finger on. He scowled when Randy drove around the park and headed out the highway. "He was not the person I expected to see on that bike. I bet he knows where Megan lives."

"Yeah, too bad you burnt that bridge," Mason said, but Jack didn't need the reminder.

It wasn't his intention to offend Randy that day at Sallee's Rock, but perceiving him as a threat, his wolf would have protected Megan had he not. Now thinking Randy might actually know her whereabouts burnt his ass. His jaw clenched as he and Mason cut across the park to Hill View Avenue. The edge-of-town neighborhood was nothing more than a few houses, three ranch-style homes on one side of the street, and a large, two-story brick on the other. "Looks like the farming business is doing well." Jack stared up at the large columned porch and hanging chandelier.

"I don't think a little lavender farm could support that kind of lifestyle." Mason glanced up at the house.

"Probably not, but whoever lives there has a pool. I can smell the chlorine."

"Which means we need to walk faster because that stuff irritates my sinuses." Mason pinched his nose as he hurried down the sidewalk. "The farm is that way." He pointed. "It's the only house on the gravel road."

"You do realize we could've walked down Walnut Street to get there." Jack glanced back at the large house, hearing laughter.

"Sure, blame it on the beta."

Jack slowed his pace to scour the area. Only a handful of houses occupied the neighborhood and turning onto Walnut was the difference between town and country. One end of the street was paved and well lit, but along the stretch of gravel road, only darkness and fields. "She's nearby, I can feel it."

"Ha, I knew I could find her." Mason bumped Jack's

shoulder.

With quick steps as the paved road turned to gravel, the two found themselves standing next to an old, decrepit mailbox. Jack looked over at the small white house that was recessed off the road. "Is there a name on the box?"

"I don't know. I'm afraid if I look, it will fall down." Mason chuckled but pulled open the door, causing the faded flag to drop. "There's mail."

Jack leaned around and pulled out a small catalog. "Wisp of Lavender Farm." He raised the booklet to his nose, but of course, it would smell like lavender. Placing the catalog back in the mailbox, he lifted the flag.

"So, back to my original question. Now what?"

It was another dead-end as far as Jack was concerned, and he blew out a breath. "It's a farm and most farms have dogs, so trying to get closer to the house might become a problem."

"We can always watch from the hill at the back of the cemetery," Mason suggested.

The hill behind the cemetery was small compared to Hunter's Ridge, which was off to the right. Jack shook his head. "I don't think we'll see anything tonight but at least we have a place to start." As he stepped back on the road, he shoved his hands through his hair and his skin prickled. Turning a complete three-sixty, he peered into the dark. "We're missing something."

# Thirteen

*Jesse*

Balanced on a stepladder, Jesse struggled to hang the newest addition to her grandmother's wind chime collection. It was a simple enough task that anyone could do, but as she reached up through the branches, Brian called out from the front yard and she startled. She grabbed for the nearest limb and shrieked when the ladder tipped beneath her weight.

"Whoa! Hold up there," Brian shouted. He hurried over to the ladder and grabbed her by the waist, causing her breath to hitch. The thought of dropping to the ground and breaking an ankle in the process sounded better than the situation she suddenly found herself in. He stood eye level with her stomach and she squirmed, hoping her shorts weren't so snug as to show the pudginess of her belly. "You smell good," he remarked as he lifted her off the ladder. It was agonizing, the whole three seconds it took for him to place her on the ground. The feel of his hands on her bare skin made her belly quiver and boom! The giddy girl was back.

"It's sunscreen." She giggled and pulled her shirt down. Her complexion was naturally dark, but that didn't stop her from slathering on the coconut-scented lotion. She claimed it was for the sun protection factor, but in reality, she just loved the smell. She rubbed over the creases that tracked from her wrist to her elbow as Brian re-clipped the hook, allowing the chime to hang freely.

"That wasn't so bad," he boasted while righting the ladder.

"For you maybe," Jesse said. "So what are you out doing today?"

"Apparently, saving damsels in distress."

*What?* Did he think she needed saving? Admittedly, he did startle her but at no point did she need him to hang the wind chime. She caged the giddy girl and banished her to the back of her mind. She was a strong, independent... well, almost, young woman, and it was time she acted like it. "I'm not completely helpless, you know."

"Says she who was hanging from a branch." Brian laughed. "Actually, I stopped by to see if you wanted to go to a movie Friday night?"

"Well, that depends. Are you going to let me hold the popcorn?" she asked as he followed her over to the picnic table on the opposite side of the yard.

"Depends on how hot the bucket is."

She rolled her eyes and motioned for him to have a seat. "I'm sure the bucket won't be hot, but I guess there's only one way to find out." She smiled and took a seat across from him, her body swaying with the music from a nearby radio.

"I take it you like to dance."

"I love to dance!" she said and her eyes lit up with the possibility.

"Funny, I didn't have you pegged as the dancer type."

Her sway faltered, and she lifted her eyes. Feeling somewhat insulted by his comment, she scowled. "Exactly what type is a dancer type?" She may not have been a skinny chick, but on the dance floor, she could move with the best of them.

"I didn't mean that in a bad way. You just seem intelligent and nothing like the usual girls that hang out at the dance hall," he explained.

"Oh, well, thank you," she said, still not sure if it were a compliment or not. "So there's a dance hall in Cloverly?"

"No, it's in Berkley."

"Berkley's not that far. We should check it out sometime." Now that she admitted she loved to dance, maybe he would take her dancing instead of to a movie. That would be the perfect first date in her opinion. "Do you go there often?" She hoped he would pick up on the hint and she waited anxiously for his reply.

"On occasion I do."

"I don't need an occasion. I just need music." She flashed a tight-lipped smile.

"I see that," he said, unaware of her mood change.

She chewed her lip, waiting for him to say more. Had she not just admitted she loved to dance? That would be a definite C- on the GAG scale if it actually worked. "Are Lori and Steve going with us?"

"They said they would meet us there. Do you mind?" He dusted the paint chips off the table and looked up.

"No, I don't mind at all. The more, the merrier." Her hand fanned the air as her snarky side emerged and she paused, looking across the yard. "I was hoping you wouldn't care if I invited Jack and Tracy. I know she was a little brazen at the boulders, but I think that was partly my fault," Jesse said and Brian shot her a confused look.

"How was that your fault?"

"Don't you remember Megan saying Tracy liked Jack?" She gestured with her hand, waiting for him to recall the conversation. "The day I met Tracy, I was with Jack. She considers me competition." Brian glanced over at the cabin, and she smirked. "We don't have to invite them if you'd rather not."

"Why do you care what she thinks? I mean, if there's nothing between you and Jack."

"I don't care, but Jack is my friend and I'd like to keep it that way." Jesse stood and even though Brian didn't seem thrilled with the idea, he walked with her across the yard.

As they approached the cabin, the music grew louder and Jesse grinned when she spotted denim-clad legs stretched out from beneath Jack's car. Singing along with the radio, he twisted to the side, his brown boots digging into the grass—and grunted. Jesse covered her mouth to stifle a giggle. Something about him tickled her fancy and she stood for a moment, taking in the view.

"Hey, Jesse," Jack said as he rolled out from beneath the car. "What's up?" He reached for a towel that was draped over the open trunk and wiped his hands.

She rolled her lip to keep from drooling because Jack without a shirt was, as Lori would put it, *hot-as-hell*. "This is my friend, Brian. He lives across the street." She didn't miss the glare Brian shot her way, but as soon as Jack offered his hand, his smile returned.

"Nice ride," Brian said. "I have a friend that drives an old bug. It's not a muscle car, but to her, it's the greatest thing on four wheels."

Jesse followed them around the car, trying to keep up with their conversation but the smudge of grease on Jack's chest was quite distracting. *Now you're acting like Lori.* When Brian looked her way, she jerked her head towards Jack and he narrowed his eyes and mouthed something she couldn't understand.

"If you're not doing anything next Friday night, a group of us are going to the movies. If you all want to stop by." Brian looked over at Jesse and shrugged. It wasn't the way she would have worded it, but hopefully it would have the same outcome.

"Sounds good," Jack said, glancing towards Jesse before returning his attention to Brian.

"Well, I guess I should go. I'm catering tonight's bunco party, and those women are never late," Jesse jested as Jack popped the hood. With a wave of her hand, she turned and headed back across the yard, leaving Brian behind.

***

Later that evening, Jesse found the bunco brigade were in a class all their own. Those old women had her in stitches most of the night with their friendly rivalry and colorful banter. Her jaws ached from laughter, and her ears from the constant slip of certain dirty words she would not repeat for fear of her grandmother pulling out a bar of soap. Once the evening wound down, and everyone departed, she headed up to her room.

After changing into her sleep clothes, she paused in front of the floor-to-ceiling bookshelf. She ran her hand over the fabrics that were sorted by color and resembled a large rainbow. Megan had done a great job organizing the material, and she had no intentions of changing it.

Sewing supplies and books filled the bottom shelf, while at the far end were several books she assumed belonged to her dad. Some were old and worn, and others looked unread, but one book caught her eye. The bright yellow tape holding the faded red cover to the spine was proof the book had been read multiple times. She scanned the title as she ambled across the room and crawled into bed. She didn't believe *Western Wolves* was referring to Western Kentucky, but the thought was intriguing.

Propped up on a pillow, she opened the book and the pages parted to an old photo that was wedged into the spine. The black-and-white picture was creased and faded, but the image was clearly that of a light-haired girl. Slender with long hair, it must have been taken in summer based on the clothes she wore. She removed the photo, but without a name, she couldn't place her. The twin creases that split the picture into three equal parts suggested that at one time it had been a cherished photo held in a billfold. As she looked down at the page, her phone vibrated on the bedside table. Tucking the picture back into the book, she answered the phone.

"Hello." She grinned when she heard Brian's voice, sounding unsure and apologizing for calling at such a late hour, which wasn't late by her standards. But since moving to Cloverly, she noticed most of the neighbors' houses went dark after the ten o'clock news. There was a pause, and then a rush of words before the call ended. "Meet me on the porch?" She repeated as she got out of bed. Placing the book and phone on the table, she hurried out of the room.

Jesse tiptoed across the foyer and opened the front door, listening for her grandmother. Dressed in boxer shorts and a thin t-shirt, she crossed her arms over her chest and stepped out onto the porch. The night air was humid, and the longer she stood there, the more moisture beaded on her skin. She rocked back on her heels as she looked toward the tree line and the damp earth smell caused her nose to wrinkle. The neighborhood was quiet and if she listened hard enough, she could swear she heard voices. Her body trembled and she considered turning on the porch light, but when Brian's clicked on, she relaxed. "Is everything all right?" she asked when he jogged up the steps to where she was standing.

Without a word, he placed his hands on her hips and walked her back into the shadows. "Sorry, I've wanted to do this since yesterday in the pool." His words brushed over her cheek and a tinge of excitement trickled through her body as his lips met hers. Soft, unsure, she wrapped her arms around his neck, urging him on. Unable to see his face, their first kiss was awkward, and nothing like what she pictured in her mind. She pulled back and took a deep breath as his hands roamed down her back and the aggravation from earlier that day dissipated. "I'm glad you moved to Cloverly," he said.

*Wasn't that the same line Randy used?* "You came over here in the middle of the night to say that?"

"No, I came over here to kiss you but I'm still glad you moved to Cloverly."

She smiled. "Well, I'm glad you came over here to kiss me. It was nice."

"I know. We should do it more often," he said. She wasn't expecting him to make a special trip across the street, but she was glad he did. *Definite A+.* "I can't stay long. I have an early day tomorrow. Plus, it's getting nippy."

"I'm a lot of things right now but nippy isn't one of them."

"That was just an excuse. I really think you should go in before Gramma gets up." His arms tightened around her waist and she giggled.

"Scared of a little, old lady?"

"Yes, I am. She has a variety of skillets, and I'm allergic to iron." His raspy voice brushed through her hair, causing her to shiver.

"Oh, I think you're safe... for now."

"But are you?" In one forward motion, he caged her against the house before his mouth crashed down on hers. The kiss was rushed, with such urgency; she tensed up, choking back a laugh when the porch light flicked on. "You should probably go before you get me in trouble." He chuckled and wiped over his mouth.

"Me? Get you in trouble? Sorry, mister, that was all you," she teased, but as she stepped around him, he swatted her on the ass.

"No, *that* was all me." He smirked and walked down the steps as the front door opened.

# Fourteen

*Jack*

Wiping the sweat from his brow, Jack stepped off the porch to where the others gathered in the front yard. He nodded as Tracy walked over beside Tucker. Lately, she was giving him space and since their last heated argument, she seemed changed. Trying to work out the differences in his head, he watched her intently. Her appearance was the same. Same clothes, earrings, hairstyle, but something told him it was deeper than that. Her attitude wasn't snide or snippy and the aggressive edge was gone. She was happy, judging by the smile that beamed on her face, and that alone was a shock. "You're in a good mood tonight."

"I'm always in a good mood; you're just never around to see it." She waved him off and turned when Tucker cut in.

"I guess biker boy brings out the best in you."

"Biker boy?" Jack repeated as he stared between the two before a light bulb flickered in his head and his thoughts traveled back to the cafe. *Something about that bike...* It was the sound of a motorcycle he'd been hearing near the cabins, and usually, it was well into the early morning hours. Oh, she was a clever one, he'd give her that. Fraternizing with a human! Who would have thought? Not him, but when she shifted her weight on her feet, he knew there was some truth to the biker comment. Despite her denial, seeing her in a good mood was unusual. Seeing her in a good mood on phase night was contagious.

"Yeah, she has a new bestie. I've been dumped," Tucker announced as he pretended to stab an invisible dagger into his heart.

"Oh, it's nothing like that, I assure you," Tracy said. The smile on her face as she played the role of an innocent was more than entertaining and Jack grinned.

"Really? Because I got the impression you were—"

"Just being nice?" Tracy cut in. But even the darkness couldn't hide her lie. She tried to sound convincing, but fidgeting with her earrings, she was not her confident self. Randy caught her attention, although Jack couldn't imagine how; but then again, who knew what or why Tracy did the things she did?

"If that's all it takes to put you in a good mood, maybe we should invite him over for supper." Tucker pulled her into a half hug and she elbowed him in the stomach.

"You have a lot of room to talk." Tracy laughed, jerking away from his tickle.

"Aww come on, Trace, don't be mean," Tucker said, flashing puppy dog eyes.

*A lot of room to talk?* Jack tilted his head, waiting to hear more. He understood Tracy keeping Randy a secret but what was Tucker hiding? Tucker hadn't been acting any differently, and he hadn't been away from the pack except for the time he spent in Kinsley, meeting with the alpha. He looked over at his cousin, but nothing out of the ordinary came to mind. Tracy was probably referring to a certain blonde female that was determined to corner Tucker into a relationship. It wouldn't be the first time she tried, and based on the way Gina was acting at the last pack meeting, she was very persistent. Jack grinned. Gina and Tracy were so much alike, to the point that they couldn't stand each other.

"I've been excited for this run all day. Are we going to the lake again? I'm fine with wherever you want to run," Tracy said, ignoring Tucker.

"No. Tonight you can run wherever you want. Just be careful, have fun... and stay away from the neighborhoods," Jack said. He preferred to let the group run where they pleased, but every once in a while, he had to place restrictions on them. Normally, it was because of the hunters in the area, but lately it centered on Tracy and her territorial ways.

Tension surrounding the last phase was forgotten as the pack disappeared down the road. Jack was the last to enter the woods, and he ducked under the nearest tree and pulled off his clothes. Without hesitation, he phased and trotted toward Hunter's Ridge. It was a quiet place he often visited when he needed to think, but also a dangerous place for the wolves during hunting season.

By the time he arrived at the ridge, his wolf was satisfied with the strenuous uphill run and he stretched out his legs before a shiver shook him from nose to tail. Prancing over to the cliff's edge, he sat down, scratched behind his ear and then phased.

The view was breathtaking and he could see for miles as he leaned back against a large rock, shifting his eyes skyward. He relaxed when a slight breeze carried the scent of lavender from the neighboring farm and his mind drifted back to Megan. He had been spending more and more time scoping out the little farmhouse at the end of the road, but with little luck. The lavender scent taunted him as he watched from a distance, hoping to see her again. He was so preoccupied with finding Megan that he hadn't been spending as much time with the pack. He hadn't even been concerned that Tracy was spending more time *away* from the pack. *Yeah, you're going to make a fantastic alpha someday.* Thankfully, he had Mason covering for him when anyone questioned his absence.

Twigs snapped at the bottom of the hill, and Jack rose up and peeked over the rock. The pack knew better than to sneak up on him; who did they think they were? He slowly stood without making a sound, and willed his wolf forward. Quietly trotting across the clearing, once he hit the tree line, he was gone in a flash.

Heavy footsteps on dried leaves confirmed his cousin was nearby. Tucker was impressive from his height to his build and all the way down to his size thirteen feet—so his wolf was equally imposing. Assuming Tucker would be hidden amongst the trees, Jack looked for the largest shadow. As he ran beneath a huge pine, he swerved to the opposite side where he thought Tucker would be waiting. He glanced back, distracted by clanging metal, and realized too late he had been double-teamed. He spun on his heels as a large shadow fell over him and Tucker landed on his back with a thud. The extra weight threw him off balance and they both tumbled down the hill. Jack wiggled around, struggling to pull out from beneath the massive wolf as Tracy raced past in a blur. Once she was out of sight, Tucker threw his head back and howled before racing off after her.

Jack shook out his fur and jumped to his feet, eager to join the chase. It was times like these when he loved being a wolf. Putting their differences aside and enjoying the pack as a family was the greatest feeling in the world. He dodged and wove through the trees, and although he was taken down, neither of them could out-run his wolf.

Jack continued to follow on Tucker's heels, but as they crossed the clearing at Sallee's Rock, Tracy ran out from behind the boulders and together, they sandwiched Tucker between them.

Tracy was the first on her feet and she shook out her fur as the copper coin earrings slapped against her head. With a slight snub over her shoulder, a howl ripped from her throat and Whitney responded from somewhere in the distance. She darted off into the woods, leaving the two males in a jumbled mess while she continued the chase.

Jack jumped up as adrenaline burned in his veins and his wolf prepared to take the lead. He passed Tracy, giving a quick nod, and she fell in behind him, while Tucker brought up the rear.

Whitney and Mason greeted them at the lake when they broke through the trees. Jack signaled for Tracy and Tucker to move forward as the other two slowly stalked back and forth, holding their ground. The two groups faced off at the edge of the water. It was a waiting game to see who would attack first.

Whitney stirred. It was she who kept the peace and her wolf shared that trait. Jack expected she would be the first to react with Mason closing the gap. Intervening for the greater good, she would put herself in harm's way if that meant keeping the others safe.

Jack threw his head back and howled, signaling the charge. The wolves wrestled, rolled, nipped, and yelped until exhaustion took over and they rested at the water's edge. He kept watch over the secluded area, his wolf satisfied at the moment. He didn't expect anyone to intrude on them but being an alpha, it was his responsibility to protect his pack.

Just before sunrise, the pack headed home with Tucker leading the way.

"That was fun! It's been a long time since we chased. It's just what my wolf needed," Whitney said, and all the others agreed.

After the stress Jack had been under, the run had definitely improved his disposition. His body was relaxed but tired, and he hoped he could finally get some much-needed sleep. As the sun burst over the horizon, he walked into his bedroom and pulled down the shade.

# Fifteen

## Tracy

The following Sunday, Tracy squeezed between pack members, searching for a seat. Always one of the last to arrive, she usually sat in any available seat and that was frequently with Travis. The room was packed but spotting a chair on the front row, she continued moving up the aisle. She sat down between two elderly males without bothering to ask if the seat were already taken. Rude, maybe, but it wasn't every day she got the chance to sit at the front of the room and far away from her uncle.

Travis stood off to the side and scowled when she glanced his way. He wasn't happy that she didn't save him a chair but he would get over it. Jack stood against the back wall, talking with a group of scouts—and Mason standing at his side. Whitney and Tucker sat in the center of the room with a group of females, all of whom were vying for Tucker's attention. *What a lush!* She smiled and turned back to the front of the room where two groups of scouts stood on the opposite side from where she sat, talking in hushed voices and she wondered what was going on.

The alpha lifted his hand to quiet the room as the last of the pack took their seats. "Settle down, everyone," he said, pausing until the conversations died out. "I've received information that a resident of Cloverly has been asking questions about wolves in the area. This is not a threat to us but I do want any of you that are living in Cloverly to be extremely careful. Pay attention to your surroundings and try not to expose the pack."

Tracy fidgeted. Travis didn't mention any questions being asked, so it had to be something the alpha had just been informed of. As whispers spread throughout the room, she cleared her throat. "What happens if we are exposed? Are we allowed to fight? Or do we walk away?" she asked, causing the room to quiet. She glanced over as Travis raked his fingers through his beard.

"No, we will not fight. We are not going to act like a pack of rabid dogs running around, nipping heels. The humans pose no threat to us and we, in return, will not threaten them." The alpha scanned the room. "Our human always controls the wolf. Is that understood?"

"If the pack is being threatened, you know our wolves are hard to control when we're put in a life or death situation," Travis argued, and Tracy bit back a smile. She had to admit, it was a ballsy move even for her uncle and clearly, the alpha wasn't impressed.

"I hardly think someone questioning wolves in the area is putting any of us in a life or death situation. It's natural for our wolves to howl when we are out running and sometimes people hear us. But most people assume what they heard was a dog," the alpha countered, directing his words towards Travis.

"But what if? There is always that one person that won't let it go. Why can't we bite them? They can't very well expose us if they are one of us," Tracy said, taking the heat off Travis. She actually enjoyed being the center of attention until the alpha glared at her.

"Do you really want to take that chance? Do you know anything about creating a new-blood or what they are? They are unpredictable for starters. Not to mention, it creates a whole new bloodline that may or may not be aggressive towards the pack or the wolf that did the changing," Alpha Cooper said, his voice unwavering.

"But we have new-bloods in the pack. I don't see what the big deal is," Tracy retorted as she glanced around the room but no one dared look her way.

"We have one and he is the descendant of a new-blood, a type B in this case. It's not the same. A type A new-blood is the actual human that was bitten by the wolf. The saliva enters their bloodstream, infecting them with the lupine virus. They develop the wolf characteristics within thirty days but after that, you cannot predict when they will phase and take the wolf form. That is assuming they live through the transition. It's a dangerous game to play and I'm surprised Travis hasn't mentioned it to you," Alpha Cooper said.

Tracy turned, unsure if Travis actually knew what the alpha was talking about and crossed her arms over her chest, scowling.

"There was no need to mention it. You make it sound worse than it was. I know. I was there. It had nothing to do with being a new-blood," Travis sneered.

"It had everything to do with new blood and you know it. She was changed against her will by your father, for reasons we won't discuss here. And when she attacked the alpha, she was killed. It took several wolves to bring her down but not before she exacted her revenge. Two died from their wounds and if I'm not mistaken, you nearly had your own face ripped off. My father saved your ass and in the process, lost his life, so don't tell me I'm making it worse than it was." The growl that resonated through the room startled everyone, and a few of the females jumped, including Tracy. "Which is why changing a human just because you feel threatened by them will result in severe disciplinary action. So again, the answer is no, Tracy. We are humans first and as such, we will live peacefully with them," the alpha said and Travis looked away.

*What the hell?* Tracy wanted to scream as she glared at Travis, but he ignored her. Did he not think that was vital information she would need to know if she were going to be Jack's mate, an alpha female? He never told her about the Type A new-bloods, which made her look like a fool in front of the entire pack. The snickers coming from behind her pissed her off and she bit her tongue to keep from spitting on them. She turned back to face the alpha as Jack silently scolded the snickering females. "Thank you," she mouthed. It was nice to know someone had her back, unlike the asshole she called *uncle.*

Jack was sharp and usually sat back and observed everyone. If he noticed anything out of the ordinary, he was quick to call it. He was definitely alpha material and Tracy was the only female in the pack with alpha tendencies, thanks to her early training. She lowered her head and kept quiet as the alpha continued in a new direction. Once the meeting was over, she waited until most of the others left the building before exiting the room.

Giggling females gathered around Jack and began bombarding him with questions. Tracy paused at the door. As he answered, they smiled and batted their lashes. They were trying way too hard to get his attention, but Tracy didn't feel threatened by the trifling fools until she noticed the wink. *Was he flirting with them?* The grin plastered across Gina's face suggested such and Tracy clenched her fist and stormed out the door.

Stragglers stood outside the building, but Tracy kept her head down as she continued across the yard and slipped into the shadows of the Canadian hemlocks that lined the driveway. She paced back and forth, mumbling to herself until the door finally opened and the group of she-wolves walked out onto the porch.

Some stopped to continue their conversations while others scurried away. But Gina stepped off the porch last, a clear indication to the other females that she was a contender for Jack's attention. Tracy waited as Gina casually strolled along the drive, humming softly. *Puke!* When she passed, Tracy grabbed her arm and yanked her into the trees. "What the hell do you think you're doing?"

"I could probably ask you the same question," Gina hissed, jerking out of Tracy's tight grasp.

"I saw the way you were looking at Jack but it's not going to work. Stay away from him," Tracy growled.

"Oh please. Your threat may work on the younger females but not on me." Gina dismissed her with a flick of her wrist.

"It's not a threat! And I am not the person you want to challenge." Tracy's eyes flared, and she snarled. It took everything she had to not grab the brassy bimbo by the throat and throw her to the ground.

"Let me guess. Your uncle is still feeding you that garbage that you are somehow better than the rest of us. Grow up, Tracy. Everyone here knows Jack isn't interested in you." Gina laughed as she stepped out from the trees.

Anger seared through her body and if it hadn't been for Jack walking out the door with Alpha Cooper, Tracy would have taken Gina out.

The ride home was quiet and Tracy claimed she was tired; it wasn't often she felt the need to cry. Facing off with Gina brought back childhood memories she didn't care to revisit. She didn't think she was better than anyone; actually, quite the opposite. Travis had filled her head with a lot of shit, but at no time did he make her think she was something special. As she walked into the cabin, she slammed the front door, and stumbled across the room before flopping down on the sofa. She was pissed at Gina, at Travis, and at the world, so she pulled her shoes off and slung them against the wall. It was bad enough she had to keep an eye on Jack because of Jesse, but to think Gina dared to challenge her was something even she couldn't believe. She narrowed her eyes when the back door opened.

"What took you so long?" Travis said, ducking as a pillow hit the wall beside his head.

"You're really asking me that question, Mister Oops-I-forgot-to-mention-new-bloods?"

"Damn! Who slipped a thistle in your seat?" he said as he walked into the room.

"Are you here for a reason? If not, I'm not in the mood to hear your mouth." The glare in her eyes was a warning, but it had little effect on him.

"Sweetheart, you will hear anything I have to say and you'll be happy about it," he scoffed. "I stopped by to commend you on doing a fine job tonight at the meeting. Planting that little seed of doubt was perfect. I just wish I'd thought of it."

"Yeah? Well, I wish you had told me about new-bloods before I made a fool of myself. It seems like I'm the one doing all the work for your benefit and glory."

"What are you talking about? You haven't done a damn thing. Your job is to hook-up with Jack and you can't even do that."

"Well, if I didn't have to contend with females on both sides of the river constantly hitting on him. It's hard to keep his attention when they're throwing themselves at his feet. So what was it you were doing again?" she asked, her voice dripping with sarcasm.

"Look, you worry about Jack. I'll take care of the rest."

"Yeah, I know. Jack, Jack, Jack. Whatever." Tracy laid her head back and closed her eyes. "Just leave. And don't slam the door on your way out."

# Sixteen

*Jesse*

"Sorry I'm late," Jesse said as she rushed into the kitchen and headed straight for the broom closet. She promised to clean the kitchen floor before Lori came over that afternoon, and she was running behind. After her interview with Dr. Stevens last week, she didn't expect he'd call so soon, but she was excited to have the opportunity to work at the animal shelter. Grabbing the blue-handled mop and a bottle of detergent, she walked over to the sink.

"Don't fret, dear. Some things are more important than cleaning a floor," her grandmother said as she placed the mop bucket in the sink. "I take it things went well." She glanced back as she turned on the faucet.

"It went great! I actually started work today."

"Well, I think you'll find Dr. Stevens a good man to work for. He's highly respected in the community,"

Gramma said, turning off the water.

Jesse lifted the bucket out of the sink and set it on the floor. Adding a cup of cleanser to the water, she submerged the mop and swished it around until bubbles formed. "He gave me a tour of the shelter and I met his wife. She's really nice. I also cleaned a few cages and fed the cats," she said, hearing a light tap at the front door. She leaned the mop handle against the sink and hurried out of the room.

"Hey, you," Jesse said as she walked across the foyer. Brian was casually leaning against the screen door wearing a pair of washed-out jeans and a light blue t-shirt that fit snugly across his chest. When he stepped back, she pushed open the door and invited him in.

"Thanks, but I can't stay. I wanted to stop by and make sure we were still on for tonight."

"I can't wait," she lied, stepping out the door as he brought a bundle of daisies out from behind his back. "For me?"

"It has your name on it." He flashed the name card and grinned at her excitement.

Jesse took the flowers and cradled them against her chest as she tipped up on her toes, drawing him into a quick kiss. "They're beautiful."

"Wow, had I known you would respond like that, I would have given you flowers." His arm snaked around her waist and she looked up and smiled.

"Well, now you know my weakness. Thank you."

"You might want to wait on thanking me until you put those in water."

"I probably should. I'll be right back."

She walked into the kitchen where her grandmother

was busy stacking chairs on top of the table. With a grin on her face, she pulled a canning jar from beneath the sink and filled it with water. She placed the flowers in the jar and as she sorted through the stems, she removed the small envelope that hung from a ribbon. *Jessie.* She smiled at the misspelling of her name, but the penmanship was beautiful. She removed the card and leaned against the counter. *Until tonight,* she read to herself.

"Those are beautiful. I love Shasta daisies," Gramma said, walking over to the sink. "What's the occasion?"

"Brian wanted to make sure I remembered our date tonight. He's on the porch, I'll be right back." Jesse tucked the card into the envelope and hurried out of the room. Brian was leaning against the porch post, deep in thought when she walked out the door. Staring into the woods, he smiled when she placed her hand on his shoulder. "What's the matter?"

"Nothing. I thought I heard thunder and I was hoping we could walk to the theater tonight."

"That would be nice." Jesse looked up at the cloudless sky. "So you stopped by to remind me of our date?"

"Yeah, and I also wanted to congratulate you on the new job."

"I haven't been home five minutes and you already know about my job?"

"A friend told me." He pushed a strand of hair over her shoulder.

"Well, did this friend also tell you I liked flowers?" She looked down at his hand, her cheek grazing his knuckles.

"Actually, she did," he said point blank. His tone confused her until she noticed the blush on his face. "I have to get to work, so I'll see you around seven."

"I'll be waiting." She stood on the porch until he was back across the street.

*\*\**

After helping with the housework, Jesse spent the rest of the afternoon sketching designs and talking to her mother on the phone. "Mom, Lori's here so I need to go," she said. "I love you, too." She ended the call and rolled her sewing chair away from the window as Lori walked up the sidewalk with her duffel bad slung over her shoulder.

Lori bounded up the stairs with a huge grin on her face, and Jesse instantly went on alert. "How was your first day?" Lori walked into the room and tossed her bag on the floor as she kicked off her shoes. "So are you ready for your date? She pounced in the center of the bed and pulled off her socks. Excitement sparkled in her eyes and Jesse grinned, not wanting to disappoint her.

After finding out the first movie was a horror flick, Jesse considered cancelling the date. There were two things Jesse didn't like, things that lurked in the dark and movies about things that lurked in the dark. "The job was great and I'm excited to see Brian, if that tells you anything."

"Would you relax? It's just a movie and more reason to snuggle with your beau." Lori bounced her brows.

"Would you stop with the brow flicking?" Jesse looked over at the jar of daisies. "Did Brian say anything to you? He seemed a little odd this morning."

"So what else is new?" Lori replied as she unzipped the duffel bag.

"Well, I appreciate you telling him I like flowers but you should have suggested he take me dancing."

"I told him you liked flowers the day he invited us to the movies. This morning, I called him to make sure we were still going tonight, and I mentioned you had a job, but you can't fault me for not remembering your likes and dislikes when my caffeine level is deficient. So suck it up, buttercup. He's a movie buff, and he's excited to be taking you," Lori said as she stuffed her socks into her bag.

"I know, but..." Jesse sighed.

"Ahh... I know that look," Lori teased.

"What look?"

"The look that says you've tagged first base, but you obviously didn't think it was important enough to share with your best friend." Lori fluttered her lashes and Jesse rolled her eyes.

"Whatever. We kissed once, and I didn't tell you because you always make a big deal out of nothing," Jesse said, untying the ribbon from the flowers. She wasn't the kiss-and-tell type, and considering Brian could be a little on the naughty side, that was one tasty tidbit she wanted to keep to herself. The memory of him pressing her against the house still lingered in her mind and she stifled a smile.

"And?" Lori crossed her arms over her chest.

"And nothing, that's it." Jesse walked over to the closet as Lori sprang off the bed, her landing rattling the room. Bracing for the impact, she laughed when Lori wrapped her in a bouncing bear hug. "Would you get off me?" She tried but failed to push her away. "See? You're doing it again. Making a big deal out of nothing."

"Say what you want but you can't fool me. You've

snagged one of Cloverly's most sought-after bachelors. I love it, love it, love it! Take that, Annie," Lori cheered, shoving her fist into the air.

"Who the heck is Annie?" Jesse asked as she pried Lori's arm loose and spun around. "Don't tell me he already has a girlfriend."

"Naw, she's this snotty twat-waffle he dated back in high school. They split when he returned home from college. Seems the long-distance relationship wasn't working for them. But never mind her; I want all the dirty details."

"Please, it's not like we're getting married. We're just... dating. I think." She stepped into the closet and removed a dress from its hanger. Remembering Randy making a similar comment, she chuckled.

"You don't have to be married to play house," Lori said and her eyes widened when Jesse walked out of the closet. "You expect Brian to watch the movie with you wearing that?"

"As a matter of fact, I do." The large floral print dress wasn't flashy, but with the faded pastel colors of teal, pink, and yellow set against an antique white background, it was perfect for the evening. "It matches the ribbon, don't you think?"

"It matches perfectly but I doubt that's what he'll be looking at," Lori said.

"Is it too much?"

"Well, that depends." Lori held up the dress and studied her image in the mirror. Flipping the dress around, she grinned. "A bit daring, aren't we?"

"How do you figure? It's knee-length and covers everything."

"It's a halter dress, which means no bra."

"Oh, act like you've never worn a dress without a bra." Jesse rolled her eyes.

"Sure I have, but my girls don't have the jiggle factor going on. You, on the other hand, are going to attract a lot of attention. Brian had better step up his game is all I'm saying."

"It's Cloverly. I don't think he has much stepping up to do."

"Excuse me. Did you forget who walked you home when you conveniently got lost in the woods? And if I'm not mistaken, you did invite him to the movie." Lori smirked at her reflection.

"There you go again," Jesse said as heat traveled up her neck. There was some truth to what Lori was saying but since meeting Brian, she hadn't really thought about Jack, and she wasn't sure he would show up at the theater.

"Me? It was you that said he was practically naked."

"I did not! I said he had on shorts and no shirt."

"That's practically naked in my book," Lori said and Jesse swatted her arm.

"See!?"

# Seventeen

## Jesse

Later that night, Jesse and Lori stood on the sidewalk in front of the theater while Brian and Steve mingled with the crowd. "Look, there's Jack," Jesse said before she elbowed Lori for gagging when she saw Tracy. Being new to Cloverly, Jesse welcomed the chance to make friends, even if they were the Cabin Crew. Expecting only Jack and Tracy, she was pleasantly surprised to see the others there as well. As the group stopped shy of the crowd, a tall, dark-haired girl continued walking towards her and she smiled.

"Hi, I'm Whitney and based on Tracy's description, you must be Jesse. You've caused quite a stir in the neighborhood," she said, returning the smile.

"Well, ya gotta be good for something, right?" Jesse laughed as Tracy walked over and stood beside Whitney, a slight frown on her face. "I'm glad you all could make it.

It's really nice to meet you."

Whitney was not what Jesse expected and standing next to Tracy, they were as different as night and day. Both were equally gorgeous but Whitney had a graceful ease about her that outshone them all, even wearing something as simple as a pair of jeans and a button-up blouse.

"Wow, I want to be her when I grow up," Lori said after Whitney and Tracy walked away.

"Get in line. I think I have a girl crush."

"Well, you have fun with that. I'm going to round up the guys," Lori said over her shoulder.

Jesse stood alone in the crowd, smiling at anyone who looked her way. When she spotted Brian talking with a group of girls, she wondered what he saw in her. The girls were dressed in shorts or jeans, with cutesy tops that showed off their slender waistlines, which made her feel like a lump of lard. Slightly overdressed and out of place, she looked down at the floral print dress. She didn't consider herself fat, just healthy, and definitely not model material; Whitney and Tracy had already cornered that market.

Deciding to make the best of the situation, Jesse walked over to the building and read all the movie posters taped to the large window. "Massacre in Carson County" sounded so cliché and she mentally rolled her eyes. Moving on to the next poster, her skin prickled when a shadow clouded the window and she spun around, her heart one beat away from bursting through her chest. *Holy smoke, where did he come from?*

"Sorry, I didn't mean to startle you. I'm Tucker," the voice said in a deep, smooth-as-chocolate tone.

Bewitched by his presence, she licked her lips and looked up at the golden flecks that sparkled in his eyes. Everything about him drew her in, from his dark complexion to his massive arms, but especially his eyes. His rich, brown eyes, framed by dark lashes, stared into hers, searching. She blinked down to his lips and fought the urge to stretch up on her toes. "I'm..." her voice stalled.

"Jesse," he said, and she nodded. "It's nice to meet you. Your hair looks lovely tonight."

Her body heated with his words and she practically melted on the spot. Unable to look away, she didn't notice Brian walking up until he pulled her to his side.

"You must be Tucker. I'm Brian," he said, instantly breaking their connection.

Jesse looked down at the hand draped over her shoulder and then back up at Tucker, his frown matching hers. If there were ever an awkward moment, that was it. From wanting to push Brian's arm off her shoulder, to pulling Tucker into a kiss, her mind went completely bonkers.

"It's nice to meet you," Tucker said, and although his smoldering gaze was still trained on her, his jaw ticked. With a curt nod towards Brian, he walked away.

"That was awkward," Brian said as Jesse twisted out from beneath his arm.

"Awkward? You have no idea," she scolded. Since arriving at the theater, Brian had spent most of his time chatting up old friends, and the one time someone paid attention to her, he rudely interrupts? She peeked over as Tucker joined Jack against the building. *What the heck were you thinking?* He was extremely gorgeous and nowhere near her type. *And Brian is?*

"There's Randy. I'll be right back," Brian said but before she could respond, he disappeared into the crowd.

*Alone again. Great!* Jesse crossed her arms over her chest as the large motorcycle pulled up to the curb. Randy helped his date off the bike, unaware Tracy stood back in the crowd. *You are so busted.* She smirked and turned back to the movie posters with a snarl.

Laughter from behind had her rolling her eyes and she twisted the end of the ribbon around her finger. *Your hair looks lovely tonight.* She could hear Tucker's voice and she brought the silk strand to her lips. Brian said she looked nice but did he notice the ribbon? *He's distracted. Give him a break.* But his distractions had her worried. She glanced over her shoulder and frowned when a tall blonde latched onto Brian's arm. It was probably an old friend, niece or cousin, and as much as she wanted to introduce herself, and be the jealous girlfriend, she wasn't the jealous type. She turned back to the posters.

Five minutes later, Brian came up behind her and wrapped his arms around her waist. "You know, I've been thinking," he whispered over her shoulder, "since you don't like scary movies, maybe we could skip out and go back to my place."

*Not likely, Casanova.* "And what would our friends think?" Jesse asked, allowing her irritation to lace her words.

"Well, I can't answer for the girls but seeing how the guys can't keep their eyes off you, I'm one lucky SOB."

"And without luck, what would you be?" Jesse muttered below her breath. Hearing a light chuckle when Tucker walked past, she bit her lip. There was no way he could have heard what she said; but seeing the grin on his face when he looked back and winked meant he clearly had. "You're up." She nudged Brian, thankful he didn't hear her snarky reply.

Being the last ones to pay for their tickets, Jesse stood back as Brian chatted up the cashier—another cousin or something. She turned and ignored them when a scraggly mutt darted across the street and disappeared behind a car.

"Come on, or we're going to miss the start of the movie," Brian said, leading Jesse back to the building.

The auditorium was packed by the time they took their seats and everyone was paired off, except for Jack, Tracy, and Tucker. Lori leaned up from behind Jesse and handed her a bucket of popcorn. "Five bucks says she's with the big guy." Lori cut her eyes to Tracy.

"I'll take that bet and raise it five more bucks that says she's trying to make Randy jealous," Jesse whispered back.

"You're on, sister." Lori sat back in her seat, snickering.

"What's with the grin?" Brian asked. Taking the bucket of popcorn, he placed it in his lap.

"By the end of the night, I'll be five bucks richer and Lori will be pouting about her inner circle of friends," Jesse said as the lights dimmed.

The movie seemed to drag and Jesse struggled to keep her eyes off the screen. Looking down at the silk ribbon, she twirled it around her finger and eyed the bucket of popcorn. *Why did I agree to this?* Her eyes traveled from the popcorn, to Brian's knee, to the huge-acious glob of blue bubblegum that was stuck to the back of the seat in front of him. *Gross!*

Then she glanced to the left at the section of seats, one row down, on the opposite side of the aisle. Tracy sat with her arms folded across her chest, bouncing her knee. Jack, on the other hand, leaned away from her with his elbow on the armrest, his chin resting on his fist. *Nope. Not a couple.* The only one of the three that seemed to be enjoying himself was Tucker, and he was staring back at her.

The heat of his gaze had her on the edge of her seat and the pull she felt toward him intensified. She shuddered. If she didn't stop acting like Lori, she would make a complete fool of herself before the night was over. She looked away when Brian leaned forward, blocking her view.

"What are you doing?" he asked.

"I dropped popcorn in the seat," she said, hoping he didn't catch her lie. She spent the remainder of the movie staring down at the lump of bubblegum in an attempt to avoid the horror flashing across the screen. She was apprehensive and for whatever reason, the feeling wouldn't go away.

Once the movie ended and the lights came on, Jesse didn't waste any time pulling Lori out of her seat. "Come on. I have to use the restroom and I'm not going alone." As the two walked up the aisle, Jesse elbowed Lori for snickering. "It's not funny. I thought I would wet myself before the movie ended."

"Well, that's your fault. You squirm too much."

"Glad you noticed. Brian didn't seem to." Jesse pushed open the bathroom door. She made quick use of the facilities and washed her hands before doing a quick once-over check of her hair and dress. All the while, Lori was busy wiping sticky soda residue from her leg.

As the room filled, a line formed against the back wall, and Jesse was glad she hadn't waited. Looking through the mirror, she eyed Tracy when she entered the room. She towered over most of the girls as she squeezed through the crowd, making her way to the sink. Standing behind Randy's date, Tracy smirked and looked down her nose. Jesse wanted to laugh at the childish display but knew it would only cause a reaction from the snarky redhead, and at the moment, she was flying under the radar. Excusing themselves, Lori and Jesse moved through the packed room and hurried out the door.

Once Jesse was back at her seat, Jack stood and walked up the aisle, his swagger hidden with the slight incline. A few minutes later, Tracy walked through the door, sauntering past Randy and flipping her hair over her shoulder. Jesse wasn't sure if she were teasing Randy or rubbing it in his face; either way, he probably deserved it. When the door opened again, Jesse expected to see Jack coming back from the concession area but instead, saw Megan who shyly waved as she walked down the aisle. "I'm glad you made it," Jesse said, noticing the slight blush on her face.

"Megan, you know everyone here except the Cabin Crew," Lori said.

Jesse froze, as did Megan, but Lori never missed a beat and continued the introductions. She definitely needed a muzzle, stat!

"It's nice to meet you all," Megan said, looking over at Mason before her blush deepened. Uncomfortable, she turned toward the nearest empty seat. "Is this seat taken?"

"Jack's sitting there but you can have mine," Tucker offered and he moved over one chair, leaving a space between Tracy and him.

Jesse frowned as Megan squeezed past Tracy and sat down in the vacant seat. Unsure how well they would get along; she was surprised to see them hitting it off. She looked over at Tucker and he winked. *Sweet mercy!*

Her heart did somersaults in her chest and her mind drifted... Her body trembled beneath his touch and he smiled as if he knew the power he held over her. What was it about him that was so alluring, enticing, mesmerizing? She looked up, and the heat continued building between them. As her hands slid down his bicep, she lightly squeezed, hoping he wouldn't notice. He was strong, rock solid, and she could imagine him pinning her against a wall. She blinked away the thought as she dropped down in the seat, and her face contorted with guilt.

"Are you okay? Can I get you something to eat?" Brian asked, concern etching his face.

"I'm good." Jesse smiled and she snuggled beneath his arm as the lights dimmed.

# Eighteen

*Tracy*

After the second movie ended and the lights came on, Tracy stood as everyone around her rushed the aisle. Waiting out the stampede, her heart sank when Randy pushed through the crowd without bothering to look back. *What did you expect?* She lowered her eyes as the thought hammered her brain. She did expect more from him, honestly, but maybe Travis was right all along and humans did only think about themselves.

It had been a week since she was teased about the biker boy, which opened her eyes to the possibility of Travis finding out about him. So after her run that night, she spent the rest of the day locked in her cabin, trying to figure out a way to undo the damage she had already done. Distancing herself from Randy, if only temporarily, seemed like the only alternative at the time, and now she was regretting her decision.

"What are you waiting for?" The whisper from behind startled her, and she looked back at Tucker.

"I didn't want to get mowed down," she said. With his hand on her back, he guided her and Megan up the aisle as her emotions peaked and tears threatened to spill from her eyes. *Trouble, always trouble,* echoed in her head, causing her lower lip to tremble. Feeling rejected, unwanted, *a failure* her uncle would say, she crossed her arms over her stomach, covering the area of skin between the crop top and the low-waisted jeans she wore.

By the time they reached the concession area, there were a few people lingering at the counter, but most of the crowd had already exited the building. She paused inside the front door and noticed Whitney and Mason standing on the sidewalk talking with Jesse and her friends. Seeing them laugh, even she had to admit they weren't as bad as she originally thought—for humans. Tucker pushed open the door, and she drew in a breath as she walked out into the muggy night air.

The group stood outside on the sidewalk, but Tracy wasn't in the mood to socialize. Instead, she worried about Randy and the situation she found herself in. As she walked away from the crowd, her eyes drifted to the motorcycle parked at the curb.

Her heart raced with the possibility that maybe Randy did wait for her. But spotting him leaning against the building, his hands shoved deep in his pockets, her hope faded. With one foot resting against the brick wall, he stared down the street and a frown marred his face. She had never seen Randy look so dejected, and her heart ached to be near him. His date, on the other hand, seemed pretty content just hanging off his shoulder as if she were trying to climb on top of his head. Tracy's breath hitched when Randy looked down at the brunette. He shifted his weight, and pushed off the wall, but that didn't deter his date. The female adjusted her hold around his arm and hugged it to her chest before looking up at him with a goofy smile.

Tracy scowled as a low rumble rattled her chest. She didn't understand why Randy was upset. It was a temporary parting of ways and based on his actions, temporary meant *over*. She chewed her nail. If anyone had the right to be angry, it was she. *Just deny the bond and let him go.* It would be the right thing to do. Hearing Travis talk, however, she never did anything right in her life.

"You look like I feel," Tucker said, seeing the frown on her face.

She leaned against his shoulder and blinked the moisture from her eyes. She needed to hide her emotions, but it was hard to do. Randy had ignored her most of the night, and that was the worst feeling in the world. At one point during the movie, she even tried to flirt with him but he looked away. "I'm tired, and ready to go home. What's your problem? Too many females to choose from?" She chuckled, but it sounded more like a lazy growl.

"Nah, I'm ready to blow this joint," Tucker said but his attempted smile faltered when he looked back over his shoulder.

"Don't try to pull the wool over my eyes. I may have been born at night but the moon was full," Tracy said, although even she couldn't muster a smile.

"You keep telling yourself that." Tucker chuckled and pulled her to his chest. He planted a kiss on top of her head and looked over his shoulder, again. Something was bothering him, she was certain, but he wasn't talking.

Wrapping her arm around his waist, she tugged on his shirt to get his attention. "See those females over there?" Tracy nodded toward the door. "They're drooling over you like you were the beef in their burrito." Tucker looked down, confused. "Yummy!" She flicked her brows and laughed. Just because her life was a cesspool at the moment didn't mean she couldn't try to cheer up her best friend.

"You're insane," Tucker said, squeezing her against him. Tucker's best asset was his caring nature, which bordered on the protective side. Coming from a large family, he had plenty of experience with both, something Tracy knew nothing about.

"I'm not, they are. They act like they're starving and you're the main course. I expect a cat fight before the night is over and most likely, I'll have to defend your honor," Tracy joked.

"Well, you can stay and defend my honor all you want, but I'm outta here," he said before following Mason and Whitney down the road.

Tracy debated moving closer to Randy, knowing there was no way she could claim him as her mate since she was destined to be with Jack—ever since the age of four. Travis had warned her many times the family's name was at stake and failure wasn't an option. But why should she give up her life when it was he who wanted the pack? A question she dared not ask out loud.

She should've walked away and left things as they were but the thought of being near Randy once more was too tempting. Standing next to him, she casually brushed his arm as she whispered in his ear. "Pick me up later." While waiting for him to respond with a nod, a wink, or anything, she frowned at the gutsy brunette trying to wedge herself between them. It wasn't in her nature to back down from a human, but trying to avoid attention, what other choice did she have? She stepped around the female and looked up at Randy. Still, he refused to acknowledge her. *"What did I do?"* The unspoken question lingered between them.

The sullen look on Randy's face as he rolled his bottom lip between his teeth stabbed her heart. Tracy only wanted to protect him, not hurt him, but how could she explain her reasoning without revealing what she was? A heaping dose of reality kicked her in the gut when she realized no matter what she did, they could never share a life together. She looked down the road, her eyes misting, and bit her lip to stop the quivering. Her world was crashing down around her and the only way to end it was by letting him go. *It's for the best,* she tried to reason and before she could walk away, Randy's hand gripped her arm and she looked up. Seeing the storm of emotions swirling in his eyes: desperation, failure, defeat, she wanted to curl up and die. Had she truly broken his spirit? It was never her intention, yet his eyes no longer sparkled. "I'm sorry," she whispered as he leaned down, his lips lightly skimming hers. He was hesitant at first, but when she wrapped her arms around his waist, he deepened the kiss. It was pure bliss for a split second before a shrill voice screamed in her ear. Tracy jumped, breaking their connection, and Randy shoved his hands through his hair.

Humiliation settled over her when Randy backed up against

the building and looked away. *Was that a kiss goodbye?* Tracy's wolf insisted she fight for what was theirs but it was pointless. There was nothing she could do to change the family obligation she was doomed to follow. *Trouble, always trouble.* Inhaling a shaky breath, her heart shattered but she turned and walked away.

Catching up with the others, Tracy settled beneath Tucker's arm. He was her best friend, he would understand, but it wasn't something she could talk about without tearing up. A desperate longing settled in her gut, and she refused to look back. If it were truly goodbye, she didn't want to see Randy leave. Her chest ached with the realization that he didn't want to be with her, but she also knew whatever they had together would eventually end. It was too dangerous for her to continue seeing him, Travis would make sure of that.

As the four turned onto Cabin Run Road, Randy's motorcycle sounded in the distance but she didn't want to think about where he was going, or whom he was with. She hated that stupid female, and wanted desperately to claim what was rightfully hers; but how could she, and still uphold the family name? She stared down the road as the roar of the motorcycle faded into the night. Noticing the lights were out at Jack's cabin, she breathed a sigh of relief. "It doesn't look like Jack wants any company." She knew she should have been a little more concerned about her future mate but at the moment, her concern rested elsewhere. "If you all don't mind, I think I'm going to follow his lead and turn in for the night," Tracy said, faking a yawn as she pushed out from beneath Tucker's arm. She needed time to sort out her thoughts and consider the pros and cons of the bond she shared with Randy—as if she had a choice.

# Nineteen

*Tracy*

Tracy didn't bother turning on the lights as she entered her cabin. Instead, she tromped over and flopped down on the sofa and kicked off her shoes. She didn't need an audience, and she damn sure didn't want company. Just her, sulking alone, was the way it had always been and there was no need to change now. *Humans are beneath you*, the words echoed in her head. But no matter how many times Travis told her that over the years, possibly thousands, she still couldn't shake the heavy sadness that gripped her heart.

She was eighteen and wanted to have fun, to laugh, not sit around like a wart on a frog's ass. She wanted to feel the wind in her hair, to fly. She wanted to be with Randy. He was exciting, spontaneous, and unlike any male she had ever met. One more night with him was all she asked... just one! *Why? The hard part is over and you didn't have to be the bad guy,* she thought, but deep down, she missed everything about him.

Taking a deep breath, she glanced over as the late-night breeze parted the curtains, exposing a dark shadow that moved along the tree line. It was most likely Travis, creeping around in the dark, the true meaning of a perve in her opinion. She wasn't in the mood to talk about the family obligation or Jack. He would probably tell her how disappointed he was and why she wasn't worthy of the family name. Not wanting to face any more of her failures, she lay down on the sofa and closed her eyes, pretending to sleep.

As a tear slipped down her cheek, her thoughts shifted and she pictured herself on the motorcycle, flying down the highway. *Freedom.* It was nice to think about but now had become something she would have to store in the back of her mind along with her memories of Randy. Because like it or not, based on Randy's behavior, she already lost him.

As the wind swept through the pine branches carrying a soft whisper, she tilted her head. *Wishful thinking.* Another tear streaked down her face. Then she heard the whisper again, louder, and her eyes shot open. She jumped off the sofa and tripped over an end-table as she ran to the window. Shoving the curtains to the side, her eyes frantically searched for the one person that made her heart zing. "I'll be right out," she whispered back and her heart landed in her stomach.

Anxiety blossomed in her chest as she quietly closed the front door. What was he thinking by showing up at her cabin? It was dangerous, and if Travis caught him there... She sprinted across the yard as his silhouette leaned against a tree and she couldn't help but admire his form. With his long legs casually crossed at the ankles and his arms crossed over his chest, he was a sight to behold even in the darkness. "What are you doing here?" she asked, scanning the woods behind him.

"I'm not letting you go. I will fight for you," Randy said defiantly.

"But I thought..." Tracy's words faltered when he narrowed his eyes.

"What you thought was I'd walk away, but I'm not. This can't be over. It can't just be your decision." The rumble of his voice sent a chill up her spine and her wolf wiggled in delight.

"I thought you didn't want me." Tracy looked down at her bare feet. She was so excited he had actually come for her; she forgot her shoes.

"Let's go. We need to talk," Randy said as he pushed off the tree.

"Wait. Where's the bike?"

"Around the corner."

She slowly scanned the area, again. "Let me get my shoes. I'll be right back."

"Take your time. I'm not going anywhere. And if your uncle shows up, I'll introduce myself," he said, resuming his position against the tree again.

Tracy knew by the tone of his voice that he meant what he said, and as thrilled as she was, she started freaking out. She shoved open the front door and hurried across the room, tripping over the end-table again in search of her shoes. After releasing a few swearwords, she grabbed her sneakers off the floor and slipped them on before hobbling back across the room. *He's insane.* A nervous chuckle escaped her and her heart lodged in her throat. Racing out the door and around the cabin, Randy was standing with his hands on his hips, obviously amused by her antics. "Hurry," she said as she grabbed hold of his hand. Careful to stay in the shadows, she dragged him down the street and prayed she would survive the night.

The motorcycle was parked where he said and despite her fear, she took comfort knowing within minutes they would be on the road. Taking the helmet he offered, she settled behind him and fastened the strap. Tracy didn't ask where they were going because one more night with him was all she wanted and she was grateful for the opportunity.

The ride was serene as they headed out the highway and she relaxed against his body. With her chin on his shoulder, she closed her eyes and let the warm night air caress her face. Able to breathe again, the events from the theater melted from her mind. When the bike slowed, she opened her eyes as they turned onto the dirt road. The old church with its boarded-up doors and broken windows was eerily beautiful, especially with weathered headstones in the background.

Randy parked the bike in front of the barn and extended his hand. Once Tracy had her feet on the ground, she removed the helmet and smiled over at the old wagon. "It's still here?"

"Yeah, it isn't used for much anymore," Randy said as he jumped up on the wagon and pulled Tracy up behind him.

Tracy wasn't what she would consider a country girl

but being there with him was undeniably appealing. "So do you bring every female here?"

"Nope, just you," Randy said. Taking a seat on the straw bales, he pulled her down beside him. "Too bad it's not a full moon." He lay back and stared up at the sky.

"It's a waning moon," Tracy said, remembering her last phase.

He glanced her way, offering a half smile. "Well, I guess it'll do." He turned back to the sky.

She waited, expecting him to say more, but when he didn't, she lay down beside him and took hold of his hand. "So you like sitting out under a full moon?"

"With the right girl, I do."

"Are you with the right girl now?" Her face heated with the question. *Don't lead him on. It has to end before things go too far.*

"You tell me." He rolled his lip, something she noticed him doing whenever he was stressing.

The smile on her face couldn't hide the sadness in her eyes. It was dangerous for her to be there, yet he made her feel safe. And she knew she would eventually have to let him go, but she could spare one more night of freedom before they parted ways. "Have you always lived here in Cloverly?"

"Not always. I lived in Texas for a year. I had big dreams that didn't include living in a small town. But it didn't take long for me to realize everything I wanted to do could be done here, so I moved back. Plus, Dad needs help with the farm and that keeps me busy." He plucked a piece of straw from the bale and stuck it between his teeth.

Tracy wondered what it would be like to make plans

for the future, plans that didn't include her uncle. She wanted to be a scout, which was the pack version of a game warden, but Travis frowned on the idea. He said it wasn't something an alpha female did. She pulled a piece of straw from the bale and placed it between her teeth. *Yuck.* She tossed it over the side of the wagon.

"Have you always lived here?" he asked and pulled the straw from his mouth and flicked it through the air.

"No, I recently moved to Cloverly. I lived across the river in Kinsley."

"Where did you go to school?"

"Homeschool," she said as he continued staring at the sky. "Is something wrong?" She rolled over against him and waited. When he finally looked her way, he smiled but the deep-seated sadness she saw in his eyes was still visible and undisguised.

"Is he your boyfriend?" His voice was barely above a whisper as he turned back to the moon before she could answer.

"Is *who* my boyfriend?" She propped up on her elbow, confused by the question.

"Jack."

Her heart skipped with the mention of his name. *Hell no, he's not my boyfriend!* She swallowed hard and an icy chill hardened her heart, reinforcing the wall she had built around her emotions. "Jack and I have a lot of history, but it's not what you think. It's not... something I can talk about."

"Why? You talk about him all the time?" Randy challenged.

Tracy could tell he wanted to say more, and she wanted to tell him everything, but she couldn't. She couldn't risk putting his life in danger and being there with him did that. *Trouble, always trouble,* the annoying voice rattled in her head. "Well, I'm with you now."

Randy chuckled as he rolled over, pinning her beneath his leg. "That's not good enough. I want more." The smile slid off her face, and he leaned down and placed a soft kiss on her lips. She closed her eyes, enjoying his scent as it mingled with hers. Holding tightly around his neck, she parted her lips and he deepened the kiss. The feel of his body caused heat to pool in her belly and a low rumble rose in her chest—she opened her eyes. His closeness made her dizzy and her wolf wanted to submit, but she couldn't surrender. Pushing him back to gain some space, she licked her lips as he ran his fingers through his hair. Just for the night, she wanted to be everything to him, but giving in would only cause trouble for them both. "It's getting late. I need to go home before my uncle finds out I'm gone."

"Stop, Tracy! You've been playing me this whole time. I know your uncle doesn't live with you." Randy rolled over on his back, and exhaled. "I wish you would stay," he said, his voice softer, almost pleading. Tracy's heart shattered for the second time that night. She wanted to stay there, but she feared things would get out of hand and she had to cut him loose before that happened. "You said *anything.*" The whisper was so low she almost missed it.

"I don't understand." She frowned.

"You said if I taught you to ride, you'd give me *anything.*"

"Okay. What is it you want?" She made the deal when she wanted him to teach her how to ride the motorcycle but never thought he would ask for payment.

"I want you to give me a chance. You owe me that."

He was right, and she wasn't one to back out of a agreement, usually. *Trouble...* She blasted the thought from her mind. "A chance?"

"Yeah. Give me a chance to prove you belong with me, not Jack." He sat up, resting his elbows on his knees and bunching his hands in his hair.

Tracy sat up beside him and stared at the church across the way. When she finally turned to face him, he flashed a crooked smile. "I told you he wasn't my boyfriend, but all right. If that's what you want."

He pulled her into a hug and kissed her cheek. "Let's get you home."

Back on the highway, Tracy relaxed against his chest. She loved being in control of the bike and the way his fingers worked circles over her belly, soothing the pain in her heart. It was easy for her to picture them together, with his body molded around hers— protecting her. Something she could never imagine with Jack. Tears filled her eyes. Although she agreed to give Randy a chance, she knew it would be their last ride. He was perfect for her, but trying to explain that to Travis was a different story. *The family name, always the family,* she thought as a tear blew off her cheek.

# Twenty

*Jesse*

Rarely did Jesse get anything over on Lori, but staring down into the cellar; she bit her jaw to hide her grin. She promised her grandmother she would bring up canning jars, and since Lori so cavalierly dismissed her fear of the movie the night before, it was payback time.

She clicked on the overhead light and a cricket hopped across the floor, reminding her why Lori hated the cellar. They had followed Gramma down one morning to explore the musty room, when a cricket jumped on Lori's leg. She slapped and kicked, swearing like a sailor at the ripe old age of eleven. That was the day Jesse knew she and Lori would always be best friends, even though her grandmother threatened to wash Lori's mouth out with soap. She had spunk, and Jesse admired her for that.

"If that cricket jumps on me, my ass is out of here,"

Lori said, glaring at the bug.

"Would you just ignore it and help me? I'm tired and I don't want to be down here any longer than necessary."

"Of course you're tired; you kicked like a mule all night."

"What did you expect? I told you I would have nightmares." Surviving the horror movie intact didn't prevent her mind from conjuring up its own version in her dreams.

"I expected it was a stupid movie and you would see the humor in it," Lori said as Jesse passed her a basket.

"You dancing with a cricket was humorous; the movie, not so much." Jesse grinned and pulled a jar off the shelf lining the back wall.

"I fondly remember a jumping spider." Lori moved over beside Jesse and placed her basket on the floor.

"It wasn't a spider; it was a camel cricket."

"Well, at least we both agree it was the size of a camel." Lori picked up a jar and scrunched her nose. "Why do people bother?"

"Probably because they don't like buying processed food." Jesse shrugged.

"Yeah, I miss buttered popcorn. That imitation shit they served at the movie sucked."

"I wouldn't know." Jesse's thoughts went back to the theater, and the instant connection she felt towards Tucker. Even now when she pictured his grin, her heart did all sorts of weird flipping thumps. Was it possible to die from an irregular heart beat? If so, he would be the death of her.

"Speaking of... What did you think about Randy last night? I don't know about you, but he seemed really ticked." Lori pinched her nose to stop a sneeze.

"I think he was being a jerk. What right did he have to be mad at Tracy? It's not like he was there alone. And since when does he get that wrapped up in a girl, anyway?"

"You got me. The worse part was his date. Did she even notice?" Lori placed another jar in the basket.

"I think she noticed but like most of his groupies, they don't care as long as they're the one hanging on his arm," Jesse said. "But... on the other side of the aisle, I couldn't get over how much Mason and Jack looked alike."

"Yeah, I was talking to Whitney and mentioned the hot-as-hell neighbor before I realized it was Mason." Lori chuckled and Jesse bit her lip to suppress a laugh. "She looked at me like I was crazy until she figured out I was talking about Jack. But to make matters worse, she called Mason over and introduced him as her hot-as-hell boyfriend."

Jesse's belly shook, and she snorted. "Karma."

"What did I do to deserve karma?"

"You called them the Cabin Crew to their faces. Luckily, I don't think they heard you," Jesse said and Lori rolled her eyes.

"Well, moving past my humiliating moments... I had the best time talking to Tucker. He's funny. He and Steve had me laughing so hard, I spewed soda out my nose."

Jesse picked up a jar and placed it in the basket in order to avoid Lori's stare. Her heart raced with the mention of his name but like Brian, she expected to see some stick-chick hanging off his arm. "He's a big guy and those girls..." Jesse shook her head.

"I'm surprised you noticed... standing next to Brian,

that is." Lori smirked and walked down to the far end of the shelf.

"Please. Until we're officially dating, the sun spot position is still up for grabs," Jesse said. It would take a lot for a guy to be the center of her world and although she could see Brian filling the role, they weren't there yet. She rolled her eyes when Lori grunted a reply and her thoughts turned to Tucker. Everything about him made her weak in the knees and if she were being honest, he was the most attractive guy she had ever met.

"Well, I'm glad everyone had a good time, although I wonder why Jack left early," Lori said, staring at the wall of glass.

"Maybe his date stood him up. Too bad he didn't stick around, though. I would have loved to seen Megan's face when she realized he was there. Considering the way she kept eyeing Mason."

"I thought it was adorable, in a Megan sort of way," Lori said, turning from the shelf. "We should fix them up."

"Are you kidding? You saw how she reacted to him at Sallee's. She was pissed."

"Fine, we'll fix her up with Tucker. He was quick to give her his seat." Lori grinned.

"I vote Jack. She was sitting next to Tucker but I don't think she noticed him," Jesse said and an unfamiliar feeling settled in her chest, for the second time in less than twenty-four hours. Megan was her friend and there was absolutely no reason for her to be jealous.

"Only because he was preoccupied with you." Lori snickered.

"No, he wasn't. He was talking with everyone and glanced my way. He probably thought I was stuck up or something, which reminds me, I owe you five bucks."

"Actually, you don't. Tracy wasn't trying to make Randy jealous, and by the way Tucker was eyeing you, he wasn't with Tracy."

"He wasn't eyeing me. But if you believe that, then he's clearly not into Megan." Jesse reached down and lifted the basket, checking its weight.

"Fine, Jack it is," Lori said, pulling a small cedar box off the shelf. "Look, a hidden treasure chest."

Jesse glanced over and frowned. "Where did you get that?"

"It was on the shelf behind those old, green jars." Lori handed Jesse the box. "Open it."

"I'll hold it, you open it."

"No way, sister. There could be a snake in there." Lori shivered.

"It's covered in dust. So it hasn't been opened, probably, for years. Never mind, you hold it and I'll open it."

"Ahh... I see what you're doing. I'm not holding a dead snake. I'll open it," Lori said. Clutching the edge of the lid, she yanked it open and jumped back as Jesse bent with laughter.

"See? You always make a big deal out of nothing."

"You say that now, but look what you're holding."

Jesse looked down and her eyes widened. "Holy cow! Someone here knows the secret."

Jesse and Lori finished filling the baskets and placed them at the back door. Excited to see what was in the box, they quietly hurried up the stairs to her room.

"This is nerve-wracking," Lori said as she and Jesse crawled to the center of the bed and Jesse opened the box.

"I know." Jesse grinned and fished out the papers before laying them out on the blanket.

"These are the same articles we have at the library."

Just seeing the collection, an unsettling chill rolled over her, leaving a trail of goosebumps in its wake. "Do the articles have dates?" Jesse asked, leaning over to scan the article nearest her. There was nothing to indicate to whom the box belonged, but being in the cellar, she assumed it must be her grandmother's. She reached into the box and pulled out an old black-and-white photo, matching the one in the wolf book. "I found a picture like this the other day." Jesse got off the bed and grabbed the book off the shelf. "These pictures are not as old as the articles, but look at them." Jesse handed the photos to Lori, pointing out the similarities.

"Is that a dog?" Lori asked, looking down at the pictures.

"I don't know but they were both taken with the same camera." Jesse thought the dog looked more like a wolf, but the picture was taken at night so it could have been a husky or shepherd.

"Okay, so either your dad had a dog or his girlfriend did." Lori shrugged.

"But what if it's not a dog? The pictures were taken from that window there. You can see the wire lock on the screen at the bottom." She pointed to the window beside her bed.

Lori looked up and grinned. "Maybe the girl changes into a wolf after dark. I mean, you did find the one picture in a wolf book." The color drained from Jesse's face as she shot a glance toward the window. "I'm joking. That's not possible." Lori laughed.

"Are you sure?"

"Yeah, only in books do shifters exist. Maybe you should ask your dad who took the picture. It was his room," Lori said, reaching back into the box.

"I would but I don't think he would tell me. He doesn't talk about his teen years."

"Maybe there's a reason. Based on this, I'm not the only one here with an active imagination." Lori handed the drawing of a pack shield to Jesse. One could argue that's not what it was, but with a clover on one side and paw print on the other, separated by a ribbon with the word *Lycan,* what else could it be?

Jesse knew what Lori was getting at, and she didn't think it would be too far a stretch to say the wolf in the picture was real. But believing it was a shifter-wolf? Even that was something she couldn't grasp.

"I'm not saying it's real, but you can't deny what you have here. Pictures, old newspaper articles, the drawing of a pack shield. This has to be the secret of Cloverly."

"So you're saying the secret is werewolves?" Jesse asked.

"No, but it wouldn't surprise me if they all believed it back in the day. Don't you remember what Steve said about Sallee's Rock? Wolves, panthers, the hillbilly beast…"

"Yeah, but he also said it was folklore."

"Maybe, maybe not."

"So how would we prove them wrong… or right?" Jesse asked, looking back at the drawing as the thought of werewolves crawled up her spine.

"I guess we'll have to wait until the next full moon and see who howls."

"Fine, it's a date. But let's keep this between us for now. I don't want people thinking the new girl is a whacko." Jesse chuckled and put everything back into the box.

"You are known by the company you keep." Lori reached for her duffel bag. "I have to go get ready for work, but I'll do some digging and see what I can come up with."

"Okay. Call me tonight." Jesse stashed the box under her bed and pulled Moose into her lap. "Don't worry, boy, werewolves are not real." To believe in something so outlandish, she would have to question her own sanity. She chuckled. *What a backward little town.*

A few hours later, Jesse walked into the kitchen holding a stack of books. "Dad, do you have a minute?" she asked as she placed the books on the table.

"Sure, what's up?" Dr. Williams set his cup down and looked over at the books. "Please tell me you're not having second thoughts about living here."

"You know me better than that." She was the happiest she'd been in years and he knew it, but that wouldn't stop his teasing from time to time. "I found some old books on my shelf, and I wasn't sure what you wanted me to do with them. I would like to keep the top book if you don't want it."

He grinned and picked up the wolf book. "This was one of my favorites. I memorized it word for word." He opened the book and Jesse waited, shifting on her feet. "I don't remember what happened to the cover though." As he flipped the book over, the picture fell out and a frown crossed his face. That pretty much told Jesse what she wanted to know based on his reaction alone.

"Who is that?" Pretending she hadn't seen the picture, Jesse leaned over to get a better view, hoping he would name the girl, but she really didn't expect he would. She studied his face as he examined the picture.

"She was one of the girls who used to run the neighborhood but I don't recall her name," he said, tossing the photo on the table. He closed the book and put it back on the stack. "Were there any other pictures?"

"I didn't see any," she lied, but no more so than he did. Clearly, he wasn't expecting the picture, and as he stood up from the table, his face went blank and their talk was over.

"I have a meeting this afternoon, so I'd better get going. You can have the books if you want them." He looked down at his watch to avoid eye contact as Gramma ambled over to the table and picked up the photo.

"Isn't that Sonya?" Gramma asked as Dr. Williams walked out of the room. "You know, she owns the bookstore on Main Street." His footsteps paused in the hallway.

"No, I didn't." Making a beeline for the door, he stumbled over the sadiron doorstop and spewed a few words beneath his breath as he hurried across the porch.

Jesse stood out of view as he backed his truck down the drive. "Wow, he sure made a hasty exit. It's a good thing I didn't mention talking to her the other day when I stopped in at the bookstore," she said, walking back into the kitchen. "Is she one of Dad's old girlfriends?" She picked up the picture and placed it back in the book.

"Well, dear, he was quite fond of her. She was a very sweet girl. I thought they would marry but something happened right before he left for college. She visited one afternoon, and afterward, I could tell your father was very upset. He didn't want to talk about it and has never mentioned her since. He really did care about her, but I guess it wasn't meant to be."

# Twenty-One

*Jack*

Jack lay back in the swing and tried to picture Megan in his mind. As entertaining as the movie was, he expected to see her there but that didn't happen. After the no-show, he had to decide whether the bond was worth pursuing. *Anything worth fighting for comes with obstacles.* His wolf seemed to agree with his line of thought but in the back of his mind, there were some niggling words of wisdom, *if it doesn't come easy, it's not meant to be.*

The morning breeze was pleasant compared to the stuffy, fragrance-laced air from the night before. The females he encountered at the theater all smelled as if they had bathed in perfume, as if that odor was more appealing than their natural scent—*they were wrong.*

Jarred from his musings, he tilted his head and listened to the soft thuds that crossed the yard and his thoughts automatically went to Tracy. *What did she do this time?*

"You are the unluckiest person I know," Mason said as he stepped up on the porch.

Jack lifted his head and glanced down the road toward Tracy's cabin. "What are you talking about?"

"Megan. She showed up at the theater." Mason pushed Jack's leg off the swing and sat down.

"Dammit! I knew I should have stayed. Did she say anything?"

"Of course she did! She kept giving me googly eyes all night. I think she was attracted to my boyishly good looks," Mason teased and Jack chuckled. "I overheard her telling Tracy she works at the cafe."

Jack blew out a breath, his body instantly relaxing. "How was she? Did she say anything else?"

"I didn't talk to her long. When she realized who I was, she apologized for the way she acted at the boulders but as soon as Whitney came out of the restroom, we left. I didn't want anyone to know I knew who she was until you told them."

"So Whitney doesn't know I have a bond with Megan?"

"No, that's your story to tell. I haven't said a word."

"Good. I'd like to keep it that way until I have a chance to talk to her."

"Well, it looks like the ball's in your court," Mason said, pushing up from the swing. "If you need me, you know where I'll be."

Jack's mind whirled at the thought of seeing Megan again. He rushed into the bathroom and stood in front of the mirror. Was he presentable? At the cafe, wearing jeans and a plain white t-shirt was common; surely his casual appearance would blend in with the crowd. His plan was to have coffee and afterward, who knows? Maybe Megan would join him for dinner later in the evening or take a walk along the river. At this point, begging wasn't beneath him and he would have done anything she wanted if it meant he could have an undistracted minute of her day.

He stared at his reflection. Would she find him attractive? Most females did, but she wasn't like the others. She had a mind of her own and wasn't easily impressed. He chuckled and tucked the tips of his hair behind his ears. *You need a haircut,* he thought as he shut off the light and headed toward the door.

***

As Jack strolled down Main Street, he nodded to the locals he passed along the sidewalk. "Beautiful day," he said to the group of women gathered outside the flower shop.

"A beautiful day indeed," the plump, little woman replied as she reached into the bushel basket she held and extended a purple rose in his direction.

Jack stopped and looked down at the rose before taking hold of the stem. "Thank you," he said and a flicker of recognition flashed in his mind. Something about her seemed familiar, but she was an elderly female and the only elderly female he knew outside the pack was his neighbor, whom he really *didn't* know.

"The name's Bridget. I play bunco at Emmalyn's house. Dr. Williams' house?" Her brow arched as she waited for him to place the location.

"Jesse's?"

"Yes," Brid said, her wrinkled hand patting his arm. It was a comforting gesture, and something he thought a grandmother would do.

"Do you have more of these?" He held up the rose.

"As a matter of fact, I do." She gestured toward the door and followed him inside.

He looked around and scanned the different arrangements but he wanted something for a younger female, not a centerpiece to set on a dining room table. Sniffing the rose, he walked over to the counter. "I'll take a dozen of these," he said and handed her the flower.

"Aww, love at first sight." She placed the roses on a sheet of white floral mesh and added a sprig of lavender. "For luck," she said as she slid the enclosure card and a pen across the counter.

"Thanks. I'll take all the luck I can get." He chuckled and neatly signed the card. "Can you deliver them to the cafe?"

"I can have them there in fifteen minutes."

"That would be great. Thank you," he said, handing her the card and some cash. Satisfied he made the right choice, he smiled inwardly as he walked to the door. Things were finally looking up and he couldn't wait to see Megan's face when she saw the roses. He pushed open the door as a voice called out.

"She watches over the wolf. She knows you. She will remember."

Jack paused, certain it was Brid's voice, but she was waiting on another customer. *Now you're hearing things.* He shook his head and walked out the door and down the street.

It was past noon when he entered the diner. Based on the number of patrons there, business was booming. Unsure of what to expect, the quaint, little cafe was appealing and the atmosphere light, even welcoming. Picking up on the conversations around the room, he blushed at the whispers he heard from a group of females in the far corner as he made his way to the counter.

"I'll be with you in just a sec," the waitress said and smiled his way. He nodded as she rushed around removing empty plates and pouring coffee. "I'm Mallory," she added as she wiped her hands on her apron and picked up a pad and pen. "What can I getcha?"

"Coffee and a slice of apple pie," he said, glancing down at the folded newspaper. "Can I have the paper also?"

"Sure can. Find a seat, and I'll bring your order to you."

"Thanks," Jack said while handing her a ten. He picked up the paper and waited until a group of men walked past before sitting down in the corner booth they had vacated.

"Here you go, sugar," Mallory said, placing the coffee and the hot apple pie on the table, along with his change. "If you need anything else, just holler."

Jack nodded and Brid walked through the door. The longer he studied her, the more familiar she seemed. He was curious not only about who she was and where she was from, but also what she meant by "she watches over the wolf."

His attention was drawn back to the window when a small, red Beetle pulled in front of the building. It was an older vehicle, and he could appreciate the classic beauty, but when the door opened, Megan was the last person he expected to climb out. He glanced back as Brid walked out the door, and quickly picked up the newspaper.

"Hey, Roger," Megan greeted the owner as she walked across the cafe.

Roger reached below the counter and then handed Megan an envelope. "You must have a hot date tonight," he said. "Mama, our girl's gonna break a lot of hearts."

Jack peeked around the newspaper as Megan walked behind the counter and stopped beside the yellow rotary phone hanging on the wall. Her finger ran across what Jack assumed was a work schedule while his eyes traveled down her body. Her blonde, spiral curls danced on her shoulders as she rested a tiny hand on her hip. When she turned, her eyes sparkled beneath the overhead lighting, and her face was a deep shade of red from the teasing.

"You know I don't have a boyfriend."

"If you say so." Roger cut a glance toward Jack. "Ester, I guess the delivery wasn't for her after all," he yelled to his wife while Jack ducked behind the paper.

*He doesn't know you sent the flowers,* Jack thought. He folded the paper and placed it on the table. Feeling like a teenager with a crush, he glanced back towards the counter and Roger grinned. *Busted!*

"Megan, a delivery came for you," Ester called out from behind the grill. "Over on the desk."

"Are you sure it's for me? I wasn't expecting anything." As Megan turned, her breath hitched when she saw the purple roses. "Ester, are you sure these are for me?" she asked again.

"The card has your name on it," Ester said, walking

over to where she stood.

"But who would send me roses?"

"That I don't know. I didn't read the card."

Jack leaned to the side and looked between the pie displays as Megan turned back to the roses. She carefully pulled out the card and her face lit up when she read the words he had written. Twisting the edge of the newspaper between his fingers, he waited for her to come back through the dining area. He wasn't exactly sure how or when he would approach her. He just prayed that when he did, he wouldn't come off sounding like a mad dog and scare her away. His knee bounced, keeping rhythm with his heart, and he glanced over at the door. *Great, just great.* Notorious for her bad timing, Tracy walked in. He grabbed the paper off the table, and opened it, noticing her reflection in the window as she walked over to the booth.

"What are you doing here? Don't tell me you came for the pie," Tracy said as he folded the newspaper and placed it on the table.

"Did you need something?" Jack asked.

"I think we should sit at the counter," Whitney said, noticing the pie.

"Don't be rude, Whit. Say hi to Jack." Tracy pulled away and slid into the booth next to him, causing Whitney to scowl.

"I'm sorry," Whitney mouthed from the end of the table.

"Since when do you like pie?" Tracy asked, glancing around the room.

"I don't. I'm here for the coffee." Taking a sip, he considered playing the alpha card but didn't want to attract any more attention than what they were already getting from the nearby tables.

"I think I'll have a slice of pie." Tracy waved to the waitress.

"Take mine. To go." Jack pulled a napkin from the dispenser and flipped the pie onto it before handing it to her.

Tracy grinned and judging by her looks, he wasn't getting rid of her that easy. She took a bite of the pie and watched the bubbly waitress in the far corner. "This is delicious, but I prefer cherry."

"Of course you do." Distracted by Megan when she walked out from the kitchen with a grin on her face, Jack forgot about the pesky redhead beside him. She was happy, a far cry from the teary-eyed female he previously met at the boulders. Her rosy cheeks and bright smile captured his heart and he couldn't look away.

"Have a good time," Roger said as she headed toward the door.

When Megan turned to wave, her eyes locked onto Jack and her smile faltered. She glanced between him and Tracy before visible confusion clouded her features. She looked down at the roses she held against her chest. Jack had no clue what was going through her mind, but when she looked up again, he could see the hurt in her eyes. "Thank you," she mouthed before bolting out the door.

"Move!" Jack growled and as he stood, his legs caught beneath the table top and he fell back against the bench seat. Whitney jumped as the table shook and Jack cursed. Following his line of sight, Whitney looked out the window to see Megan ducking into the car before it sped off. Jack dropped back into the seat and fisted his hands to keep from wringing Tracy's neck. His plans were ruined, and thanks to her, Megan now thought they were together. He stared down at the mess he made as Whitney grabbed a stack of napkins to soak up the black liquid spilling across the table.

"I am truly sorry," Whitney said, blinking back tears.

"What are you sorry for?" Tracy asked, licking the apple filling from her finger.

"Shut-up, Tracy! Just shut-up and eat your pie," Whitney snapped before she stormed out the door.

"What's her problem?"

"You wouldn't understand," Jack replied, pushing Tracy out of the seat. Following Whitney, he was out the door in a flash. With his wolf on edge, he darted between the lunch hour traffic in an effort to put as much space between him and what his wolf considered *the enemy*. He ignored the blaring horns and raced across the park as his wolf fought to come forward. It had every intention of protecting its human, even if that meant exposing the pack. *It's all right, buddy.* He tried to calm the beast, but when Tracy yelled for Whitney to wait up, his wolf snarled. He didn't dare look back. The game Tracy played was not one his wolf eagerly participated in, and he was ready to take her down.

Using a shortcut through the neighborhood, Jack passed the two-story mansion—and a mixture of chlorine and lavender filled the air. Crossing Walnut, he sprinted through the cemetery, jumping over the headstones in his path. Running as fast and as hard as he could, when his foot landed past the tree line, he phased.

His wolf was lightning fast as it sped up the hill towards Hunter's Ridge. Erratic and beyond reasoning,

Jack had no choice but to let him run off his frustration. As he paced the cliff's edge, he snarled and lashed out at anything that moved. Even something as simple as the wind triggered a reaction. His wolf stood trembling until the adrenaline faded. And in one final act of defiance, he threw his head back and howled— a vicious sound that would have best been reserved for the moon. When all was said and done, the loneliness that seeped from his wolf crushed his spirit and he yelled out as he phased and dropped to his knees.

How had he gotten so mixed up with a human that she affected every minute of his day? Holding his head in his hands, he rocked back and forth for what seemed like hours. It was now his turn to release the two months of frustration, tension, and worry that had taken over his life. His fist connected with the ground and the bones cracked beneath the force, but he didn't care.

Their bond was instantaneous but as the days stretched without completing it, he could feel it slipping away. His thoughts turned to Lizzy as the realization hit his already frazzled mind. *If you had a bond with Lizzy, you would've had to deny it in order to have a bond with Megan.* Proof that what he thought he had years ago was wrong.

Jack drew in a deep breath and struggled to understand what led him to Megan. Watching the sun slowly set, he remained silently still while the dark shadows devoured him, letting his wolf simmer below the surface. He didn't realize how late it was, but time no longer mattered—he was dangerous. His wolf, although calm at the moment, was still wired-out and every few minutes, a zap of electricity shot through his body. After months of trying to find Megan, it was becoming harder to appease his wolf and more thoughts of denying the bond entered his mind. "It's there for a reason." He could hear Mason scolding him.

For his own sanity, he pushed Megan out of his head and tried to figure out what his next move would be. How could he deal with Tracy if he couldn't calm the beast that threatened to explode at the mention of her name? *If you can't control your own wolf, how will you control a pack?* He wasn't sure he could answer that question.

He groaned when he realized he wasn't wearing clothes, but thankfully it was dark and the chance of running into anyone so late in the woods wasn't likely. He trekked downhill, looking for the pine tree Tucker hid behind the night they chased. Ducking under the low-hanging branches, he unfastened the black bag that was tied to the trunk. *Way to go, wolf,* he thought as he pulled a pair of black sweat pants and a t-shirt from the bag. He quickly dressed and after re-tying the bag back to the tree, he jogged up the hill and retraced his steps back to the cemetery. He slipped on his shoes and gathered the tattered clothes before carrying them back to Hunter's Ridge. The walk did him good, but not enough to go home and risk the chance of running into Tracy. Taking a seat at the edge of the cliff, he stared out over the farmland. *Get comfortable, you're going to be here a while.*

# Twenty-Two

*Tracy*

Tracy crossed the ditch and was on her way home when Tucker came barreling up the street and grabbed her in a bear hug. "Gosh, I've missed you," he said, swinging her around until she laughed. "Wanna hang out?"

"Might as well. It's not like I have anything better to do," she said, wiping the sweat from her brow. Tracy loved spending time with her best friend, but since meeting Randy, things had been different. Between trying to get Jack's attention and not wanting to give up Randy's, she had no time for the one constant relationship in her life. Tucker was the rock that had kept her grounded for the past two years. When he moved to Kinsley, she figured he latched onto her because she was the self-proclaimed outcast of the pack. Being raised by her uncle, she kept mostly to herself, but Tucker changed that. He listened and talked to her, and soon became the true reason she was now living in Cloverly.

Randy, on the other hand, was human and the best disaster she ever ran into. The feelings she had for him were unlike anything she had ever experienced. He was funny and kind and the warmth of his smile radiated around him like sunshine on a dreary day. In a perfect world, they could have been the ideal couple, but her world was anything but perfect. Her eyes misted over and she frowned. Life was cruel that way. Giving you a glimpse of heaven and then stealing it away.

"Is everything all right?" Tucker asked.

"Everything is as right as rain, now that you're here," she said and she honestly meant it. She smiled and wrapped her arm around his waist.

"So where are the others?" Tucker glanced over at Jack's cabin.

It had been days since Tracy last saw Jack. Apparently, he was avoiding her, and she had no idea what she had done to Whitney, so she gave her plenty of space. "I don't know. I figured you all were hiding out, together, avoiding me." She lifted a brow in question.

"It's nothing like that. I've been training with Alpha Cooper for the past few days."

"Brown-nosing again?"

"No more than usual." He tapped her nose with his finger. "So what have you been up to?"

"I was taking riding lessons but now I'm just trying to stay out of trouble," she said, stepping up on the porch.

"No way!" He stopped her at the door. "You expect me to believe you've been sitting on the rump of an old, broken down saddle-trap? Not likely." His exaggerated laugh filled the air.

"Would you keep it down? I don't want the whole world to know." She glanced down the street and whispered. "I was referring to a motorcycle, not a horse." The folly of his comment had her fighting back a grin. He was silly at times but she knew he was only trying to make her laugh, which he usually did.

"Really?" He chuckled, still not believing.

"Yes, really. And I'm pretty good at it." Pride reflected in her eyes and she smiled as if she had just won the lottery.

"Oh, so that's the story between you and the biker dude. I'm surprised you gave him the time of day," Tucker said. "You've been holding back."

"What can I say? I like motorcycles and he was willing to teach me how to ride. End of story." Truth be told, she would have liked nothing more than to finish out her story with the sexy playboy but the more time she spent with him, the harder it was to walk away.

"Wow, I'm impressed. Way to go, Tracy! A hog-mama." He nudged her with his elbow. "Does Jack know?"

"No! And you can't tell him," she hissed, looking around as if she expected Jack to pop out from behind a tree.

"What's wrong with him knowing? It's not like he would stop you. Heck, he would probably encourage it. You're young. You need to enjoy life and not be so serious all the time. If not, one day you'll wake up as a miserable, old biddy with fifteen cats and you'll have no one to blame but yourself," he joked. Four years difference between them didn't make him an authority by any standards, and she rolled her eyes. "And why do you always feel the need to prove yourself? Can't you just be you? Not the Tracy with the chip on her shoulder, but the one that has a sparkle in her eye when she talks about riding a motorcycle. That Tracy is pure gold."

"If I could be that person, don't you think I would? I have to prove my worth. It's what I'm destined to do. You don't understand, no one understands," she said. Walking into the cabin, she slipped off her shoes and planted herself on the sofa. She slid the hairband from her hair and stuffed it between the cushions.

"Come on, Trace. I'm your best friend. Make me understand." Tucker sat down beside her. "I promise I won't tell a soul." She shook her head as he crisscrossed his finger over his heart.

"What happened to you Friday night? You were being a little snarky if I remember correctly. Did you not like the movie?" she asked, changing the subject.

Tucker sighed loudly and his shoulders dropped. "The movie was fine, but I don't know. There's this female I wanted to talk to and..."

"Please tell me you didn't cross over to the dark side." She laughed, making him smile.

"Not yet, but I sincerely hope to."

Tracy's eyebrows shot up with his answer. "You've been corrupted! How will I ever go on without you?" Her theatrical performance had him pushing her away and she laughed. Tucking her feet under her legs, she leaned back against his side. "Seriously, all you had to do was wink and she would have followed you home. That's like Dating 101...01." She snorted.

"I don't think she would fall for that. She's not like most girls, but I know she's attracted to me. I could see it in her eyes."

"Then what's the problem? Throw her over your shoulder and pound on your chest a few times. She'll get the message when you drag her to your cave." Tracy tried to lighten the mood but she could tell whatever the problem was, he was taking it personally.

"It's complicated," Tucker said as he brushed his dreads back over his shoulder.

"Complicated as in a love triangle? This is getting better by the minute," Tracy said.

"What the heck is a love triangle?"

"Never mind." She rolled her eyes. "Tell me more about this female."

"No, I'm not telling you who she is, so don't bother asking. You would be at her door in an instant. I know because I'd do the same for you."

"How can you deny me that privilege? It's what friends are for. Plus, I would love to see the look on her face when she answered the door." Tracy's voice dropped. "Yo, sugar-puss. Pack a smile and leave your attitude at home. There's a gorgeous male waiting for you in the wolves' den."

"That is exactly what I'm afraid of." He laughed.

"Well, if she likes you, but has a boyfriend, their relationship can't be serious. You should try talking to her. She may be more into you than you realize. Trust me. I have a feeling she's waiting for you to make a move." She snuggled closer and looked up through a fan of brown lashes.

"I gave her flowers."

"You didn't! What did she say? Did she like them?"

"She didn't know they were from me."

Tracy's excitement dropped a notch, and she placed her hand on his thigh. "Honey, if you're going to give a female flowers, it's an absolute must to sign the card! How else will she know who adores her?"

"I was going to mention the ribbon she had in her hair, but that lucky SOB showed up and interrupted our conversation."

"Tucker Wilson! I can't believe you said that." Shocked, she covered her mouth and laughed.

"That wasn't my choice of words. I was repeating what he called himself."

"Well, at least now you know why their relationship isn't serious. Any male that refers to himself as a *lucky SOB* must have an ego the size of Mars." She snarled her lip.

"All right, enough about me. What was your problem? I felt the change in your attitude when we left the theater. I know something happened and I assume it involved your biker friend."

Tracy shook her head, again. Randy was the least of her problems, but exposing her uncle's plan to take over the pack would no doubt find her face-down in the river by morning. He hadn't actually come out and threatened her life, but certainly insinuated it. "Have you ever wanted to escape? Like, get away from all the politics of pack life?" she asked, catching him by surprise.

"What? No!" He frowned. "The pack is everything. Have you ever met a rogue? If you do, you'll understand why being in a pack is so important for the wolf. Without an alpha, they do as they please and eventually, the wolf takes full control."

"I'm not saying I want to go rogue, but maybe an

escape... to another pack. One where I have more control over my life and can do the things I want..." She paused when he squeezed her hand. "I want to be the me you see. Is that too much to ask for? I want to have fun and laugh, to find that special someone..." She paused again. "Forget it. There are things expected of me, which I can't discuss with you or anyone else. I appreciate your concern, but I can't." She turned her head to hide her tears. *Stop it! You're not a weak female.*

"Does this have anything to do with your uncle?" His voice sounded harsh as he switched to big brother mode. "I know he's been hanging around lately. He thinks he's being slick coming up behind the cabins, but I've seen him," Tucker said with a slight growl in his words.

"He's an idiot," Tracy said, trying to play it down. She wished she could tell him the truth but he would go grizzly on Travis, and the thought of her uncle being mauled by her best friend wasn't something she wanted on her conscience. Not that he didn't deserve it, he did. He was a smug, nasty, old toad, and known for fighting dirty. So risking Tucker's life for hers would not happen. "He's working for the alpha at the building site and stops by to check up on me before he goes home. He's afraid I might have too much fun living away from him and Vivian."

"I knew he was a control freak, but that's messed up."

"Ha! You should be in my shoes."

"I don't understand him. You're eighteen. Old enough to do as you please, but he still treats you like you're twelve. You know, I could run interference for you."

"That's not necessary." She laughed. "So what do you want to do? Are you hungry? 'Cause after that depressing conversation, I need comfort food. You up for some chicken pot pie?"

"Double crust?"

"Double crust." She grinned when he jumped up and pulled her off the sofa, practically dragging her to the kitchen.

# Twenty-Three

*Jesse*

Jesse hauled the mop bucket across the back porch as the ear-splitting sirens wailed, disrupting the uneventful day. She dumped the dirty water on the ground and placed the bucket upside-down on the edge of the porch and wondered *how many people in Cloverly would miss lunch if the tornado sirens weren't tested daily?* Glancing across the yard as the sirens wound down, a repeated thud taking their place, she spotted Whitney standing next to Jack's car and waved.

"Hey, Jesse," Whitney yelled as she jogged across the yard. "Are you busy?"

"I'm meeting Lori for lunch. You want to join us?" Jesse asked, walking over to the fence. Since meeting the Cabin Crew at the theater, she hoped to hang out with them more often but so far, they kept mostly to themselves.

"Are you sure? I don't want to intrude," Whitney replied, looking back towards the cabin. "I didn't get a chance to talk to Megan at the theater. Will she be there also?"

"Megan's on vacation, but Lori and I would love to have your company. It'll be fun," Jesse said as her eyes drifted towards the thumping sound. Between the noonday sun and the tree branches, it was hard to see who was on Jack's roof but that didn't stop her from trying. "Is that Jack?" Surprised to see him wearing a ragged t-shirt with the sleeves cut out and jeans with holes in the knees, she lifted her hand to shield her eyes. *Whoa!* His hair stuck out in all directions and a shadow covered his jaw. She wrinkled her nose and Whitney chuckled.

"Jack wears stubble from time to time, but what you just witnessed is an untidy mess," Whitney whispered as she stepped over the small fence and followed Jesse across the yard. "I've been tempted to lock him in his room but knowing him, he would crawl out the window."

"Something tells me it probably wouldn't be the first time." Jesse grinned and looked back over her shoulder.

"Not hardly. He and Mason were notorious for cuttin' capers when they were younger.

"So are they brothers, or cousins?"

"Neither, just best friends," Whitney said as they rounded the house. "Tucker is Jack's cousin from Tennessee. He moved here a couple years ago."

Jesse smiled, thinking back to the theater. "Was that Tucker on the roof with Jack?" she asked, casting a glance across the street to Brian's house. *He hasn't asked you to be his steady, so stop with the guilt trip.*

"That was Mason. Tucker's with Tracy."

"Oh." Jesse told herself Tucker and Tracy weren't a couple, but who else would he be with? He was drop-dead gorgeous, and she was sex appeal wrapped-up in a skimpy, little package. She chewed her lip as Lori bounded up the sidewalk in a pair of cut-off shorts and a tank top.

"And where are you lovely ladies off to?" Lori asked, stopping in front of the house.

"Lunch at the cafe," Jesse said as they started down the sidewalk.

"Good, I'm starved." Lori popped a piece of candy in her mouth and followed behind Jesse and Whitney.

"When are you not?" Looking over at Whitney, Jesse rolled her eyes. "I swear, she eats more than three men, and I gain all the weight!"

"I can't help if I have a high metabolism." Lori puckered. Passing the package of sour candy to Jesse, she pulled her hair into a ponytail. "Gosh, I hate this time of year!"

Jesse laughed her agreement as the afternoon heat shimmered atop the asphalt, typical for a summer day. Plucking her shirt away from her skin, "Where's all the traffic coming from?" she asked as they turned onto Main Street.

"They're having a plant swap at the park, and the local churches are hosting a Summer Fun Fest. There's not much to do here, so they try to keep the little ones entertained at least one weekend a month." Lori reached out and took the package of candy from Jesse and stuffed it in her pocket.

"That's a nice thing to do for the little ones. I'm sure they enjoy it." Whitney said.

"Yeah, it's a big hit every summer but the fall festival is the best," Lori said as a break in traffic allowed them enough time to run across the street.

Stepping up on the curb, Jesse instantly locked her eyes onto the vast assortment of flowers displayed beneath the overhead awning in front of the flower shop. Thinking about the pink asters waiting on her porch that morning, she wondered if that was where Brian had gotten the flowers.

"Brian gave you flowers again?" Lori asked.

"What makes you think that?" Jesse grinned when Lori reached over and tugged on the ribbon. "Well, as beautiful as the flowers were, the card was much, much better." The soft smile and dreamy look on Jesse's face had Lori sticking her finger in her mouth, pretending to gag.

"Since you brought it up, you could tell me what the card said instead of making me work for every little detail."

"Are you sure you want to know? I mean, I wouldn't want you to choke on your finger or anything." Jesse snubbed her nose in the air. She didn't intend to reveal the true message on the card. It was personal and for her eyes only, but after opening her big mouth, she felt obligated. "My heart now beats for you," she said, placing her hand on her chest, another dreamy look crossing her face.

"Back at-cha, babe." Lori winked.

"Dream on, chicklet. That was for me, written on my card and attached to my flowers."

"Yeah? Well, I wonder how long it took McCheesy to come up with that line." Lori snorted.

"I think it's sweet, even if it is cheesy," Jesse admitted. As soon as she got home, she intended to call Brian.

Seeing how he was the only guy not affected by Tracy's charm, she needed to make sure it stayed that way.

"I don't think it's cheesy at all. It means you stole his heart," Whitney chimed in.

"Aww, that's so romantic. I never thought of it like that," Jesse said, walking away from the flower shop. She preferred to stay there and sniff each individual blossom until she lost all sense of smell, but with the heat of the day upon them, it would have to wait. Standing at the corner, she looked back one last time before crossing the side street.

"Hey, isn't that your dad's truck?" Lori asked, pointing to the blue pickup parked next to the bookstore.

Jesse looked over at the truck, and then at the bookstore. The store was only open four days a week, Monday through Thursday, and it was Friday. "He's probably at the park," she said as she followed Lori and Whitney into the cafe.

Once their order was placed, the three headed over to the corner booth, and Jesse was surprised to find the cafe practically empty. As they waited for their food to arrive, she looked out the window to scan the crowd across the street, but there was no sign of her dad. She turned back to the conversation. It was nice spending time with Whitney and Lori, but she wished Megan had been there as well.

"Thanks for inviting us to the movies last Friday. It was nice to meet everyone," Whitney said.

"It was, although I'm not really sure what the second movie was about. I was too busy trying not to choke on my drink," Lori said, squirting ketchup over her fries.

"That's because you were sitting near Tucker. Never

sit with Tucker—ever." Whitney laughed and sliced into her pie.

"Yeah, he's a blast," Lori said before shoving a fry in her mouth.

"Oh, he can be quite entertaining; that you can be sure of, but he's not someone you should take to the movies. It's a wonder he didn't get us all kicked out."

"So that's why everyone moved their seats. Thanks a lot for including me," Jesse said.

"Hey, you looked pretty comfy where you were, and we didn't want to interrupt." Lori grinned and looked over at Whitney. "Which reminds me, are Jack and Tucker dating anyone? Jesse and I were talking and we thought...well, Megan's been a little down in the dumps lately and—"

"—we want to fix her up with Jack," Jesse blurted out.

"Or Tucker." Lori narrowed her eyes and jabbed Jesse in the ribs.

"I didn't see that coming," Whitney said, setting her cup on the table.

"Are they available? Either will do."

"Lori!" Jesse scolded. "Way to be subtle."

"Me? You have a lot of room to talk."

Whitney grinned. "Believe it or not, they're both available."

"But I thought Tucker and Tracy were dating?" Jesse asked. Taking a sip of her tea, she glanced over at Whitney.

"Nope, just friends. And between Jack and him, I think Jack would suit Megan best. And that's not saying anything bad about Tucker. He's pretty amazing himself."

"Well, let's not get ahead of ourselves here. We're

assuming she'll agree to the date, but you know how she is," Lori added.

"I have a better idea." Whitney looked between the two. "Let's have a party! That way we can hang out and she can meet him on her own terms without feeling obligated to date him."

"I like your way of thinking," Lori agreed.

"Well, my cabin isn't huge, but it has an oversized backyard with a nice view of the river, and the patio is large enough for dancing. Tucker could provide the music. I know he wouldn't mind."

"That would be perfect, except I don't think Brian would go," Jesse said.

"Please. It's for Megan. He'll be there," Lori assured her.

Once they decided to have the party, the date was set for the Saturday after Megan returned from vacation. Jesse felt somewhat relieved when they agreed Jack was the better fit for Megan, but now she was questioning the relationship between Brian and her. Did one date, maybe two, if she counted the pool party, make them a couple? Was that what the flowers signified? Brian never came out and said so, but if he were solely dating her, wouldn't he have? Not that it mattered. She knew nothing about Tucker and although she sensed a connection to him, she wouldn't allow her thoughts to sabotage what she may or may not have had going on with Brian. "This will be so much fun, and I have a closet full of dresses if anyone needs something to wear," Jesse said.

"Don't let her lie to you. She has more than a closet full," Lori said, shoving another fry in her mouth.

"Why do you have so many dresses?" Whitney asked.

"Secretly, I'm a fashion designer," Jesse whispered as if it truly were a secret. "When I was a freshman, my mom talked me into joining the dance squad. Turns out I was a good dancer, but an even better costume designer."

"Wait 'til you see her dresses. She really knows how to dazzle with the material," Lori bragged.

"It sounds wonderful. It's not often I get the chance to strut my stuff. I think I'm more excited to wear a new dress than the party itself," Whitney admitted.

"Oh, I have a dress that would look amazing on you," Jesse said. She had enough dresses to fit the whole group, and would have loved nothing more than to see the others wearing her designs. "I also have a little gold dress that would look perfect on Tracy."

"So are we talking a formal dance?" Lori asked, and Jesse could see the cogs turning in her head.

"No, the guys can wear whatever they choose. I just thought it would be fun for us to dress up. Why?" Jesse narrowed her eyes.

"I'll let you know in a minute," Lori said, bumping Jesse out of the seat.

Jesse and Whitney watched Lori walk across the diner and disappear into the kitchen. Only Lori would act like she owned the place and enter an area posted *Employees Only*. Patiently waiting, the two finished eating before Lori waltzed back over to the booth. "I've got great news," she said, butt-bumping Jesse to move over in the seat. "Ester said she would cater the party if you wanted."

"Are you kidding? That's great! I'll have Mason round up some tables. How much will it cost? I can go get the money right now," Whitney said excitedly.

"It's free! Ester and Roger consider Megan their

daughter. Ester said she noticed Megan seeming a little depressed lately, so she thought it might cheer her up. Plus," Lori looked over at Jesse, "she hoped whoever sent Megan the purple roses would be there."

"Megan got purple roses and didn't tell us?" Jesse asked as small creases formed between her brows.

"It's not that she got the roses, but the sender's identity that we need to know," Lori said. "I'd hate to fix her up with Jack if someone else is sending her flowers."

"Jack sent the roses. I was here the day she got them. I didn't say anything, and you all can't tell them you know. But Tracy was here and Megan thought Jack was with Tracy because she bolted out the door and down the road before Jack could stop her. It was not a good day for either of them."

"No way," Lori said. "He sent her flowers after she ripped him a new one?"

"What are you talking about? I was under the impression she didn't even know him. She really told him off?" Whitney asked.

"Oh yeah, she was hot. We don't know exactly what happened. She wouldn't say. But he must really like her if he's sending her flowers." Jesse's eyes misted when she thought about Brian sending her flowers. *He must really like you.*

"That could be why he sent her the roses," Whitney said. "I'm pretty good at reading people, and judging by the way he was acting, he's really into her."

"Well, what are we waiting for? We have a party to plan," Lori said.

# Twenty-Four

*Jack*

Early the next morning, Whitney appeared at Jack's front door. Barely awake, she tucked her unbrushed hair behind her ears and knocked. "Jack, I need to talk to you," she said before the door completely opened.

"Would you like some coffee?" Jack offered, adjusting the sleep pants on his hips. She nodded, taking a seat on the edge of the porch without saying a word. Jack was clueless as to why she was there so early, but seeing the worried expression she wore, he knew something was definitely bothering her. *Why else would she be knocking at such an ungodly hour?* he thought as he walked into the kitchen.

Jack on caffeine was like listening to an all-day talk-a-thon. More than one cup and he prattled on for hours, not to mention the wiry effect it had on his wolf. Pouring a cup of coffee for Whitney and milk for himself, he carried the mugs out to the porch. "Here you go," he said, pushing open the screen door. "It's strong, but I figured you could use it."

Whitney took the coffee and wrapped her fingers around the mug before taking a sip. "Thanks. The stronger the better," she said, resting her head against the porch post.

As the silence stretched between them, Jack stared down at the alpha shield resting against his chest.

"Penny for your thoughts," Whitney said, looking down at the shield.

Jack looked up and chuckled. "Just a penny? I thought females wanted to know what males were thinking. Seems like my thoughts should be worth more than just a penny."

"That depends on the thought," she said, meeting his eyes.

Jack tilted his head, thinking back to the past couple of days. He remembered nothing unusual happening. He was pissed at Tracy, but that was normal in their world. "My thoughts are in the same place they've been for months, so you probably don't want to spend that penny."

"You're probably right. But that's not why I'm here. There's something I need to say, and I need you to listen and hear me. Okay?"

Jack nodded, giving her his full attention. He had no idea what she was about to say, but obviously, it was something she had been thinking about for a while, based on the small crease he noticed between her eyebrows.

"You know I think a lot of you and I trust your judgment one hundred percent. I wouldn't be here if I didn't," Whitney said. "I know what happened at the cafe was hard for you and you said everything was all right when you came home from Hunter's Ridge, but I don't think so. I've watched you for the past week and you haven't been yourself. Even Jesse commented on your appearance."

"But?" Jack prompted as she gathered her thoughts.

"You've changed, and I'm here to call you out. I mean no disrespect but you know I'm not one to sugarcoat things." She glanced up to see if he were still listening. "You look unkempt," she said. "If Megan saw you today, what do you think she would say?"

Jack grimaced but said nothing.

"What is wrong with you? You're not one to give up; and based on your actions, you have. I want you to go inside, clean yourself up, and shave that crap off your face! I know you're worried about Megan. I understand that. But I'm worried about *you*." She frowned before a slow smile spread across his face.

"So you don't like the new look?" He grinned when she narrowed her eyes. He knew she wasn't trying to knock him, and there was truth in what she said. "I admit it was hard watching Megan leave, and my wolf wasn't happy knowing I was the reason for her tears, but we're fine now," he said. "I needed time away... to regain control of my thoughts, nothing more."

"Then why does it look like you've been sucked through a knot hole? And if I remember right, you weren't the cause of her tears. I think we all played a part in that. It was a misunderstanding."

"Yeah, I know and as much as I want to blame Tracy, I can't. If I had only talked to Megan when I had the chance, and made her listen, who knows where we would be now?" He poured the remaining milk on the ground.

"What do you mean, *made her listen*?" Whitney tilted her head.

"I have a bond with Megan, but I didn't want to say anything until after I talked to her."

"Why didn't you tell us to leave? Talking to Megan was more important than Tracy eating pie."

"I know, but going alpha in a public place would have only attracted attention, and I was hoping she would leave before Megan came back through. Not to mention, that Roger guy at the counter. Somehow he knew I was the one who sent the roses, and I didn't want him to think I was an ass. I consider that about ten times worse than Megan thinking I was with Tracy."

"True. A misunderstanding can be explained away; a first impression, not so much." Whitney chuckled as she looked down at her cup. "I heard Megan told you off at the boulders, but you know she's on vacation and not trying to avoid you, so that has to make you feel somewhat better. You sent her roses. She's a female. After she thinks about it, she will want to talk to you. Wait and see."

"I hope you're right." Seeing Megan walk away, twice, had Jack second-guessing their bond. And knowing his wolf was dead-set on bonding with her, if she walked away again, he wasn't sure he could handle the rejection. He would have no choice but to end it for the sake of his sanity, not to mention his wolf.

"I am right. So would you please go clean up before the others get here? I'm sure they'll be glad to see the old Jack." Whitney stood and handed him the mug. "Thanks for the coffee."

Jack took the mug and watched Whitney walk across the yard. There was nothing like an early morning scolding to set the mood for the day. He chuckled and went inside.

*** 

Later that evening when the group gathered at the cabin, Jack whispered *thank you* in Whitney's ear and she nodded. Taking a seat on the porch swing, he turned his attention to Tracy who was chipping bright red nail polish off her fingernails. She was unusually quiet, and not at all aware of the conversation around her.

"Are we running at the lake tonight?" Tracy finally asked when Tucker stepped off the porch and walked over to where she was sitting.

"It would probably be best," Jack answered. He kept avoiding Tracy after the cafe incident until he could reason with his wolf. Now, he looked at her with pity. She had proven herself to be a royal pain-in-the-ass and he had every intention of sending her back across the river until a gut feeling warned him against it. Moving to Cloverly was good for her, but lately, something had changed, and he assumed that had to involve her uncle. He picked up Travis's scent in the area and although he was a member of the Kinsley Pack, he wasn't a member of the Cloverly Pack, and needed to know his boundaries.

"Don't worry about me, Jack. I've got it under control," Tracy said as Tucker swatted her hand, if only to stop her from picking her nails. Jack was leery, but Tracy had done nothing lately to warrant a restricted running area. And as weird as it sounded, she wasn't harassing him about where he had been.

"If you all want, we can hit Hunter's Ridge and from there go east past the cemetery," Jack suggested.

Tracy stood and high-fived Tucker, a silent celebration between the two. As the sky darkened, the group of five jogged down the road toward the ditch. The shadowy bend was the darkest area for entering the woods unnoticed, especially since Jesse had moved in with her grandmother.

"What a great night for a run," Whitney remarked, jumping the ditch and following the trail behind Tracy.

"I don't think so. There are more storms forecast," Tucker said, looking skyward.

"Well, I hope we get a good drenching. I love running in the rain." Whitney looked up as a web of lightning skittered across the sky.

"Eww. Wet dog smell is not my idea of a good run," Tracy grumbled. "I hope the rain holds out until after. It will absolutely destroy my hair."

"As tight as you have that braid, you've nothing to worry about," Whitney said, tugging on the lime green scarf twisted in Tracy's hair.

"Yeah, you have a better chance of ruining your shoes," Mason added as they continued deeper into the woods.

"I think we can rule out the storms for now," Jack interjected. Ducking beneath a large pine, he undressed and phased.

Racing towards the cemetery, Jack's wolf wasn't in the mood to run so he phased at Hunter's Ridge, and watched the others race past. Slightly depressed, his wolf had forgiven Tracy, but he still didn't entirely trust her. He sat down on the edge of the cliff as the remaining

clouds moved out and moonlight lit the area, exposing
small stones and boulders peppered across the ground. He
tossed a rock over the ledge and listened to it splash down
in the creek below. Resting back on his elbows, he stared
at the ring around the moon before an ominous feeling
settled over him. Jack wasn't superstitious but if trouble
brewed for the pack, he took comfort knowing Megan was
out of town and safely out of harm's way. He inhaled a
deep breath as he stood and phased with the intentions of
heading back toward Sallee's Rock. Instead, shaking out
his fur, his wolf threw its head back and howled—a long
drawn-out howl of a lonely wolf summoning its mate.

# Twenty-Five

*Tracy*

The heart-wrenching howl resonated through the trees, halting Tracy's run. Her heart understood Jack's sorrow, so deep, it cut her to the bone. A sad smile crossed her face when she phased and looked up the hill. A lonely wolf desperate for its mate; she knew that feeling all too well. Standing beneath the pine trees, she could hear the others returning the call before racing past the cemetery. How could she continue the run when there was so much pain and anguish behind that one howl? Her heart went out to Jack, knowing he felt as trapped as she did, although she had found her true mate. A tear slipped down her cheek when she thought about Randy and what could never be.

"I thought you said you had this under control?" Travis hissed as he stepped out from behind a tree to confront Tracy. "You know what you have to do! What the hell are you waiting for?"

Tracy startled, bringing her hand to her chest. She didn't realize Travis was lurking in the shadows and wondered if the others detected his scent. She shifted nervously. Had she known he was there, she would have never phased, and now she stood like a deer caught in headlights. A low growl rumbled in her chest but she silenced her wolf when she noticed the flare of his eyes. Travis was the last person she expected to see, especially considering how the others could turn back that way at any time. Despite the sense of dread that washed over her, she knew she was on her own. Whatever he had to say would only cause more heartache.

"I told you I have everything under control. I'm not the one who's going to screw this up. Have faith in my charm," she said glibly, but in reality, she wanted to spit in his face and run for the hills. "And why are you here anyway? Are you intentionally trying to get caught?"

"Well, unless you're the one Jack is smitten with, your charm isn't working, sweetheart. So don't worry your pretty, little head about me, you have bigger fish to fry."

Tracy wanted to smack the grin off his smug face. "Smitten? You honestly think Jack is smitten? I'm with him most days and there are no other females around besides Whitney and myself. So chill out. I got this."

She was thrilled the day she moved to Cloverly and got away from her uncle's house. His rules were tough while he constantly plotted ways to take down the alpha, always using her as a shield. He hated living under Alpha Cooper's rule, and he especially hated being civil to humans. He was a thorn in her side and she despised the way he always made excuses to antagonize her.

"Maybe you do and maybe you don't. Either way, I think I'll hang around a bit longer and have a look-see for myself. See what you've been up to, and for your sake..." He stepped back and cocked his head—listening.

"Suit yourself, but don't underestimate me." She couldn't resist rolling her eyes at the brazen fool.

"Well, from what I heard, it sounds like lover boy is lonely, but I don't think it's you he calls to. So maybe you should explain to me where you've been sneaking off to lately. You haven't been with Jack. He made that perfectly clear to basically everyone."

"For the love of the moon, would you stop already? I don't owe you any explanations so go chase a rabbit or a deer, or something." She was angry and didn't understand what gave him the authority to question every move she made. It was her business, but clearly, he still thought he was in control of her life. He made his threats known, so there was no reason for him to continue pushing her buttons, which was starting to grate on her last nerve. She was an adult by most standards and he needed to understand that, back the hell off and give her breathing room.

"Don't overstep your bounds, sweetheart. Your worries should be with Jack, not me. I'll be chasing whitetail before the sun comes up," he grunted. "You, on the other hand, had better hope a certain male is chasing your tail before the night is over. You know what you have to do! So put on your best seductive smile and make your move tonight... or else!"

"Are you seriously threatening me?" Tracy asked.

Hearing footsteps in the distance, it was safe to say the pack was headed in the opposite direction. "I'm your niece, you raised me! You don't threaten your own family!" She sneered and fisted her hands at her sides. Huffing out a breath, she tried to calm herself but with Travis, it was nearly impossible. "I don't need you to tell me how to seduce Jack or when. It will happen, and on *my terms*, not yours. So back off and let me handle this."

Travis stalked forward as a low growl echoed through the trees. Grabbing Tracy around the throat, he glared into her eyes. "I will not allow you to destroy everything I've worked for. Is that understood? The pack belongs to me, and I will kill anyone who tries to stop me from taking what is rightfully mine, even you! So don't overestimate your value, my dear, you have none." Shoving her back, he slammed her head against the tree and she crumpled to the ground.

Tracy pushed up against the tree as pine needles stabbed her backside and black spots clouded her vision. She was a strong female, but Travis was bigger, outweighing her by at least eighty-five pounds. Her body trembled and tears filled her eyes but she quickly blinked them away. He was the only family she had left. Surely that meant more than his precious pack? Looking up at the man that raised her, his nostrils flared and the evil was fairly radiating from him. His wolf loomed just beneath the surface, its eyes locked on her. One sudden move was all it would take and he would be on her faster than she could phase. "I said I would take care of it. I will. Okay?" Her voice cracked and she rubbed her neck and swallowed, trying to regain her composure.

"Well, let me give you a little incentive, sweetheart.

You thought by moving to Cloverly, I wouldn't know what was going on, but you're wrong! I know you've been sneaking out, and I know why." His lips curled into a wicked grin, and a cold shiver inched up her spine. "You see, I'm always watching, and that little scene at your cabin was truly heartbreaking, to say the least. But you really should have explained to your little friend, confronting me was the last thing he would ever want to do. I would hate to see biker boy have an untimely accident, wouldn't you?" His eyes flared—Randy was as good as dead.

"No! Leave him out of this! He's a friend; nothing more," Tracy insisted as nausea roiled her stomach.

"Oh, you tell that lie so well. You're a slick one, I'll give you that, but there is more. I've seen it with my own eyes. You on the back of that motorcycle rubbing up against him like a dog in heat. You knew the danger, yet you still think what you did was all right. I can see it in your eyes," he growled.

"That's crazy. You see nothing."

"Really? Then explain why your heart rate jumped when I mentioned him. Why are you so defensive? I've smelled his scent on you. Oh, I think he's more than what you admit."

Tracy looked away to avoid letting him see her lie. Randy was clueless to the danger she put him in, and now she wasn't sure she could protect him. Fear surged through her body as her heartbeat thundered in her chest. She inhaled a rickety breath. "No, you're not right. You know me better than that. He's a human, a male that I've been using to make Jack jealous." She pushed away from the tree and stood to face him. She knew if she cowered now, Randy would be dead by morning and she could never live with herself. "So before you jump to conclusions, you need to get your facts straight. Jack will be an alpha, and there is not one male in the pack that intimidates him. Randy, on the other hand, is his sole competition." She placed her hands on her hips, hoping he bought her lie. "So if you want your plan to work, you need to leave now and let me handle Jack. I've already told you, *I've got this.*"

"Fine, but for your sake, I hope you know what you're doing. If not, your friend will pay the ultimate price." Travis phased and disappeared into the shadows.

Tracy slumped against the tree and hot tears stung her eyes. Struggling for a breath, she rested her hands on her knees as her vision blurred and her pulse echoed in her ears. Trying to control her breathing before she blacked out, she slowly inhaled through her nose. The panic rushing her body was foreign to her and she needed to gather her wits. *Trouble, always trouble.* She phased and raced up the hill.

By the time Tracy arrived at Hunter's Ridge, all was quiet and Jack was no longer in the area. She phased and looked out over the farmland, wondering if her life would ever truly be her own. It wasn't fair that Randy was the most important male in her life, and now because of her uncle's determination to take over the pack, she would have to let him go. But she was also smart enough to realize Travis's threat shouldn't be taken lightly. He was cruel and evil; and apparently, the only thing that mattered to him anymore was power. She wiped her eyes.

The brief time she spent with Randy was wonderful, but what choice did she have now but to walk away? Her wolf protested. It wasn't happy about the turn of events and insisted it could protect him. A plan formed in her head and she closed her eyes and drew in a long breath while mulling over the idea. She would have to make a showing at Jack's; that was for sure, but would it be convincing enough for Travis? Sending a silent prayer to the moon, she phased and headed back toward Sallee's Rock, knowing failure wasn't an option.

# Twenty-Six

*Jack*

It was early morning by the time Jack rounded the boulders at Sallee's Rock. A few lingering clouds and the occasional streak of lightning off in the distance were all that remained of the storms that besieged the area earlier that night. Phasing, he quickly dressed then climbed to the top of the boulder and waited for the others to return from their run.

Dreading the pity his pack would more than likely shower on him, he intended to hold his head high. He wasn't ashamed of his wolf but that didn't mean he wanted the others to hear just how depressed and lonely he truly was, although Whitney already knew. He tried his best to hold back the pain but once his mind centered on Megan; he lost control again and his wolf did the only thing it knew—it called to her.

One by one the others arrived at the boulders, Tracy

being the first to join him with Whitney close behind. Silence stretched the hour, but once they were all there and accounted for, they headed down the trail towards the ditch.

Jack remained quiet, listening to their hushed conversations as he followed them through the woods. A low chuckle from time to time drew his attention to Tucker, who was attempting to distract the others with lame werewolf jokes and riddles. Jack smiled, trying to work out the answers in his head, but his mind wasn't in a humorous mood. He had no idea what kind of market a werewolf would avoid, so he cocked his head, waiting for the answer.

"A flea market." Tucker laughed and jumped across the ditch. Jack just shook his head.

"Get some sleep, we'll meet up later," Jack said as Tucker walked across the street to his cabin. He expected Tracy would follow him but seeing her expression, he knew something was bothering her and he didn't think it was the punchline. Waving to Whitney and Mason as they veered off to their cabin, he hoped whatever was troubling Tracy would hold off 'til later.

Trudging onward, he tromped through standing puddles, sending water droplets flying through the air. His body was drained and although he had cleaned himself up, he still felt beaten down by his own mental thoughts. *You were such a fool to let her leave. You made her cry.* His jaw clenched and he sucked air in through his nose. It was his fault that his wolf was so miserable, and until he could speak with Megan, he didn't expect that to change.

"Jack," Tracy's voice shattered the silence and he groaned inwardly. "Would you like some company?"

"Not tonight, I'm tired," he said without turning to acknowledge her. Tossing his shirt over his shoulder, he continued down the road with her following at a distance, trying to avoid the splashing water. He glanced up at his cabin, and the brief chance of him falling asleep anytime soon became impossible, but she didn't need to know that.

"Jack, I really... wish you would let me help you." Tracy jumped over a puddle and landed in his front yard.

Jack's shoulders slumped as he stopped and slowly turned to face her. He didn't want to deal with her at the moment, but apparently, she refused to walk away. "I don't need your help. What do you not understand?" Running his fingers through his hair, he turned and strolled up the sidewalk.

"You may not need me, but your wolf does. Can't you see that? Why do you continue to fight it? Your wolf wants a mate. I could... I *can* be that for your wolf," Tracy said.

The uncertainty of her words surprised Jack and he stopped. He stood quietly as she continued speaking, never failing to notice the slight waver in her voice. It was hard to admit, but for once, she was right. His wolf was frustrated and lonely, *but not for her.* "The man controls the wolf, not the other way around. But since you feel I should listen to my wolf, then maybe you should take your own advice and listen to yours. If you did, I'm sure you wouldn't be standing here right now," he replied but his words missed their target.

She slowly stepped forward, her hands trailing up his back. "Let me help you," she whispered. "Let me be the female your wolf desires. You're running out of options. Even Jesse has found her mate. You don't need her. When you become the alpha, you will need a strong alpha female to stand beside you, to rule. A human isn't strong enough to handle that position. You know that. She could never control the pack."

He closed his eyes as her breath brushed across his ear, sending a wave of queasiness to his stomach. He was lonely, his wolf frustrated, and both were tired of searching and always coming up short. But Megan was the one he wanted to be with, not Tracy. Chills traveled up his arms as her scent mixed with the pine aroma in the air, smothering him. What he intended to do probably wouldn't score him any karma points, but if games were what she wanted to play, he would join her... at least for the night. Glancing up at the halo around the moon, he took that as a warning.

Spinning on his heels, Jack appeared behind Tracy. "Just for the night," he whispered so low, she barely heard him. His fingers squeezed her waist and her body stiffened, causing him to rethink what he had in mind. But he would give her the night, knowing she most likely wouldn't enjoy the outcome. Jerking her back against his chest, he guided her up the sidewalk and she paused at the door, her body trembling.

He smiled and pushed open the door with one hand, keeping the other gripped tightly at her waist. She was hesitant at first but eventually stepped forward. "Relax, this is what we both need," he assured her as he moved her into the living room. He was calm, pursuing her, and she was as fearful as any prey. *A taste of her own medicine*, he thought as he loosened his grip, allowing her to step away. He was tired, and really didn't want to contend with her but he knew if he didn't give her the attention she craved, she would never leave him alone. "Make yourself comfortable and I'll get us something to drink. To celebrate." He tossed his shirt over the back of the recliner as he walked past and she shifted on her feet. She was nervous—*good.*

Tracy smiled when he entered the kitchen but he could feel the tension in the air. Why wasn't she stopping him? It was clear she didn't want to be there; but was she that stubborn she would go against her wolf? As he walked over to the sink, he could hear her shifting on the sofa and he scowled.

He pulled two large glasses from the cabinet and filled them with ice before turning on the faucet. A nervous giggle sounded from the living room when he shut off the water. He closed his eyes and forced his body to calm. After a minute, he walked into the living room, his shoulders back, and his game face on.

Sitting on the sofa, her long hair draped over her shoulders. Her lime green scarf was removed and now tucked beneath her leg. She was probably one of the most beautiful females he had ever seen but her fake persona was lacking, which made her as ugly as dirt. She stood and adjusted her halter top, exposing more skin than necessary. *How far was she willing to go?* He wondered as he bit his tongue, to keep from growling and ruining his plans. Past the point of no return, he would finish what he started and by daylight, she would know her place in the pack.

Anticipation was thick in the air, his more than hers. "Here you go," he said, standing before her bare-chested, his eagerness almost unbearable. "A tall glass of ice water after a run is always refreshing." His sultry voice gave nothing away as his eyes drank her in.

"I don't want to be refreshed, I want to be ravished," she said, meeting him in the center of the room. There was no mistaking the dread that flashed across her face, which she quickly hid behind a smile.

"Damn," he said when she flipped her hair over her shoulders, exposing her cleavage. Slowly his gaze traveled downward, seductively caressing the bare skin of her chest, her stomach, and gradually descending to the tight, little miniskirt that displayed her long, slender legs. She fidgeted and he smirked as his eyes continued downward to the black leather ankle boots she wore. She had an amazing body, and most males would have killed to be in his position. Moving his eyes slowly back up, he waited for her next move.

"Well, what do you think?" She clasped her hands behind her back, and swayed from side to side.

The pleasure of what was about to take place caused his heart to race and he flashed a crooked grin. "Let's do this," he said, his alpha card coming into play. She swallowed hard and her breath hitched when he stepped into her personal space. "I think it's time." The vibration of his voice caused her to shudder, and she glanced up through her lashes. "Time for you to cool down." No sooner had the words left his mouth, when his arms went up, pouring both glasses of ice water over her head, drenching her right where she stood.

For a split second, she couldn't comprehend what happened, and the frigid water pooled around her feet. Shock registered in her eyes, and she rubbed the goosebumps on her arms. "What the hell did you do that for?"

"Because you're like a damn dog! All you do is dig, dig, dig! You may one day be the mate of an alpha, but that alpha won't be me. So bury that bone tonight. It's dead!"

"Screw you, Jack!" Tears filled her eyes as she stomped across the room. "I never wanted this!"

"Well, tell me something I don't know. I've seen the way you've changed over the past few weeks. Why would you settle for something you don't want when what you do want is easily attainable?" he asked as he motioned her back to the sofa.

"Because Travis thinks if I seduce you, it would force a bond between us," Tracy blurted out.

"He can't honestly believe that." Jack ran his fingers through his hair and sat down in the recliner. "Are you serious?"

Tracy nodded. "He wants me to be an alpha female." Her voice was low and she stared down at the spilled water, unwilling to meet his eyes.

Jack walked out of the room and returned with a towel. Handing it to Tracy, he paced the floor, trying to make sense of her statement. He knew there was more to the story, but she didn't trust him enough to confide in him, or anyone else for that matter. Just hearing her finally open up about Travis was huge. Usually, if Travis were mentioned in a conversation, she stayed out of it. She was always loyal to him, but now Jack wasn't so sure. "Is that what you want?"

"No. I want to be a scout, but it doesn't matter. I don't have any choice. It has to be his way, or else."

"Or else, what?" Jack stopped and faced her.

"Or else I must leave the pack."

"No! You can't leave. We'll work this out. I don't know how, but I'll figure something out," he said, coming to kneel before her. "I know lately we've butted heads, but I don't want you to leave. The pack needs you."

# Twenty-Seven

*Jesse*

The morning light shone through the window as Jesse rolled over and stared up at the roof hatch. After she and Lori spent the better part of the night on the widow's walk, she was tired but eager to talk to Brian.

She glanced over at the clock on her bedside table. They had less than an hour before they had to meet Steve and Brian, and part of her was dreading it. Brian told her that trying to figure out the secret of Cloverly was a waste of time, but Lori thought he was just being a protective boyfriend when he acted that way. Based on his counselor position and dealing with groups of hyped-up kids, he wasn't used to anyone bucking his authority. But Jesse wasn't any kid, and she didn't need his protection, much less, a guy ordering her around. What she wanted from him was a steady relationship, and he had yet to ask.

*He kissed you.* She rolled her eyes at the thought. Were guys now so entitled that they didn't bother asking the girl to be their steady? Was it assumed a kiss was all that was necessary? She would have preferred he asked her to be his girlfriend like guys did back in the day. Then she smiled. He *was* her boyfriend. Why else would he send her flowers? She kicked off the sheet and jumped out of bed. Suddenly, facing Brian and Steve didn't seem so stressful. Once she and Lori were dressed, they hurried out the door and across the street, careful to avoid her grandmother.

After finding the box of old newspaper articles, she and Lori researched the history of Cloverly. The town was established in 1854, which oddly enough, was about the same time gray wolves disappeared from the state. So maybe the wolves did linger in the area longer than originally thought; but keeping it a secret made absolutely no sense to her.

She grinned as Brian stood in the doorway waiting for them to cross the yard. Wearing a pair of snug-fitting jeans and a yellow muscle shirt, he smiled. "This way," he said, leading them through the house and out the side patio doors to where Steve was waiting.

Jesse glanced over her shoulder as she placed the backpack on the table. Behind the privacy fence and out of sight of her grandmother's house, she pulled out the wooden box. She cleared her throat to get Brian's attention, and handed him and Steve the newspaper clippings. Whether or not they agreed with what she and Lori were doing, it wouldn't hurt them to show a little support or at least *act* like they were interested.

"Okay. I understand there was a secret, or is still a

secret that some of the residents have kept over the years. What I don't understand is how you tie wolves into the mix," Brian said after scanning the articles.

"It has nothing to do with the articles, it's this right here," Lori said, digging through the papers until she found the drawing of the shield. "The word *Lycan* is what ties wolves to the secret of Cloverly."

"Werewolves? You've got to be kidding," Brian said.

Jesse didn't fail to notice the shared look of disbelief on their faces and the slight grin on Steve's. She knew they wouldn't buy the werewolf theory and quite frankly, she wasn't sure she did either. "Have either of you seen a shield like this before?" She shifted her weight and leaned against the table.

"Did you ever think that maybe the secret wasn't an actual secret, but a secret group?" Brian suggested, tossing the paper back into the box. "Mascots could be many animals, which means that drawing proves nothing."

"Sorry, but I'm with the big guy on this one," Steve said.

"I'm talking about a town secret, not a team mascot! There is a difference, and if what we heard last night was a wolf, then there's got to be more than one," Jesse said.

"So you heard a dog howling and you assume it was a wolf, based entirely on a drawing?" Brian leaned back in his chair and laughed. "That is ridiculous."

"I'm not assuming anything. I'm from the city and I know dogs will howl at passing fire trucks or tornado sirens, but they don't do that here. So I think it's highly unlikely that one would run into the woods just to howl at the moon," Jesse said, her snarky reply causing Brian to frown.

"So now you're bringing the moon into this? Unbelievable," Brian remarked. The scowl on his face made Jesse rethink telling him anything more, but she needed his help; and if that meant biting her tongue, she would.

"I'm not bringing the moon into this but it was a full moon last night and I don't know of any dog that howls at the moon just because... although I remember a dog named Kira that barked at thunder," Jesse said, her voice growing sweeter as she played up to him.

"For the sake of argument, let's say what you heard *was* a wolf. There's nothing stopping wild animals from traveling through this area. It's not like wolves have never been seen in Kentucky. And where were you last night when you heard the howl?" Brian asked while Steve put his head down on the table to hide his grin.

"We were on the widow's walk, where else?" Lori piped up.

Steve and Brian both looked over towards Jesse's house. "Up there?" Steve asked.

"Don't look so surprised. It wasn't that big a deal." Lori chuckled.

"How did you get up there?" Brian glanced back at Jesse with a slight sneer on his face.

*Oh, no, you didn't!* Jesse knew the guys wouldn't believe them, but at that point, she didn't care. "I'm not allowed to disclose that information. It's top secret. If I told you, I'd have to kill you."

Lori snorted.

"So you think what you heard was a werewolf? Does that also mean you believe in vampires, ghost, and aliens?" Brian asked, growing more annoyed.

"Of course not. Everyone knows vampires don't have blood pumping through their veins, and without any circulation, they're dead."

"And ghosts aren't?" Brian smirked when Jesse palmed her forehead.

"Ghosts are different. They don't need a body. They just appear—to float—kind of."

"Yeah, and years ago, people thought the earth was flat." Steve swatted Lori away when she bopped him on top of the head.

"Well, before you ask, I do believe in aliens. The universe is huge. So what?" Jesse smartly replied.

"You can't pick and choose. Either you believe in everything or nothing at all," Brian said as a light breeze pushed his hair into his eyes.

"That's stupid." Jesse crossed her arms over her chest, determined to stand her ground. He may have been her boyfriend but that didn't mean she would cut him any slack. "I believe there are intelligent life forms on other planets and I believe in ghosts but not the haunting kind. And until you can prove they *don't* exist, I'm going to continue to believe they do."

"So you have proof vampires don't exist?" Brian grinned.

"No!" Jesse huffed. "This is getting us nowhere."

"Well, the way I see it, you have two choices. If you really think you heard wolves, we can go look for wolf tracks. If they were in the woods last night, the ground was wet," Steve suggested.

"What's the second choice?"

"Ask your grandmother whose box it is." Steve smiled.

"I can't do that. It was hidden in the cellar and I don't want her to think I was snooping."

"Weren't you? If you had merely stumbled over the box, you would have shown it to her, but instead, you went through it. Sounds to me like you *were* snooping," Brian said.

"Well, it wasn't intentional. We just saw the articles and..." Jesse frowned and looked over at Lori.

"Lace up your boots. It looks like we're going for a walk." Steve winked at Brian.

"Do you really want to go right now?" Jesse asked, glancing towards the woods.

"I'm not. I'm staying right here," Lori insisted.

Brian and Steve got up and started across the yard. "I take that as a yes," Jesse said, hurrying to catch up with them.

The three headed out the back gate, leaving Lori alone on the patio. Jesse wasn't thrilled about going to Sallee's after hearing the howls the night before, but surely she could survive one more trip, even if she were a bit leery.

The trail that ran behind Brian's house wasn't as noticeable as the one by the oak tree. It was narrow, and the area was thick with trees and brush, concealing the ground beneath. Jesse looked up as the sky disappeared behind the canopy of green and crossed her arms over her chest. She wasn't claustrophobic but in the midst of all the greenery, she felt like the trees were closing in around her. "I don't like this path at all."

"This is just the start, once we get past that pine tree up ahead, it will open up to the trail we were on the other day," Brian said. True to his word, as soon as they passed under the pine, Jesse recognized the trail. Feeling better about their location, she made a mental note of the path and how it branched off. She wouldn't get lost again.

When they arrived at Sallee's Rock, all was quiet as they walked across the clearing to the boulders. Spreading out to cover more ground, Jesse didn't expect to find any tracks since the howl came from the opposite end of town, but she had yet to mention that small tidbit to Brian. With his take-charge attitude he would have them hiking through unknown terrain just to prove a point, and as much as she wanted to prove that what she had heard was a wolf, she wasn't thrilled about finding evidence in their territory. *Which is where you are now.* Blaming her skittishness on her imagination, she scanned the ground in front of her. "I don't see anything."

"I found one," Brian yelled.

Steve and Jesse ran over to where he was stooped next to the boulders. Looking at the ground, Jesse wrung her hands.

"It's a print but how can you tell the difference between a dog's paw and that of a wolf?" Steve asked.

Jesse held her breath and waited for his answer. *Stop worrying, it's probably a dog.* Jack had confirmed it was a dog that ran through her yard and since she was no expert on wolves, maybe he was right. She chuckled and stepped around Brian. Freak-out averted. "Look, there's another," she said, feeling confident that Jack probably knew more about wolves than they did.

Steve followed the tracks to the backside of the boulder. "It looks like a whole herd came through and stopped here, only there's no watering hole."

"You're right," Brian said. "If these are wolf tracks, do you know what that means? We haven't had wolves in

Kentucky for well over a hundred years. This is epic!"

Jesse glared. They would think it was epic, seeing the tracks for themselves. She rolled her eyes. Maybe now they would be more interested in finding out what the secret was, rather than making snide remarks about it.

"Let's get the cameras. I bet we could get some great pictures of the pack," Steve said.

"But I thought they were dogs." Jesse tensed up and her eyes darted around.

"Probably, but there's only one way to be sure. Come on, let's go." Brian grabbed her hand, and the three hurried back down the trail.

The woodsy smell tickled her nose as Jack's words played in her head. *The woods can be a dangerous place.* Feeling somewhat better after ducking under the pine tree, upon seeing the privacy fence, she relaxed. Walking through the gate, Jesse expected Lori to be happy they were back; instead, she sat at the table, pouting.

"Please tell me you didn't find anything."

"You should have gone with us. It was unbelievable the number of tracks we found." Jesse laughed as the nervous energy moved through her body. Taking a seat beside Lori, she put her hands between her knees. "That was the scariest thing I've ever done," she whispered.

"Well, you could have fooled me," Lori whispered back. But when Jesse raised her shaking hands, Lori's mouth fell open. "What the hell?"

"Shh, I'm fine. It was a little freaky but I'm good now. Just trying to wind down," Jesse said.

"So what are they doing?" Lori asked as Brian and Steve rushed around the house.

"Gathering supplies. We're going back." Jesse knew

Lori wasn't thrilled with the idea. She would have preferred to spend her day reading about nature, rather than experiencing it. She hated wearing mosquito repellant, and bugs irked her. Her list of complaints grew longer every time they went into the woods, which was entertaining in itself.

"You're kidding," Lori said, laying her head down on the table. "I don't want to go."

"No one said you had to. You can wait here."

"Do you know how scared I was sitting here alone, unable to see past that large-ass fence? Well, let me tell you, every noise I heard, I expected something to either come through the gate or fly over the fence. I stood by the back door the whole time you were gone. No, thank you! I'm not staying here by myself again."

Within ten minutes, the four set out across the backyard and Brian held the gate open while Lori and Jesse followed behind Steve. Jesse wanted to suggest using the path beside her house, but there was no way they would be able to sneak past Gramma, especially if she were working in the garden.

"I can't believe I'm doing this," Lori said.

"I can't believe you freaked yourself out." Jesse chuckled.

"Couldn't we have done this on a day that wasn't so humid?" Lori fanned her shirt as she stepped out from beneath the pine tree. "That tree makes me itch."

Jesse snickered.

By the time they arrived at Sallee's Rock, Lori's voice was hoarse, and there was no way they could've snuck up on anything with her constant complaining. Lori squealed and swatted the air, then ducked behind Jesse.

"What is it now?" Jesse laughed as she looked over her shoulder.

"I hate horseflies," she screamed and swatted the air again.

"That wasn't a horsefly. It was a grasshopper," Steve said.

"Whatever. It's the size of a horse and it flies. Same difference," Lori retorted as she patted down her hair and shivered.

Standing at the edge of the clearing, Jesse held Brian's duffel bag as he and Steve went to work installing hunting cameras around the area. The plan was to place two cameras low to the ground and one higher up, for an overhead view. If the cameras worked as well as Brian said they would, they should know within a week or so if wolves or dogs had been running the woods. That was reassuring to Jesse, and she hoped it was just a pack of stray dogs. If not, she would have to rethink the whole werewolf angle and that wasn't something she was looking forward to.

The secret of Cloverly and the wolves in the area were probably no more than a coincidence or at least that's what she told herself. Her dad admitted he thought wolves were cool when he was a teenager and she could see him drawing the shield based on a description from something he read back in the day. Just because the word, *Lycan* had been written across the drawing wasn't proof of anything, even though Lori seemed to think otherwise. Taking a seat on the ground, Jesse and Lori waited until the last camera was put into place, tested, and reset. A few minutes later, Brian took a bottle of water and a bowl of powder and mixed up a white, soupy mess. Explaining how to make castings of the prints, she could imagine how the kids felt at camp.

"Now that's cool," Lori said as she hurried to find her own print to cast. "If this works, I'm going to use mine as a paperweight." It was amazing how quickly Lori switched gears, but Jesse wasn't about to remind her that her paperweight might actually be a wolf print.

"It would make a great conversation piece," Jesse said after she made her casting. "I'm going to paint mine pink." Listening to Brian and Steve discuss the size of the paw prints, she placed her hand beside the print, to gauge its size.

"How big is big?" Lori asked, glancing between Brian and Steve.

"Big as in huge, enormous, massive, gigantic... take your pick," Steve said.

"I call bull. You're just trying to scare me." Lori scoffed.

"No, I'm not. These are huge prints and whatever made them must be pretty darn big."

"Well, that just ended my trail-walking days," Jesse said as she scanned the tree line. She knew there was a chance there were wolves in the area but it never crossed her mind that they would be that *big*. She counted the trails that led into the clearing. Five, from what she could see.

"See? That's what happens when you let your imagination run wild," Brian said, glancing over at Jesse. "It's probably just a pack of dogs."

"That doesn't make me feel any better. Not all big dogs are teddy bears." Jesse walked over and stood next to Brian.

"Oh, that's great. Compare them to bears. What's next? T-rex?" Lori sneered.

Once Steve had finished taking pictures and their mess was cleaned up, Brian handed everyone a plastic zip-seal baggie. Showing them how to lift their castings, they placed them inside the baggies as thunder rumbled in the distance.

"Okay, It's time to leave," Jesse said, looking up at the sky. It was still clear for the most part, but she wouldn't chance getting stuck out there in the middle of a thunderstorm. Shoving everything into the backpack, they headed back to Brian's.

# Twenty-Eight

*Jack*

Singing along with the radio, Jack tapped out a tune as he stared down at the little, white farmhouse surrounded by lavender fields. Lost in the rhythm, he didn't hear anyone coming up behind him until Mason pulled the earbud from his ear.

"What's up?" Mason asked, taking a seat beside him.

"Nothing, just trying to figure out Tracy." Four days had passed since their phase and Tracy was spending most of her time in the company of Tucker or Whitney so Jack assumed it was her way of avoiding Travis.

"Is she still threatening to leave?"

"No, but that doesn't mean she won't." Jack wasn't sure what was going on between Tracy and her uncle, but when he offered to talk to him, she became hysterical to the point of making herself sick. Until she opened up to him, there was little he could do. "She's afraid of Travis; that much I know. I just don't know why."

"He's a jackass," Mason said, pushing the earbud into his ear. Staring up at the cloudy sky, he grinned and slammed his head to the beat.

Jack laughed and yanked the bud from his ear. "Dude, you are no headbanger." He shoved the earbuds into his pocket.

"Now I know why. That was harsh." Mason pressed his hand on the back of his neck. "Since when do you listen to country music?"

"It's a mood thing," Jack said, leaning his head back to rest. Thinking about everything that had happened over the past couple months, Megan was the unexpected factor, but Tracy's recent confession troubled him too.

"It's no wonder you've been a crank-ass lately. That's cryin'-in-your-beer-'cause-your-sister-dumped-ya-and-your-dog-won't-date-ya, music," Mason said in his best country boy twang.

Jack tried not to laugh but failed. Pushing the hair out of his eyes, he pointed at the farmhouse. "Any minute now." No sooner had he said the words than the front door swung open and an elderly male moseyed down the gravel drive toward the mailbox. He pulled the newspaper out of the paper slot, then headed back to the house. "Do you think that's Megan's dad?" Jack asked as the old timer disappeared behind the pale lavender door.

"I thought Whitney said they were on vacation?"

"She did, but I've been here every morning since then and every morning, it's the same routine. Never anyone else. Just him." Jack stretched out his legs.

"Maybe he's a hired hand, just keeping an eye on the

place."

"Could be." Jack pushed off the ground. Casting one last glance towards the farmhouse, he and Mason set off down the hill.

The jog home was more about checking out the neighborhood than the exercise it provided. Even after Whitney told him Megan was on vacation, something loomed at the back of his mind. Perhaps the timing or hearing that damn motorcycle, again. Jack glared towards Main Street. With Megan's scent at every turn, his wolf was antsy and he could barely contain it. Slowing to a walk, he looked up when the screeching of brakes sounded in front of them and Steve's truck came to a sudden stop.

"I wonder what that's about," Mason said, staring ahead.

"Whatever it is, it doesn't look good." Jack picked up his pace as Steve jumped out of the truck and ran over to where Lori and Jesse were sitting on the ground. Brian's restless pacing caused Jack concern. Something was definitely wrong, and his intuition told him whatever it was, Megan was involved. *You were warned,* he thought, remembering the ring around the moon. His thoughts scattered as Randy blew the stop sign and pulled up at the curb, meeting them at the corner.

"Where's Megan?" Brian's voice came out harsh but Jack didn't think he was angry. It was more of a panicky, demanding tone. One that sent shivers down his spine.

"Her parents haven't seen her since Sunday night," Lori said as Steve moved in to replace Jesse in holding her.

Jack drew in a calming breath that did little to relax his mind. The nagging tick was a warning, but not understanding at the time, he wrote it off as anxiety. He wanted to scream when his thoughts went back to Lizzy. *How could life be so cruel?* "I thought she was on vacation." Surprised by the panic in his own voice, he swallowed and looked over at Lori.

"This is Thursday. How did her parents not know this sooner?" Brian cut in.

"I don't know," Lori said, defensively. "When they arrived home and found Megan's car in the garage, they called the police."

Jack spun around, and Mason grabbed him by the shoulders. "Control," Mason said, pulling him away from the others.

Control was the last thing on Jack's mind, and as much as he would have loved to turn his wolf loose, he couldn't. The animal in him fought frantically to come forward, a struggle so fierce, he could hear the threads of his clothes snapping along the seams. *Not here!* He demanded. *We'll find her.* There had to be a way.

"All this time, we thought she was on vacation, and she's been missing? I think I'm going to be sick." Jesse covered her mouth with her hand.

"I saw her early Monday morning, around one o'clock. She was at home sitting by the pool," Randy said, looking confused.

A protective rumble settled in Jack's chest and he shrugged off Mason's hand and clenched his fist. "What were you doing at her house?" The accusation in his tone didn't go unnoticed, nor did the underlying growl. Jesse's eyes widened, and she backed up against Brian. Jack struggled with his anger, which was fueled by fear, causing his wolf to emerge. Mason placed his hand on his shoulder and Jack acknowledged the subtle reminder. He had to control the wolf even though it was there for his protection; or in this case, Megan's.

"Do you even know Megan?" Randy's haughty tone had Jack stepping forward.

His eyes flared as his wolf simmered just below the surface, and knocking the smirk off Randy's face was more than just tempting.

"Don't," Mason whispered another reminder as he stepped up beside Jack. With another pack member there, Randy didn't seem as threatening and Jack's wolf backed down.

Lori placed her hand on Randy's arm. "Just answer the question. We need to know what you know."

"On my way home, I noticed the back light on at Megan's house, so I stopped."

"What were you doing there?" Jack asked again, but quickly swallowed the growl.

"It's none of your damn business," Randy spat.

Mason swung his arm out, catching Jack across the chest. "Control," he hissed as the rumbling growl grew louder.

Jack pushed Mason's arm down and took another step forward. "That's where you're wrong. Megan *is* my business." He gave Randy a pass the first time they butted heads, but if the smartass biker didn't watch his mouth, he couldn't guarantee the same outcome.

Jesse had every right to be frightened by his stance, and he should have been more concerned that she collapsed to her knees, but he wasn't. Standing off against Randy, his focus was on finding out what Randy knew, but to do that, he would have to resist the urge to knock him on his ass. He side-glanced Mason, who was on edge, but ready to intervene if needed. Normally, he would have remained in control, but since meeting Megan, his control was waning.

"Could you two alphas hash this out later? Right now we need to find Megan. So, Randy, why did you stop at Megan's house?" Lori asked, pushing between them.

"I wanted to apologize. She is still my friend, you know." Randy combed his hands through his hair.

"Which is why I'm asking. We need to know how long you were there, so we know how long she's been missing," Lori explained and a tear rolled down her cheek.

"Maybe thirty minutes."

"Where was she when you left?"

"She was sitting by the damn pool." Randy threw his hands up in frustration as Jack turned and whispered to Mason. It was clear Randy was telling the truth, but that didn't mean he had to like the guy.

"Where does she live?" Mason asked once Jack had backed away from Randy.

"Right down the street. Turn left at the cemetery. It's the house on the hill," Brian said.

Jack turned to look in the direction Brian pointed. "Are you talking about the big, brick house?"

"Yeah."

"Has anyone been searching for her?" Jack asked.

"Not yet. Everyone is gathering at the middle school. Officer Riley is organizing the search party from there," Lori said and turned to Jesse. "Are you okay?"

"I'm fine, let's go find Megan," Jesse said.


Jack pulled over to the side of the road and parked

behind Steve's truck. Looking across the schoolyard, Megan had a lot of friends if the crowd that gathered around Officer Riley were any indication. Seeing his old teacher, he breathed a sigh of relief knowing Riley was an excellent tracker. "There they are," Jack said when he spotted Brian.

"Small town news travels fast," Tracy said, drawing everyone's attention to the backseat.

Jack looked through the rearview mirror and his forehead creased with concern. "What's that supposed to mean?"

Tracy squirmed. She wasn't acting her normal self and until she opened up about Travis, he wasn't ready to trust her. She was annoying him, though, one minute hot, and the next cold. He had half a mind to take her over to the Alpha house in Kinsley and let his dad deal with her, but he gave his word, and that was something he didn't take lightly.

"Don't worry, Jack, we'll find her," Mason said.

"Whatever. We are not their protectors." Tracy glared from the backseat.

"You're right, we're not," Jack said, waving his hand towards the people walking across the yard. "But we are Megan's."

"That's the dumbest thing I've ever heard. She's not..." Tracy's voice trailed off.

Jack looked over his shoulder and smiled. "She is now. I have a bond with her and that makes her a pack member." He left out the part where Megan hadn't actually accepted the bond, but that was a mere detail Tracy didn't need to know.

"When?" Tracy demanded.

"It doesn't matter. It's over and done now and nothing will change it." Jack knew Tracy would be pissed when she found out about the bond, but the fear that flashed in her eyes was not something he expected. What did she fear? Megan?

He tilted his head, waiting for her to chime in with some smart remark but she dropped her head to her hands and mumbled something that sounded like, "I'm dead."

Still feeling uneasy about Tracy, he opened the car door and got out. Sending the others ahead, he waited for her to get out of the backseat. She stood staring down at her feet as she worked the toe of her shoe against the gritty concrete. "Tracy?" She looked up through a fan of damp lashes. "I wasn't trying to hurt your feelings, but it is what it is."

"It's not that, Jack. I understand." She lowered her eyes.

"Can you do this? Will you help me find Megan?" he asked. She stood up straight, drawing her shoulders back, but Jack saw the panic in her eyes. "Tracy, what's going on? I can't help you unless you tell me."

"Nothing, I'm here to help you find Megan. We can worry about my problems later." She smiled and moved past him.

He stepped back against the car as she joined the group that was gathering in front of Officer Riley. She was right, they needed to find Megan first, but as Jack watched her, he couldn't shake the unease that settled in his gut. Something about Megan obviously put Tracy on edge, but he couldn't imagine what that could be. Running his hand over his jaw, he walked over to join the group.

The search for Megan continued late into the evening and as the sky darkened, Officer Riley called everyone back to the school. "Meet here first thing sun-up and we'll resume the search." Marking the locations on a map, he looked over at Jack. "We can't risk them getting lost in the woods," Officer Riley said while glancing over the lingering crowd.

"I know, but I'm going to keep looking. Did you by any chance talk to her parents?"

"I went over to the Smiths' last night. I'm not sure what's going on, but with the chlorine so thick in the air, I couldn't get a good hit on Megan's scent. It was there, but too indistinct. Do you have any reason to believe the Grayson boy might be lying? Or that he may have caused her harm? He was the last person to talk to her as far as I know."

Jack looked over as Randy quietly talked with Jesse and Lori. He shook his head. "He annoys me, but I don't think he would harm Megan."

"After talking to him, I don't either. But since her car was in the garage, we have to assume she left on foot or she left with someone else, and the only scent we could pick up was his."

Jack looked back, only this time, Tracy was standing with Randy. "I talked to him this morning when he first found out she was missing. He was confrontational towards me but as far as Megan goes, I think they're close friends and if anything, he'd protect her."

"I thought so, too," Officer Riley said, rolling up the map. "But don't let your guard down. There's something going on here, and someone knows more than they're saying."

# Twenty-Nine

*Tracy*

With the whole town in a tizzy over Megan's disappearance, Tracy was confident Travis would stay away until the commotion died down. Sooner or later, though, she would have to face him. She had stalled his plans for as long as possible, but now there was nothing she could do to keep the ball from rolling except spend whatever time she had left with Randy. "Can you stay for a while?" she asked as she pulled her leg across the black leather seat. Standing next to the motorcycle, her heart raced and she looked up at the cabin. She had never invited Randy in before and hoped she wasn't making a mistake by doing so now.

"I thought you would never ask," he said, flashing a naughty grin. "Are you hungry? I could run down the road and grab us some burgers."

"I'm starved. Burgers sound good." Tracy watched him turning the bike around in the street. He had no idea what she had pulled him into. Not on purpose, mind you, and so dangerous. Her wolf was happy and content to be spending time with him, while she, in the meantime, was nervous as hell. Randy would never be the alpha Jack was destined to become, but damn! If he weren't the best thing to ever cross her path! Remembering the day she plowed him down, she smiled weakly.

Nothing unusual stood out to Tracy until she turned and headed up the sidewalk toward the cabin. Her scalp prickled and her body stiffened. *Deny everything.* It was an instant thought and not the most brilliant plan, but it would buy her time until she could come up with something better. *Trouble, always trouble,* echoed in her head as she pushed open the front door.

As soon as she entered the cabin, the smell of river water assaulted her nose and she looked around for the fishy source. *He knows nothing. Deny. Lie.* Her thoughts raced, and her stomach churned. She knew Travis would hold her responsible for Jack's bond with Megan and she would pay dearly. That was guaranteed.

"What are you doing here? And why are you wearing an eye patch?" she asked as he peered around the kitchen door.

"Where have you been?" Travis hissed while walking out of the kitchen, circling her.

"I've been with the others." Tracy turned to face him. *Don't get excited. He'll smell your fear.*

"Liar! Do you think I'm blind? What were you doing with that boy again? This is how you repay me for allowing him to live? Look at you. You aren't worthy of the Hudson name," he said and his face twisted to a sneer.

"If you were as smart as you thought you were, you would know I wasn't with him! He just gave me a ride home. We were out searching for Megan." She closed her eyes, listing as he paced the room. *Open your eyes or he'll think you're lying.*

"How do you know Megan?" He stopped in front of her.

"Does it matter?" She studied his face. His wolf stirred just beneath the surface; something wasn't right with him. The warning glint in his eye was proof of his agitation. *It's a set-up. He's not ballsy enough to attack you here.*

"Don't act like you don't know what's going on," he said and sweat beaded across his forehead. He was tense and not like his normally controlled self. "As usual, I've taken care of your problem."

"What are you rambling about? I never had a problem. You're the one with the problem," she said, bracing herself against the sofa. Tracy didn't dare take her eyes off him. Having been on the receiving end of his temper one-too-many times, she believed he would slit her throat and not think twice about it if he thought it could benefit him. He was callous, a trait all the Hudson males shared.

"Sweetheart, you have no idea how big a problem you had. You owe me dearly."

"For what? What did you do?" Her throat tightened and she knew whatever it was, Megan was in big trouble.

"I, unlike you, eliminated the problem. But this is the last warning you get! The last chance to make things right before biker boy pays the price. You will do as planned and you'll do it by the end of the week," he growled before walking back through the kitchen.

"I will not take the fall for you!" she yelled.

"You don't have to. Someone else already has," he said over his shoulder.

"What's that supposed to mean?" Deep down, Tracy knew she would never be with Jack and honestly, she didn't want to be. She had failed at a lot of things over the years but she never failed to honor her wolf.

"Aww, poor Tracy. You're in it as much for the power as I am. So don't play innocent."

"But I wasn't going to hurt anyone."

"Sure you were. How else could you get rid of Megan?"

She wanted to smack the grin off his spiteful face and he deserved it. "You need to leave. Leave before Jack finds you here."

"Yeah, because we both know that will happen! You're the least of his worries, for now. But just so you know... you're in this as deeply as I am. If he finds out about me, he finds out about you." Travis laughed and walked out the door before vanishing along the riverbank.

"Stupid, stupid, stupid," she mumbled to herself. Walking through the cabin to the front porch, she sat down in the swing. *The only thing worse than a power-hungry werewolf was a pissed off werewolf, jacked up on testosterone, seeking revenge.*

As the motorcycle came around the corner, Tracy walked out to the curb and waited for Randy to park the bike. "We're going to Jack's," she said, taking his hand.

"Really? I mean, when you invited me over, I didn't expect to be hanging out with the all-powerful Jack. I can't compete with him. He's like what I want to be when

I grow up," Randy said as he pulled the keys from the bike and pushed them into his pocket.

"Please, he's not all that, but he's okay, I guess." Tracy smiled. Not realizing they had already met, she eagerly led him down the street.

"I beg to differ. You're the one that's always talking about him." Randy frowned and looked up at the cabin.

"Jack has nothing on you. You are amazing." Tracy winked, but Randy didn't look convinced.

"That's easy for you to say, you're not the other guy."

"You're not either. You're the *only* guy, and I wouldn't ask if it weren't important," she said, noticing he stood a little taller. "For me."

"Only for you," Randy said as they crossed the street.

Tracy's smile widened as he tightened his grip on her hand, and she looked up when Jack walked out his front door. "Jack, I need to talk to you!" she yelled.

Randy glared and tugged Tracy back off the curb. The scowl on his face caught her offguard, and she wondered what she had missed. Pulling her hand from his, she hurried across the yard. She didn't have time to worry about his ego, not when Megan's life was in immediate danger.

"I don't have time," Jack said, looking past her with a scowl.

"It will only take a minute. It's really important," she pleaded as she looked back at Randy. His stewing expression promised trouble to come.

"Right now, I'm only concerned with finding Megan. So speak fast, you have exactly thirty seconds," he said as he walked to his car and opened the driver's door.

"Megan's in trouble. I don't know what Travis did,

but I know he did something," she blurted out.

"What the hell are you talking about?" Jack growled and sparks of fire lit up his eyes. "Get in the car."

Tracy shivered at his somber tone but made no sudden moves. His wolf was at the surface, and she didn't want to provoke it. She looked back at Randy, who was still standing on the side of the road, clearly irritated and glaring at Jack.

"Whatever, just get inside the damn car." Jack waited until Randy slid into the backseat behind Tracy before starting the car. Looking through the rearview mirror, he backed out of the drive and Randy stared back at him. "Do you have a problem?" Jack asked, his tone dangerously low.

Randy looked between Tracy and him. "This is Jack? The Jack you talk about?" There was no mistaking the sneer in his words. It was obvious they knew each other, and she assumed it was from the theater.

Ignoring his foul mood, Tracy turned to Jack. Retelling the encounter she had with Travis a few minutes earlier, she could feel the tension in the air. She explained how he schemed to take back the pack and said he "took care of the problem." She confessed everything, knowing she was also incriminating herself.

Randy sat quietly in the backseat as the conversation bounced back and forth. Finally, he put his hand on the seat and leaned forward. "What the hell are you talking about? Alpha? Family revenge? What are you? The Mafia?"

Tracy looked over at Jack. "He doesn't know."

"Know what?" Randy's words were demanding and Tracy flinched.

"Is it serious?" Jack asked.

"It could be," Tracy said, using her finger to trace the stitching of the leather seat.

"What's stopping you?"

"Travis. I've known all along but..." She looked down.

"But you were afraid of what he would do to Randy?"

"Yes," she whispered.

"I'm perfectly capable of taking care of myself," Randy chimed in defensively.

Jack looked through the mirror as Randy glared at Tracy. "Tracy, I can't tell you how to live your life but if what you say is true, don't let Travis steal your happiness."

"I know; but I don't want anything to happen..." Glancing back at Randy, she could tell he was pissed. The thought of Travis and his threat sent daggers to her heart, and she tried hard to swallow the lump that lodged in her throat.

"If you're talking about me, I'm still here," Randy said, clearly irritated by the ping-pong conversation about him.

"How do you feel about Tracy?" Jack asked, looking over his shoulder.

"What kind of lame-brained question is that?" Randy shot back.

"It's a serious question that needs a serious answer," Jack said, pulling up in front of Dr. Stevens' house.

"You really want me to answer that?"

"Yes, I do." Jack turned in the seat. "And the sooner the better. I don't have all night," he added as Tracy blinked back tears, trying to look unfazed.

"I must be out of my everlovin' mind." Randy ran his hand through his hair. "Look, I've been chasing after

Tracy since the day I met her. Even knowing she wanted Jack, or you, or whoever. I don't play second fiddle to anyone, yet I can't seem to walk away from her. So you tell me. How do I feel about Tracy?"

Jack grunted. "I think you two need to take a walk. I'll see you back at the cabin."

Tracy leaned over and hugged Jack. "Thank you, but I want to help you find Megan first."

"No, you need to talk to Randy. If you share a bond, the pack will protect both of you. Now go before Travis realizes his mistake."

# Thirty

*Tracy*

Feeling a light squeeze on her hand, Tracy looked over at Randy. She wasn't sure how to start the conversation. She worried how he would react to her once he found out what she was, but it was time to come clean. Her shoulders sagged a bit when he smiled. "I'm tired of trying to please everyone. I'm not perfect."

"That's good to know because I'm not perfect either. I hate brussel sprouts and cupcakes with sprinkles, and I cried when that ol' yeller dog died." His stormy eyes gave nothing away, and she pressed her lips together to keep from giggling.

Looking out as the porch lights cast a soft glow over the lawns, Randy took hold of her hand. Tracy wanted to tell him about her wolf, and Jack seemed confident it was the right thing to do, but deep down, she feared he would walk away. *Trouble, always trouble* whispered in the back of her mind and she briefly squeezed her eyes shut.

"Over here," Randy said, dragging her across the yard and pulling her down beside him in a swing that hung from the tree's largest branch.

"What are you doing? Do you know who lives here?"

"No, I just like their swing." He wrapped his arm around her shoulder and pulled her closer to his side.

The night was unusually quiet, and in a small town like Cloverly, a missing person was a big deal. Everyone was family, another reason she hesitated to tell Randy she was a werewolf. Not only was she an outsider, but a freak. It was times like these when she hated what she was. To be normal and live a normal life, she envied the human females.

"I've never lied to you. I'm not a bad person, but no one sees that. All they see is this pretend me. I never wanted to be with Jack." She swallowed hard.

"I know you're not a bad person; remember? I took you to the barn." He waggled his brows, and she snickered. "I want you to be that girl. That's the true you. I've seen her with my own eyes." He kissed her hair when she laid her head on his shoulder. "But if that was Jack, who was the guy you were hanging on at the theater?"

"Who? Oh, that's Tucker, he's my best friend." She looked up and smiled.

"So there's nothing between you and Jack?" Randy's brow furrowed and he rolled his lip. The uncertainty in his voice tugged at her heart.

"No." She squeezed his hand. "I was raised to believe Jack would be my mate. My uncle wanted to challenge the alpha for the pack. He thought it would be easier to take control if I were an alpha female."

"Hold up. I don't understand," Randy said. "Alpha? Mate? Who talks like that?"

"That's what I'm trying to tell you," she said, her voice growing softer as if she were afraid someone else might hear. Her eyes scanned the area. "I'm not like you. *We're* not like you." She looked up at the confused expression on his face. "We're not all bad, like the Mafia, but we've had our moments."

"What are you?" Randy looked down. "There's something different about you, I could see it in your eyes the first day we met."

"You noticed?"

"Yes, they're just like Jack's." His confession shocked her and a tear slipped down her cheek.

"I'm afraid you won't want me if you knew my true nature."

"Nothing could ever make me not want you. You have to trust in that."

She pushed up out of the swing, and he followed. "We're werewolves. I know it sounds crazy but I promise: it's the truth." She turned to face him, expecting to see disgust in his eyes. But instead, he seemed intrigued, even curious.

"How is that possible?"

"It's in our DNA. We are what some call shape-shifters," she said, hoping he wouldn't think she had completely lost her mind.

"How did you become a shape-shifter? Were you bitten by a rabid wolf?"

"No, I was born this way." She looked down to avoid his eyes.

"Sorry. I didn't mean to offend you."

B. S. TODD

Tension lingered between them as they continued down the street, and the voice in her head insisted he would never settle for the likes of her. She blinked back the tears that rimmed her eyes. *Trouble, always trouble.* She pressed her palm against her head.

Crossing Main Street, Randy still hadn't said a word and the anxiety of scaring him away kept her silent. But she knew if he didn't say something before he left, she would probably never see him again. When they stopped in front of her cabin, he dropped her hand and looked around the area. When he finally met her eyes, she expected the worst.

"Prove it."

If Randy didn't accept her wolf, she would have no choice but to deny the bond and skip town in order to protect him. She drew in a nervous breath. *No sudden movements*, she thought to her wolf. *We don't want to frighten him away.* Taking his hand, she led him to the cabin and switched on the light as he walked through the door.

"Wow, this is a nice place," Randy said, looking around the room.

"It's small, but it works." Tracy closed the door and Randy moved over to the sofa and settled on the arm, resting his hands on his knees. She walked across the room and pulled the curtains, then kicked off her shoes. Normally, she wouldn't think twice about shedding her clothes, but Randy was a human and exposing her wolf was strictly forbidden. *He's your mate.* The thought didn't make the task any easier and her face turned three shades of red. Moving back to the center of the room, the overhead light sparkled in his eyes as she slowly unbuttoned the black vest that complimented her curves.

"Why are you undressing? Not that I mind," he said as he leaned back to watch the show.

"I don't want to risk ruining my favorite outfit." *You're a confident, young female and he's as nervous as you are,* she told herself when she dropped the vest to the floor. Lifting her eyes, her face heated with his grin.

"So do you always strip naked in front of men?" His point-blank question made her blush even more.

"Don't tell me you're the jealous type. I would have never guessed that," she said while slipping out of her jeans. "Are you ready?"

"You know me, I'm always ready." Sliding down onto the cushion, he rested his ankle on his knee.

"Ready or not...." She phased.

"Holy shit!" Randy jumped up on the sofa, trying to gain more space between him and the wolf that was now standing in place of Tracy. Leaning against the back cushion, the sofa flipped and he slid down the wall to the floor. He sat there for a minute, expecting the wolf to attack him and held up a cushion to shield his body. Hesitantly, he inched up and peeked over the edge of the seat. On the opposite side of the room where Tracy undressed stood a beautiful gray wolf with red undertones that grazed the ridge of her back and muzzle. As the wolf pranced over to the sofa, Randy looked into its eyes. "Tracy?" He stood and righted the sofa, trying hard not to make any sudden movements that might scare the noble animal. Stepping over the back of the seat, he lowered himself down onto the sofa. He offered his hand, and the wolf licked his palm. "Oh hell! You're wearing... earrings!" He laughed nervously when Tracy's wolf moved to sit between his legs. Leaning forward, he ran his fingers along her muzzle and then up behind her ears and she nuzzled his neck. "I don't believe it. This is crazy. You're even gorgeous as a wolf," his voice cracked.

When Tracy phased back, she was still sitting on the floor between his knees, and his hands were resting on her shoulders. As she looked up, he pulled her into his lap, wrapping an arm around her waist. "That was beyond anything I've ever..." he shook his head, trying to regulate his rapid breathing.

"I have that effect on males." She chuckled. "Do you remember the day we met in the woods? That day was the start of a bond between us. My wolf really likes you." She giggled timidly while twirling a strand of hair between her fingers. "But now that you know what I am, do you still want to be with me? I can't force you. You have to accept me as I am. If you do, the bond will connect us and you will be my bonded mate." She was pretty sure he would accept her by the way he responded to her wolf, but he still needed to confirm it. "If not, the bond will break and you will be free to go."

"Wow, this is a lot to take in." He closed his eyes and rested his head back against the cushion. Things had changed over the course of a few minutes and she prayed he would accept her. "So there's nothing between you and Jack?"

"No," she said, pushing out of his arms. "Just think about it. I don't want to rush you." She walked over to the discarded pile of clothes and pulled on her jeans.

"If I do this... what's in it for me?" Randy opened his eyes as she slipped the vest over her shoulders.

"All I have to offer you is me." Her heart flip-flopped,

and she took in a long breath to calm the jitters. *What if he says no?* She fidgeted with the buttons on her vest.

"So, *bonded mate,* does that mean forever?"

"Yes. When we find our mate, it's for life."

"What about you? Do you want to be with me forever? I mean, if I have to accept you, shouldn't you have to do the same in return?" He leaned forward, resting his elbows on his knees.

"I chose you that day in the woods. That's why the bond is still intact. Had I wanted to, I could have said no to the bond and we would have gone our separate ways, but I didn't. I wanted to see where things could go with you."

"Even though you were chasing Jack?" He lifted a brow in question.

"My wolf would never accept Jack as long as I shared a bond with you."

"So I wasn't your second choice?"

"I did what I had to, in order to survive my uncle. Once I met you, you were my first choice," she said and slipped on her shoes.

"And if Megan were out of the picture, would you still feel the same way?"

"Yes. I had the bond with you before I knew about Megan. But I won't lie. I tried to hook up with Jack after Travis threatened your life, even though we shared a bond. My wolf was against it, but it would've done anything to protect you, even if that meant letting you go. Thankfully, Jack wasn't interested." Standing there feeling like a fool, she anxiously ran her fingers through her hair.

"Well, I'm interested, but... will I become a wolf too?" His brows furrowed as if he were thinking about the possibility.

Tracy laughed. "No! The only other way to become a wolf is for a wolf to bite you and that is strictly forbidden."

Randy thought for another moment before responding. "Good, because you being a wolf is badass, but I like me the way I am. I mean, it's nothing against you but I kinda like my humanness." He blushed.

"I understand. I'm quite fond of your humanness, as well."

"Well, I'm still interested. I may be sealing my fate but like I told Jack, I can't walk away. It looks like you're stuck with me," he said before leaning back on the sofa.

She squealed and ran over to the sofa and threw her body onto his. Running her hands through his hair, she peppered his face with kisses as tears fell from her eyes.

"Tracy," he mumbled. "I. Can't. Breathe." His laughter filled the room and he wrapped his arms around her waist. "Thank you for choosing me."

Tracy wiped the tears from her eyes and kissed him one last time. Her wolf was delighted, and the cooing growl that rumbled in her chest told him so. He was a good match for her and now he was officially her bonded mate. "I can't believe you said yes."

"Would you rather I said no?"

"If you did, I would have begged you to reconsider," she looked up.

"Damn, I knew I should have held out longer!"

"I'm glad you didn't. I don't think my heart could take it," she said, and he pulled her into a kiss. With their bond intact, the sensation of his lips sent a wave of electricity through her body, settling deep in her core. Her heart strummed as he ran his hands up her back. "We need to go," she panted, not wanting him to stop.

"So soon? I mean, isn't there some kind of bonding ritual we need to complete first?" He flipped her on her back and pinned her against the sofa as mischief danced in his eyes.

"Yes, but until we make it official, the bond we have will do," Tracy purred and rubbed her nose along his neck, savoring his scent.

"Damn, you make me crazy. And I love crazy."

# Thirty-One

*Jack*

After Tracy's confession and the bond Jack shared with Megan fading fast, he needed to speak to Dr. Stevens now more than ever. Stepping up on the front porch of the small, two-bedroom house, he was surprised when the front door swung open.

"I've been expecting you," Dr. Stevens said, motioning him inside. "I just talked to your dad. He's on his way to see Officer Riley."

"Then you know what's going on?" Jack asked as he followed Dr. Stevens to the kitchen. Worrying over Megan without sealing their bond wore Jack down emotionally and it showed on his face.

"Yes," Dr. Stevens said.

"Well, things have changed and I desperately need your help." Jack pulled out a chair as his mind clouded with thoughts of revenge. And that wasn't good, considering how eager his wolf was to settle the score with Travis. He took the cup of coffee Dr. Stevens offered and waited as he poured another for himself.

"I'll help in any way I can. What do you need me to do?"

"I need to find Megan, and to make matters worse, I just discovered that Travis had something to do with her disappearance." Jack set the cup on the table and pulled out a chair.

"Does the alpha know?"

"Not yet. I learned about it on my way over here." Jack rubbed his hand over his face and covered a yawn. "I should have told Megan about the bond when I had the chance but at the time, I hadn't totally accepted it," he said. Dr. Stevens pulled out a chair and sat down on the opposite side of the table. Embarrassed by what he was about to say, Jack lowered his eyes. "I considered denying the bond but my gut feeling told me it would be a mistake."

"That's because it's a game changer. The attraction between you and Megan has been simmering for years. And when the time is right, it pulls you back together."

"So you're saying Megan was already attracted to me and this wasn't just a chance meeting?" Jack asked. "Is that possible?"

"Anything is possible, and that's the beauty of it. We don't know why a person is chosen, but at some point, you two had to cross paths. It's been lying dormant inside you for years, waiting to emerge. Fate is funny that way, leading us down the path we're destined to follow. So if you are considering denying the bond, think long and hard before you do so."

"I have; and now I need to protect her, but the bond is getting weaker and there are times when I don't feel it at all. It's strange. It's like it wavers in and out." Jack thought for a minute and then added, "These past few days, it's been a steady strum but very, very faint.

"That is strange. I'm not sure why it would waver unless something is interfering with it." Dr. Stevens stared down at his coffee. "Can you feel the bond now?" He glanced up.

"It's faint, but it's there."

"That's good, we can work with that." Dr. Stevens said, leaning back in his chair. "The pull you feel towards Megan and the need to protect her come from the bond you share with her. You can tap into the bond. It's hard to break through a human's shield, but it can be done."

"Even without her knowing?" Jack asked.

"Yes. The pull may not be strong right now, but it *is* there. Just don't overanalyze it and don't get frustrated. Find a quiet place and let it lead you."

"Thank you," Jack said as he hurried through the house.

"Let me know when you find her," Dr. Stevens said, closing the front door.

The bond Jack shared with Megan was a mere whisper between two souls that had wavered in and out for months. It was frustrating and now, since changing into a constant hum in his head, irritating. The static ringing in his ears had disrupted every part of his life. His mind never settled, and he was emotionally exhausted. But he hoped Dr. Stevens was right and he could eventually connect with Megan. He turned into the driveway and shut off the car as Mason pulled open the driver's door, the burden of finding Megan weighing heavily on his mind.

Greeting the pack, Jack walked around the cabin, taking a lounge chair in the backyard. He stared up at the night sky. It was after eleven and the thought of Megan being in the woods all alone terrified him. Making a wish on the first star he saw, he closed his eyes. Whitney and Mason waited quietly at the small patio table while Randy and Tracy stood back in the driveway.

Concentrating on the bond that seemed out of reach, he shifted uncomfortably. The night was quiet, *as still as death*, a thought he quickly pushed out of his head. After a few minutes, he opened his eyes. "I can't do this. I get nothing." His voice cracked and he pinched the bridge of his nose.

"You can do this and you will," Whitney replied, walking over beside him. "Block out everything around you and focus only on Megan."

Doing as she instructed, Jack closed his eyes and cleared his thoughts of everything except Megan. But with his wolf on high alert, it was hard to keep all the distractions out of his head. Crickets and tree frogs, burrowing mice, he gritted his teeth, pushing harder for the silence he needed to focus—but nothing. Taking a different approach, he pictured Megan at Sallee's Rock. Her blonde curls touching her shoulders as the sun cast a soft, red halo about her head. The slight upturn of her nose and her dainty little sneezes made him smile. Then she tilted her head and stared into their hideout. His breathing grew rapid, matching the beat of his heart, and the world spun around him. Her eyes flared, locking onto him as they did that day— their bond becoming stronger.

He drew in a deep breath and opened his eyes. The connection was strong, vivid, and his mind whirled with fear. He looked over at Mason and a soundless message passed between them before Jack took off across the yard. Dodging the wind chimes that hung from the oak branches, he entered the woods and raced along the trail, holding tightly to the bond that connected them.

Mason and Whitney kept pace behind him, and off in the distance, he could hear Tracy yelling at Tucker. He was grateful for his friends, but especially, Tracy. If it hadn't been for her, he would have no idea what enemy he faced. Now he would find Megan, and once she was safe, he could settle the score with Travis.

He sped past Sallee's Rock. A run he had made a hundred times over, in and out of wolf form. The thought of bringing his wolf forward entered his mind, but he was too afraid of losing the connection, so he dismissed it and continued running east. The area was familiar, every tree, every boulder and every path that trailed along the south side of town. Forty minutes later, he came to an abrupt stop at the top of Hunter's Ridge. His body shook from exhaustion and the rush of adrenaline flushed through his system. The bond was stronger than he remembered and he looked around, glancing over the cliff's edge. He sniffed the air and cocked his head as the sweet smell of lavender drifted on the breeze. Expecting Megan, he turned and glared when Tracy walked out of the woods. "You're not Megan!" A growl rose in his chest as confusion muddled his mind. "Dammit! What did you do?" he demanded. "What the hell did you do?"

"Whoa! Don't jump to conclusions," Mason said,

stepping between Jack and Tracy.

Tucker broke through the trees just in time to pull Tracy behind him and out of harm's way. The deep growl that rumbled from Jack was threatening and Tucker threw his arms out to prevent him from attacking.

"Jack, stop!" Whitney yelled before he could phase. "Stop, please, it's Tracy. She didn't hurt Megan. You know her better than that." She stepped in front of him and placed her hands on his chest.

"What the hell did I do? Obviously, by telling the truth, I've put a target on my own damn back! You're frickin' welcome!" Tracy spat, standing behind the buffer the others created between Jack and her.

"Tracy!" Mason snapped. "One more word and you can deal with him on your own. Got it?"

"Got it," she huffed. "Jack, I don't understand what's happening. I didn't do anything." Tracy spoke softly, trying not to enrage his wolf. "I'm the one that came to you, remember?"

"Why do you smell like Megan? I can't smell you. I smell her!" he growled as Mason's grip tightened on his shoulders.

"You're nuts. I don't smell like Megan. It's perfume. *Fortuity*." Tracy grabbed the tiny glass vial that hung on a ball-chain around her neck. "Is this what you smell?" Unsnapping the necklace, she handed it to Whitney, who passed it to Jack.

Jack popped the cork and dropped to his knees, utterly defeated. He was certain the bond had led him to Megan, but perfume? His head fell back on his shoulders as the lavender scent wafted around him. *I almost attacked Tracy over a damn bottle of perfume! How am I*

*supposed to find Megan if her scent is everywhere?* He
stared at the sky as if waiting for a divine answer. When
he looked back at Tracy, he did not fail to notice the fear
in her eyes. "Where did you get this?" he asked in a
dangerously low voice.

"Megan gave it to me at the theater. She said it was
her favorite fragrance. I was showing Randy when you
ran into the woods. Then—"

"I ran up and grabbed her. I thought it would make
biker boy jealous, and that's when the perfume spilled
down her shirt," Tucker said, defending her like any big
brother would.

"I don't know what's going on. I haven't talked to her
since that night. I wouldn't hurt her. She's my friend."
Tracy blinked back tears.

"She's masking her scent," Tucker said.

"But this is lavender, not bloodroot," Jack countered.

"It doesn't matter what plant you use, its only
purpose is to cover the underlying ingredients," Tucker
said. "I've been around females wearing something
similar. It was a way of blocking their scent from the pack
males."

"But she's not a wolf. She wouldn't know to block her
scent." Jack dropped his chin to his chest. *It was like
standing next to Whitney* echoed in his head. Whitney
was wrong. Why would Megan mask her scent if she
weren't trying to avoid him? His heart took a nosedive
into his stomach.

"Which is why I didn't say anything. She told Tracy
she was testing new fragrances, so I figured it was a
coincidence." Tucker shrugged.

Jack got to his feet and shoved the necklace into his

pocket. "I'm sorry, Tracy, but my wolf doesn't trust you. This is Megan's scent, the only scent I have. And when you came into the clearing..." his voice trailed off.

Tracy smiled and brushed it off as if it were nothing, but there was no mistaking the glassy sheen in her eyes. *You assumed, and you were wrong. Own it.* He did own it, but that didn't make him feel any less of an ass.

"I wouldn't trust me either, knowing what you do, but right now we need to put that aside and find Megan." Tracy pushed past Tucker and bravely walked over to Jack. "You were following the bond, not her scent."

Jack looked over his shoulder and realization flashed in his eyes. "I'm going to kill him!" he growled. Crawling along the jagged cliff, his eyes scanned the darkness below. As he focused on the bond, the ground crumbled beneath his hand and his face crashed into the dirt.

"Jack!" Whitney screamed and Mason threw his arm out to keep her away from the edge.

"I've got him," Mason said.

"She's down there." Jack pointed and jumped to his feet, looking for a way down that didn't include falling and breaking his neck. Knowing his only other option was to go around and come in from the farmland side, it would take more time than he was willing to allow. Finding a fairly safe area, he lay down on the ground and slid his legs over the ledge. "Get Officer Riley," he said before dropping out of sight.

# Thirty-Two

*Jesse*

Jesse stared out the window as her thoughts swirled around Megan. *Was she hurt, cold, afraid... dead?* A tear rolled down her cheek, and she pulled the quilt around her shoulders to ward off a chill. She was exhausted and so tired; she needed sleep but her mind wouldn't shut down. Apparently, she wasn't alone.

It was late, so upon hearing Randy's motorcycle and watching him park beneath the street light, her fear factor hit the roof. He sat on the bike and leaned forward, resting his elbows on the handlebars as he stared into the woods. *Surely he's not thinking...* She headed downstairs to investigate.

Jesse walked out the front door and stood in awe. Megan was well liked by everyone in the community as became apparent in the support they showed by leaving their porch lights on. A warm feeling engulfed her, giving her hope, and she said a silent prayer.

"Come on," Lori yelled and Jesse followed Steve and her to the end of the road where Randy was waiting.

"Did they find Megan?" Jesse asked, crossing her fingers at her sides. Standing within ten feet of the tree line, she inched her way behind the motorcycle. It wasn't her idea of protection, but just another layer between the darkened trees and her.

"Not yet, but he will," Randy said.

"Who will?" Jesse asked, glancing over when Brian jogged across the yard. The thought of being in the woods after dark wasn't something she could imagine herself doing, or anyone else for that matter.

"Jack will," Randy replied.

"Right, because he's going to run out there in the woods at night and find her. He'll be lucky if he doesn't get lost himself," Brian said while wrapping his arm around Jesse's waist protectively.

"What the hell!" Lori exclaimed and glared at Brian. "Would you stop with your play-by-the-book bullshit? I don't care what Officer Riley said. If Jack thinks he can find Megan, dark or not, more power to him! At least he's not standing around with his head up his ass."

"Jack will find her. On that you can bet the farm," Randy said as Lori stormed past. The tone of his voice emphasized his bad boy image, something Jesse had never noticed before. Dark and dangerous, alluring, he had it *all*. She looked up as Brian scowled. Clearly, they weren't as friendly as she originally thought.

"Lori, wait." Jesse stepped around Brian and walked over to where she was sitting on the sidewalk. "You need to calm down," she said, taking a seat beside her.

"No, what I need to do is help Jack find Megan," Lori replied, angrily swiping at a tear.

"I'm sorry. I wasn't trying to criticize Jack. I'm worried about Megan and wasn't thinking," Brian said. Stooping down, he lifted Lori's chin. "I do hope he finds her."

It was sweet of him to apologize, but Jesse didn't think it was necessary. Everyone knew Brian and Megan were close, he just didn't show his emotions to the same extent. Jesse offered a weak smile, rubbing her hand over his shoulder.

"We all hope he finds her," Steve said. Taking a seat, he pulled Lori into his lap and she buried her face in his shirt.

Jesse reached over and squeezed Lori's hand as her body shook from silent tears. Trying to comfort Brian, and wanting to comfort Lori, she struggled to hold back her own emotions.

Needing a distraction, she focused on Randy, who tapped his knuckles against the gas tank. He was the rebel of the group and she couldn't help wondering what was going through his mind when he got off the bike and paced back and forth. She knew he was worried, as they all were, but his behavior was odd. He stopped and listened, then paced some more, and the frown never left his face. Then without warning, he bolted across the yard to the tree line.

"What's he doing now?" Steve asked, looking over his shoulder.

"He's talking to someone," Brian said, pulling Jesse to her feet. "Back there by the oak tree.

From the sidewalk, Jesse could barely make out Randy's form as he stood beneath the tree. Moving closer to Brian, the wind chimes clanged before a couple of swear words and a giggle could be heard, and her heart raced, hoping Jack had actually found Megan. Then she saw Tracy and her excitement faltered. *What the hell?* Jesse thought as Jack's warning played in her head. *The woods can be a very dangerous place.*

"They found Megan at Hunter's Ridge. We'll meet you there," Randy said as they ran past, to the bike.

"Let's go, Steve," Brian said, fishing his keys from his pocket.

"Wait, we're going too." Jesse had no idea where Hunter's Ridge was, but if it were safe enough for Tracy, it was safe enough for her. She grabbed Lori's arm and pulled her across the street, climbing into the Jeep. "Hurry! We don't have all night."

Based on the look Brian gave her when he climbed into the driver's seat and started the Jeep, he was not happy. "Buckle up," he barked as he backed out of the drive. Heading down the road, he turned right toward the cemetery, Randy turned left.

Looking through the side mirror until Randy was no longer in sight, Jesse rubbed the goosebumps that prickled her arms. She glanced over at Brian who was lost in thought and decided not to disturb him. Common sense said Hunter's Ridge was probably a gathering place for gun-toting rednecks—a log cabin or campsite. She wouldn't ask.

"Steve, there're flashlights in the box behind the seat," Brian said as he turned onto the gravel road that ran alongside the cemetery. Driving past the rows of headstones, Jesse's teeth chattered and anxiety exploded in her chest. Scanning the area, it was dark and ominous; she swore she saw a shadow ducking behind a tree. She shivered.

"This is as far as we go. Now we walk." Brian parked in the darkest corner of the lot, far from the road and pushed open his door. "Grab a flashlight and stay together."

Jesse had never been to Hunter's Ridge, and honestly wasn't that impressed when she looked up the hill. "This is it?" she asked when Brian came around the front of the Jeep. It was no bigger than a molehill, nothing compared to what her mind had conjured up, and nothing about it screamed *ridge*.

"This is just a stepping stone to that there." He pointed to the right and Jesse crinkled her brows. The darkened ridge looked mountain-ish beneath the dim moonlight, and her stomach dropped. Unable to hold the flashlight still, its beam bounced across the ground.

"You've got to be kidding. It will be daylight by the time we get there," Jesse said, trying to keep up with Brian.

The uphill trek wasn't as difficult as she thought, considering she could barely see her hand in front of her face. Surrounded by trees, darkness, and more trees, she felt claustrophobic and sweaty while wondering if they would ever reach the top. But when they did, she froze as the light she held cut through the darkness and across the clearing. Whitney and Mason were standing there, dressed in black.

"Where is she?" Lori asked. Pushing past Jesse, she darted across the clearing.

"Over there." Mason pointed down to the side of the cliff.

Shining her light in the direction Mason indicated, Lori screeched and stumbled backward.

"It's all right," Tucker said, catching her under her arms. As Tucker helped Lori to the ground, Jesse fought the urge to empty her stomach, where she stood. Tucking the flashlight under her arm, her body swayed, and she rested her hands on her knees until the wooziness diminished. Squeezing her eyes shut, she pushed back against the panic that threatened to take her breath.

"Jesse?" Tucker said before appearing instantly at her side. A calming sensation flowed through her body when he placed his hand on her back.

Wiping the sweat from her face, she peeked through her hair and prayed he would walk away before the queasiness returned. It was humiliating that he had to come to her aid when Brian didn't, and barfing on his feet wasn't any kind of a memory she wanted him to have. *Where are his shoes?* That was the question of the day until she noticed he was dressed in all black. Feeling slightly disoriented, she stood and placed her hand on her stomach. "I'm good now. Thank you," she said and her body swayed, exposing the lie she told.

"You're not okay," Tucker said, but when she held her hand out to ward him off, the flashlight fell and her knees buckled. Tucker brushed the hair off her face as he lowered her to the ground. "Jesse, let me take you home. You don't need to be here."

"I can't leave. I need to know Megan is safe." Her words slurred against his chest as she fought to keep her eyes open.

"And I need to know you are," he countered.

Her eyes grew heavy as his musky scent drifted around her, and for just a moment, she managed to forget the nightmare she was starring in. Her thoughts concentrated on his hand as it raked through her hair. *Heaven.* Then Mason's voice shattered the silence. Her eyes shot open and her face flushed. Considering she could only see Tucker's outline, he probably didn't notice. "I'm fine really," she repeated, although she wondered if she had actually said the words.

Tucker lifted her off the ground, wrapping his arm around her waist until she was steady on her feet. He led her over to where Lori was sitting, catching her every time she stumbled over a stone. Releasing his hold when she was firmly seated on the ground, he turned to Whitney. "Keep an eye on her."

Jesse moved closer to Lori, unsure of what was going on and definitely way out of her comfort zone. Without Tucker to keep her calm, she felt cold, alone, afraid. *Where did that come from?* Searching for Brian, who was standing next to Steve, she saw that both had their flashlights aimed down at something she couldn't see. "Are they looking for Megan?"

"Yes, but Jack will take care of her," Whitney said, stretching out her legs.

"Wh... where's Jack?" Jesse stuttered, trying not to worry about why Whitney didn't have on shoes.

"Down there," Whitney nodded.

Jesse held her breath and Lori spotlighted Jack at the bottom of the cliff. Feeling relieved that he was dressed like his normal self, her body relaxed but only for a split second. "Megan's down there?" Panic laced her words and her breathing grew shallow as she jumped up off the ground and stumbled back towards the woods. Drenched in sweat, she darted into the trees in an attempt to get off the mountain.

"Jesse, wait!" Whitney yelled, but she was already heading downhill fast.

# Thirty-Three

*Jack*

Jack knew the outcome wouldn't be good when the bond he shared with Megan led him to the woods. Although the first time he met her, she was in the woods at Sallee's Rock, things hadn't fared well between them. Rushing to her side, he made the mistake of thinking she would be instantly receptive to the bond, but instead, she was quick to put him in his place.

His race through the woods was stressful, and with Megan injured and alone, he was growing desperate to find her before Travis realized she was still alive. She had crossed his path at some point, but he wasn't sure if she were targeted because of their bond. When she went missing, only two people besides him knew about the bond, and Tracy wasn't one of them.

Looking over his shoulder as dirt and rock rained

down the cliffside; he could see the ground below and slid another three feet. With less than ten feet to go, he pushed out away from the wall and dropped, twisting his ankle when he landed on solid ground. It wasn't the first time he injured his leg, which left him with a slight limp to his gait.

Ignoring the pain, Jack ran alongside the creek until he came to the area beneath the overhanging ledge. It was dark and hidden from view by a massive tree that had fallen over it. Searching through the branches, his breath caught when he saw Megan's naked, battered body. Unable to grasp the sight before him, his heartbeat echoed in his ears as his world spiraled out of control.

Jack dropped to his knees and winced, but the pain he felt was nothing compared to what he deserved. *You should have protected her!* Guilt shimmered in his eyes as he checked her body for injuries. Satisfied it was safe to move her; he yanked his shirt over his head. Her perfumed scent lingered, but the underlying scent he detected startled his wolf. Gently lifting her, he quickly pulled the shirt over her head and once she was covered, scooped her up in his arms and carried her over to the creek.

Carefully placing her on the ground, he looked up at Mason. Giving him a thumbs-up, the news rapidly spread through the small crowd that watched from above—she was alive.

Jumbled thoughts twisted in his head as he turned back to Megan. *It's Lizzy,* his wolf insisted. *Where did you go? Where are you now?* The unanswered questions resurfaced, and he banished them to the back of his mind. Not a day went by that he didn't think about Lizzy, and no matter how hard he tried, he couldn't keep his thoughts from traveling back to the night when all hell broke loose in the pack.

"I'm not a pup, I'm six years old," Jackson said as he tried to explain why he snuck out of the house to find Lizzy. "But Dad! She's only five. She needs me."

The scolding he received had angered him because he didn't understand why Lizzy's mother would leave her at the river alone. He may have been small, but he had the heart of a warrior, even though he wasn't old enough to phase.

It was the following day when he learned the truth: Lizzy's mother had taken her to the river to hide her. Under Alpha Hudson's rule, the pack was instructed to do away with the half-bloods and all the human mates, which was when the pack split. Half of the pack wanted to protect the "impurities" as the alpha referred to them, while the other half wanted to purge them from the pack. It was a strategic move designed to expand the pack by allowing only the strongest bloodlines, and by doing so, the alpha believed he could take over any other packs in the region, and eventually rule the entire state.

A challenge was put forth, and under the rule of Alpha Cooper, the pack eventually reunited. After an extensive search of the area, most of the members were all accounted for, but a few pups were missing and Lizzy was one of them. The elders said she probably drowned, but her body was never found, and that gave Jack eternal hope. But the area was also known for poaching, and where there were poachers, there were traps.

So later that night, Jack crawled out his bedroom window, again thinking Lizzy might have stepped into a trap. But when he did, no one was there to help him. It was morning before the alpha set out looking for him. He was found three miles downriver, lethargic, but breathing. Dr. Sanders tried to repair the crushed bone, but his leg was never the same. The limp became a constant reminder of how he failed to save Lizzy. She was gone, and he would have to live the rest of his life without her.

Jack took a deep breath as he recalled the memories that still haunted his dreams. Did he dare allow himself to believe that Megan could be Lizzy? He wanted with all his heart to believe his wolf but he worried that he could not handle losing Lizzy again if Megan were not her. Staring down at her lifeless body, her skin seemed so pale and she shivered but never made a sound.

"I need your shirt," he yelled to anyone that was listening. Tucker pulled his shirt over his head and tossed it over the edge. Jack caught the shirt as three more floated down, one landing in the tree. Spreading the shirt over Megan's body, he suddenly realized just how small she was. His heart shattered knowing she didn't stand the slightest chance against the likes of Travis. Most females could not have faced off against a male wolf and won. Gathering the other shirts, Jack smiled and looked up as Tucker pulled the half-naked Lori back from the ledge.

Placing two shirts under Megan's head, Jack dipped the other in the cool creek water. It was well after midnight and he looked up at the moon, wondering how long it would take before help arrived. Folding the wet shirt, he knelt down and lightly wiped it over Megan's lips, gently removing the dirt from her face. She shuddered, but he assumed it was from shock, and not the night air. It was a pleasant night, warm with a slight

B. S. TODD

breeze, but seeing her lying there, fighting for her life, sent a chill up his spine. *I'm coming for you!* His jaw clenched and he took hold of Megan's hand. "Hang on, Megan, help is on the way," he soothed her before lying down beside her. A constant tremor traveled through her body. *If she were a wolf, why wasn't she healing?* A lone tear rolled down his cheek.

"I hope you can hear me," he said, nearly whispering. Gradually, he explained why he was at Sallee's Rock, and the bond they shared. He told her how the bond helped him find her and how he wanted her to remain in his life. He explained the roses and Tracy at the cafe. But when the thought of her almost dying tormented his heart, he choked up and sobbed. "I'm so sorry." And with nothing else left to say, he started singing.

Megan let out a whimper and he brushed his hand over her hair. "I'm right here, always," he said, but she didn't respond. Watching the ambulance pull up alongside the creek, he was glad to see Dr. Williams when the back doors opened. Jack kept watch while they loaded her into the ambulance. He didn't trust Travis and sensed he was probably lurking somewhere nearby. He gave him a subtle warning. *In time, my friend. In time.* Muffling a growl as the ambulance drove away, Jack jumped the creek and ran over to the patrol car, asking, "Can I get a ride?"

The distinct smell of disinfectant, blood, and latex gloves hung in the air as Jack held his head in his hands. Sitting on the far side of the waiting room, away from all the others, his stomach rumbled, his eyes burned, and mentally, he was spent. However, he refused to leave the hospital. The gossip mill was in full swing, and word of

Megan being found traveled faster than a bullet train. It wasn't necessarily a bad thing, *unless there was some crazed wolf out to kill you.* A threatening growl rose in his throat and he coughed into his fist.

"How are you doing?" Alpha Cooper said, stopping in front of Jack.

"He tried to kill her," Jack said, getting to his feet.

"I know. I talked to Tracy and I've stationed scouts around the building." The alpha's voice was low as he looked back over his shoulder.

"No need. I'm not going anywhere; besides, I'm the last person Travis wants to run across." Jack reached into his pocket and pulled out the bottle of lavender liquid, which he handed to the alpha. "She's a wolf, Dad. She's been masking her scent," Jack said as Dr. Williams entered the room.

"Ben, how are you?" Dr. Williams asked, extending his hand.

"I've been better. How's Megan?"

"She has a rib contusion, a slight concussion, and suffering from dehydration, but she's going to be fine." He looked over his shoulder as her parents left the room and turned back to the alpha. "I sent her parents in to see her. What happened? Did you know she was a wolf?"

"I just recently found out." The alpha looked over at Jack. "We don't know what happened, but based on the information we do have, she was masking her scent, and it was a pack member that attacked her," Ben said.

"Is there any way I can see her?" Jack cut in, not wanting to be rude, but impatient and unwilling to wait any longer. He shifted nervously.

"David, this is my son, Jack. He shares a bond with

Megan."

Dr. Williams nodded. "You're the one that found her. She's been calling for you."

"Yes, sir," Jack said, raking his hands through his hair. He was trying to stay calm, but hearing that she was calling for him only made his wolf push harder to take control.

"Give her parents a few minutes to visit before you go in," Dr. Williams said, "but there will be no other visitors allowed until later this afternoon."

"Thank you," Jack said, and his wolf backed down.

A few minutes later, Jack quietly entered her room and closed the door. Through the dim light, he could see Megan and he blinked to clear his eyes. Nearing the bed, she looked so small, defenseless... and human. The color in her cheeks had returned, and the dirt was gone, but the bruises remained. The soft pink of her lips complemented her olive complexion, and her light brown lashes fanned over her cheeks. He reached out and touched the strawberry-blonde ringlets that framed her face. *She looks so peaceful*, he thought as he leaned down and softly kissed her forehead. Noticing the light, mossy-rose scent that drifted around her, he inhaled a long breath through his nose. She was a wolf, and that eased his mind, but where had she come from? Pulling up a chair next to the bed, he sat down, unable to keep his eyes off her. She was his mate and he would do whatever it took to convince her to be with him, even if that meant begging.

"I'm sorry. I didn't think anyone was here," Jesse said, stepping into the room. "Dad said she couldn't have company, but I couldn't go home without seeing her. How is she?" she whispered, walking further into the room.

"She looks better," he said, glancing down at Megan.

"Are you going to stay with her?"

"Yes."

"Good. I don't feel comfortable leaving her alone. I was prepared to sleep under the bed if I had to. I'm not sure what happened, but I have a bad vibe about it. I know it's probably stupid to say, but I feel better knowing you'll be here," Jesse said as she watched Megan sleep. "If you need anything at all, call me."

"Thank you, I will," Jack said, knowing she was trying to be helpful, but if he needed anything, he would call on the pack. He took the paper she wrote her number on and watched her lightly rubbing Megan's leg.

"Looks can be deceiving."

"How's that?" Jack asked, unsure of where Jesse was going with her comment.

"She looks so fragile but she's the strongest person I know." Tears welled in her eyes as she turned to leave.

"She'll be all right. I'll see to that," Jack said, trying to ease her mind. "I'll let her know you stopped by." Jesse looked over her shoulder and nodded once, then quietly closed the door after she walked out of the room.

It was just before noon and Jack had fallen asleep, his body utterly exhausted from the events earlier that morning. The comforting massage from fingers running through his hair brought a smile to his anxiety-creased face. It was a dream; and dreams like that he wouldn't have minded having every night. Relaxing with the soft touch, a low giggle in the background caused him to stir. *It's not a dream.* He opened his eyes and a bolt of electricity zipped through his body. Seeing the shy smile on Megan's face and the way she lowered her head reminded him of Lizzy and his heart thundered. She was awake, she was touching him, she was beautiful.

"Thank you for finding me, and for staying with me there in the dark. I thought I imagined the whole thing until I woke up." Her feathery voice matched her smile and tugged at his heart.

He had fallen asleep with his head on the bed and his arm stretched across her legs. "I'm right here, always," was the last thing he told her before she was loaded into the ambulance, and now he was glad he stayed. "Lizzy, please tell me it's you." He lifted her hand to his lips as he sat down on the side of the bed. "I was told you were de..." he couldn't bring himself to say the word. He would never say that word. "No one knew what happened to you. I searched for you. Where have you been all this time?" he asked as a tear slipped down the side of his face.

Recognition sparked in her eyes. "Jason! I can't believe it's you," she said, placing her hand over her mouth as visible shock shone on her face. "I've been here in Cloverly for most of my life."

Jack smiled upon hearing the name he had long forgotten. His parents named him Jackson, but at five years old, she pronounced it *Jason*. She was the only one that ever called him that, and by the time he was twelve, his parents shortened his name to Jack.

"That night on the cliff, I realized the dream I'd been having was actually a memory. I remembered it all. I know what happened the night we were attacked. I was terrified. Travis was trying to take me from my mother. He grabbed her by the throat, but my dad jumped him from behind and yelled for my mother to run. I was scared, and I didn't understand why they hated me. Right before we ran into the woods, I looked over Mom's shoulder and saw three males pulling my dad off Travis. He fought hard, but in the end, they took his life." She wiped away a tear. "My mother took me to the river where a boat was waiting. She said I would be safe. She said she would come for me, but nothing she said made sense. I was so, so scared. I woke that night screaming, but my mom never came back, and I couldn't keep the image of my dad's death out of my head. So I blocked it. I didn't understand it. I couldn't handle it. I blocked everything and everyone. Eventually, I accepted the Smiths as my parents; it was easier for me that way. I simply allowed myself to forget, but Travis brought all those memories back. He killed my parents." She wiped her eyes and inhaled a shaky breath. "How could I be so heartless? How could I just block out the memory of my parents? I loved them," she said, sobbing pitifully.

Jack moved up on the bed, and wrapped his arms around her. "You had no control over what happened," he said, restraining his anger. She wasn't a pure-blood, and that's why she and her mother were targeted. Fighting back his own tears, he added, "No child should ever have to go through the emotional trauma you were subjected to, human or wolf."

"He's right, Megan." Jack turned to see Dr. Williams standing in the doorway. "I'm sorry, I wasn't trying to eavesdrop, but I didn't want to interrupt you. I never realized how bad it was that night," he said, stepping into the room. "Your body has a way of dealing with trauma, and in your case, your mind chose to block it out. You did nothing wrong, Megan, and I'm glad to see you have your memory back. No matter how painful, eventually, it has to heal." He stood at the end of the bed, looking over her chart. "I'm on my way home but I wanted to stop by and check on you. If you need me, you know the number." He smiled. "Try to rest; it's the best thing for you right now." Nodding towards Jack, he turned and walked out of the room.

"Can you tell me what happened? Is Travis the alpha? I can't go back to the pack, he will kill me," Megan whispered.

"No, he will never touch you again. After what he did, he is no longer a member of our pack, and he will be dealt with as justice dictates. As for your question, Dad's the alpha so you don't have to worry, you will be protected. I swear, I will never let anyone hurt you again." He placed a kiss on her forehead and she wrapped her arms around his waist.

"Thank you for saving me."

Jack held her until she drifted off to sleep before he gently placed her head back on the pillow and pulled the blanket up to her chest. The afternoon sun hung high in the sky and as much as he needed to speak with the alpha, he refused to leave her side. Quietly, he closed the blinds and sat down next to the bed, guarding the most precious thing his heart had ever known.

"I love you, Jason. I've always loved you, even when I couldn't remember why," she said and his heart melted.

"I love you too, Lizzy."

# Thirty-Four

*Jesse*

After a long night without any sleep and a morning of working at the shelter, Jesse was ready to crawl into bed before she collapsed on her feet. She wasn't one to defy the Sandman, and he was now shouting her name. She went into the kitchen and the first thing she noticed was a bundle of orange dahlias in a jar of water. "Are those for me?" she asked.

"Yes, there's a card," Gramma said. "I wasn't sure how long you would be gone, so I put them in water."

Jesse nodded her thanks as she searched for the card that was stashed between the stems. She loved the flowers Brian left for her, but it was the card she looked forward to the most. *I can make you happy if given a chance.* She smiled and ran her fingers over the soft blooms.

"How's Megan?" Gramma asked as she opened the

oven door. The smell of roast beef filled the room, and Jesse's stomach rumbled.

"She's doing good, considering." Jesse pushed the flowers to the side and poured a cup of coffee. Her mind was numb and she stood there in a sleepy daze.

"Thank the Lord. I was worried about her." She closed the oven door and followed Jesse over to the table where she sat down across from her.

"Gramma, is something bothering you?" Jesse studied her face as she struggled to keep her eyes open.

"No. I was just thinking about Megan," she said. "Is everything all right with you? You look tired."

"Last night was exhausting, and waiting at the hospital this morning, plus, working at the shelter, I'm pooped. But more than that, I'm frustrated about what happened to Megan. I feel like there's something not being told, and that irritates me to no end." She frowned. "Everyone's just happy Megan's safe, but what happened to all the questions? Like why was she in the woods? And who was with her? There had to be a reason."

"I'm just happy she's safe, and right now, that's all that matters. As for why she was there, well, I guess that is her business, and unless she's willing to tell it, we may never know."

"Well, can I ask you something?" Jesse took a sip of coffee and set the cup on the table. She wasn't sure how to ask her grandmother about werewolves without sounding insane, but there was no getting around it. There was more going on in Cloverly than people admitted, and it was a feeling she couldn't shake. "What do you know about the wolves?"

"What wolves?" Gramma shifted uncomfortably

before she got up and went over to the counter to pour another cup of coffee. "I don't know anything about wolves," she said, returning to the table.

Jesse glanced over at her. "I know there's this big secret that's been kept for like, a gazillion years. I've read about it in old newspaper articles, and I've got proof there are wolves in the area but I just want someone to tell me the truth." Her grandmother looked down at her coffee. "Just between you and me, Gramma, I know there are things going on and no one wants to talk about them. I need to know. I need to know if what I discovered is the secret of Cloverly."

"What makes you think I know?" Gramma looked her dead in the eye and for a minute, Jesse was thrown off by her blank expression, but then, she grinned.

"Because you're trying to protect me by pretending you don't know. I can see it in your eyes." It was clear her grandmother was holding back, so Jesse had to think fast. "Wait here, I want to show you something."

Gramma got up from the table and dumped her coffee down the drain, just to pour another cup. She paced around the kitchen and finally sat back down.

"Look at this," Jesse said, unzipping her backpack as she rushed back into the kitchen. "We went to Sallee's Rock the other day and these are pictures of wolf prints we found there." She arranged them on the table. "And here, I made this from one print." She placed the plaster casting on top of the pictures and continued shuffling through the bag.

"Well, dear, I guess it could be wolves, but it could also be dogs. I wouldn't know the difference between the two," Gramma said, picking up the molded print that was as big as her hand. Setting it aside, she examined the pictures.

"Well, I've never seen a wolf print, so I'm not sure you can. But the one I made a casting of was too large to belong to a dog unless there's a bullmastiff on steroids running loose." Jesse pulled out the wooden box and set it on the table in front of her grandmother. "Does this look familiar?"

"Where did you find this?" Gramma asked as her hand caressed the top of the cedar box. "I haven't seen this box in years. Your grandfather made it." She lifted the lid and pulled out the old newspaper clippings.

"Then he must have known the secret," Jesse said, sorting through the papers until she found the drawing of the shield. "This shield stands for Cloverly Pack, doesn't it?" Jesse left out the werewolf part for her own sanity. She wasn't ready to admit anything of that nature could exist, not just yet. "Gramma, I just want the truth. There are three cameras set up in the woods right now, and sooner or later, we will catch something on them. I would rather know firsthand what I'm getting into, instead of stumbling onto something unknown. Please, Gramma, I just want the truth."

Gramma turned back to the articles as the kitchen clock ticked off the time. "I don't want to be responsible for any harm coming to my family," she finally said, thirty-two seconds later. Jesse was counting.

She placed her hand on Gramma's arm. "What is the big deal about wolves being in Cloverly?" She could see the burden she placed on her grandmother but her need to know the truth outweighed it.

"I wish you would leave this alone. It would be in the

best interest of the whole community," Gramma said, placing the top back on the box.

"We're talking about wolves... just wolves. How is that hurting the community?"

"Jesse, did Megan know about this?" she asked, waving her hand over the box.

"No, she wasn't with us. Why?" Jesse pulled out a chair to sit down.

"You are not dealing with normal wolves. They're werewolves and they are very dangerous."

Jesse looked up to meet her eyes. "Do you believe that? That the wolves are werewolves? Have you ever seen one?" She could feel the cold shiver inching up her body and goosebumps dotted her arms. *That's crazy. There are no such things as werewolves, just overactive imaginations.* Now she was thinking like Brian.

"No, I haven't, but I know people that have. And I was so worried about Megan. I was afraid..." Her grandmother paused.

"Afraid the wolves attacked her?"

"I worried about what you all had seen, or who might've seen you in the woods. If they suspect you know their secret, you will be marked."

"Who are you talking about and marked... how?" By now, Jesse was more than confused as she stared at her grandmother in disbelief. Kicking around the idea that wolves were in the area was fun, but werewolves? Ridiculous.

"Jesse, the secret isn't necessarily the wolves, but what they will do if you tell what you know. They will kill you."

"You can't truly believe that," Jesse said, looking

down at the plaster cast. She tried to hide her disbelief, but it was impossible. It was something straight out of a storybook, and only Lori could talk about such things without sounding totally whacked.

"There are several people in this town who believe just that, and it would do you good to heed my warning. You must not tell anyone you know the secret. Not even your friends."

"I can't do that. I can't just stand by and do nothing. If you honestly believe the wolves are dangerous, you have to fight back. Kick them while they're down," Jesse said, and that's exactly what she planned to do. Glancing down at her high-tops, she wondered if it would be wise to invest in better footwear with a steel toe. "We can stop them. Do you know who the wolves are? Does anyone know?" *Would you stop! You're allowing yourself to be sucked into a world that doesn't exist.* Again sounding like Brian, she fought the urge to roll her eyes.

"I thought I did, but I was wrong," Gramma said, looking down at the table. "I'm ashamed for assuming something that wasn't true and because of that, I've treated some people less kind."

"How do you know you were wrong?" Jesse lifted her eyebrows in question.

"Because he saved Megan and they would never save a human. They hate all humans." Gramma looked back at Jesse.

"You thought Jack was a wolf?" Jesse stared slack-jawed as she leaned back in the chair.

"I did until he found Megan. Now I don't know, and that is just as frightening."

"Who else knows? Does Dad?"

"If he does, he has never mentioned it to me, and I have no intention of telling him. The less people that know, the safer everyone will be."

"Well, then I won't tell him either, but we need proof. We can stop them if we have proof. Or everyone will think we're crazy."

"Maybe we are. Maybe we should drop it. If they find out you know..." she warned again.

"No, they can't kill us all and no matter what they do, there are people willing to confront them. We can stop them," Jesse insisted. She wasn't sure how she could defeat something she didn't yet believe in, but she knew she had to try.

"Just be careful. I don't want anything happening to you or anyone else for that matter." Gramma frowned and drank down her cold coffee.

"Don't worry; we'll be fine," Jesse said, gathering everything into her bag. "I'm going up to bed. I'm tired and I need to think." Zipping the backpack, she slung it over her shoulder and picked up the flowers before heading to her room.

Maybe she would have been better off not knowing about the wolves, but seeing the look on her grandmother's face made Jesse angry. Her jaw clenched as fear traveled through her veins, and the sudden need to expose the mangy wolves amplified. *Breathe!* She told herself as she entered her room. Jesse wasn't the type to go ballistic, but mess with her grandmother, and anything was possible. She flopped on the bed and stared out the window, a seething scowl on her face. Thinking about everything her grandmother told her, and trying to figure out her next move, she finally lay down and drifted off to sleep.

She tossed and turned for the better part of the night as a pack of wolves mocked her in her dreams. *Fed up with their attempt to rule the town, she slowly stalked through the woods with a shotgun across her chest. In search of what she considered a nuisance, she dropped to one knee and brought the weapon up against her shoulder. As the howling grew louder and twigs snapped, she took aim. Waiting until the last possible second, she pulled the trigger, and the rifle kicked back, sending her into the underbrush. Swearing a blue streak, she dusted herself off and grabbed the double-barreled shotgun off the ground. Taking aim again, her eyes widened when a large wolf, as big as a house, stared down at her with glaring, green eyes. She swallowed hard and pulled the trigger, hoping her aim wasn't off. As the red-tipped, plastic dart left the gun,* her eyes shot open and her heartbeat pounded in her ears. *What the hell kind of nightmare was that?* She clicked on the bedside lamp.

By the time she settled into a steady sleep, sunlight was streaming through the bedroom window, and she rolled over to shield her eyes. Her body was exhausted, but knowing Lori would be waiting for her at Brian's, she hauled herself out of bed and quickly dressed in a pair of denim shorts and a sleeveless blouse. Somewhat excited, she hurried down the stairs and out the door, her nightmare soon forgotten.

Greeted by a sleepy Brian, he handed her a cup of coffee and motioned her through the kitchen and out to the patio. After telling them about the conversation she had with her grandmother, Jesse and Lori agreed they would find a way to stop the wolves. But Brian and Steve had a very different reaction.

"I think you're taking this a bit too far," Brian said. Pacing the patio, he ran his fingers through his hair. "This is nothing more than storybook tales. It's crazy, werewolves are not real." He continued his path around the patio. "Plus, Gramma said she had never seen one, so it's probably something that was told and retold years ago to keep kids under control. She's an old woman and the first thing to go is the memory."

Steve sided with Brian, which Jesse expected. "That's the best explanation I've heard. The tale was probably told to keep kids from playing in the woods. I remember my grandmother telling us if we ate raw potatoes we'd get worms. And I believed it. Although sometimes I tempted fate and snuck out of the house with a raw potato in my pocket. I loved raw potatoes. To this day, if I catch Mom peeling potatoes, I'm eating one... with salt. To hell with the worms!" Steve said.

"But that's not the same," Jesse said, trying not to laugh. "There are people that believe werewolves are living here in Cloverly. We need to expose the so-called wolves, for the benefit of those that believe in them. Whether we believe it's true or not."

"People will think you're crazy. I think you're crazy for suggesting it. Plus, if they aren't real, how will you expose them?" Brian was obviously tired of their discussion and Jesse assumed he would get up and go inside. "Look, I'm not trying to upset you. I just don't understand your obsession with werewolves."

"What if I get proof? Something more than what we already have?"

"How can you prove something that doesn't exist?"

Brian raked his fingers through his hair, but the slight roll of his eyes was starting to tick her off.

"Isn't that what the cameras are for? I mean, we haven't checked them, so maybe we'll actually see something. If not, I haven't figured that part out yet," Jesse said, but Brian didn't seem at all convinced.

"I got it! You could always ask people. Who knows? There may be wolves right here in the neighborhood." Brian looked over at Steve. "Are you a wolf?"

"Do you think that would work?" Lori asked, trying not to smile, but Jesse knew she would back her up no matter what the guys thought.

Steve snickered. "I don't think that would work because if I were a wolf, I wouldn't admit it."

"We can't just walk up to a complete stranger and ask them if they are a werewolf. Gramma said if they find out you know their secret, they mark you. So we'll have to come up with proof without the wolves knowing," Jesse said, staring across the yard.

"I'm sorry, Jesse. I'm not trying to discredit your grandmother, but I quit believing in fairy tales when I was six." Brian pulled out a chair and took a seat across the table from her.

"What about you, Steve, are you willing to help us?" Lori asked.

"Well, I have to admit I did question the size of the prints we found, and I'm not saying I believe it, but if there are such things as werewolves, I prefer not to know."

There was no winning with those two, but Jesse wasn't ready to throw in the towel just yet. "Would you at least think about it? Please?"

"Yeah, although I highly doubt it will do much good," Brian said. At least he agreed on something and to Jesse, credibility was half the battle.

# Thirty-Five

*Jack*

Megan whimpered while she slept, and as much as Jack
wanted to wake her, he knew she would have to work
through the nightmare in order to heal. He held her hand,
comforting her. If there were any way that he could
remove all of the nightmares, he would have done so. He
rubbed over her knuckles and slowly breathed in her
scent. She no longer smelled like the lavender perfume,
but instead like a wolf. "Hey," he smiled when she opened
her eyes. "How do you feel?"

She claimed she was fine, but there was no mistaking
the sadness he saw in her eyes and the hiccupped
breathing. He rubbed down her arm, wishing he could
take the pain away, and that he had done things
differently. Still, she was there and although she wasn't
fine, he knew she would be in good time.

Not wanting to rush her, he put off their bonding as long as possible, but with her in immediate danger, his wolf insisted they seal the bond in order to protect her. Pressing his forehead against hers, he inhaled the mossy-rose scent and smiled. "Lizzy, I know you can feel the bond, but do you understand what it means?"

"Yes. You said if I accepted you for what you are, we would be bonded. My eyes may have been closed, but I heard every word." She lowered her head to the side, a shy gesture, reminding him of when they were younger.

"Lizzy... Megan." The slight quiver of his hand as he held hers didn't go unnoticed; and she chuckled, causing him to blush. Placing her hand over his heart, "Do you accept me for what I am?" he asked, resting his other hand on the bed with his fingers crossed.

She picked up his hand and kissed his fingers before placing it over her heart. "Jason... Jack, I accept you for what you are. I always have. Even when I couldn't remember what you were."

Jack leaned down and lightly kissed her, keeping the bond between them intact. "That's more like it," he said and he kissed her again. She giggled when he nipped her bottom lip. "I think we might need to save that for later." He winked and got off the bed. "As much as I would love to keep you all to myself, you have visitors." He sighed and the weight of the world lifted off his shoulders. He had finally found Lizzy and nothing, and no one could ever take her away from him. On that, he would stake his life.

"Are my parents here? I can't imagine what they're going through," she said, twisting her hands in the blanket.

"They've been in and out since you got here. Why, is something wrong?" He watched her expression change with her thoughts, and he paused at the door.

"I want to see my mom, but I feel a little awkward. I know they aren't my real parents, but I love them as if they were. What if they don't want me anymore? Have you met them?" she asked, her nerves causing her to ramble.

"Yes." He grinned and opened the door.

"Can I come in?" Mrs. Smith smiled, leaning in from the hallway.

"Mom!" Megan exclaimed and tears filled her eyes.

Jack relaxed as Megan's excitement filled the room. "Let me help you," he said as he reached down to adjust the bed so she could sit more comfortably.

"Mom, this is Jack."

"Yes, I know. How are you this morning?"

"I'm fine, thank you." He leaned down and kissed Megan on the cheek. "I'll be right outside."

"Stay. I want you to stay," Megan said, placing her hand on his arm.

"No need to leave, Jack. I know who you are," Mrs. Smith said.

Jack was stunned by her admission, but he nodded and sat down in the chair next to the bed. How much she really knew, he wasn't sure, but very eager to find out. Maybe it was a figure of speech. Either way, he sat quietly and listened.

"You knew?" Megan asked, squeezing Jack's hand.

"Yes. I wanted to tell you everything, but it would only put you in danger," she said, holding back her own tears.

"It's okay, Mom, I understand." Megan blushed. "Can I still call you Mom?"

"You had better, young lady. I am still your mother. That hasn't changed." She smiled and patted Megan's leg.

"But how did you find out?"

"Your mother was my best friend. Growing up in a family of boys, she was the sister I always wanted. There were no secrets between us. And I swore that night on the boat that I would do whatever I had to, in order to keep you safe. I knew it would be risky, but a risk I was willing to take for Beth."

"And you told no one? Does Dad know?"

"Yes. I explained it to him that night. Your mother asked if we would meet her at the river. She told us where to dock the boat and we waited. When she ran out of the woods, we knew it was bad. Then we saw your face, and you were terrified. She handed you over and said she needed to go help your dad. She asked us to keep you safe and not let anyone take you. After that night, we waited, hoping she was all right, but we never heard anything more about her or the wolves. It was your dad's idea to move out of town for a couple years, and when we returned to Cloverly, we told everyone you were my niece and that we had adopted you."

"Excuse me. I hate to interrupt because I know there is a lot you all need to talk about, but how do you know me?" Jack asked. Mrs. Smith's face was familiar, yet he had a hard time placing her.

"Beth came to my house one afternoon and you and Megan were with her. I know you probably don't remember it."

"You were mixing things together, a recipe or

something." His eyes widened with faint recognition. "The woman from the flower shop, she was there as well."

"She was. We were working out a formula to mask Megan's scent. Brid is a seer. She has the ability to see things that are certain to be. It was she who warned Beth to cover Megan's scent. Her visions aren't always complete; and usually, they are just enough to warrant a change in behavior. It was also Brid who gave me the idea for the business. She said if I made a variety of lavender products and sold them, no one would suspect we were shielding Megan. And that's how WOLF was born." Mrs. Smith winked at Megan.

"Well, that explains the lavender," Megan said.

Jack followed the conversation fairly well until her mother threw in the *wolf* part. Now he was confused, but more importantly, he needed to know what *wolf* was. "What do you mean, how *wolf* was born?"

"Wisp of Lavender Farm. The business," she said.

"Brid said she would remember. She said she watches over the wolf. It didn't make any sense at the time," Jack said. "But if she knew about us, why not tell me if only so I could protect her?"

"Megan, Brid said as you grew older it would be impossible to block your wolf. The nightmares you've been having since you were thirteen came from your inner wolf, trying to force you to remember," Mrs. Smith said. "Her memories had to be restored before she could move forward. 'He that destroyed the family releases the memories.' That was the last vision Brid had, but like all visions, they don't come with directions or expiration dates as to when or how."

"But why didn't her wolf help her heal? Why has it

taken her longer?" Jack asked.

"Her human DNA slows down the healing process, but she still heals faster than most."

"How do you know that?" Megan asked.

"Your mother was half-wolf, and your father was a pure-blood. She healed slower than he did because of her human DNA." She placed her hand on Megan's cheek. "When I look at you, I see her. She would be very proud of you today. I'm proud of you."

Megan smiled as more tears filled her eyes. "I love you, Mom."

"I love you too, sweetie." She leaned over and hugged Megan. "You know, Dr. Williams said you could come home tomorrow if you're feeling up to it, but for now, you have more visitors." She kissed Megan's hair. "I'll be back later."

Jack stood when his dad entered the room. "Megan, this is my dad, Alpha Cooper."

"How are you doing, Megan? It's nice to see you awake."

Her mouth parted as her eyes followed the alpha across the room. He looked similar to Jack, just slightly bigger in build, but about the same height. His hair was cut short against his head and dark in color. "Alpha Cooper," she acknowledged without looking him in the eye.

"It's okay. I'm not that strict." He smiled when she looked up. "Do you feel like talking? Can you tell me what happened and how you ended up on Hunter's Ridge?"

Jack sat down beside her and held her hand in his lap. "It's okay. You're safe."

Megan cleared her throat and looked between the two. "It all started when I was thirteen, or that's when my nightmares started. I didn't know at the time that it was because of my wolf, but every month during the full moon, I would always have the same dream. It was horrible and I could never get back to sleep afterward. That's when I started sitting out by the pool, finding the moon somewhat comforting." She shrugged, her mind drifting back to that night.

*The sound of a motorcycle startled her, and she looked back to see Randy walking up the driveway. "What are you doing here?" she asked when he sat down in the chair beside her. Randy was her friend, and usually, she wouldn't have talked to him in such a harsh tone, but she was still embarrassed that he had thrown her over his shoulder, in front of everyone.*

*"I was in the neighborhood and saw the light on. I took a chance that you would be out here," he said as he flipped his keys back and forth across his hand. "Look, I want to apologize for being an ass. It wasn't my intention to embarrass you. You mean a lot to me as a friend, and I miss talking to you."*

*"You came here in the middle of the night to say you were sorry?" Megan glared, trying to hide a grin but failing as a smile crossed her face. "I'm sorry. I should have never yelled at you. You are one of my best friends, and I would hate to lose you. Who else would I have to talk to at one in the morning?" She chuckled. "Apology accepted. So now give me the scoop on you and Tracy."*

"After he left, I started to go inside, and that's when I heard the howl. It was you. You called to me. I remember." Megan looked over at Jack, hot tears filling her eyes. "I ran. I didn't know where I was going, but I had to find you," she said, slipping back to her memory.

*Standing alone on Hunter's Ridge, an icy shiver rolled over her. Glancing around the clearing, moonlight filtered through the trees, casting soft shadows on the ground. Her first instinct was to run, but not knowing the area, she dropped down, pretending to tie her shoe as her right hand slid over a large rock.*

*Twigs snapped, drawing her eyes to a darkened shadow, and she stood, holding the rock at her side. "Jack?" she called out, but when he didn't answer, she turned to leave.*

*"No need to leave on my account, sweetheart." She froze, not wanting to see who was behind her. She knew Jack, and it wasn't him.*

*"Who are you?" she said, turning as the large shadow moved into the clearing.*

*"So you are the one he calls. How interesting," he said, ignoring her question. He took a step closer, his head tilted upward, sniffing the air. "What a nifty, little trickster you are."*

*Warning bells rang at the sound of his voice, yet she was confused as to whom he was. "Do you know me?" she asked.*

*"I'm a friend... of the family, you could say." His eyes moved down her body, causing her to shiver. "You have grown into a shapely, little female."*

*Megan shuddered at the evil that reeked from him, reminding her of her worst nightmare. "Where's Jack? I was supposed to meet him," she said.*

*"Yes, I know. He did call for you, but when you didn't show up, he chose another. Sorry, sweetheart, you're too*

late."

"Late for what? Where's Jack?" She held her ground and her skin crawled beneath his gaze.

"My dear, you are nothing to Jack, can't you see that? He found his mate when Tracy answered his call. By sun-up you will no longer matter." He laughed.

"I don't understand."

"Of course you don't. And that's the beauty of it. Here you stand without knowing your full potential, and now it doesn't matter! But if you do as you're told, I may be able to right the wrong."

"And if I don't?" She didn't intend to be so brassy but anger seeped through her veins and she bit her lip to stop the tremble.

"If you don't, I'll kill you just like I killed your mother."

"You have the wrong person. My mother is not dead!" she yelled, hoping to attract attention. But who else besides her would be stupid enough to run into the woods alone?

"Are you sure? Sometimes things aren't as they seem." His snarl echoed around the clearing and he took another step closer.

She wanted to throw the rock and run, but instead, she stood there in a daze. The images of her nightmare flashed before her eyes, her wolf reminding her of her past. Run, Lizzy! Get out of here, the voice yelled in her head. Slowly, she backed away. All those years, what she thought was a dream, was actually a memory she kept buried deep in her mind. "Stay away from me," she hissed.

"Now that's no way to be towards your future mate." He closed his eyes and inhaled as if he couldn't get enough air. "I love the smell of fear," he said in a low, raspy voice. Megan's eyes darted around the clearing. "Don't try it. You can't escape me." He continued making her retreat toward the cliff. "We can do this the easy way, or your way. Either way, I always win."

She could see the edge of the cliff but couldn't tell how far down the drop would be, so she decided against jumping. "I don't know what you want, but I have to go." She raised her chin defiantly, her wolf pushing to come forward. She turned, and there he stood, two feet in front of her.

He ran his finger along her jawline and lifted her chin, tilting her head to the side. "I can't wait to see the look on Jack's face when I—"

"Don't touch me!" she growled. Jerking her head away, she stepped to the left to distract him while swinging her right arm around and slamming the rock against his head. He bellowed out in pain.

"You'll pay for that," he said and his eyes flared with anger.

Megan gasped at the sight of the monster before her. Blinding fear coursed through her body, launching her wolf forward. In an instant, bits of clothing scattered at her feet as her wolf hunkered back. With a low growl, she attacked, grabbing him by the arm. He roared viciously as he twisted around, slamming her to the ground. As her wolf dangled over the edge of the cliff, he placed his boot on her neck.

"Well, now, seems you're right where I wanted you," he said, his voice dangerously low. "What a waste. Another female that doesn't know her place." Stepping down, he grinned as her wolf struggled, clawing at the *ground. "Audacious, just like your mother." Lifting his boot, the wolf yelped when he kicked her in the head. Black spots danced in her eyes but she kicked away and phased.*

*"No!" she screamed as her body fell backward and everything went black.*

"I heard the howl and I knew it was Jack. I felt a pull to him, like I did the first day I saw him in the woods. Only this time I had no control. I had to find him. I don't remember anything after I fell until Jack found me. I remember him," Megan said. Her face flushed as she lifted her eyes.

"Wow. I don't know what to say except I'm sorry. At the time, I didn't know you were a wolf. I never thought my wolf would affect you that way." This time, it was Jack that blushed as he looked over at his dad. "We need to find Travis, *now.*" The thought of him hurting Megan set Jack's wolf on edge and he knew, if given the chance, Travis would attack again.

"I agree," Alpha Cooper said, a crease lining his forehead. "Until we can locate him, you are not to be left alone. You are still in plenty of danger, which is why I've called in scouts to patrol the area. Once you get home, there will be more scouts stationed around your house. They're here now. I want you to know who will be guarding you," he said walking towards the door.

"I will protect her," Jack growled. By protection, he meant he would kill Travis if he attempted to get near Megan again, and he knew the alpha could see how serious he was in his eyes.

"I know you will, Jack, but you can't be with her every minute of the day, so I've assigned Sage to shadow her. You or Sage will be with her at all times and the others will monitor from a distance." Alpha Cooper opened the door and the four scouts walked in. "Megan, this is Sage, Seth, Nigel, and Brayden. They will be guarding you until Travis is located and apprehended."

"Do you really think I need guards? Do you think he will come back for me?"

"Yes, you are definitely a threat to him," Alpha Cooper said.

"Why? I'm nothing compared to all of you. I'm no threat to anyone."

"Because he knows eventually, you will be an alpha female," Jack said, "and if he is out for revenge, you make the perfect target."

"Me, an alpha female?" Megan whispered, lowering her eyes. Jack squeezed her hand, and she looked up to see him shaking his head.

"Don't look away. You're stronger than you think."

Hearing a light tap at the door, they all looked back as Mason entered the room.

"We'll get out of your way now. Sage will be right outside the door if you need her and the others will be close by." The alpha led the scouts to the door. "Megan, I'll see you soon."

"Come on in." Jack motioned for Mason to join them.

"How are you, Megan? You had us all worried, especially this guy here," Mason said and squeezed Jack's shoulder.

"I'm doing much better, thanks to Jack." She blushed, staring between the two.

"Glad to hear it because I brought company. Sorry, Jack, but they followed me here." He winked at Megan before walking over and opening the door. Whitney was the first to enter the room, and she ran over to the edge of the bed and took a seat. She gushed over Megan, making Jack smile.

"Megan, I think you know everyone," Jack said as Tucker entered the room.

"How's my girl?" Randy asked, moving past Tucker to stand at the foot of the bed. Hearing a low growl from Jack, he laughed. "Down, boy!"

Pushing past Randy, Tracy walked over and stooped down beside the bed. "Megan, I'm so sorry about everything. If I had known..."

"Tracy, it wasn't your fault. You are not responsible for what Travis did," Jack said.

Randy pulled Tracy up and draped his arm over her shoulders. "Megan, I know you've met Tracy, my mate." He grinned.

"Oh my gosh, are you kidding? That's wonderful!" Megan squealed.

# Thirty-Six

*Jesse*

Jesse waved Whitney over as she walked into the cafe. "I ordered you a coffee," she said, pushing the cup across the table as Whitney took a seat.

"Are you alone?" Whitney asked, adding a packet of sugar to her cup.

"No, she's over there." Jesse pointed when Lori walked out of the restroom.

Whitney looked over and smiled. "Thanks for coming on such short notice."

"Not a problem, we're meeting the guys for lunch," Lori said, sliding into the seat next to Jesse and picking up the menu.

"I've already placed our order so you can't eat until we get to the park." Jesse took the menu and placed it between the chrome napkin dispenser and the wall.

Turning her attention back to Whitney, she didn't miss the snarly face Lori made. "I assume you know Megan is home now."

"Yeah, Jack told me," Whitney said.

"You mean they really are a couple now?" Jesse asked.

"He climbed down the side of a mountain to rescue her. What did you expect?" Lori rolled her eyes.

"Yeah, but they didn't even have a first date," Jesse whined.

"Well, from where I was sitting, they passed first date status while lying on the ground that night." Lori flicked her brow and Jesse elbowed her.

"Actually, that's what I wanted to talk to you about. I visited Megan earlier today and she said she still felt a little dehydrated, but she was up and walking. She looked good and seemed to be in good spirits, so I was hoping you all would agree to go ahead with the party. I know she may not be able to dance, but after everything she and Jack have been through, I thought it would be nice to just relax with friends. Plus, I had my heart set on dressing up," Whitney said.

"We could get together Saturday. It doesn't have to be anything fancy," Lori said.

"It gives us five days, and we've got everything we need," Whitney blew the steam off the cup as she looked across the table.

"Which reminds me." Jesse pulled the garment bag off the back of the booth. "I have Megan's dress and I want your opinions before I show it to her. We've talked about opening a store, so I'm hoping I can use the dress to seal the deal." Jesse stood with one knee on the seat as she unzipped the bag. The ripping noise drew the attention of the couple in the neighboring booth. Bringing the dress out of the bag, she held it up in front of her. "What do you think?"

"Wow. It's beautiful," Whitney said.

"And she'll be able to wear it on their first official date." Jesse grinned.

"I think she'll love it. And she won't question why you're giving it to her. It's brilliant," Lori said, holding the bag open as Jesse secured the dress inside the vinyl. "But I thought you all agreed the store had to be on Main Street?"

"It will be, but until I talk to Megan, mum's the word." Jesse winked.

"But I'm your best friend." Lori pouted. "You can't leave me hanging."

"Don't worry; you'll be there, but until then." Jesse zipped her lips.

"So, is Saturday good for you all? I've already told Jack we wanted to do something for them, but I didn't tell him what because I want it to be a surprise. He's just waiting for me to get back with him on the date and time. And he'll suspect nothing with the party being at my cabin," Whitney said.

"That works for me. We'll talk to Megan on Friday morning, and you can tell Jack Saturday morning. Just make sure he has her wearing the dress," Jesse said.

"I love surprise parties. Plus, I want to talk to her new boyfriend. Mister Tall, Dark and Damn Fine." Lori fanned herself.

"Lori, have you no shame?" Jesse blushed as she looked around the cafe.

"Girl, don't go acting like you didn't notice. I know all

about him and his swagger and it didn't come from Megan." Lori laughed. "Now if you'll excuse me, I have a caterer to talk to."

"Don't worry, Jesse. I grew up with Jack and I'll admit he gets better with age," Whitney said after Lori walked away.

As they walked out of the cafe, the first thing Jesse noticed was Steve staring from across the street. He and Brian were sitting at the far end of the park, which was good considering how irritated Brian could get, and the chance of anyone overhearing their conversation wasn't likely. Nudging Lori, they waved at Steve before walking over to her dad's truck that was parked in front of the bookstore. Normally, she would've walked to the cafe, but since she had Megan's dress, driving was the better option. She placed the dress bag over the seat and closed the door, waving as Whitney headed down the street.

She shielded her eyes against the noonday sun as they crossed the street to the park. Steve was talking to Brian, who was facing the opposite direction. Hopefully, by bringing lunch, they would be more inclined to listen to what she had to say without objecting every three minutes. "I brought lunch." She said, holding up the bag.

"I told you they were going to bribe us with food." Steve laughed.

"We're not bribing you," Lori said. She opened the bag and handed them their burgers before she and Jesse took a seat across from them.

Jesse set her food on top of the bag and glanced over at Brian. "Did someone drop a pin?" she said, breaking the silence.

"Fine, I'll start. We know you invited us here for a reason. Now would you like to get to it, or do you want to continue pretending this has nothing to do with wolves?" Brian said and Steve snickered.

"Talk about forward." Jesse frowned and her throat tightened as she fought the urge to spew a few cuss words. He deserved it. "Actually, we wanted to invite you to a surprise party for Megan next Saturday, but since you brought it up." It was a flat-out lie and she knew it, but it was better than letting him think the only thing they had to talk about was wolves.

"Look, I don't know what you expect us to do. I mean, how are we supposed to know who is or isn't a wolf? Most people don't even know about them, so why bother?" Brian said, taking a bite of his sandwich.

"So you agree there are werewolves in the area?" Lori asked.

"I agreed there were wolves in the area because I was trying to be polite. Honestly, I think you two have plunged into the deep end and now you're trying to drag us in with you."

"So your solution is to tell us what you think we want to hear?" Jesse asked, unable to hide her aggravation.

"What did you expect me to say? There are wolves terrorizing the town? I don't think so," Brian replied. His voice took on a tone that didn't sit right with Jesse. Harsh, bitter, and determined to control the situation. "Look, I'm not trying to sound hateful, but if there were such things as werewolves, why expose them to begin with?"

"Because they are dangerous." Jesse sighed and her shoulders slumped. She didn't think she could change his thinking, and that bothered her more than anything. Why he chose to make this harder than it had to be was beyond her. She stared down at her burger, no longer hungry.

"You don't know that, first off. And second, no one will come forward and admit they are a monster. And third, if they were real, do you know how many hunters would invade this place?" Brian dropped his sandwich down on the wrapper. "Okay, let's try this. What if I told you I was a werewolf? Would you expose me and risk the chance of someone trying to kill me? Would you risk my life to expose the wolves?" he said, meeting her eyes.

Would she expose him? He was Brian, her boyfriend, but if he were a wolf, he was dangerous, wasn't he? Okay, she could see his point, but that didn't mean her point wasn't equally important.

"Well, I guess your silence answers my question, but I have to admit, if you were a wolf, I would never expose you or put you in any danger. I thought you'd see how people could be hurt by your actions, but evidently, you don't care," Brian said before stuffing his half-eaten sandwich in the bag.

"Hold up. That's not fair. You didn't give me time to answer the question; and you didn't see the look on my grandmother's face. She believes there are werewolves, and she believes they are dangerous, so don't start preaching your do-good attitude to me. I know you insist there's good in all people, but not all people are good." Jesse could feel the frustration rising from her core, and if she were a cartoon character, steam would have billowed out her ears.

"I'm done. I think it's a stupid idea. But if you're right, and I highly doubt you are, you'd be putting a lot of people in danger, and for what? So you can brag that you discovered the secret of Cloverly? Sorry, but your grandmother isn't the only person who lives here. And to risk the safety of a town because of one person… well, that's just plain selfish." Pushing up from the bench, Brian turned and walked away.

"Wait!" Jesse jumped up from the table and ran over to catch him. "You've had your say, and I listened. Now you're going to listen to me! Despite what you think, I'm not intentionally trying to hurt anyone so don't make me out to be the bad guy here. My grandmother is just one of the elderly residents that knows the secret, and she has feared them long enough. And I admit, I'm confused and I don't have the slightest idea what the hell I'm doing, but know this," she said, placing her hands on her hips, "you may not agree with me, but if there are wolves, I will expose them, and I will protect my grandmother. It really, really sucks that we don't agree, but I guess it's better to know where we stand now than finding out later." She spun on her heels, her hair fanning out as she stomped back to where Lori and Steve sat with stunned expressions.

"I'm sorry. I don't know what came over me," Jesse said. Tears filled her eyes and Lori jumped to her feet and wrapped her in a hug. She was fuming mad and basically told Brian to go to hell, which he deserved for calling her *selfish*. Some boyfriend he turned out to be! If he truly thought that about her, why did he send her flowers? Lowering her chin, she knew her flower receiving days were over.

"What a total bonehead, and to think I actually thought he had half a brain." Lori looked around Jesse and glared.

"Wait up," Steve yelled as he got up from the table. "You know, I've got your back on this one."

"Why does he have to be so damn stubborn?" Jesse asked. She knew by the way Brian stalked off, there was no changing his mind.

"Ignore him," Lori said, packing up their lunch. "We've got wolves to hunt."

# Thirty-Seven

*Jesse*

The week flew by with Jesse and Lori spending most of their time walking around the village, sightseeing, and taking pictures. Being a small town, there weren't many places to look for clues, so hanging out at the cafe was their best option. By the time the weekend rolled around, they were exhausted, frustrated and had pretty much thrown in the towel. Hearing Brian and Steve say, "I told you so," was not an option. They needed to come up with a different plan.

"What about the cameras?" Jesse asked, flopping down on the bed.

"Nope, out of the question. I'm sure Brian's already taken them down, plus, there's no way I'm going into the woods even if he didn't. I think we should just ask around. What's the worst that can happen? It's not like they can throw us in jail for asking stupid questions," Lori said, kicking off her shoes.

"You mean the nut house," Jesse replied, looking over at the closet. "Let's forget about the wolves for a while. If we don't get a move on, we'll be late for the party and Whitney will skin us alive."

Five days, seven hours, and thirty-nine minutes was the amount of time that passed since Jesse and Brian's disagreement at the park. He walked away when she told him what she thought, and because of that, she wasn't sure he would show up at the party. Lori, on the other hand, believed he would be there, but only because of Megan. Finishing up the final touches, Jesse refused to let her argument with Brian ruin the night. Standing back as Lori moved from table to table, lighting candles, Jesse savored the fresh pine and citronella aroma that hung in the air.

She glanced up at the tiny lights, draped between the overhead branches. The twinkling bulbs, set against the dusky sky, cast a soft glow over the yard. The effect was breathtaking. What was once a backyard of pine trees and concrete had been transformed into an outside dining area worthy of a magazine cover. With a makeshift dance floor on the left, and eight, two-chaired tables dotting the grassy area on the right, it was the perfect place for an informal, yet romantic dinner and dancing. She frowned. *So much for romance.*

"You did a fantastic job decorating the yard."

Jesse turned to see to whom the unfamiliar voice belonged. "Hi, I'm Jesse. Are you here for the dance?"

"It's nice to meet you, Jesse. I'm Seth." He bowed his

head and she grinned.

"I've seen you before," she said, admiring the man bun twisted high on the back of his head. It was obvious he had long blonde hair, but how long? She couldn't tell.

"Yes, I know." He flashed a smoldering smile. "It's a beautiful night for a dance."

"That it is." Jesse looked back to see if Lori spotted the new arrival, but she had already gone inside. "Well, it was nice meeting you, Seth, but I need to go before Whitney starts looking for me. So I guess I'll see you later?" The question lingered between them as he looked out over the yard.

"If you promise to save me a dance," he said, and his smile shone in his ash-gray eyes. His playful personality and teasing ways reminded her of Randy, and she could envision them being best friends. From his height to his build, they had a lot in common based on looks alone.

"I'm sure that won't be a problem," she said as she walked toward the back door. He was a natural beauty if a guy could be called such, and his personality fit him to a tee. Always asking questions, never answering, she wondered if he, too, was a player. Imagining what Lori would say, she grinned and pulled open the door.

"See you later," Seth called out as the door shut behind her.

"There you are! We need to hurry and get dressed or we're going to miss the party," Whitney said, jiggling her hips. "I don't know what I'm more excited about, the party or the dress."

"Speaking for myself, the dancing," Jesse said, following Whitney down the short hall to the bedroom. The room felt cozy and her eyes drifted to the quilt-covered bed against the far wall. A hint of cinnamon swirled in the air and she looked up at the ceiling fan. Everything around her was wood. The walls, ceiling, even the furniture was handcrafted and rustically designed. Returning her attention back to Whitney, she asked, "Who is Seth?"

"Ah, that explains the smile when you walked into the kitchen. He's pack," Whitney said as she opened the closet door.

"Duh, are you blind? He's the hunk on the front porch," Lori said, walking into the room. Picking up her dress bag off the bed, she hurried back down the hall.

"Where are you going?" Jesse called after her.

"I have to pee, do you mind?"

Jesse rolled her eyes and shut the door. Lori would say anything, no matter where she was. Leaning over the bed, Jesse unzipped the first bag, exposing a short, sapphire-blue dress. "What did you mean by *pack*?" She looked over her shoulder as she kicked off her shoes.

"We grew up together. When we were little, we made a pact to remain friends forever. You know how silly kids are. The whole clubhouse, no one allowed in without the secret password. But don't worry, Seth is harmless," Whitney said.

"Harmless? I don't think so. It wouldn't take much to get lost in those silvery eyes. I think he could be dangerous in all the right ways." She chuckled at her confession. Slipping out of her clothes, Jesse stepped into the lace-covered dress and pulled it up to her chest before unfastening her bra. She wasn't usually so modest around Lori and Megan, but with Whitney, she wasn't ready to expose her less-than-perfect body. The lace caressed the satin material of the underskirt as she walked over to Whitney and turned, lifting her hair.

"Seth can be quite charming when he wants to be; he's only dangerous to the heart," Whitney said, zipping up the dress.

"Well, for a minute there I thought you meant *wolf* pack." Jesse laughed at Whitney's surprised expression. "If all the wolves in the area looked like him, I'd be happy."

"Oh, I'm sure he can be wolfy when he wants to." Whitney said as she moved across the room to the bed.

"Yeah, I know it sounds crazy."

"I'm not saying that at all. This area is the perfect location for wolves. With the woods and the lakes, I imagine one could see just about anything if they were really looking," Whitney replied as she picked up the empty dress bag, moving it to the side.

"I know, right? Just don't repeat that around Brian or he'll think I've brainwashed you."

"I promise I won't if you show me my dress." Whitney pulled the bag to the edge of the bed.

"Wait!" Jesse said as she hurried across the room. "We have to be careful with this baby. It's a work of art."

Jesse held her hand beneath the zipper as Whitney slowly unzipped the bag. When the bag fell open, white feathers bubbled out, and Whitney sucked in a sharp breath. "It's beautiful!" she said, running her hand over the feathers. "Oh hurry, hurry, hurry! I can't wait to see it on."

Jesse laughed as Whitney hopped around the room, modesty no issue with her. Lifting the dress out of the bag, she unzipped the bodice and held the dress open so Whitney could step into it.

"This is going to be a blast," Jesse said.

Running her fingers over the fancy needlework design, Whitney walked over to the mirror. "How do I look?" she asked, a smile beaming on her face. The antique white dress was perfect against Whitney's dark-olive complexion, and the beaded bodice along with the white-feathered skirt looked very feminine.

"You look beautiful. Mason won't be able to keep his eyes off you." Jesse reached over and smoothed down the skirt.

After putting on their shoes, Jesse followed Whitney through the cabin to where the others were gathering on the front porch. When she walked out the door, she blushed at Seth's wink.

"Hey, beautiful," Brian said, walking over to hug her. Memories of the theater came to mind, and she cut a glance back to Seth. Yeah, he was still staring, which was why Brian was standing at her side. *Men!*

"Hey, yourself." Jesse was glad Brian was there although he seemed a little distant based on the one-armed hug. She brushed it off, fully determined to have a great night.

"Is everyone here?" Lori asked, stepping off the porch. Wearing a knee-length, halter style dress, she twirled, causing the plum-colored skirt to flare out, which made her squeal. Dropping her arms down, her face turned a deep shade of red and Jesse snickered.

"Mrs. Rani, you look amazing," Mason said as he slipped his arm around Whitney's waist. Most women worked hard to obtain grace and beauty, but Whitney had it without even trying. Her tall, slender frame and long, black hair, pulled into a braided bun with a few loose strands framing her face, made everything about her seem perfect.

"Why, Mr. Rani, are you flirting with me?" Whitney giggled behind her hand.

"Now children," Seth teased before being sidetracked by Randy's motorcycle as he turned into the drive.

Watching Randy help Tracy off the bike was quite entertaining. Her stylish red hair stood out against the shimmering gold dress she wore, and whether Jesse liked her or not, she couldn't look away. Tracy loved to be the center of all the attention, and that was exactly what she got. Clearly, she liked the dress, but how she managed to ride on the back of the motorcycle and not show her cooter, was a mystery in itself.

Randy was in seventh heaven, and his smile matched Tracy's as they greeted the group. But when Tracy's eyes zeroed in on the hand resting on Jesse's hip, she frowned. "Where's Tucker?"

"He's in the back setting up the speakers, which is where we need to be," Mason said, walking off the porch. He put his hand out to help Whitney down the step, and everyone followed them around the cabin as Tucker walked out the back door.

"Jack and Megan just turned the corner," Tucker said and his eyes locked onto Jesse. With a dimpled smile, he nodded.

Jesse grinned, but Brian didn't give her a chance to say anything. He grabbed her hand and pulled her over by the back door where the others were waiting. Standing behind the small crowd, she peered around Seth to get a better view. There was something about Tucker that made him stand out. Maybe because he was the only guy there that had actually dressed for the occasion. He wore black slacks and a charcoal gray shirt that shimmered in the dim light. He even pulled his dreads back off his face, which made him even more *striking*.

Tucker lifted his hand to quiet the group as he peeked around the corner of the cabin. Hearing the car door slam, he moved beside Seth. "Ready?"

"Surprise!" They yelled when Jack and Megan rounded the corner.

# Thirty-Eight

*Jesse*

Megan's eyes lit up as she curled into Jack, and he wrapped his arm around her waist. "Did you know about this?"

"I knew they were planning something, but I didn't expect this," Jack said.

Moving under the canopy of lights, a smile graced Megan's face. She looked beautiful standing there in the strapless green dress, and the color matched her eyes. When she stepped out of Jack's arms and turned, the sheer overlay skirt danced against the scalloped hemline, resting mid-thigh. "I can't believe this. It's beyond words." She slowly turned toward her friends. "Thank you."

The food was served and although the tables were evenly spaced apart, somehow over the course of dinner, they were pushed together. Everyone seemed to enjoy the party, except Jesse. It probably had to do with the cold shoulder Brian was giving her since Megan arrived, which made no sense to her at all.

Tucker smiled as he walked over to the neighboring table and Jesse studied him from the corners of her eyes. The thin material of his pants hugged his butt nicely when he pulled out a chair for Sage. *A+ for the view.* Jesse thought, but when he looked her way, she quickly averted her eyes. *Busted!*

Dinner was quiet, or at least it was between Brian and her. By the time the sun had completely set, the tables had been cleared and soft music played in the background. She turned and smiled at Brayden who was sitting with Sage and Nigel.

"Jack, Megan, if you're up to it, the first dance is for you," Tucker said as he reached over and cranked up the volume. The stereo was pre-programmed with a random mix of music and wired to surrounding speakers, carefully concealed in the trees.

"Shall we?" Jack asked as he stood and extended his hand.

"I don't like being the center of attention," Megan replied but followed him across the yard.

"I know, but right now you're their hero." Jack chuckled when she poked him in the ribs. In the middle of the dance floor, he pulled her into his arms, resting his cheek against her head, "You look beautiful tonight."

Jesse smiled as they moved around the dance floor, perfectly in tune with each other. Everyone seemed captivated by the couple as if their presence were something to worship. She elbowed Lori and whispered, "Do you feel that?"

"What?" Lori whispered back.

"The energy in the air." Jesse looked around the yard and rubbed her arms. The darkness that surrounded them would normally have her shaking in her boots, but after what she'd been through, how much worse could it get? Her greatest fear was tested on Hunter's Ridge and in her eyes, she passed the challenge, even though she still felt leery.

She gazed in Tucker's direction. Just being around him was like snuggling with a warm, fuzzy blanket. He was kind and compassionate, the complete opposite of Brian. She never mentioned to Lori or Megan how he helped her overcome her panic attack on Hunter's Ridge. Practically a stranger at the time, he held her until she calmed down and regained her composure. With all the commotion going on, no one noticed him, but she could never forget. It was Tucker that made her realize not everything in the dark was dangerous.

The applause brought her from her musings as Jack and Megan took their seats. Megan fidgeted with the necklace she wore and a slight blush filled her cheeks. Jesse grinned, but what she really wanted was to have a peek at that necklace. It looked vaguely familiar; like the one Jack was wearing the first day they met.

"Are you having a good time?" Jesse asked, trying to strike up a conversation with Brian so Megan wouldn't think she was staring.

"Good enough, I guess."

Jesse sat back in her seat; now it was she who fidgeted. With their argument still hanging over her head, it was childish to let it ruin their night, but clearly, Brian refused to let it go. The secret of Cloverly was probably some old-timer's overactive imagination, but that was something she had to prove to her grandmother. She smiled when Brian looked her way. She missed the closeness she once felt when she was around him, and it just wasn't there at the moment.

She turned toward Tucker who was standing off to the side with his hands clasped behind his back as his chest stretched the seams of his shirt. Jesse noticed the light tap of his foot, but other than that, he stood still as a statue. His eyes scanned the area before coming to rest on her. She wasn't intentionally staring but realizing he had caught her again, she felt guilty as sin. Turning back toward Brian, she frowned at the social butterfly. Now engaged in a conversation with Jack, she wondered if it was his way of avoiding her altogether.

"Would you like to dance?" Tucker asked when he approached the table. She looked up, then over at Brian.

"I don't mind," Brian said over his shoulder. That told Jesse he was paying attention to what was going on, yet purposefully ignoring her in the process.

As she followed Tucker to the dance floor, she looked back, growing annoyed. All afternoon she wondered if Brian would show up for the dance, and when he did, she was excited. Standing on the front porch, he wrapped his arm around her waist, but even that was temporary; it lasted a total of three minutes, tops. It wasn't until they were seated at their table that his mood shifted. Jesse loved to dance, and it was obvious she would have no partner in him.

"I hope I didn't interrupt," Tucker said as he wrapped his arms around her waist.

She looked up. "Brian doesn't really like to dance,"

she said as a slow song played. *Stop making excuses. He's a jerk.*

"Do you?" Tucker held her stare longer than necessary, and she melted beneath his blazing, brown eyes.

"Absolutely." Her voice came out wispy and she took a deep breath, trying to blink away the tingling daze that clouded her mind. As she wrapped her arms around his neck, electricity shot through her body. "What was that?"

"Chemistry." He smiled.

Jesse and Tucker drifted around the dance floor, an unsettling mix of emotions washing over her. She was thrilled to be dancing with him, but confused over what passed between them. Desperate to get closer and savoring the moment, she rested her head against his chest. *You're a pushover.* Ignoring her inner thoughts, she inhaled the wild, woodsy fragrance that wafted around him as her body relaxed against his.

"Snap out of it," Lori said before disappearing behind Tucker.

*Is it that obvious?* The question echoed in her head as if her deepest, darkest desires had been exposed for all to see. Still reeling from the close contact, she didn't notice the song had changed until Tucker twirled her around. Catching her, he pulled her to his chest before dipping her back. Nose to nose, he leaned in and whispered, but she couldn't hear the words over the music.

By the time the song was over, both were exhausted, but neither wanted the dance to end. "I need a drink," Jesse said, hurrying over to the table. After taking a sip of water, she leaned her head back, resting the glass on the side of her neck. The icy chill was a welcome relief from the hot flashes she was experiencing, which were probably due to a summer cold coming on. Offering the glass to Tucker, she watched him drink down the last of the water before placing the glass on the table.

"You want to go again?" His lazy grin drew her in and she smiled.

"I think I do." She slipped off her shoes and tossed them beneath the chair as she took Tucker's hand. Like two kids chasing after an ice cream truck, they ran over and joined the others before the tempo slowed. The soft rhythm moved through her body as she swayed in his arms.

"You're beautiful," Tucker said, and she opened her eyes at the compliment. Comfortable resting against his chest, she noticed Brian glaring her way. She stared back, not trying to piss him off, but did he really expect her to sit on the sidelines all night?

Once the music ended, Tucker walked Jesse to her seat, keeping his hand on her lower back. "Safe and sound," he smirked, aiming his comment at Brian.

Brian seemed unfazed as he turned back toward Jack and Megan. *What the hell?* Jesse wanted to scream, but she refused to make a scene. Frustrated, she got up and walked to the back of the yard, enjoying the cool breeze that blew across the river. It was dark where she stood, and she patted herself on the back for her bravery.

Not expecting Brian, she jumped when he walked up behind her and wrapped his arms around her waist. "Do you want to dance?" he whispered in her ear.

*Is the sky blue?* She looked over her shoulder. She couldn't very well turn him down and then complain because he wouldn't dance with her. But seeing that sourpuss smirk on his face, she did consider it. "Sure," she said, flashing the biggest, goofiest grin she could muster.

Brian actually seemed eager to dance as he led her across the backyard. But his grip was the betraying factor, and that spoke volumes. She wasn't an expert on body language, by no means, but the hold he had on her hand wasn't a flirting maneuver either.

Humiliation settled over her as she joined him on the dance floor, her stomach knotting, and the fleeting thought of faking an ankle injury crossed her mind.

Dancing with Brian differed greatly from dancing with Tucker. At least Tucker was lively and laughed as if he enjoyed her company. Brian was as dry as dust. Proving her point, he didn't seem at all enthused, and the conversation between them was awkward and forced.

Jesse's skin tingled as Tucker flashed her another smile and she smiled back. He looked extremely sexy standing there in the shadows, but she was crushing on him, nothing more.

As the dance went on, Jesse tried to keep a conversation going with Brian. Anything to take her mind off of the big lug that stood guarding the night, but Brian had little to say. She huffed out a breath. She didn't know whether to laugh or cry when she thought about the situation between them. Everything was fine until a few weeks ago when she brought up the wolves. Then everything went to pot. *Maybe he's a wolf.* She glanced up to meet his eyes. "This is nice," she said, hoping he would at least agree, but when he said nothing, she stopped dancing.

"What are you doing?" He narrowed his eyes, clearly embarrassed by the abrupt stop.

"What I'm doing is calling you out for being an ass," she hissed. "You came here for Megan, not as my date. But as soon as another guy takes an interest in me, you decide maybe you made a mistake. Well, I'm nobody's mistake, and if you're looking for a girl that bows to your every whim, you need to look elsewhere. I refuse to let a man tell me what to do, what to think, or what to say. I have a mind of my own; and right now my mind is telling me I don't want to dance with you." She spun around, her hair fanning out, slapping against his chest. Ignoring the confused look on Lori's face, she stomped back to the table.

"I'll get something to drink," Brian said and he hurried to the cabin. But what he was really doing was trying to save face or some crap like that. More macho BS as far as she was concerned.

*Well, look at the bright side; you're right where he wanted you.* Tears rimmed her eyes and she looked down, hoping no one would notice how upset she was. She didn't want a drink. She wanted to have a good time, but Brian ruined that.

Tucker kneeled down and placed his hand on her shoulder, but she didn't look up. "Do I need to take out the boyfriend?"

"No, I'm fine. Just taking a break." She kept her head down, not wanting him to see her eyes. *Who's saving face now?*

Seth cleared his throat as he walked up beside Tucker, kneeing his shoulder. "Ten o'clock."

Tucker looked up and nodded. When he turned back to Jesse, his hand slid down her arm, leaving a trail of warmth that stopped at her fingertips and her body calmed. "If you need anything, Tracy knows how to find me." He stood up and walked away.

Jesse drew in a deep breath as the calming energy spread through her body. She glanced through her hair when Seth looked back over his shoulder. The frown on his face was disturbing, and she wondered if he knew she was lying. *Maybe he's a wolf,* she thought as they disappeared around the cabin. *As if a wolf-man could look that good.* Facing the patio while the others continued dancing, her mind wandered. *What if she were wrong in her thinking? What if the wolves weren't nasty, vile creatures?* She smirked. Even she found that hard to swallow.

"Here you go," Brian said, but she looked away.

When the song ended, Jesse motioned for Whitney and leaned down and grabbed her shoes off the ground. Whitney excused herself and Jesse stood and followed her through the cabin to the front porch. "I'm sorry to pull you away from the party, but I need to leave. I'll come by tomorrow and help you clean up."

"Does this have anything to do with Brian?"

"You noticed?" Jesse looked surprised.

"Yeah, he's been ignoring you most of the night. Look, don't let him get you down. There are plenty of guys that would love to spend the evening with you. I saw the way you and Tucker were laughing. He was having the time of his life, and if you don't want to dance with him, Seth has been keeping a close eye on you as well," she said, "not to mention the others."

Jesse stared down the street. She hadn't noticed any of the others, but it was a shame she wouldn't get the chance to dance with Tucker again. "You know, I wouldn't leave if I didn't absolutely have to, but I need to do this for me. I don't want Tucker to get pulled into the middle of Brian's piss-pot. I know Brian's not jealous, but he's using Tucker to get back at me, and it's just so damn immature."

"I understand, but what am I supposed to tell them when they ask where you are? Tucker will be back in ten minutes and be so disappointed if you leave, especially if he thinks it was because of him."

"Tell Tucker I had a wonderful time and tell the others whatever you want." She sucked her bottom lip between her teeth and blinked back more tears. She swore she would not let Brian ruin her night, and yet, he had.

"Ladies, the party's in the back," Nigel said, interrupting their conversation when he walked out from beside the cabin.

"Nigel, would you walk Jesse home? She's not feeling well," Whitney asked. Jesse knew the excuse was for her benefit, and she wondered if Brian would use it as a reason to stop by and check on her. But after telling him off, twice, she wasn't about to hold her breath.

"Sure. Are you leaving now?"

"Yes." Jesse hugged Whitney and then she and Nigel walked across the yard.

Whitney's cabin was just down from Jack's, but the road itself was dark, so Jesse was glad to have a chaperone. Cutting across Jack's yard, the breeze kicked up and a shiver prickled her skin. She had an eerie feeling she was being watched, but with Nigel beside her, she pushed the suspicion out of her mind. "Thank you for walking me home."

"Not a problem." He nodded and waited until she was inside before he turned to leave.

Jesse walked over to the refrigerator and took out a can of soda. Standing next to the sink, she sipped the grape cola as Nigel walked back across the yard.

Nigel was nice looking, a little older than the others, about thirty-five, she guessed. He had grayish green eyes, an odd color she had never seen before, and dusty blonde hair that touched his shoulders. He was somewhat tall but lean, and seemed friendly enough. Once he was out of sight, she put her soda back in the fridge and went upstairs.

*Well, isn't this an unusual turn of events?* Jesse snarled at seeing her image in the mirror. She wasn't one to leave a party early, especially if there was dancing, yet there she stood. She should have ignored Brian and danced with the other guys, but she was tired of kissing up to him in order for him to acknowledge her.

She changed into her favorite worn t-shirt, and crawled into bed, trying not to think about the party. She pulled the curtain back as the night air drifted across the room and stared out the window. The music carried on the breeze and she dropped the curtain and rolled over on the bed, thinking back to the conversation she had with her grandmother. She didn't really believe the werewolf story, even if there were wolves in the area. The Loch Ness monster and Sasquatch had attracted a large following through the years, but neither had ever been proven true. She shivered and pulled the sheet up to her chin. *It's just a myth. They're not real.* And that was exactly what she intended to prove.

# Thirty-Nine

*Tracy*

"I'm in here," Tracy yelled from the sofa when Randy walked up on the porch. With her feet propped up on pillows and ice packs strapped around her ankles, she wasn't about to get up. After a night of dancing in heels, her ankles throbbed, her toes ached, and her feet were swollen.

"Hey, sexy she-wolf…" Randy sang as he strutted through the door. He shuffled his feet and spun around, then dropped to his knees in front of her.

"Stop! Don't remind me," Tracy said, putting her arm over her eyes. "If I never dance again…."

Randy laughed. "I told you not to wear the stilts, but would you listen? Nooooo," he said, placing his helmet on the floor.

"I listened," she said when he went into the kitchen. "I

thought you had to work today?" She couldn't keep the
grin off her face when he walked back into the room. He
was so damn good-looking, she didn't know whether to
lick him or kiss him. Either one sounded pretty frickin'
fabulous.

"I did, the day is about over," he said, handing Tracy a
cup of coffee. With a quick peck on the top of her head, he
grabbed the pillows out from beneath her feet and tossed
them to the corner chair. Sitting down at the end of the
sofa, he placed her feet in his lap.

"What are you doing?" Tracy complained as she
placed her mug on the small side-table.

"I'm gonna make your feet happy." He sat back and
rubbed the sole of her foot. A little pressure here, a light
touch there, then he switched to the other foot.

"Oh, that tickles, but feels so good." She laughed, her
head hanging back over the arm of the sofa as her nails
dug into the cushion. "Like I died and went to heaven."

"Yeah, I have that effect on women." He smirked.

"Well, you had best forget about those females, or this
one will hog-tie your ass and..." Her head jerked around.
"What are you doing? You can't just bust in here like you
own the place," Tracy yelled as she jumped off the sofa.
The ice packs that were strapped around her ankles flew
through the air and landed on the opposite side of the
room.

Randy jumped too when the door banged against the
wall. He didn't know who the dark-haired woman was
standing in the doorway, but she looked like a bull ready
to charge.

"It doesn't look like you can stop me," Vivian sneered.
"Travis had a foolproof plan, and you blew it. Do you

know where I've spent the past several nights while you're lying up with this... this... human?"

"Whoa there, nelly," Randy said as he stood up to confront the ill-mannered woman. "I don't know who you are, but don't talk about me like I'm a piece of shit on the bottom of your shoe." Moving over beside Tracy, he narrowed his eyes.

"Sit down and shut-up. This is between me and her," Vivian growled.

"Oh, no you don't." Tracy glared and stepped forward. "In my house, you will show respect," she warned. She understood why her aunt was pissed because she, too, had been brainwashed by Travis, but if Viv thought for one minute she could come in and attack Randy, she was deadly mistaken.

"Respect? As if you know what that means! You are nothing but a spoiled brat. Always getting everything you want, having it your way. Do you know what I went through because of you? No, because you are a self-centered, useless female. But today it stops. I've done nothing but support you and Travis, and now it is me who has to pay? I don't think so. You are a traitor, and that is punishable by death."

"Whoa, whoa, whoa!" Randy said, raising his hands to ward off the raging bull as he stepped in front of Tracy. "You'll have to go through me first."

"Is that a challenge?" Vivian smiled.

"Call it what you want." He smiled back.

Tracy bit the side of her jaw to keep a straight face. Randy stood tall and tense, and if she didn't know better, he could have probably handled the old hag. But she wasn't about to let it come to that. It was her life and her mess to clean up. She started by telling Jack the truth, and she would finish the mission by taking out the trash.

"Spoiled? Self-centered? That's what you think of me?" Tracy stepped out from behind Randy. "The little girl that wanted to play with the others, but was told she couldn't because they were half-bloods?" She walked up to Vivian. "Or the little girl that cried herself to sleep because nobody loved her?" She circled behind her. The loathing she harbored for the woman that raised her was evident on her face. "Or maybe it was the teenager that tried to escape the hell-hole she lived in, only to be caught and locked in her room for a month. Alone! Should I go on?" Anger seeped from her core as she stopped in front of Vivian, but there was no reply. "Yeah, that's what I thought. I lived through hell, and now you have the audacity to call me a spoiled brat? Well, guess what? Karma's a bitch," Tracy said, taking a step back, and trying not to lose control of her wolf.

"Oh, poor Tracy, so mistreated. You're pathetic. We should have kept you locked in that damn room. I knew you would be trouble," Vivian spat.

"Your plan backfired. Deal with it. Alpha Cooper is a good man no matter how much you deny it. But you are right about one thing. I *am* trouble, and you have five seconds to get the hell out of my house or I will put you out." Tracy felt a hand rest on her shoulder and she knew Randy was there to back her up. "One... two... three..."

Vivian's laugh turned to a snarl, and Tracy flashed a warning glare. *Surely she wouldn't shift in front of Randy.* Or at least, she hoped she wouldn't. The cabin was small, and there was no way to keep Randy safe if she attacked. She narrowed her eyes as Vivian stepped forward, and

Randy grabbed his helmet off the floor and hurled it across the room, hitting Vivian in the head. He winced when her body crumpled to the floor.

"Oh, shit! Did I kill her?" he asked, turning to Tracy. "I didn't mean to hurt her. I just didn't want her to hurt you." He shook his head. "I've never hit a girl before."

"Oh, you've done it now," Tracy said, seeing Vivian sprawled out in an un-ladylike manner. "You're in trooouble." She had never seen a werewolf taken down by a human, and she couldn't help but laugh. "I can't believe you just did that. Come on, we need to go or else there will be hell to pay when she wakes up."

"I didn't mean to hurt her. She was just..."

"Never mind that, we need to go. It's about to get real hairy." She giggled at the pun.

"We can't leave her there. What if she's hurt, like really hurt... or even dead?"

Tracy could hear the concern in his voice, but it wasn't necessary. "Trust me, she's a wolf and in a matter of minutes, she will heal, so we need to go."

"But she's bleeding," he said, looking down at the floor.

"I've seen more blood from a hangnail," Tracy said, pulling him out the door. She wasn't afraid to stay and fight; she knew Vivian wasn't a threat to her. But if Viv attacked Randy, her wolf would have to take her out. The anger was in place; all her wolf needed was a reason.

"Where are we going?" Randy asked as he followed her across the yard.

"We need to find Jack. I think he's at Megan's house. Do you know where she lives?"

Randy straddled the bike and turned the key. Within

ten minutes, they were pulling up in front of Megan's house. Standing at the side yard next to the shrub line, Seth turned, hearing his name. "Where's Jack?" Tracy yelled as she ran towards him.

"He's in the house, what's wrong?"

"It's Vivian; she tried to attack me at the cabin."

"Where is she now?" Jack asked, coming across the yard.

"When we left, she was on the floor by the front door. I didn't want to wait around for her to wake up. I was afraid she would attack Randy."

"Why?" Jack asked, confused.

"Because he knocked her out," Tracy said before she laughed. "I told her to leave... when she started to phase, he hit her with his helmet."

"Wait here," Jack ordered, and he and Seth took off down the road.

Tracy knew Randy would go back to the cabin to ease his mind, and as she pushed open the back door, she paused. *He defended you against a crazed she-wolf. Without question.* As the motorcycle roared down the road, she sighed. Randy may not have been a wolf, but in her eyes, he was an alpha.

Thirty-five minutes later, the motorcycle pulled into the drive and she ran out the back door. "Did you find her?" Tracy asked when Jack climbed off the back of the bike.

"No, she was already gone. Seth is with Mason and Tucker, they're checking the area," Jack said. "And what's this?" He nodded towards Randy who was walking up behind him. "I said to wait here."

"Hey, I saw you naked. I promise, you needed my

help," Randy said. Walking past Jack, he chuckled and put his arm around Tracy, leading her back into the house.

Jack grinned and followed them into the kitchen where Sage and Megan were waiting. "I don't think it's safe for you to stay at the cabin. Not until we find Vivian and Travis." Jack looked over at Tracy. "I'll contact Alpha Cooper and find out what he wants to do. Until then, you can't go home."

Tracy looked through the sliding glass doors and stared out at the pool, her stomach flip-flopping with what she knew would come next.

"I think you should stay at the pack house," Jack said.

"But... can't I stay with Whit?" She looked down at the concrete patio and blinked back tears.

"It's too dangerous. You know Travis will watch the cabins," Jack said. Tracy rested her forehead against the glass.

"Fine." But the thought of going back to pack grounds even for a day was not something Tracy wanted to think about. She loved living in Cloverly, and now that she and Randy shared a bond, she felt like she was losing him.

"Why can't you stay with me?" Randy asked and she looked back. "I think it's time you met my parents. If we're together and we share a bond, you need to get used to being around my family."

"But will they let me stay there?" she asked, bracing herself for a letdown.

"I guess if you want to stay with them, they might, but I have my own place."

"Wait a minute. If you don't know where he lives, it's safe to say Travis and Vivian don't either," Jack said, looking between the two. "It's a good idea. I think you'd be safe there. I'll have Mason and Whitney meet you at the cabin so you can get some clothes, then you and Randy need to go to his house as soon as possible and stay there." Jack narrowed his eyes at Randy.

"I won't let anything happen to her. I'll protect her with my life," Randy said, and Tracy knew by the look in his eyes that he would protect her, or die trying.

# Forty

*Tracy*

It was just after nightfall when Tracy and Randy crossed the grassy field behind his parents' house. The smell of straw and manure filled her nose, and she looked over the acres, noticing the old weathered barn where she and Randy spent their first night together. She smiled. "Your parents are really nice, I like them a lot," she said. Her eyes skimmed across the lake to the yellow porch light that lit the white cottage Randy called home. The house sat at the back of the property, facing the lake, which separated his house from his parents. The barn was off to the right, on the far side of the field, and security lights hung from wooden poles, randomly spaced about the farm, lighting the area.

"Well, I know firsthand they were taken with you. It's not every day Mom winks her approval." Randy looked down, and she blushed. "And I'm not sure, but I think I have competition. Oliver has a crush on you." Randy's nephew took up with Tracy the minute she walked through the door. The rambunctious three-year-old clung to her side, even sitting between them on the couch.

Tracy swatted Randy before wrapping her arm around his waist. "Yeah, he was adorable. One day I'll have my own little Oliver." She smiled, but sadness glimmered in her eyes.

"What's wrong?" Randy asked, pulling her to a stop. Wrapping his arms around her, she looked down to hide the tears that welled in her eyes. "Was it something I said?"

"No, it's nothing. I was just thinking." A good cry was what she needed, but she wasn't the type to show weakness. Her exterior shell was as tough as steel, and although she could feel him breaking it down, she still struggled to keep it in place.

"It's something or you wouldn't be teary-eyed. You can talk to me. We do share a bond," he said, kissing her hair.

"I guess, meeting your family, they were exactly what I pictured a family would be like. The way your dad smiled at your mom and Oliver bounced around, trying to get everyone's attention. It felt real, and right. See? Now I'm rambling." She exhaled a breath that lifted the stray strands of hair off her face. "I miss my parents so much. I was only four when they died but I still remember the way Mom used to braid my hair, and Dad too, he was the strict one. I never wanted to cross him. But they loved me and I loved them. I still dream about them from time to time. What it would be like if they were still here. I grew up with a pack family, but it's not the same." The last part came out as a whisper, and she closed her eyes and turned away.

"I'm sorry." He pulled her to his chest. "Tracy, I would trade my life to give you back your parents, if that would take the sadness from your eyes. But life doesn't work that way," he said, and she opened her eyes, staring at the lake. "Nothing can replace what you've lost, but I can make you happy." She looked up. "You picked me to share a bond, now I pick you to share my name. Marry me, Tracy! Let *me* be your family."

The grit of his voice sent butterflies to her belly, and she melted against him. *Marry me?* She knew eventually it would come to that, but she wasn't expecting it so soon. She lifted her hand to his cheek, rubbing her thumb across his bottom lip. He pleaded in silence as she stared into his eyes, his emotions clearly etched on his face. *Could it be that simple?* "You want to marry me?" she asked.

"Of course I do. I love you." Wiping a tear from her cheek, he smiled. "I know we have a bond and for a wolf, that's major, but I'm human, and I want you to have my last name." His eyes held the promise that he would always love her, and knowing that made her heart flutter. Her breathing increased, matching his, and he leaned closer, his scent mixing with hers. The desperation in his kiss sent her pulse spiraling out of control and she held tightly around his neck. Her body trembled and she closed her eyes as the last of her shield crumbled. Randy was everything she knew she could never have, yet there he was, holding her as if she were the most valuable asset in his life. Feeling dizzy, she pulled out of the kiss, but his arms stayed locked around her waist.

"I love you, too." A soft growl formed in her throat as her wolf wordlessly approved. Her heart exploded with happiness, and the thought of him loving her was the most amazing feeling in the world.

"So... is that a yes?" he quirked a brow.

"Yes!" Tracy said as he captured her mouth in an earth-shattering kiss that curled her toes. When he pulled away to draw in a breath, she whimpered.

"Come on, let's get you settled." Randy hugged her against his side as they continued toward the cottage. "Are you hungry?" he asked, pushing open the front door.

"I'm starved," she said as she walked into the house. The open floor plan made the house seem larger than it was, which was roomier than her cabin. "You have a nice place." She looked up at the loft. "Do you paint?" Somewhat surprised by the unfinished painting resting on an easel, she grinned.

"Yeah, every once in a while, but I'm no Picasso," he said, walking over to the kitchen. "Go ahead, make yourself at home and I'll fix us something to eat." *Home.* She liked the sound of that.

She slowly walked up the stairs, her eyes taking in every detail. Looking out over the banister, she admired his backside as he moved around the kitchen. *Yeah, you are a perve.* Her thoughts made her giggle and she turned and stared at the painting. It was a picture of a dark-haired girl sitting by the lake, a very pretty girl. Tracy continued looking around as she made her way back down the stairs. Wrapping her arms around his waist, she savored his scent. "Something smells good," she said over his shoulder.

"I hope you like spaghetti," he replied and she grinned.

"I was referring to you, but spaghetti works too," she

purred in his ear and he shook from the shiver. Tracy set the table while Randy took the garlic bread out of the oven. Once everything was in place, she sat down and waited for him to join her.

"One more thing," he said, placing a candle in the center of the table. "Our first meal deserves a candle." Knowing she would see his smile every day for the rest of her life made her heart zing.

As he served the food, he talked about growing up on the farm and Tracy felt content being there with him, listening to the stories. Finally, working up the nerve to ask the question that kept lingering on her mind; she leaned in on her elbows. "Who is the girl in the painting? Should I be jealous?" She secretly hoped it wasn't an old girlfriend, but as gorgeous as he was, she wouldn't rule it out.

"Don't tell me you're afraid my sister will steal me away from you! You know there are laws against such things." He laughed when she blushed and hid behind her hands.

"Oh, aren't you the funny one," she said, peeking between her fingers. She had smiled more in the last twenty-four hours than she had for her entire life and it was all because of the wonderful man that shared a bond with her. She loved the way his eyes lit up when he talked about his family and the way he rolled his bottom lip when he was deep in thought. Who was she kidding? She loved everything about him, but his laughter made her weak in the knees. *He's perfect.* A knock at the door caused her to jump.

"Stay back, I'll get it." Randy made his way across the room with Tracy right behind him. "Can I help you?" he said, moving his body to block the view of the man standing on the small slab porch.

"I'm Ben Cooper. Could I speak with Tracy, please?"

"Alpha Cooper, come in," Tracy called out from behind Randy.

Randy paused before stepping to the side to let the man enter. "Randy, this is Jack's dad, Alpha Cooper." Tracy introduced them before taking her place at Randy's side.

"It's nice to meet you, Randy, and welcome to the pack," he said, extending his hand. "I don't have much time but I wanted to stop by and make sure Tracy was safe, and I can see that you are. Thank you for agreeing to let her stay here. If there's anything you need, just ask."

"We're fine. We were having dinner. Can you join us?" Randy asked.

"I'm really in a hurry," Alpha Cooper said, looking over at Tracy. "On second thought, I would love to."

Randy grinned as Tracy hurried over to the cabinet and pulled out another plate. "You have company, I'll get it," he said and kissed her cheek.

The evening went well, and Tracy was surprised at how relaxed she felt around the alpha. Never in a million years could she have imagined the alpha sitting at Randy's table, having a meal with them. He was a busy man, yet he made time for her. Travis was so wrong, she wanted to say, but she refused to ruin the moment by speaking of someone so undeserving.

"Tracy, I know things have been hard for you over the years, but I want you to know that we appreciate everything you've done for us. You are a part of the pack family and we will protect you. You have my word," Ben said.

She smiled and a tear slipped down her cheek. "Thank you, it means more than you know." Feeling a slight brush against her leg, she looked over at the smile on Randy's face.

Alpha Cooper pushed his chair back and stood. "Never doubt your place in the pack. You are my family," he said, pulling Tracy into a hug.

Randy snickered when Tracy escorted the alpha to his truck later that night. When he pulled out of the drive, she waved until he was out of sight before turning back to the house.

"What's so funny?" Tracy asked, smiling at the silly smirk she saw on Randy's face. She would never in a million years get tired of seeing that smirk.

"You're what's funny. You've guarded your heart from people for so long that you don't realize how many people actually care about you. You're not the person Travis tried to make you out to be. You may not be able to see past that, but it looks like everyone else can. Tracy, there are plenty of people that love you. You just need to accept that and trust not everyone is out to get you." He stared into her eyes as he closed the door behind them.

"It's not easy for me, but I know they love me. Why else would they put up with my crap for all those years?" She loved how Randy made her feel like a princess, making her very own fairytale come true.

"Because they see the same thing I see when I look at you," he said, lightly brushing his lips across hers.

"And what do you see?" she asked, her eyes misting. Staring at his face, she noticed the slight upturn of his lips.

"I see one hot, sexy hog mama." He jumped when she

slapped at him.

"You did not say that," she yelled as he darted up the stairs. "You and Tucker are in sooooo much trouble. Wait 'til I get my hands on you." She raced after him.

"Promises, promises..." he yelled back, his laughter echoing through the house.

# Forty-One

*Jesse*

Jesse watched out her back bedroom window as Seth fired up the grill. If she hadn't humiliated herself, she would have invited herself over, but after the way she left the dance, she wasn't sure they would appreciate her crashing the party. She inhaled the smoke from the grill when it drifted up to her window, reminding her of the cookouts her dad used to have in Indy.

She hated to admit it, but she was missing their studio apartment and the neighbors that lived across from them. Located in the business district, it was noisy day and night with all the traffic in the area. But even that was better than constantly feeling like someone was trying to beat you down, and that was how she felt about Brian at the moment.

So what if she wanted to uncover the secret of

Cloverly? What boyfriend wouldn't be supportive or at least, chalk it up as silly girl stuff? But to get angry over the mere mention of it? That wasn't right. She frowned and looked down as Whitney carried a large bowl out the back door. Whitney was nothing but nice to her since their meeting at the theater and she hoped she wouldn't hold it against her, now that she had ruined her party. "Jesse?" she heard as she reached up to close the curtain. Leaning down to the screen, she waved.

"Can you join us?"

Jesse fidgeted, but Whitney was smiling, and so was Seth. Apparently, they weren't pissed after all. "I'll be down in a minute," Jesse yelled back.

Twenty minutes later, Jesse walked across the backyard, carrying a pan of fresh baked brownies. "Speak of the devil," she heard Seth say.

"I don't think the devil is what you see when you look at her. I saw you Saturday night. I'm just glad Brian wasn't paying attention."

"Damn, Whitney, do you have to be so blunt? You embarrass me sometimes." Seth chuckled. "But I'm not the person Brian needs to worry about," he said as he flipped the steaks and the grilled aroma carried in the evening air.

"Care to share?" Whitney asked, leaning toward him.

"Guys, I'm right here," Jesse said and her face held a slight blush.

"Nope, I gave my word." Seth checked the fire before looking back at Whitney. "Jesse knows I like her... as a friend, unfortunately. But I like any female that has meat on her bones."

"You mean curvy females." Whitney grinned and turned toward Jesse. "I'm glad you could join us. Seth is

.  S.  TODD

grilling steaks."

"Why else would I be here? I smelled the grill as soon as you lit it. My room smells delicious."

"Smoke follows beauty," Seth said over his shoulder as he sprinkled pepper over the meat. "I hope you're hungry. There's plenty."

Holding up the pan of brownies, Jesse smiled. "Here's my contribution."

"And she brings chocolate! Why couldn't I have met you first?" Seth grabbed a brownie and took a large bite. "Damn, I'm glad Tucker's not here. Brownies are his favorite."

"I'll keep that in mind," Jesse said, following Whitney over to the table. Placing the pan beside a bowl of freshly cut cantaloupe, the sweet smelling fruit made her mouth water.

"Here, have a taste, is it ripe enough?" Whitney handed her a toothpick and Jesse speared a chunk.

"Perfect," Jesse said as she looked around the yard. The thought of sitting on Jack's patio two weeks ago would have caused her grandmother to cringe. But since he had rescued Megan, her feelings towards the seasonal tenant had changed. Sending Jesse over with a pan of fresh-baked brownies was her grandmother's way of being neighborly.

Relaxing back in the chair, Jesse glanced up at the darkening sky. So many things had changed since moving to Cloverly. Her paradise was tainted with a secret that could destroy the town. *To believe that, means you believe werewolves are real.* She pushed the idea out of her head. It was probably an extension of the Sallee's Rock lore and believing in the hillbilly beast, her imagination didn't stretch that far. She looked over and smiled when she noticed Whitney watching her.

"You've been on my mind these past few days," Whitney said.

"Oh?"

"I consider you a good friend and I worried about you after what happened with Brian. Did you get things straightened out?"

"No. Actually, I haven't talked to him since the party." Jesse shrugged.

"What do you mean, you haven't talked to him? I told everyone you left because you weren't feeling well. I was trying to do him a favor by giving him a reason to stop by and check on you." Whitney shook her head as she stared across the yard.

"He was only there for Megan. And considering I wasn't sure he'd show up, it is what it is."

"Well, if it makes you feel any better, he seemed miserable after you left."

"I don't think he was miserable, just embarrassed. He was being a jerk," Jesse said. "I had a great time, by the way."

"Yeah, I wished you'd stayed longer. There wasn't much dancing after you left. We mostly sat around and talked."

"Well, I would love to blame it all on Brian, but honestly, I wasn't feeling good. Maybe hay fever or a summer cold. My head was fuzzy most of the night, and hot flashes like you wouldn't believe."

"Are you all right now?"

"I'm fine. Nothing a good night's sleep couldn't cure."

"Whit, could you bring me that jug of water?" Seth

"I'll get it." Jesse took the pitcher of water over to Seth as flames shot up through the grate, illuminating the smooth lines of his face. He really was a good-looking guy, and she loved the way his hair was braided, hanging down his back.

Looking past Seth, to the woods, Jesse didn't feel the familiar shiver that normally followed because she refused to let the darkness control her. She should have been terrified, knowing what she did, but she wasn't the weakling Brian made her out to be, and still had every intention of proving that to him. She was on a mission, and if it meant she had to get up close and personal with the darkness, she would. "It's awful quiet tonight. Where is everyone?" Jesse asked, walking back to the table.

"Well, we all know where Jack is." Whitney chuckled. "And Tucker could be anywhere. I think Tracy and Randy are together, and Mason had to run an errand for Jack. He should be here soon." Whitney moved her chair around, making room for Seth. "Those look delicious," she said when he set the tray of steaks on the table.

"We have salad, bread, and cantaloupe if you like," Seth said, handing Jesse a plate. Taking a seat between them, he filled his plate before adding a couple chunks of cantaloupe to Jesse's.

"This steak is really good! Too bad the others missed out," Whitney said between bites.

"I'm glad you like it." Seth smiled as he glanced over at Jesse.

The three talked and laughed over the silliest things as the night went on, something Jesse missed. Other than Lori, she had no one to hang out with, so spending time with them was extra nice. After what turned out to be a pleasant meal and great company, she completely forgot about her problems with Brian. "Seth, thank you for supper," she said before placing the plate back on the table.

"There's more if you want seconds," he said, adding more salad to his plate.

"No, I'm stuffed. I couldn't eat another bite."

"So this is what goes on when I leave for a few hours!" The scowl on Mason's face caused them all to laugh, and he smiled. "Please tell me you saved some scraps. I'm starving."

"There's plenty," Whitney said, pushing out the chair between Jesse and her.

"Hey, Jesse," Mason said, reaching for the plate Seth held out to him. "What are we celebrating?"

"Nothing, we just wanted to entertain the neighbor." Seth winked.

Jesse chuckled, knowing with Mason there, the cuttin'-up would probably start over again. She sucked in her jaws, trying to work out the ache as she glanced around the table.

"I'm glad I got here before Tucker," Mason said as he filled his plate and grabbed a brownie.

"He'd better show up. It was his idea," Seth said, and Jesse grabbed a napkin, wiping her mouth to cover her grin. Her heart raced at the thought of seeing Tucker again, and she hoped the others didn't notice.

"It'll be awhile yet, he's with Gina," Mason said as he grabbed a piece of cantaloupe from the bowl and popped it into his mouth—Whitney swatted his hand. "What?"

"Use a fork, mister," she scolded.

Jesse struggled to keep her disappointment from showing as the others continued talking. Tucker hadn't mentioned a girlfriend when he was flirting with her at the dance, not that she expected him to. But then again, Gina could be his sister for all she knew so she would leave it at that. Plus, Brian was still her boyfriend, maybe, and Tucker was someone she had only met twice. Other than dancing, they probably had nothing more in common, or so she surmised. "So, Seth, did you enjoy the dance?" Jesse asked, pushing Tucker to the back of her mind.

"Well, I would have enjoyed it more if Tucker had let me dance with you."

Mason coughed and jumped out of the chair before Whitney followed him across the patio, pounding on his back. "Are you all right?" she asked, and he nodded.

"Damn, don't do that to me." Mason looked over at Seth as he sat back down in the chair.

"All I said was Tucker wouldn't let me dance with her."

Mason dropped his head and looked up through thick lashes and chuckled. \

Jesse expected Mason would have a comeback, but considering he was still hacking up a lung, she giggled, which didn't help him any. "All you had to do was ask," Jesse said, glancing between the two snickering fools. "I doubt Tucker would have cared."

"Yeah, about that..." Seth looked over at Mason and they both laughed again.

"You two behave," Whitney warned as she pushed back her chair. "Would you like help cleaning up?"

"No, this was my treat."

"Well, then if you all don't mind, I have a date tonight," Whitney said, bumping her hip against Mason's shoulder. "Jesse, we need to do this again. It was fun."

Jesse agreed and shortly after Whitney and Mason took off down the road, she looked over at Seth. "I hate to eat and run, but it's past my bedtime." She chuckled. "Thanks for the steak, it was delicious."

"Do you have to leave? The radio plays loud, and the patio is just the right size for dancing."

Jesse closed her eyes for a minute and rested her head against the back of the chair. The warm breeze felt good against her skin as she listened to the crickets and tree frogs, reminding her that summer was upon them. Then she thought about Brian and mentally slapped herself. *He's not worried about you. Get that through your head.* It was hit-and-miss between them for over a week, but somewhere in the back of her mind, she thought he would eventually come around. "No, I don't think my feet could handle another night of dancing right now but thank you for asking." She pushed back her chair and set her plate on top of the others.

"Well, at least let me walk you home." Seth took the remaining steaks off the grill. "Tucker likes his well done."

"You really think he's going to show up tonight?"

"He'll be here and probably feel disappointed he missed you. I can't wait to rub it in," Seth said as he set the tray of steaks on the table.

"Rub it in all you want, but make sure you save him at least two brownies."

"Yes, Mother, but I can't guarantee any more than that," Seth teased as they walked across the yard.

Jesse was glad she crashed their cookout; it was the

best night she'd had in a long time. Being able to relax and laugh, or just enjoy the company was nice for a change. Lost in thought, a peaceful silence settled between them until she stepped up on the porch.

"Would you have lunch with me tomorrow? I hear the cafe has great food, but I'd rather not go alone," Seth said once they were standing under the porch light.

Seeing the silver flecks sparkling in his eyes reminded her of a child on Christmas morning. How could she say no? Not that she trusted those mischievous eyes, she didn't. He and Randy had a lot in common, well, everything except for the hair. He even had the same flirty nature, which made her believe he was a player. "Sure. I'll meet you here when the siren sounds."

It was half past noon when Seth and Jesse walked into the cafe, the brass bell announcing their arrival. "Let's sit over here." Jesse motioned to the red padded bar stools that lined the counter. She didn't like sitting on the stools, but she didn't want to give anyone the impression that their lunch date was anything more than two friends. Taking a seat, she grinned as the waitress did a double take when Seth walked past. He didn't notice her though. He was too busy looking back at the bell.

Once Seth took his seat, the waitress came over and pulled the order pad from her pocket. "Hi, I'm Mallory. What can I get for y'all today?" she asked both of them, but quickly kept her attention fastened on Seth.

Jesse looked up at the overhead menu to block out the drooling. Mallory was charming, but her crushing on Seth had his ego expanding tenfold. She wasn't a slim girl, like the other waitresses that worked at the cafe, but he still seemed taken by her.

"What would you suggest?" Seth asked, his voice sounding raspy.

"Country fried steak. It's delicious," Mallory replied as she bit down on her pen.

"It sounds delicious. Thank you." He winked, and she grinned from ear to ear.

Jesse cleared her throat, drawing Mallory's attention away from Seth. "I'll have a tuna sandwich and sweet tea, please." After Mallory walked away, Jesse pulled a few napkins from the dispenser and swatted Seth on the arm. "Here, I think you'll need these." It didn't take long for him to figure out what she was talking about, and he snickered.

"Sorry," he said, chewing on his fingernail—a rosy hue coloring his cheeks.

"No, you're not," Jesse replied and his blush deepened. It was adorable watching him trying not to stare at Mallory, but his eyes kept drifting her way.

The cafe was busy for a Thursday afternoon, a clear indication that the food was good. "This is a nice, little place. I see why the locals like it," he said as Mallory answered the yellow rotary phone that hung on the wall across from them. Pulling a pencil from behind her ear, she quickly jotted down an order.

When Mallory returned with their meal, Jesse had to look away. The girl was totally crushing now, and Seth was eating it up. She coughed into a napkin to cover her laugh. Watching them flirt with each other, Jesse wondered if she looked as awkward when she first met Brian. *Of course you did.* "So... you're not from around here? I mean, you mentioned the locals as if you weren't,"

Jesse said.

"I live on the other side of the river near Danbury, at the edge of the county." Seth glanced up as Mallory emptied the coffee pot.

"Then you're not from out of town, you've just never been to Cloverly before?"

"Well, technically I'm from another town, but in the same county." He laughed. "I've been here, just never at the cafe. Usually, I'm just passing through."

"So how do you know Tucker? Are you friends, family, co-workers perhaps?" Jesse asked.

"I haven't known him as long as I've known Whitney, but long enough that he's one of my best friends. What about you?" Seth wiped his mouth with a napkin before placing it beside his plate.

"I don't really know him." Jesse shrugged and picked up her sandwich.

"I find that hard to believe. You seemed pretty comfortable with him at the dance, yet you were there with Brian. Imagine that." His mischievous grin made her squirm and she shook her head as she swallowed her food.

"Don't bother. I know what you're thinking and that's not the case. Tucker's a great dancer and I love to dance. That's it," Jesse said.

Seth leaned against her shoulder and grinned. "And what I heard was 'I loved dancing with Tucker'."

She could feel the heat moving up her neck as he waggled his brows. "Oh, no! I'm not falling for that pretty boy smile of yours. I'm not telling you I loved dancing with Tucker so you can run back and tell him! I know how guys are. You pretend to be all macho and grunt while you compare muscles, but in reality, you guys gossip worse than girls. You're probably his wingman, sent to do the dirty work." She pushed back against him. "I can hear it now, 'She said you're funny and sweet and yummy'," her voice cracked as she tried to mimic his.

He laughed.

"No! Do not tell him I said that or I'll skin you alive!" She wanted to crawl under the counter after the embarrassing display. That was until Mallory walked over and asked if they needed anything else. Jesse considered playing matchmaker between the two of them, but then something else came to mind. She smiled wickedly. "You know, I bet Mallory would take a shine to Tucker. I mean, he is the most gorgeous man to walk the face of the earth." Placing her finger against her lip, she glanced over at Mallory who was waiting on another customer. "Yeah, I bet when she finds out you're married, her interest in you will drop like a hotcake."

"That's cruel. I can't believe you would do that to me." He looked over at Mallory and then back at Jesse. She winked. "Okay, you win. I promise I won't say anything to Tucker about you if you promise not to spread tales about me."

By the time they left the cafe, Jesse's nerves were finally settled. Seth was a sly one, that much was clear. She wanted to know more about Tucker, not to date him, although that thought had also crossed her mind. She blamed it on Brian. Even Seth noticed the cold shoulder Brian gave her at the dance, and for a guy, that was huge. As they strolled down Main Street, she wanted to reach over and knock the silly smirk off his face. It was obvious he knew something she didn't, but she didn't dare ask any more questions.

# Forty-Two

*Jesse*

Another Friday night found Jesse staring out the window as she waited for Brian to get home. He was working extra hours at the station and she figured it was his way of avoiding her. Maybe he was embarrassed by her plan to expose the wolves *because that doesn't sound crazy at all.* She wanted to take his side; and had it not been for her grandmother, she might have. That was the problem. If she had dropped the whole wolf thing in the beginning when Brian said it was a stupid idea, she wouldn't be sitting there alone, of that she was sure. But pride cometh before a fall and their relationship had fallen about as far as it could without hitting rock bottom.

Frustrated and a little annoyed, she flicked her pencil across the desk and closed her notebook. Her days and nights seemed to mesh together. She was spending most of her time working at the shelter or hanging out with her sewing machine. She had no luck uncovering the secret or anything wolf-related and at the moment, she didn't care.

Turning out the light, she crawled into bed and yelled for Moose. "Come on, boy. I know you love me." She pulled the cat up on the pillow as she reached over and pushed the curtain to the side. It was nine-thirty at night, too early to go to bed, but that had become her life.

Brian's light was off too so there was no chance of seeing him, not that it would do any good. It was obvious he wasn't used to girls standing up to him, and she wasn't one to back down.

Her bedroom lightened, and she looked up at the intricate design cast across the ceiling, coming from the lace curtains that covered the back window. Depending on what her neighbors were doing, she may have to crash another cookout. She chuckled. Even that was better than going to bed at such an ungodly hour.

She threw back the cover and walked over to the window, pushing the curtain to the side. Jack's porch light lit the backyard, and she frowned at seeing Seth and Mallory dancing on the patio. *Party for two. Great.*

As she dropped the curtain, she noticed the silk ribbons hanging on the cork board. The thought of throwing them out the window at Seth made her laugh. He'd probably use them in his hair to spite her, and then she would want them back. She rolled her eyes. The only difference between his hair and hers, besides the color, was the ribbons she usually tied in hers. It was her way of showing Brian she appreciated the flowers, but he never seemed to notice. She went back to bed.

Punching her pillow once or twice, she rested her

head near the open window, breathing in the night air. "Calm down, Moose. I don't know what you're growling at but I'm not in the mood." She stared across the street and her mind drifted back to the night Brian kissed her on the porch and she huffed. If only they could go back to that night, would she have done things differently? She flopped over on her back and closed her eyes, willing the Sandman to work his magic. Eventually, she drifted off to sleep.

*She stood on the porch as he wrapped his arms around her waist and walked her back into the shadows. Just out of reach of the streetlight, he slid his hands down her body and lifted her up, pinning her against the house. She wrapped her legs around his waist as a lazy grin spread across his face. He smelled of nature, woods, heaven, and she breathed him in as her heart somersaulted in her chest. Trailing kisses up her neck, he nipped her earlobe before pulling back— her body responding automatically to his touch. Heat rose between them and he leaned back down, his mouth covering hers. His lips were soft, gentle, and with each movement, the intensity increased as he deepened the kiss.*

Her eyes shot open as her chest heaved and she tried to control the shock waves that ricocheted through her body. She reached up and touched her ear, the nip still creating goosebumps on her arms. Admitting she was attracted to Tucker would be easy, and she closed her eyes, allowing her body to relax into the mattress. His eyes reflected warmth, and she thought of his smile, a tenderness that felt so real, if she dwelled there long enough, she could still feel the tingles set off by his kiss. She grumbled and looked over at the clock.

The nightlight cast a subtle glow around the room and she reached over and turned on the bedside lamp. Needing a distraction from the big lug that crept into her dreams, she got out of bed and grabbed the wolf book off the shelf. With the intentions of reading herself to sleep, she propped herself up on a pillow and opened the book.

\*\*\*

Bright and early the next morning, Jesse walked out on the front porch. Thanks to her new sleep schedule, Saturday mornings felt more like Mondays. She tilted her head, allowing the sun to warm her face as a soft summer breeze blew through her hair.

The neighborhood was fairly quiet except for the baseball card that clicked against the spoked wheel of the red bicycle the paperboy pedaled down the street. Tossing the daily news onto the sidewalk, she smiled and waved at the dark-haired boy. *To be a kid again*, the thought made her chuckle. *Stomping through mud puddles, and catching lightning bugs, or playing tag in the dark.* She was quite brave at eight years old until a group of neighborhood kids got together to play hide-and-seek late one night. Looking for the perfect hiding place, she dashed alongside her house and stopped when she heard a growl rumble from beneath a peony bush. The raccoon was just as frightened as she was, although she screamed louder. After that night, she never went out to play in the dark again.

Picking up the newspaper, she turned as Brian walked around the house. "Brian!" she squeaked, a little too eager to get his attention. It was the first time she'd seen him since the dance and she wanted to apologize, if only to make things right between them. *He's been deliberately ignoring you.* She pushed the thought to the back of her mind because like it or not, she felt equally responsible for how that night ended.

"Hey," he said while walking over to the steps. Running his hand through his hair, he stared down the street.

"You're the last person I expected to see this early in the morning." It was a joke, intended to lighten the mood, which failed miserably.

"I forgot to take down the cameras and considering there are werewolves in the area, I figured it would be safer to get them this morning before I go to work, rather than after dark." He looked up at the door and frowned.

"Did you get any pictures?" She wanted to say more but considering the way he said *werewolf,* she didn't dare press her luck. Glancing over at the woods, sometimes she wished she knew nothing about the wolves. Life seemed much simpler back then.

"I don't know. I've got to be at work in fifteen minutes, so I don't have time to check right now," he said, looking down at the cameras. "If you want, you're welcome to come over when I get home tonight."

"Great. I'll see you then," she said and just like that, he turned and walked away. Trying to rein in her excitement, she would do whatever she had to, and mend fences while she was there, even if she had to lie. Exposing the wolves shouldn't have been an issue between them, but apparently, it was a touchy subject with him. She stood on the porch until Brian got into his Jeep and drove away. She waved and he nodded, but he seemed distracted.

As she turned back to the door, she noticed a bundle of yellow lilies resting on the small side table. She walked over and placed the paper on the table and picked up the flowers. *He leaves flowers, and then frowns?* She carried them over to the swing and sat down, searching through the stems for the hidden treasure card. "I never knew how much you meant to me until..." she read to herself. *Until I told you off?*

Brian's Jekyll-and-Hyde personality was really irritating her and she blew out a breath. The day began perfectly until he walked out of the woods. His snide wolf comment and the frown he displayed were enough to tempt her to take the flowers across the street and stuff them through the mail slot on his front door. But looking down at the flowers, she tucked the card back into the stems and headed into the house.

"Flowers again?" Gramma asked when she walked into the kitchen.

"I know, aren't they beautiful?" Jesse said, repeating the same routine she did every time Brian gave her flowers.

"He must really like you," Gramma said as Jesse filled the jar with water. "We may need to go down to the cellar and get more jars." She chuckled.

"I'm surprised he gave me flowers considering we haven't talked much in the past few weeks. We disagreed over how to handle the wolves. He doesn't think I should expose them."

"Well, maybe he's right."

"He may very well be, but we've already talked about it, Gramma. For safety reasons, they need to be exposed and I'm going to find a way to do it. I just don't know how yet." She rested her hip against the counter. "So far, it's not looking good, but I promise not to do anything unless I have proof. Which is why Lori's stopping by later."

"If you're sure this is what you want to do, I'm behind you. But if you change your mind, I will back that as well. Now would you like some breakfast?"

"No, thank you. I need to straighten up my room before Lori gets here." Jesse walked out of the kitchen carrying the jar of flowers. Maybe he was trying to change her mind about exposing the wolves, but it would take more than flowers to do that.

Jesse was restless by the time Lori arrived but hearing her voice as she climbed the stairs, she relaxed. "I thought you forgot about me."

"As if." Lori grinned. "How's it going, any changes?" She asked as she walked over and sat down beside Jesse on the bed.

"No, he gave me flowers this morning but he's still acting really strange."

"I would tell him to take a flying leap. No guy is worth sitting home alone on the weekends."

"I guess, but I miss hanging out with all of you." Jesse dropped back on the bed.

"Well, if you would forget about Mister Macho across the street and call, I'd hang out with you, but I can't deal with his attitude right now." Lori lay back on the bed and rolled over facing Jesse.

"I don't want to be the third wheel."

"Jesse, I love you like a sister, and sisters can't be a third wheel." Lori tweaked her nose.

"I love you, too." Jesse grinned.

"So, what are you doing tonight?"

"I'm meeting Mister Macho as soon as he gets home. We're going to check the cameras," Jesse said and Lori rolled her eyes.

"Mom's going out tonight, and Steve's working, so call me afterward and we'll hang out."

By the time Lori left that afternoon, Jesse's mood had lifted. She missed her best friend, and although she planned to spend as much time as she could with Brian, Lori had a point. He was bossy, and she really didn't want to listen to him tell her how stupid she was for wanting to expose the wolves. She needed some good old-fashioned girl time, and after she checked the cameras, she intended to call Lori.

The distant honk of a horn had Jesse pulling the curtains back for the umpteenth time. Looking out the window, the sun had already set, and the sky was dark. When Brian said she could come over that night to check the cameras, she didn't think he meant after dark, but she'd go regardless of the time.

She pulled a lily from the jar and held it against her cheek. The flowers on her bedside table were a constant reminder that she needed to stand her ground. Since Brian was willing to show her the pictures, she figured he either hoped they would prove her wrong, or prove nothing at all.

To be honest, she didn't believe in werewolves. Based on what she read in the wolf book, wolves in general rarely attacked humans. So why was she trying to expose them? Jesse asked herself that question numerous times, and each time, it came down to the newspaper articles. Why did the city feel the need to warn the residents if the wolves weren't dangerous?

Sharing the bench seat with Moose, she looked out into the treetops. She couldn't imagine what Megan went through, so helpless and alone in the woods. Or why she was even in the woods. *Did anyone ask?* She didn't notice Moose bristle until he growled and bolted out of the room. Leaning closer to the screen, a shadow moved, and she squinted as if it would make seeing in the dark easier. "Who's there?" she whispered down from the window.

"Jesse, is that you?" The female voice that called out from beneath the oak tree was one she didn't recognize. "Can I talk to you?"

"About what?"

"Wolves."

Jesse looked around. "Give me a minute," she said, trying to locate her phone. She didn't feel comfortable meeting the girl in the dark, especially next to the tree line, but if the girl had information about wolves, she had to go. She grabbed her phone off the bed and called Lori as she tiptoed down the stairs. "Call me back in ten." As she passed the living room, her grandmother was fast asleep in the recliner and the evening news was on the television.

She flipped on the porch light as she opened the back door. The screeching hinges echoed through the kitchen, and she paused. She could hear the TV, which meant her grandmother probably didn't hear the door, so she stepped out onto the porch. "Where are you?" she whisper-yelled.

The night was dark, the shadows even darker, causing her to rethink her decision. Her heart pounded in her chest as she waited for her eyes to adjust. The rustle of leaves set the scene as her imagination conjured up all sorts of scenarios. Something told her to run and get inside, but it was too late. She was outside, and nothing could stop her from finding out if there were any truth to the wolf theory.

"Over here," the girl said as she stepped out from behind the tree. She stood in the shadows, but at least Jesse could make out her shape.

"This is as far as I go," Jesse said, placing her hands on her hips as she stepped off the porch. "I need to see who I'm talking to or I'm going back inside." What was it about that tree that everyone wanted to stand under it?

"Can you see me now?" the irritated female said, dodging a wind chime when she stepped out from under the oak branches.

Jesse studied the girl who inched forward. She was shorter by about three inches or more, and had curves that put Jesse's to shame. Her short, black hair caught on the breeze, and she tucked it behind her ear. She didn't look threatening, and that, alone, set Jesse at ease. "What can you tell me about the wolves?" She only had ten minutes before Lori would be calling, and she was down by three.

"They're werewolves," the girl whispered as she looked over at the cabin, and then back at Jesse.

"Yeah, about that," Jesse scoffed. "I've heard the stories, but that doesn't make them true. So if you have actual proof, I'm all ears. If not, I don't have time for this." She didn't mean to sound annoyed, but in all honesty, she was. Brian would be home any minute and she didn't want to be hiding out in the dark when he came over. She could imagine what he would say. Speaking of, the clanging wind chimes didn't go unnoticed, and she jerked her head around.

"Be careful what you wish for," a male voice said before moving out from the shadows.

"Who are you?" Jesse demanded, taking a step back.

"You can call me Ginseng."

Not liking the attitude of the male visitor, Jesse scowled. "How did you know about...?" Her words trailed off and she swallowed hard. "You've been stalking me?"

"Don't flatter yourself, sweetheart. Stalking would imply I'm obsessed with you."

"Then why were you following me?"

"To give you the proof you were looking for."

Jesse pursed her lips against her better judgment, and stepped forward. The two strangers seemed normal enough, but something about the man was familiar. When she was within five feet of the two, she stopped. "Give me proof, or get out of my yard." Being pissy wasn't the smartest thing to do, but feeling confident in her own yard, she refused to allow them to intimidate her. She smirked as the man looked over at the woman, but when he turned back, his eyes flared.

She jumped as bits of clothing rained down around her and a large, gray wolf snarled. "What the..." Fear grabbed her to her core and she clamped her mouth shut to keep from screaming. *Think, think, think. What did the book say? Back up slowly,* but she couldn't move. *No eye contact,* she looked down at the tattered material. *Do not run. Stay facing the wolf.* She sucked in a breath as a growl brought her attention back to the beast. Feeling faint and afraid the animal would surely attack, she knew she couldn't make it back to the house. Her eyes frantically searched between the wolf and her surroundings as her fight-or-flight instinct propelled her backward toward the shed. "Stay away from me!" she yelled, diving behind the holly bush. Prickly leaves scratched her body, but that was nothing compared to the rusty nail that dug into her side. Kicking at the branches to retreat further against the shed, her heart drummed in her ears.

"My, my, aren't you a delight?" The man laughed. "Your fear is intoxicating, and my wolf... well, he just wants to play."

"Go away!" Jesse shouted, hiding her face against the shed.

"But, sweetheart, you wanted proof." He chuckled. "It's been way too long. A shapely female such as you... has excited my wolf."

Jesse closed her eyes and drew in a slow breath. She knew he would not walk away, and as much as he seemed to enjoy her distress, he gave her the proof she asked for. She opened her eyes and looked over at Jack's cabin. Any other night Seth would've been out on the patio, but it was just her luck, the lights were out. She bit the bullet and moved out from behind the bush. *Don't back down. He won't hurt you.* She placed her hand against the cut on her side. "Omygawd, you're naked!" she screeched and looked away.

"Considering the company you keep, I highly doubt your innocence is anything more than an act." He sneered.

Jesse drew down her brows as she locked eyes with the stranger. Who did he think he was, judging her when he was the one standing there without clothes? Replacing fear with fury, she clenched her fists. "I don't know who you think you are, but whom I choose to keep company with is none of your concern. And this," she waved her blood-smeared hand in the air, "change thing you do will not help me. I need solid proof that I can take to the council meeting, so your disappearing wolf act won't work."

"Won't work?" he repeated. "You, sweetheart, are so enticing."

Her eyes widened and a lump of dread settled in her stomach. The sinister look in his eyes made her shiver, but there was no way in hell she would back down after the way he insulted her. Reminding herself as to why she was there, she lifted her chin. "Obviously, you can't provide the proof I need. So you better leave now or I'll call the police," she said, pulling her phone from her pocket.

"Don't let my 'man' fool you. I'm not one of your little wolf buddies! I despise humans and you, sweetheart, are tempting the wrong wolf." His eyes flared.

"Travis, NO!" his companion yelled as he phased.

Jesse threw her hands up to shield her face before the wolf slammed her against the shed. Her scream, silenced by the impact, caught in her throat and the air whooshed out of her lungs. Pain radiated in her chest as her body fell forward and her vision blurred. Unable to hold onto her phone, it flew across the yard. Collapsing to the ground as the wolf slid out from beneath her, she rolled over onto her back. Straining to catch her breath brought tears to her eyes, and she prayed her grandmother wouldn't hear the commotion and come out the back door.

Unable to block out the snarling growl that vibrated around her, she frantically kicked her way back behind the bush. *He will not hurt you*, she thought, but the broken branches that sliced across her skin said otherwise. Shock set in as the green-eyed wolf stared through the branches. Hearing muffled voices, her body jerked and she fought against the pull on her leg. She kicked with everything she had, but as her body shifted, pain shot through her head and exploded in her ears. *I'm going to die*, she thought as the world around her went black.

# Forty-Three

*Jack*

Jack was overlooking the pool and the smell of chlorine drifted around him. Remembering the night he and Mason walked down the gravel road in search of Megan, he chuckled. As he stared out through the darkness, he could picture himself standing in the center of the road, confused. In hindsight, he realized what he had missed. The bond was there, and he could feel it faintly, but being thrown off by the chlorine, he walked right past her house. She masked her scent with lavender but the chlorine hid her completely. The overpowering chemical was a blessing in disguise. It whitewashed her scent, which was why Travis never picked up on her being in the area when he traveled to the gas station, two miles further down the highway.

Turning back toward the house as a wailing siren

disrupted the night, he looked over to see an ambulance flying down Main Street. He was a bit on edge knowing Travis was still in the area, but reminded himself that Megan was safe and Tucker was guarding Tracy. Shaking off the edginess, he rolled his shoulders to relieve the tension that settled there. But when his phone vibrated, an ominous feeling churned his gut as he pulled the phone from his pocket. He stared down at the unknown number, his heart thundering in his chest. Taking a deep breath, he answered the call.

Hearing the panic in Whitney's voice, his blood ran cold. "Stay there. I'm sending Nigel," he said. Jack ran across the patio and pushed open the door, sliding to a stop in the center of the room. Startled by his abrupt entrance, Sage spilled a bowl of cheddar popcorn in Brayden's lap.

"What's wrong?" Megan asked, her face a mixture of fear and dread.

Jack wasn't sure how she would handle the news after everything she'd been through, but he wasn't about to lie to her either. "Travis attacked Jesse," he said, wrapping his arm around her shoulders. He looked down when tears filled her eyes and didn't fail to notice the anger flashing across her face. She was fierce when it came to her friends and he was about to see it firsthand if he didn't take control of the situation.

"Nigel, take my car. Whitney's at Jesse's house in the backyard." Nigel was the oldest of the scouts and being one of the few members from the previous pack, he had no problems working under a new alpha. Ben was his third. "Sage, you and Brayden stay here and guard Megan."

"Jack!" Megan hissed, spinning out from under his arm. Unable to hide her disapproval, she crossed her arms over her chest, her stance at once intimidating.

Jack turned as Nigel walked out the door in order to hide his grin. Megan was adorable when she was pissed, and he was pretty sure that wasn't the look she intended to portray. With flushed cheeks and a glare that would put the sun to shame, the little firecracker was getting ready to explode.

"Megan, I need you to call Dad and let him know what happened," Jack said, but the tone of his voice couldn't appease her. A low growl echoed around the room and all eyes shifted to the floor. "Do not go outside until I get back." Playing the alpha card against his mate wasn't something he practiced very often, but it was the only thing that could keep her from following him. He hurried out the door before she challenged his authority. As spunky as she was, he expected she would at least try. He pulled his shirt over his head and tossed it to the ground before running across the patio. Pausing at the pool house to remove his jeans, he phased and took off across the yard.

Under the cover of darkness, he was confident no one would notice his black wolf running down the street. Even if they did at the late-night hour, they would probably assume it was just a dog. But that was the least of his worries! Finding Travis before he could attack anyone else was top priority, even if it meant exposing the pack.

Determined to head Travis off, he raced down the street, heading toward the cemetery. Hunter's Ridge was an easy trek for his wolf and the same place Travis attacked Megan. That in itself was enough to push him forward.

He stood just inside the tree line and scanned the perimeter, but saw no sign that anyone had traveled through the area. He waited, listening, and a soft breeze rustled the leaves overhead. With his ears erect, his instincts were usually right on the mark and he expected no less. He knew Travis was fast on his feet when in wolf form. Vivian? Not so much. The lingering question as to why he attacked Jesse remained unanswered. Travis had definitely overstepped the boundaries there. Attacking a human while in wolf form was strictly forbidden.

Jack moved to the opposite side of the clearing and hunkered down behind a large pine tree. Drawing in a deep breath to calm his heart, it continued to throb inside his mind, distorting the silence. At the sound of twigs snapping, his ears flicked, and he cocked his head. Slowly, he rose, readying himself for the fight of his life and his adrenaline filled his veins.

Travis was no better than a rogue, with nothing to lose, which made him a dangerous adversary. As the large gray wolf ran into the clearing, followed by a smaller brown wolf, Jack shot out from the shadows. He knew they had picked up his scent. Once Travis noticed him, he stretched taller; his fur bristling along the ridge of his back. He didn't seem intimidated, nor did Vivian, who moved closer to the tree line. Knowing she would attack if it meant keeping Travis alive, she became another distraction he had to avoid.

Jack never took his eyes off the gray wolf even when Vivian moved out of his sight. With his ears back and his hackles raised, he snarled out a growl so harsh it could have stripped the bark off a tree, and that was just a preliminary warning. It took years of training, self-discipline, and inner courage to be an alpha and Jack was prepared to put his hard work to the test.

Without warning, Travis crouched back and launched himself forward, meeting Jack in the air. Snarling growls echoed through the trees as the wolves locked limbs in a heated battle. Circling as the attack unfolded, Vivian did her best to distract Jack, but his eyes never left the target.

Both males fought with the skill and precision of alphas, but with Vivian also there, Jack knew he would have to outwit both of them to win. One wrong move is all it would take; so he calculated every step in his head. Two against one weren't the best odds, but anytime Travis fought, the odds were stacked in his favor.

Jack jerked around when Vivian jumped on his back, biting his right shoulder savagely. She attacked from the rear and swiftly darted away just as fast as she appeared. Taking advantage of the diversion, Travis moved in for the kill, but Jack was quick on his feet, disrupting his plans. Winded and his body tiring, Jack drew in a heavy breath as Vivian crashed into his side, flipping him to the ground with a thud. Pain shot behind his eyes and a red haze clouded his vision. He was as still as death, no more than a mound of black fur at Travis's feet, and he bit back a snarl when he looked through his lashes. The little she-wolf was ecstatic. She crouched on the ground, anticipating the imminent kill.

Seth and Mason phased as they slid to a stop at the edge of the clearing, unable to interfere in the fight. A challenge was a challenge, and until only one was left standing, the others had no choice but to wait it out.

As Travis turned to warn the newcomers, Jack jumped to his feet and his eyes flared. Giving Jack enough time to rebound was a fatal error on his part, an error that Jack was expecting.

Lunging forward, Jack's jaws clamped around the neck of the gray wolf and sheer shock registered in its eyes. *This is for trying to take what was mine!* And with one harsh jerk, the wolf slumped to the ground, his neck ragged and broken.

Vivian's eyes widened with fear as she slowly inched backward, hunkering low to the ground. When a celebratory howl ripped from Jack's wolf, she darted into the woods.

"Are you all right?" Mason asked, running over as Jack phased.

"I'm fine," he said, looking down at the lifeless heap of bloody gray fur. "I need to get back. I'm sure Dad is waiting." It was his first kill, and although it was necessary, deep down, it bothered Jack. His wolf? Not so much.

"Go, we'll take care of him," Mason said.

By the time Jack arrived at the pool house, his dad was pacing. "What happened, are you all right?" he asked while Jack phased.

"Nothing that won't heal in a few hours," he replied, stepping into the shower stall to rinse off the dried blood. "How's Megan?" Shutting off the water, he grabbed a towel from the shelf.

"Megan's fine, but when she sees your shoulder? That will leave a scar," the alpha said while handing Jack his shirt and pants.

Jack looked back at his shoulder. "It stopped bleeding

so it should be pretty easy to hide."

"I take it you found Travis?"

"He's dead," Jack said, looking the alpha in the eye. "I had no choice. It was me or them."

"So you fought *both* of them?"

"Yes. Vivian ran but I don't think she's a threat anymore. Not without Travis to back her."

"No, she wouldn't dare step back into pack territory now that Travis is gone," Alpha Cooper agreed as they walked out of the pool house.

# Forty-Four

*Jesse*

Jesse's eyes shot open as the smell of rubbing alcohol assaulted her nose. Blinded by the overhead light, she bit her lip and jerked her head to the side. The sudden movement sent a stabbing pain through her head and she winced, squeezing her eyes shut.

"How do you feel?" Dr. Williams asked as she turned and opened her eyes again. She was in the emergency room, that much was clear, but how and when she had gotten there, she couldn't remember.

"What are you doing?"

"I'm trying to clean the scratch on your face. Now hold still," her dad said as he daubed an alcohol swab over her torn cheek.

Jesse sucked in a deep breath and her body trembled. She pushed up on the bed and looked around the room.

"Where's Gramma?" The distress in her voice alarmed her dad and he grabbed her shoulders to recline her gently on the bed.

"Calm down, she's in the waiting room. Is something wrong?"

Trying to calm herself, Jesse closed her eyes to avoid his stare. Her grandmother tried to warn her about the wolves but because she wouldn't listen; and now, she had become a target, just as surely as if there were a bull's eye on her back. Unsure of what to do, she needed to talk to her grandmother, but with her dad there, she had to figure it out on her own. "Yeah, there's something wrong. You're trying to burn out my sinuses," she said, opening her eyes.

"What happened to you?" The stern look on his face made her feel like a child. And the truth serum in his voice forced her to confess.

"Gramma was asleep in the living room and I was in the backyard. I fell and blacked out," she said, pinching the bridge of her nose in another attempt to hide her eyes.

"That's it? That's all you remember?"

"Well... no. I mean... everything happened so fast. I remember hearing the wind chimes." The wind chimes hung in the tree, like the bell over the cafe door. When the man stepped out, the chime rang its warning. Apparently, her grandmother was a lot smarter than she gave her credit for. "I dropped my phone. I could hear it ringing," she said, lifting her hand to touch the bandage that was wrapped around her head.

Dr. Williams tossed the alcohol swab in the trash and walked around to the other side of the bed. Pulling Jesse's hand away from the bandage, he looked at her with disbelief in his eyes.

"What time is it?" she asked, trying to change the subject.

"Just after eleven."

"Where's my phone? I need to call Lori."

"She was here earlier, but I sent her home. She'll see you tomorrow."

"Dad, I'm fine. I don't want to stay here overnight."

"Stop trying to change the subject," he said. "Jesse, were you attacked? You have multiple scratches along your arms and legs, plus, a pretty nasty cut on your left side, not to mention the goose egg on your head. The EMTs said you were out cold when they arrived. That doesn't happen because of wind chimes." His eyes pleaded with her, but she turned away.

"I was in the backyard... in the dark. That in itself was enough to freak me out." She looked back at him. "I left my phone on the picnic table and went out to get it. I heard the wind chimes, so I walked over toward the tree. I thought I saw a shadow or something, and it scared me. I fell into the holly bush, and the nail on the shed caught my side. I guess my head hit the ground harder than I thought," she said, her impromptu performance worthy of an award.

"Well, you're staying here tonight, like it or not. I'm not releasing you until I get off work. I want to make sure you're okay, and your grandmother will be in shortly to sit with you."

"Dad, that's not necessary! I'm not a child. I think I can manage to stay in bed 'til morning." She rolled her eyes and flinched.

"I'm sure you can, but I'm not taking any chances. I want to know you both are safe," Dr. Williams said, handing her a cup of water and a pill. "This will help you sleep."

Jesse was exhausted by the time she was released from the hospital the following morning. Happy to be home and in her own bed, she pulled the curtains back and stared out the window.

Learning the secret of Cloverly sounded like fun in the beginning. It gave her a chance to discover more about the town she loved, not to mention spending more time hanging out with her best friend. It was the perfect way to pass the summer but she never in a million years thought the secret could involve werewolves. As she pieced together the events from the night before, she never really believed in werewolves even though she insisted on exposing them. And if it weren't for the scratches and bruises on her body, she could almost tell herself it *was* a dream. Hearing a light knock on the door, she looked back and Lori walked into the room. "Hey," Jesse said.

"I hear you've been causing trouble in the 'hood. What are you trying to do, give the neighbors a heart attack?" Lori asked. Closing the door behind her, she walked over and handed Jesse her phone. "I thought you might need this."

"Where did you find it?"

"Whitney gave it to me last night. You sure know how to draw a crowd. That was the most excitement we've had around here in years." Lori snickered and took a seat beside Jesse on the bed. "I tried to call you back. What happened?"

Drowsy from the medicine, Jesse rubbed her eyes and yawned. "Not so loud," she whispered. "He was a wolf."

"What do you mean *he was a wolf?* You said it was a girl," Lori whispered back.

Jesse's arm dropped on the bed and she bit her lip to keep from swearing. "It was a girl, but there was a guy with her. I saw him change into a wolf," Jesse said as she rolled over on the bed. "But you can't tell anyone."

"Right, because they would so believe me." Lori smirked. "Actually, I think I've seen them before. I was eleven at the time, and it was late. I was looking through the blades of a window fan. It was hot in my room, so I snuck out of bed to turn the fan on high."

"Were you scared?"

"Not really. I thought they were dogs until one stopped and looked up at the window. Then I thought I was dreaming."

"Why didn't you say something?" Jesse hissed.

"Because I was more afraid of my mother than a stupid dog." Lori rolled her eyes.

"No, why didn't you tell me about this earlier?"

"Because I thought it was a dog. It's not like I knew the difference back then, and I'm not sure I would today."

"You'd definitely know the difference," Jesse said, unsure if what Lori saw was actually a wolf.

"So where was Brian when all this went down?" Lori glanced out the window.

"He never showed up," Jesse said, closing her eyes, evidently not wanting to talk about him. She spent most of the night waiting for him to get home, and from the looks of it, he still hadn't. She hissed out a breath as stress settled in her chest.

"Imagine that," Lori sneered, moving over to the sewing chair. She cursed below her breath as she spun around and Jesse clamped her mouth shut, the movement making her nauseous. It was obvious Lori was unhappy with Brian, but she didn't know the reason why.

It was noon before Jesse opened her eyes again. Expecting to see Lori, her room was quiet and the only noise she heard were the wind chimes in the oak tree. Being close to the tree line made her uncomfortable, and chills prickled her arms. Questioning her own memories, she worried she was crazy and everything that happened over the past twenty-four hours was nothing more than a dream. But as soon as she sat up, her head throbbed and she lay back down on the pillow. Her mind was a jumbled mess and she couldn't remember Lori leaving, but clearly, she had.

A car door shut, and Jesse pulled back the curtains to see Brian walking up to his house. Hopefully, he would check on her later, but after the way Lori ranted about him, that probably wouldn't happen. She dropped the curtain back into place and her eyelids drooped.

Hearing a distant knock, she shifted her body but never opened her eyes. "Jesse, can I come in?" the voice sounded in her head.

Finally, she blinked open her eyes to the pink curtain hanging in front of her face. *You're dreaming.* She rolled over and yelped, grabbing for the blanket.

"Calm down, it's me," Brian said, taking a seat beside her on the bed.

"You... you scared me. I thought..." Her hands trembled as she held the blanket against her chest. When it finally sank in that Brian was sitting beside her, she relaxed against his leg.

"How do you feel?" He frowned, and she looked down

when his fingers traced the bandage on her arm.

"I'm fine, it's no big deal." She tried not to be snippy, but if he came there to pity her, he needed to head back across the street. She felt like crap for the past several weeks because he was avoiding her, and now that she was hurt, he stoops to visit her?

"What happened to you?"

She avoided the question by adjusting the blanket. Her teal-blue house coat with white bunnies and yellow butterflies wasn't exactly the outfit she wanted him to see her in. "It was a wolf," she said, glancing up to observe his reaction.

"Where were you when this *supposed* wolf attacked you?"

She scooted away from him and moved to the head of the bed. Keeping the blanket pulled up to her chest, she leaned against the headboard. "Well, if you must know," she said in her snarkiest voice, "I was waiting for my *supposed* boyfriend to get home from work. But considering he never showed up, I decided to hang out with the local werewolves. At least they were willing to give me their time." She glared at him.

"It's not like that and you know it!" Brian ran his hand through his hair, and she could tell the snide remark hit its target.

"It is like that! I've been sitting here night after night hoping you would stop by so I could apologize for how I acted at the party, but instead you avoided me. I mean, look," she said, fanning her arms out as the blanket dropped to her waist, "I moved the damn bed over by this window, thinking I might get a glimpse of you when you came home at night. And do you know what I saw?

Nothing. Not one damn thing! Hell, I had a better view out the back window."

Brian looked across the room and a hateful glare appeared in his eyes. "I've been busy with classes. I have to finish them before the end of the year or I won't be considered for the fire chief position."

"Just stop with the excuses," she said, lifting her hand to shush him. "You invited me to your house, so I highly doubt you would do so if you had classes to attend. I don't know where you were and I don't really care because my days and nights of sitting home waiting for you are over."

"I'm sorry. I wasn't thinking," he said and the guilt he felt seemed to consume him, causing her to frown.

"That was obvious when you didn't show up."

"I'm here now."

Jesse rubbed her fingers across her forehead and blew out a breath. Her irritation was hard to disguise, but sometimes he made her mad enough to spit nails. After weeks of being a butthead, there was nothing in his words to suggest he had changed. And as soon as she told him about the wolves, she figured his true colors would show. "Why?"

"I wanted to see how you were doing. I got a phone call last night that you were hurt, and had to be taken to the hospital." He swallowed hard and looked down at her hand. "So are you going to tell me the truth or not?"

"I'm sorry Lori interrupted your classes, but if you must know, I was talking to a couple in the backyard. They said they had proof of werewolves, and then poof! He changed into a wolf."

"How many times do we have to go over this? That's crazy. There is no such thing as werewolves. Maybe you hit your..." He cut the sentence short, but she knew what he was implying.

"Well, you know me. All about crazy!" she said. The thought of slapping him upside the head was very tempting. *Jerk!*

"So he attacked you? That's his proof?"

"When you put it like that, maybe he didn't attack me. I told him I needed proof. You and I both know I can't go to the council meeting without it. So maybe that was the only proof he had," she smartly replied.

"If you really believe what you're saying, do you think you should continue to pursue this? I mean, the next time you may not be so lucky. He could have killed you. He may even come back in the future to finish the job. Did you ever think about that?" He narrowed his eyes, "Forget about the damn council meeting! I won't let you do this."

Anger bubbled in her chest and she stiffened. "Oh, so now you want to be the protective boyfriend? Well, I'm not asking for your permission, Brian. This is something I *have* to do. I have proof now and I know they're real. I will expose them if it's the last thing I do."

"Are you even listening to what you're saying? If this is what happens when you ask for proof, what will happen when you expose them and really piss them off? They could slaughter the whole damn town and no one would know. Remember the lost colony of Roanoke? Stranger things have happened."

"Nothing you can say will change my mind so save your breath. I'm going through with this, and I will protect my grandmother."

"You really are crazy. Why would you put yourself out there like that? Plus, you come from a large city, but in a small town, neighbors are like family. I know almost everyone, and I will not be responsible for any of them getting hurt because you believe there are monsters roaming the woods."

"I don't want anyone getting hurt either and if you knew me, you would already know that. But at the same time, the elderly residents that are aware of the wolves living here shouldn't have to live in fear. There is such a thing as safety-in-numbers, so jump aboard the crazy train because it looks to be one helluva ride."

*That played out well,* she thought as Brian stormed out of the room. She gritted her teeth so tightly her jaw hurt, which in turn, made her head hurt. *Is he intentionally trying to piss me off?* She stomped over to the closet and sorted through the clothes. Grabbing a pair of sleep pants and a t-shirt, she went into the bathroom to change. Staring at her reflection in the mirror, she tried to recall the conversation she had with Lori that morning. It involved Brian, and something about him being in a foul mood, but she didn't know why. Anxiety rolled over her as the vague details of the night flashed before her eyes.

Returning to her room, she sat at the sewing machine and stared out the back window. The wind chimes rang softly in the breeze, and she listened to the different tones. Her grandmother hadn't placed them in the tree for their musical charm; they were her foolproof alarm system.

"Knock, knock," Mallory said from the bedroom door, and Jesse turned in the chair.

"Come in." She had no idea why Mallory was there unless it had something to do with Seth. "Have a seat." Jesse stood, turning the sewing chair around for Mallory before she walked over to the bed.

"I know you don't really know me, but I need to talk to you," Mallory said in a low voice as she glanced fearfully toward the door.

"If this is about Seth, I already have a boyfriend," Jesse replied, with a slight roll of her eyes.

Mallory ignored the comment and smiled sweetly. "I was hoping you could help me understand what I saw last night." She motioned toward the back window. "I was at the cabin looking out the kitchen window."

Jesse froze, and for a moment, she thought she was dreaming again. "You saw the man that attacked me?" The question came out a little too fast, and she crossed her fingers, hoping she had heard right.

"Yeah, I saw a man talking to you, and then he changed into a wolf."

Jesse smiled, seeing the uncertainty in Mallory's eyes. Although she truly saw the wolf, she still questioned her sanity. "It was a werewolf," she whispered, "but you can't tell anyone. At least, not right yet."

Mallory's expression changed and she grinned. "And to think I was going to call my mama and have her commit me to a mental institution. I knew I wasn't crazy."

"Well, if you're crazy, you're not alone." Jesse laughed.

"Mama always said a giggle becomes a laugh when shared with a friend, and she *was* crazy." Mallory chuckled.

"So tell me, does knowing about the wolves scare you?" Jesse asked. "Because you seem pretty calm about it."

"I'm only calm because I'm armed and dangerous." Mallory tapped her purse and Jesse's eyes widened.

"You have a gun?" The thought of Mallory with a gun was almost as frightening as the werewolves roaming the woods.

"Heck no," she said, opening her purse and pulling out a slingshot. "If I'd been outside, I'd have tagged that wiry tail!"

Jesse laughed so hard, she had to hold her head to stop the throbbing. "Maybe one day you could teach me how to use that thing," she said when she finally stopped laughing. "Does anyone else know you saw the attack?"

"Naw, I didn't say anything. I'm really good at playing dumb when the circumstances call for it." She grinned. "Sometimes it's the only way to get tips. You wouldn't believe the men that prefer to tip a dippy waitress. I guess it's their way of saving the world."

# Forty-Five

*Jack*

Glancing over as Megan rolled down the passenger side window, Jack snickered. Her brows creased with worry and she chewed her lower lip, like a pouting child. Unsure of what her first real phase would be like later that night, she was stressing over it for the past several days, even though he tried to ease her mind. She knew most wolves phased at puberty, or at least by the age of fifteen, and she resisted it for over five years. Not to mention, she still wasn't sure how she phased on Hunter's Ridge, but more than likely, it was pure fear that pushed her wolf into action.

"Where are we going?" she asked when he turned onto the highway.

"I need to talk to Tracy."

"Does she know about Travis?"

"I'm sure Dad has already stopped by and told her, but I wanted to make sure she was all right. She has a tendency to put up a contented front." Part of the alpha's role is to tend to family matters, but because Jack killed Travis, that burden now lay heavily on Jack's shoulders. Tracy may have been a pain in the ass, but Travis was the conniving snake behind all the drama that surrounded her.

"That's silly." Megan frowned. "I hope she's okay. I'll talk to her if you want me to."

By the time they arrived at Randy's house, Megan had forgotten about her phase and was focused exclusively on her friend. Determined to do whatever she could to make things better, she jumped out of the car as soon as Jack pulled up in front of the little, white house.

Randy stepped out on the porch and pulled Megan into a hug before leading her inside. Jack smirked, remembering the day he met Randy at Sallee's Rock. To say he couldn't stand the sight of him was putting it mildly. Now seeing Megan and him together didn't bother him or his wolf.

"What's the holdup? You need a hug, too?" Randy asked from the door.

*Smartass.* Jack grinned as he shut the driver's door. "I think I can manage without." He chuckled as he walked up to the porch. "Has Dad been by today?" he asked when Tracy peeked out the door and waved.

Knowing the details of what Travis made Tracy endure, Jack understood why she acted the way she did. But once Randy came into the picture, it was amazing to watch her transforming right before his eyes. With no one constantly criticizing her or putting her down, Tracy was free, and with her freedom, she was an entirely different person.

"Yes, he told me everything and I'm good," Tracy said, looping her arm around his when he walked into the house. "It's not your fault. He plotted to take you and Alpha Cooper right out of the picture. It's bad no matter how you look at it, but he brought his death on himself. I hate it. He was the last male to hold the Hudson name, but with all the bad things the name presently stands for, I'm good and ready to get rid of it now." Tracy looked over at Randy.

"Tracy Grayson has a nice ring to it," Randy said when Tracy walked over and joined him at the table.

Jack grinned as Megan realized what Randy said. She had been through hell and back over the past month and to see her so exuberantly excited was like a breath of fresh air. Megan spouted off questions left and right, and at one point, Jack feared if she didn't slow down, she might actually hyperventilate. He leaned against the counter and pulled her back against his chest. Holding her in place, she bounced on his toes and he laughed.

"Stop it," Megan said, looking up at him. "I'm excited." She rested her head against his shoulder. "I prayed they would get together because I knew how much he loved her, and now they're getting married!"

"Well, there is just one thing," Tracy said, bringing Megan's bounce to a halt. "It will be a while before we make it official. Randy has to court me first. I need to make sure he's worthy." She grinned.

"Oh, I'm worthy and as soon as they leave, I'm going to show you just how worthy I am," Randy said and

Tracy's face burned red. Pulling her into his lap, he nuzzled her neck.

Leave it to Randy to blurt that out for all to hear. Jack leaned down and whispered in Megan's ear. "We may need to get out of here." Megan nodded her agreement as she looked over at the two and grinned again. "Does Dad know?" Jack asked.

"Yes, we've already talked to him. He wants to stand in place of my dad. I hope you don't mind," Tracy said.

"I don't mind at all, sis." Extending his hand when Randy got up from the table, Jack congratulated them before turning to Tracy. The burden Jack was carrying slipped off his shoulders and he opened his arms. "You deserve to be happy," he said, pulling her into a hug.

"I am. Thank you," Tracy replied, wrapping her arms around his waist.

Jack knew Megan wanted to stay longer and discuss the wedding plans with Tracy, but there wasn't enough time. The alpha was waiting for him at the pack house, and Jack would have to get there before nightfall if he planned to talk with Tucker. Keeping the situation quiet until they sorted everything out, only a select few knew Alpha Cooper detained him. Tucker was pissed when he found out Vivian tried to attack Tracy, and they understood why. But when Tucker heard about how Travis attacked Jesse, he exploded into a fit of rage and the alpha had no choice but to restrain him. It was only after the alpha told him Travis was killed that Tucker finally calmed down and even then, the alpha refused to let him leave. Jack wasn't sure what was up with his cousin, but he intended to find out. He knew Tucker liked Jesse, but even that couldn't justify his anger.

"We're meeting at Sallee's tonight," Jack said as the four walked out the door.

"That's right, this is your big night," Tracy said and Megan blushed. "You'll do great, just don't wear good clothes."

Megan blushed redder.

"You worry too much." Jack laughed. He and Megan congratulated the couple once more before heading to the car. As he opened the driver's door, he looked back at Tracy. "If you're interested, there's a scout position open."

"When do I start?"

"It's yours whenever you're ready."

"Thanks, Jack," Tracy said, waving from the porch.

With all the events the pack had been through during the past few weeks, everyone was looking forward to letting their wolves run. The night would sport a *super moon*, as the humans called it. To the wolves, however, it meant a time to let loose and stretch their legs, to thoroughly enjoy the pack family. The strain of constantly being on guard was draining on everyone, Megan included. Now that Travis was no longer a threat, everyone was excited to abandon their worries and celebrate the night, even Tracy.

The night was hot and sultry when the small pack met at Sallee's Rock. Lounging on the boulders, they talked until just after midnight. Megan had only been to the boulders once, when she first connected with Jack, so it was fitting that she chose to have her first phase there.

"Tracy, how is Randy handling you being here without him?" Jack asked. It was her first phase since they bonded, and because Randy was human, he wouldn't be running with them.

"He had to work tonight, but plans to meet up with everyone later. He seemed pretty excited, though."

Randy was good for her. Although he pushed the boundaries of pack authority, *he was still a pretty cool guy*, Jack thought.

"You should bring him with you the next time we run. We can play Chase the Biker Boy." Jack chuckled when Tucker laughed and ducked away from Tracy's swat. Seeing them teasing each other after everything that happened was a welcome relief.

After an evening of interrogating Tucker, he finally cracked and told Jack everything, but only after Jack swore on his alpha shield not to repeat it to anyone. He rubbed his fingers over the alpha shield that dangled around his neck. It was good having Tucker back with the group although none of the others realized he'd been detained. It was all done in secret and considering Tucker was spending time with the alpha and finely tuning his training schedule, no one suspected a thing.

"I'm telling him you said that," Tracy said.

"Hey, it's no worse than him saying he would get a paintball gun and use us for target practice," Tucker replied as he stood up and stretched.

"He did not say that... did he?"

"Yes, he did. He said he would give us a five-second headstart and then he was going to paint the town," Whitney chimed in.

"Ha! That is such a lie! Sorry, Whit, but I'm calling you out." Tracy smirked.

"How do you know I'm lying?"

"Because your mouth does this little twitchy thing," Tracy said before she jumped down from where she was sitting.

"Well, I tried," Tucker said jumping down and following Tracy. "Good luck, Megan."

"Have fun and stay safe," Jack added as the group quickly undressed at the tree line before phasing and racing into the woods.

"What about you?" He looked over at Megan. She was silently listening to the banter between the others, and when they phased, Jack could see the apprehension in her eyes. She tried to hide it, but biting her nails was a dead giveaway. "Are you ready to do this?" He flicked his brows and she giggled.

"I am... maybe. No," she admitted. "It scares me."

"Don't be afraid. I'm here with you. Always." Jack took her hand and together, they climbed down the boulders.

"Can you phase for me?" she joked, wrapping her arms around her waist. Swaying from side to side, she looked up at the sky.

"No, but I can help you if you need it."

"Okay. Let's do this before I chicken out. What shall I do first?" Megan asked as she squared her shoulders and lifted her chin.

"First, you control your thoughts at all times, even after you phase. Second, you control the wolf. Just don't let the wolf come forward too fast. Bring it forward slowly. And third, the phase will probably be a little uncomfortable, but even that will pass. So let your wolf run. It needs exercise just like we do."

"So what happens if the wolf comes forward too fast?"

"Nothing will happen unless you're wearing clothes,

and they'll be destroyed."

"Oh. So that's what happened at Hunter's Ridge." Megan shifted on her feet and blushed. "I've never undressed in front of..."

"It's who we are and there's nothing sexual about it. But if you would rather phase with your clothes on, that's fine. We have extra clothes scattered throughout the woods for that very reason." He didn't dare tell her he was the one to dress her at Hunter's Ridge.

"Do I have to take off everything?" She chewed her lip.

"No, but if you don't, you'll be wearing something different home," Jack said and Megan slowly pulled her shirt over her head and tucked it under her armpits, shielding her body. He grinned, and she stuck out her tongue before sliding her shorts down her legs, and kicking them into the air. She caught them and placed them on a boulder. After a minute, she mustered the courage to drop her shirt, exposing her pink bra and panties as the tips of her ears turned red.

"I'm not comfortable enough to take off the rest," she said.

"That's fine. After a few phases, you'll get used to it." He tried not to stare, knowing if he did, she would probably put her clothes back on. "You know, I still remember my first phase. Dad had to talk me through it. I could feel my wolf but I was so excited to shift that I couldn't concentrate. It took over an hour before I calmed down enough to bring my wolf forward." He smiled and her body relaxed. "I know it feels awkward right now, but the trick is to *relax*. Can you feel your wolf?" he asked.

"I know she's there."

"It's easier if you close your eyes. Picture your wolf in your mind."

"But what about my clothes?"

"They'll be here when you phase back." *Hopefully*. He kept that part to himself. Rarely did their clothes disappear, but when they did, it was usually because of a raccoon's interference. Those little bandits would steal anything that had candy or food crumbs in the pockets.

Megan gave a thumbs-up and closed her eyes. Jack could tell by the way she rocked back on her heels, she was still uncomfortable. The wrinkles that formed on her forehead as she tried to connect with her wolf made him smile.

"Keep your eyes closed," Jack said, stepping forward and pulling her against his chest. He relished the contact of her body next to his. It wasn't the way his dad coached him, but the end result would be the same. Leaning down, he nuzzled her neck and she squeaked.

"That tickles."

"Shh. Let your wolf respond to me," he said, inhaling her scent.

She tilted her head, offering her neck as her breathing grew heavy. As her wolf pushed forward, her body trembled beneath his touch. Megan stood silent and Jack pulled her closer, his hands trailing down her back. "Just go with it," he whispered. "It feels strange at first, but it won't hurt you. It's like..."

"Like what?" she asked, and he blushed.

"A burst of energy."

"But what if I don't change back?"

"I promise, you will change back. You control the wolf. All she wants is to be released so she can run."

"Okay. Let's do this, Sadie."

"Who's Sadie?" Jack asked as he rubbed his nose down her neck.

"My wolf," she said breathlessly.

Feeling her knees buckle, Jack nipped her neck and her wolf came forth. Stepping back, his heart raced at the sight of the light-gray wolf with silky blonde tips. Seeing how small she was, he kneeled down to eye level with her. "Hello, Sadie," he said, lifting his hands to her head, then rubbing one hand down her neck. "That wasn't so bad, was it?" When Sadie placed her head over his shoulder, he laughed. "Are you ready to run?" The wolf jerked back and wiggled around, giving him her full attention. The others would probably think he was crazy talking to Megan's wolf as if she were a person, but she seemed amused by it so he continued. "Step back and I'll phase." Sadie ran a tight circle around him before backing away.

Jack quickly undressed and tossed his clothes over her shredded undergarments, then phased. His wolf, excited by Sadie when she brushed against him, circled around her with his tail held high. He wanted all the males of their pack to know she was off limits. Hopping from side to side, he quickly darted into the woods with Sadie close behind.

As the two wolves raced along the worn trails, Jack looked over his shoulder, never losing sight of his mate. Leading her deeper into the woods, when they came out by the lake, he phased. Sadie stopped and stared as she tilted her head, questioning him. "It's okay, Sadie. I just wanted to show Megan where we were." Jack chuckled when Sadie shook her body and Megan appeared.

"I did it!" Megan squealed as she rushed toward Jack.

Without paying attention to the fact that she was totally naked, she jumped into his arms. Throwing him off balance, they fell back into the water with Megan landing in his lap.

Images of Mason choking on a bug flashed in his mind. *Eww, bacon.* He shivered. "That was unexpected," he said, although he was thinking about that damn bug. It was a distraction his... well, you know... mind needed. She leaned in, her lips brushing over his.

"That was amazing but a *burst of energy* isn't how I would describe it." Her chest rose with each breath as she rode the wave of desire, enhanced by her phase. The moonlight reflecting over the water heightened her excitement and he groaned.

Enchanted by her smile, he memorized every small detail of her face, from the fan of her lashes when she blinked, to the spray of freckles across her nose. He glanced down and quickly closed his eyes. *Bacon, bacon, bacon.* The sight of her in his lap and the irresistible urge to touch her, and be with her, combined to cloud his judgment.

"Sorry about the water," she said and he opened his eyes. But when she looked down and realized she was naked, she blushed. "Awkward." She leaned into him and a nervous giggle rattled against his neck causing him to growl.

"You think this is funny?" he joked as he reclined her slowly in the shallow water, his body pinning her in the soft mud. The warm water lapped against them and Jack leaned down, his breath brushing across her lips. He didn't intend to kiss her, but when he pulled back, she nipped his bottom lip, urging him on. He tilted his head and a slight glow graced her cheeks. *Bacon, bacon.* Her mossy-rose scent sweetened the air, causing his heart to thump in his ears and he licked his lips. At times like these, he had to remind himself that she was real, and not a cruel dream. Staring down into her green eyes, his wolf stirred when she smiled at him and wrapped her arms around his neck, pulling him into a kiss. As the sound of crickets played softly in the background, for just a moment, time stood still.

The feel of her soft curves beneath him sent pulsating waves throughout his body and he broke from the kiss. "We should head back now," he whispered against her cheek. He sat back on his knees, pulling her up with him. He didn't want to return to the boulders, but she was caught up in the phase, and its accompanying sensation of bliss, and he refused to take advantage of the situation. After a few phases, when she had more control of her emotions, he would welcome anything she offered but it was obvious she needed a distraction right now as much as he did. "Sorry about the mud," he said trying to occupy his mind with a different subject, but his hands were too busy rubbing down her backside.

"I'm not." She giggled and wrapped her legs around his waist.

Jack pictured Mason hacking on the bug as he carried Megan out of the water. "You ready to go?" he asked, tightening his grip.

"No. I'd rather hang out here with you."

"You really shouldn't tempt me. I would rather..." He waggled his eyebrows and grinned.

"I'll do more than tempt you," she said, "but I'm giving you a pass this time." She loosened her legs and dropped slowly to the ground. "Next time, don't start something you can't finish."

Jack's brows creased and he moved forward, pretending to stalk her. "Oh, I can finish," he said in a deep, sultry voice. As his grin grew wider, Megan giggled and inched back towards the trees. Jack kept his eyes locked on hers before closing the gap between them. In a flash, Megan phased and darted into the woods and Jack roared with laughter.

As Megan ran into the clearing at Sallee's Rock, she phased with Jack seconds behind her. She was so preoccupied with the black wolf that she never noticed the others waiting on the boulders.

"Well, now that's interesting," Tucker said to the late arrivals.

Megan did a quick squint with her brows, silently questioning Jack.

"Who knew running through the woods could get one's backside covered in mud?" Tucker said and the grin fell from Megan's face when she remembered she wasn't wearing any clothes.

A deep red bloomed in her cheeks as she stepped behind Jack and giggled against his back. "You are going to pay for this, Jason."

Jack pulled her around to his side and she buried her face against his chest. He laughed and leaned down to whisper in her ear. "Imagine what you would look like if I finished what *you* started." He reached over and grabbed her clothes off the boulder. Obviously, Whitney had folded the shirt.

Handing her the clothes, he pushed her behind him, giving her privacy from the others.

"Ignore them, Megan," Whitney said as she walked over and stood beside Jack, helping to shield Megan until she was dressed. "It's their man brain talking." Whitney shot a dirty look at Jack and Tucker. Once Megan was dressed, Whitney led her across the clearing. "So how was it?"

"It was so amazing! I can't wait to do it again." Megan's face beamed with unmasked enthusiasm.

"You know, it's still early... we can finish what you started," Jack yelled from behind her, and she blew him off with the flick of her hand.

The girls walked along the path and Megan bravely told them what they wanted to know. Jack, Mason, and Tucker followed behind, and every so often, Megan would look over her shoulder and smile. Jack winked in return.

# Forty-Six

*Jesse*

By the time Thursday rolled around, Jesse and Lori were busy distributing flyers along the business strip of Cloverly. It was a last-minute idea to remind the citizens of the council meeting scheduled for later that night. "I hope this works," Jesse said, taping a flyer to the cafe window as passersby stared. Most business owners allowed them to put out the flyers, some even found it amusing, but the looks and laughs they received irritated her. "They think we're crazy."

"So what? It helps them sleep at night," Lori said.

On their walk home, Jesse glanced around the neighborhood to the neatly kept houses and manicured lawns. Cloverly was oddly quiet compared to Indy where the hustle and bustle carried on for most of the day. "Lori, where are all the kids? The ones that were at the Fun

Fest?"

"They live on the other side of Main Street. This is the elderly side of town," Lori said, stopping in front of her house.

It sounded plausible, actually, and Jesse frowned. "Dogs too?"

"Mr. Tully has a dog," Lori said with a glance across the street. "But it's an inside dog, which is why you never see it."

"So he never lets it out to use the bathroom? His house must stink to high heavens."

"No, silly. He has a kennel behind his house." Lori pointed to the small, brick house next door to Brian.

"Then how do you know he has a dog if you never see it?"

"Ask the mailman. Bones goes ballistic every time he steps up on the porch."

That settled it. Pulling a Lori by making a big deal out of nothing, she had apparently lost her mind. "Don't be late. I want to get to the meeting early," Jesse said before continuing down the sidewalk. Glancing across the street, it was obvious Brian still wasn't home, and no big surprise there. After their last heated exchange, he practically disappeared.

She held her hair against her head and sweat trickled down her back. It was a hot, steamy day and she should've worn it up, but in her haste to get going that morning, she forgot her hair clip. As she walked up the steps, her hair fell into place when she reached for the bundle of bright blue carnations lying on the table. *How sweet.* She lifted the flowers up and walked into the house, not bothering to put them in water. In the beginning, the flowers meant something to her, a blossoming relationship with a wonderful guy. Now, they were just further proof of how flawed the GAG scale was, and it was time she stopped rating guys according to it.

She walked into her room and kicked off her shoes before sorting through the flower stems to find the small paper card. Reading the words of wisdom, "Life was simple... until you." She rolled her eyes. *Yeah, I know what you mean.* She pinned the ribbon and the card on the corkboard and opened the closet door where she stared at the double rack of clothes. Her fingers skipped over the various fabrics, looking for something cool and comfortable to wear to the meeting, and pausing at the floral dress she had worn to the theater. The following morning was when they found the cedar box. She frowned. If she could go back to that day, would she have opened the box? Again, she rolled her eyes. Deciding on a simple skirt and a button-up blouse, she pulled the hangers off the rod and closed the closet door.

A car door slammed, drawing her attention to the front window and she hurried over, thinking it might be Brian. As aggravated as she was, a part of her hoped he would come back to plead his case; or if she dared to ask him, go with her to the meeting. She pushed the curtain to the side and grinned. Megan stood there waving from the sidewalk as Jack backed out of the driveway.

She rushed down the stairs when Megan walked up on the porch. "I'm so glad you're here." she said, pushing open the screen door. She wanted to question Megan about Hunter's Ridge, but with Jack as her shadow, that hadn't been possible until now. "So are you and Jack serious? What about Tracy? Has she threatened to claw your eyes out?"

"Jack is wonderful," she said with a smile. "Tracy and Randy have kicked things up a notch. They're getting married."

"Get out of here! When?" Jesse couldn't help but smile.

"They're at the courting stage, but I expect it will be sooner than later."

"Are you good with that?"

"Actually, I am. You should see them together, they're adorable," Megan said before changing the subject. "How are you feeling?

"I'm fine. Just a few scratches." Jesse dismissed her concern as she crossed the room and sat down on the edge of the bed. "I've been worried about you, since we don't see each other as often as we used to."

"You could have called. I'm really surprised you didn't," Megan confessed. Taking a seat at the sewing machine, she pushed back the curtain as Jack walked around the cabin.

"I didn't want to interrupt." Jesse grinned.

"You're like a sister. You're allowed to interrupt." Megan turned in the chair as the curtain fell into place.

"What were you doing on Hunter's Ridge if you were sick?" The question was unexpected, and based on the stunned look on Megan's face, it was probably rude to blurt it out like that, not to mention being none of her business. But isn't that what sisters were for? She smiled sheepishly.

"The short version of a long story," Megan said. "I wasn't sick. I had insomnia and didn't feel like going on vacation and walking around all zombie-like. As for

Hunter's Ridge? You know how much I love hiking."

"So you hiked up the ridge and then what? Fell asleep and rolled off the cliff? Yeah, I'm calling BS." Jesse pinned her with an unbelieving stare. The whole explanation sounded rehearsed, and she wasn't buying it.

"No." Megan laughed. "I hiked up the ridge and was sitting on the cliff. The view is amazing. But when I got up to leave, I tripped over a rock and you know the rest."

That sounded somewhat convincing, Jesse admitted. "But who in their right mind walks in the woods at night, especially alone?"

"Guilty." Megan lifted her hand. "Plus, if it hadn't been for that night, I might not have met Jack."

"Well, actually we were planning a party."

"The dance?" Megan picked up a carnation and sniffed. "That reminds me. You left early, and I didn't get the chance to thank you. Whitney said you were sick, but I talked to Brian and I know that wasn't the case."

"I don't know what's going on with him. One minute he's mad, the next he's sending me flowers. Are we together or not? Frankly, I just don't care."

"Obviously, he's not mad if he sent you flowers," Megan said, putting the flower back with the others.

"And messages." Jesse got up and walked over to the corkboard. "Five so far." She placed the cards on the table in front of Megan.

"Are you sure they're from Brian? I mean this..." she waved her hand over the cards, her head shaking, "just doesn't sound like something he would write."

"Well, you know him better than I do." Jesse frowned and looked down at the cards.

"*I can make you happy if given a chance.*" Megan

chewed her bottom lip as she read the other cards. "Brian didn't write that. He's too..."

"Macho?" Jesse said, pinning the cards back on the board. "Yeah, it definitely doesn't fit his personality."

"Brian told me about the flowers," Megan said. "But he thinks you're sending them to yourself."

Jesse's smile dropped and her jaw ticked. "Why would I do that?" She glared at the front window.

"He thought you were trying to make him jealous, but I told him you would never do something like that."

"How dare he! If I had sent the flowers, I would have at least spelled my name right, don't you think?" Now she was pissed. It was a good thing he wasn't home or else she would have marched across the street and given him a piece of her mind.

"I didn't realize it was spelled wrong," Megan said as Jesse reached over and grabbed the carnations off the table.

"It's not for a girl, but I was named after my grandfather on my mother's side," Jesse said, turning to the trash can.

"What are you doing? You can't throw them away." Megan pushed her hands out to stop her.

"Why not?"

"Because you don't know who sent them. You obviously have a secret admirer."

"Yeah, and according to Brian, it's me!" She handed Megan the flowers and walked over and flopped down on the bed. "He gripes my ass."

Megan laughed and put the flowers on the table before moving closer to Jesse. "I wasn't trying to upset you. I told Brian I would talk to you. That's how I know about the flowers. He seemed troubled you were getting them."

"But the jerk thought I was sending them to myself. How messed up is that?" Jesse paused. "That's all right; after tonight, he'll probably never speak to me again. I'm a lot of things but desperate isn't one of them." Jesse fell back on the bed.

"You're not going to confront him, are you?" Megan asked, glancing towards the window.

"No, I'm going to piss him off by exposing the secret of Cloverly."

"Why would you do that? It's an old, outdated, secret," Megan said, her disapproval plain on her face. "Most people here don't even know it exists."

"It's not outdated and if you truly do know the secret, how can you sit there and defend them?" Jesse asked, but when Megan didn't flinch, she continued. "Gramma is afraid they'll kill her if they find out she knows their secret."

"Jesse, that's wrong. I don't know where you got your information, but they aren't killing anyone. They're not monsters, or whatever name you've labeled them. They are humans with the ability to shift forms; and if you knew them, you wouldn't be so quick to expose them," Megan argued.

"Can you honestly say the wolf that attacked me wasn't threatening? I don't think so," Jesse said, a little harsher than she intended. "Megan, you didn't see the look in his eyes. It was terrifying. If it hadn't been for the neighbors, we probably wouldn't be having this conversation right now."

"Just talk to them. Give them a chance to explain."

"It's too late for that. The council meeting is in an hour and I will be there. And now I have a witness," Jesse said, getting off the bed.

"But the secret has nothing to do with them," Megan insisted as Jesse stared out the back window.

"We're friends. We're supposed to stick together. But if you know so much about them, tell me who they are." Jesse looked back.

"Why can't you just assume I know what I'm talking about, and leave it at that? Is it too hard to believe I might actually know more than you do? I've known the secret for years. I live with it. Please don't do this. For all you know, I could be one of them and there is nothing about me that's threatening." Megan stomped across the room and out the door as Jesse called out behind her.

"Who are you protecting?"

# Forty-Seven

*Jack*

Jack was surprised to see Megan running across the yard as if her tail were on fire. Her arms pumped with her legs and he made a mental note to reduce her caffeine intake. Scowling, he couldn't imagine what could have upset the little spitfire, but he intended to find out. "What's wrong?" The frown on her face suggested the talk with Jesse must not have gone as planned.

"We need to see Alpha Cooper. Jesse is going to expose us at the council meeting tonight!" Megan said, opening the car door.

"She told you that?"

"No, she just said she was exposing the secret of Cloverly."

"And that is?" Jack slid behind the wheel and started the car.

"You drive. I'll explain," Megan huffed as he backed the car out of the driveway. "Years ago, the people of Cloverly were threatened by a pack of wolves. Cloverly is a rural area, and the hunters depended on the woods for food to get them through the winters. So late one evening, a group of five hunters was bringing in their haul when a pack of starving wolves surrounded them. As the wolves stalked closer, a nervous, trigger-happy hunter shot and killed the largest of the pack. Based on the legend, the hunter celebrated and talked about the money he would make from the pelt while the other wolves watched from a distance. Later that night, the pack paid the hunters another visit, and from there, the story grew and grew."

"But what does that have to do with us?"

"Over the years, the original story was forgotten, but the few that knew the secret apparently kept the newspaper articles that were published as a warning to the residents. Lori stumbled over one of those articles at the library, and that was all it took to pique their curiosity. Brian said they were talking crazy after Jesse found a box with more articles, and consequently, they are now linking all of them to werewolves.

"How do you know about the secret? I vaguely remember the story."

"I work at the cafe, and over the years, I've picked up bits and pieces from the old-timers."

"So basically, the Hudson pack killed the hunter, and what? Threatened the others?"

"Yes."

"Great! That's all we need," Jack said. Turning off the highway, the Alpha house sat on the edge of a five hundred-acre spread, overlooking the river. The old, weathered barn had been converted to a house with a wall of windows two stories high.

"Wow, I remember this," Megan said as soon as she got out of the car.

"Jack, Megan, come in," Alpha Cooper said in greeting as he held the door open.

Megan glanced around the large entrance hall and followed Jack. The house was cozy, with an open floor plan, and more cabin-like than a barn. With afghans draped over the back of the sofas and pillows conveniently placed in the chairs, the room was more than just welcoming. She glanced down at the large area rug that silenced her footsteps. It looked nothing like the dirt floor she remembered.

Closing the door behind them, Ben walked over and leaned against the mantel where a large wolf tapestry hung above the stone fireplace. "To what do I owe the pleasure?" he asked as they sat down on the sofa.

"Have you ever heard about the secret of Cloverly?" Jack asked, and Megan nudged his arm. "Jesse is going to expose the secret tonight at the council meeting."

"I've heard some stories, but I didn't realize it was a secret. I remember my father talking about it when I was younger." Alpha Cooper walked over to the desk and picked up a box of index cards.

"Well, maybe it wasn't a secret to the pack, but to most of the residents of Cloverly, it was. They were actually threatened," Megan said. "Jesse's grandmother knew the secret and I guess she told Jesse."

"That happened way before our time. Why is it so important now?"

"Actually, it's more current than we realized. We all

know the Hudson alphas were using scare tactics to control the pack, and eventually the people of Cloverly as well. And from what Jesse reported, Travis may have said something in that vein the night he attacked her," Megan said.

"He also threatened Megan, Tracy and Randy," Jack added.

"And those are just the ones we know about," Ben said, running his hand over his jaw. "This is not good. He worked at the gas station for how many years?"

"As long as I can remember," Jack said.

"Has anyone talked to Jesse?" the alpha asked, opening the box.

"Megan tried."

"She's Dr. Williams' daughter, right?" Ben pulled out a card and quickly dialed the number. "Answering service. He's out of office today. Do you know what time the meeting starts?"

Jack looked over at Megan. "Six o'clock."

"How close are you to Jesse?" the alpha asked, turning to face the window.

"Sisters," Megan replied.

"If you can catch her before she leaves, stall her," Ben said. "If that doesn't work, tell her the truth."

"The truth?" Megan asked as the alpha pulled his keys from his pocket.

"Yes. Explain to her that we are not under the Hudson rule, and Travis never had the authority to issue any threats against anyone. She needs to know that we will protect her, along with the rest of the people of Cloverly."

"Yes, sir," Megan said, following Jack out the door.

"Do you think many people will show up?" Megan

asked as she slid into the passenger seat and closed the car door.

"I'm sure there will be a few, but don't stress over it. It will be all right," Jack said before he started the car and took off down the gravel road, leaving a trail of dust in their wake.

"Maybe, but I'm worried how the pack will view Jesse once this is over. She's not a vindictive person and she would never intentionally do anything to hurt me; of that I know for sure." Megan let out a breath. "She's scared, and she already knows about us. I should have trusted her enough to tell her the truth when I had the chance."

"I haven't been friends with Jesse as long as you, but even I know she isn't doing this out of spite. She's trying to protect her grandmother, and I admire her for that. Few people would stand up against a pack of wolves." Jack reached over and rubbed her shoulder. "Whatever happens, we'll deal with it."

Megan tried to call Jesse as they crossed the bridge to Cloverly, but she wasn't answering her phone. Deciding their best option was to go straight to the council meeting, Jack stopped and picked up Whitney and Mason on the way. As he parked in front of the town hall building, Megan was the first out of the car. *Spitfire*, he thought as she hoofed it across the parking lot.

Cracking the door, Megan peeked into the room and Jack pointed the others toward the parking area. "Do you see them?" he whispered over his shoulder.

The meeting was scheduled to start in less than twenty minutes and, according to Randy, the council members were never late. Megan leaned back, bumping into Jack as the door shut. "They're standing on the left side of the room," she said, following him around the building.

Jack wasn't sure how the meeting would go, or if Jesse would actually carry out her plan to expose them, but in the event she did, they needed to be prepared. "Listen," he said, once they were all gathered in the parking lot. "Let's go in, but spread out. I don't want it to look like we're together."

"We'll go in first," Randy said, holding Tracy's hand. "I've been attending these meetings for years. I know everyone so we can provide a distraction until you all get seated."

"Jack, we've got a bigger problem." Tucker said, joining the group. "I found this lying on the counter at the automotive store." He handed the flyer to Jack and walked back towards the front of the building.

"Shit," Jack grumbled, wadding up the paper as a car turned into the lot.

"What's going on?" the woman asked as she pulled up alongside them.

"The meeting was canceled," Tracy replied, walking over to the car. Jack was a second behind her. He held his breath, not knowing what she was up to, but at that point, he wasn't sure what to do either.

"What's this werewolf nonsense?" The lady handed Tracy the flyer, and she quickly scanned it.

Shaking her head, Tracy looked back at the woman. "I don't know how many of these are floating around town, but it's a stupid hoax. A few teenagers set up an elaborate story about werewolves so they could get people's reactions on camera. It's all part of a fake documentary for a school project," she said without missing a beat.

"Kids these days will do anything for fifteen minutes of fame." The woman spewed out a few choice words as she put the car in reverse and exited the parking lot.

"That was impressive," Jack said, "I believed every word."

"Just doing my part."

As more cars drove into the parking area, Randy and Tracy continued to send them away while Jack spread the word and they all followed Tracy's lead.

"The meeting's getting ready to start, so we need to go," Jack said, leading them around to the front door. "The alpha's in the building too, just in case things get out of hand." He looked down at Megan and said, "Don't leave my side."

Tucker was the last to enter the room, and although Jack was relieved to see him, he knew what was going through his mind. Draping his arm over the back of Megan's chair, when Jesse moved to the front corner of the room, he leaned in and whispered. "That must be the witness."

"Mallory?" She glanced over at Jack.

"I'm not sure, but I think she was at the cabin the night Jesse was attacked. She must have seen something."

"What was she doing at the cabin?"

"Well, if she's the waitress from the cafe, probably dating Seth."

"This will not end well," Megan said, interlocking her fingers as she placed her hands in her lap.

After the last council member took a seat, the meeting started. Oddly enough, no one seemed interested in the barn tour or how much to charge for the corn maze, but the werewolves were a different story.

As Jesse moved to the center of the room, the small crowd silenced. Wiping her hands down the front of her skirt, she scanned the room with uncertainty in her eyes.

"I tried to get you on the phone. Jesse is going to expose us here tonight," Alpha Cooper whispered when Dr. Williams took the seat beside him.

"Why would she do that? She wouldn't even admit she was attacked! After you told me about it, I thought it would be best to wait until I had a day off so I could bring her to the Alpha house and explain everything to her there. I wanted to introduce her to the pack," Dr. Williams said, glancing up at Jesse, "But she was gone by the time I got up this morning."

"She never admitted Travis attacked her?" Alpha Cooper asked.

"No, but I ran the test to see if she was infected. Thankfully, the results came back negative," Dr. Williams said as Jesse started to speak.

# Forty-Eight

*Jesse*

"Thank you all for meeting today. Although I was hoping to see more people in attendance, I'm grateful to those of you that did come. My name is Jesse Williams. I'm here to discuss the secret of Cloverly." Whispers were audible in the room as Jesse continued. "Years ago, hunters stumbled onto a pack of wolves here in Cloverly. These wolves weren't normal wolves, they were werewolves," Jesse said. Expecting more whispers she was startled by a man dressed in camo who yelled back, "Is this a joke?"

But before Jesse could answer, Brian chimed in. "Shut-up, Eugene, and let her speak. Then you'll find out if it's a joke."

"Hear me out, please," Jesse said, squaring her shoulders. She would not allow Brian to distract her with his false gallantry anymore. She was on a mission to protect her grandmother and nothing short of a miracle would stop her. The people listened as she continued to talk, and Lori chimed in from time to time. Almost everyone thought she was crazy, although the few who knew the secret, nodded, spurring her on.

"Do you know how crazy you sound? And we're supposed to believe you?" Eugene yelled out again. Hearing agreements from several people in the room set Jesse on edge.

"Yes, I know it sounds crazy, but I also believe the more people that know, the safer we will be. We have elderly residents that fear them and have even been threatened by them. You can believe what you want. I'm just telling you what I know. My grandmother fears the wolves, as well as the safety of all the residents of Cloverly. I'm here to do whatever I can to protect her and others like her," Jesse said while Eugene swatted the air in front of him.

"Ignore him. He's just one person," Lori whispered and Jesse smiled.

"Ms. Williams, can you prove there are wolves? You have to admit your story is a bit out there," one council woman said.

"Mrs. Adams," Jesse said, reading the nameplate that rested in front of the dark-haired woman, "I was attacked by a wolf four days ago."

The room erupted with chatter, and the mayor rushed to Jesse's side, trying to get control and quiet the room. After a few minutes, everyone calmed down and directed their attention back to Jesse.

"You look fine to me," another council member replied as he turned his nameplate so she could read it.

The smirk on his face told her exactly what he thought.

"He wasn't trying to kill me, Mr. Moran. He was giving me the proof I needed to come here today and expose the wolves."

"Okay, Ms. Williams, I'm game. Why would any werewolf want to expose himself? And what proof did he give you?" Mrs. Adams asked.

"He showed his wolf, and I have scratches and cuts on my body from where I hid behind a holly bush."

"How did you escape the big, bad werewolf? Did you shake hands and part ways?" Mr. Moran asked.

"I don't remember how I got out from behind the bush, and I don't remember the ambulance ride to the hospital. But I have a witness that saw the attack." Jesse was getting pissed, and Eugene's snide remarks and comments weren't helping any.

As the crowd waited, another man called out. "Where are these wolves?"

"That, sir, I don't know," Jesse said before Mallory joined her at the front of the room.

"Ms. Williams," Mrs. Adams said, dismissing Mallory, "I understand you wanting to protect your grandmother, but witness or not, unless one of you can produce an actual werewolf, there isn't much we can do. I'm sorry."

"Mallory, you saw the attack; was anyone else with you?" Jesse asked.

"No, just me."

"What about Seth or Whitney? Didn't they chase him into the woods?"

"Seth and Mason did. Whitney stayed with us."

"So there are at least four people who saw the wolf and you still think I need the wolf itself for proof?"

"Yes, Ms. Williams. Unless you have proof that the man can actually turn into a wolf, we have to assume it was just a normal wolf or a large dog. What time did this attack happen?" Mrs. Adams asked.

"It was late, about ten or so," Jesse replied.

"Then it was dark, which means, it may have been a dog," Mr. Moran said.

"Well, yeah, it was dark, but he was standing right in front of me. I'm not blind." Jesse glared in defiance.

"Maybe not, but I find it hard to believe your witness could see the attack from her kitchen window, especially at night," Mr. Moran said. Jesse knew he was trying to discredit her with his comment so she had no other choice but to call out her best friend.

"Megan, you know. Yesterday at my house, you said you would talk to them. Who are they?" Jesse asked, and the room grew quiet. Knowing she was putting her friend on the spot, she intended to beg her forgiveness later. Megan never said a word, but the frown on her face told Jesse she wasn't happy.

Scanning the crowd, Jesse homed in on Tucker and he rose to his feet. He looked uncomfortable standing at the back of the room, his face a mixture of shock and disbelief. He stared for a minute and then lowered his eyes, mouthing something she couldn't understand. But as the door shut behind him, Jesse stood there in a daze. The attraction she felt towards Tucker became a heart-wrenching emptiness that she couldn't explain. Gasping for air as the dark sorrow clouded her vision; she lowered her head and listened to the disparaging remarks floating around the room. When the realization finally settled over her, she looked back at the doors. *He's a wolf.* Her heart dropped to her stomach and a wave of dizziness overwhelmed her. She grabbed for Lori's arm. "Panic attack," she whispered as she tried to slow her racing heart. "I was wrong."

"What are you talking about?" Lori asked, holding her steady with the help of Mallory. "We need to get you out of here."

"No. I have to finish this." She leaned over and placed her hands on her knees, waiting for the dizziness to pass.

"Are you sure?" Lori looked at Mallory as she wrapped an arm around Jesse, trying to hold her in place.

Jesse nodded and took a deep breath, exhaling slowly. As she stood up, her body swayed and she prayed she wouldn't pass out in front of everyone. She turned to address the council members before several people got up and walked out of the room. "Mrs. Adams," she said, her voice shaky, "I came here today to expose the wolves in Cloverly. I thought by having a witness, I had all the proof I needed. I only wanted to protect my grandmother and anyone else that knew the secret. I thought I was doing the right thing, but I was wrong. Thank you for allowing me to speak." Jesse excused herself and hurried out the side door, eager to escape the crowd. How could she be so stupid? Tucker was a wolf, which meant Jack was a wolf. They were cousins, and Mason had grown up with Jack, so was he a wolf as well? And Megan? How did she fit into the mix? *For all you know, I could be one of them.* A tear trickled down her cheek, remembering Megan's words.

"Jesse, where are you going?" Lori ran toward Jesse, who headed down the road.

"I'll call you later," Jesse said, motioning her back. She

needed to clear her head and catch her breath. She had to calm down. How could she ever face her friends again? *What friends? You ratted them out!* Then she thought about Whitney and tears again filled her eyes. They talked about wolves the night of the party. She didn't deny there were wolves in the area; actually, she said it was the perfect location for them. Maybe Whitney wanted to tell her then, but since Jesse convinced herself that the wolves were something evil, she couldn't see what was right in front of her eyes.

"Get in and I'll give you a ride home," Brian said when she crossed the street.

"I don't need a ride." Jesse shot him a hateful glare. He was the last person she wanted to talk to, considering he just witnessed her making a complete fool of herself. And he would be the first one to say *told-you-so.* Turning down an alley, she looked back, but he continued down the road.

She wiped the tears from her eyes, remembering the look on Tucker's face before he walked out the door. He would never forgive her, of that she was sure. Cutting across a field, she had no idea where she was going and she didn't care. The further away she went, the better off she would be.

Sweat beaded on her forehead as she kicked the rocks along the gravel road, and she looked up at the sky to gauge the time. She wasn't sure how long she'd been walking, but once she got to the end of the road, she recognized the area and the *Welcome to Cloverly* sign. She turned right. Another half mile and she would be at the gas station. At least she could rest there for a minute and get a drink.

She crossed the empty lot as hot tears stung her eyes. "Closed?" She should have known! Just her luck. She sat down on the wooden porch and stared across the highway. It wasn't that long ago when they pulled into the station for gas. Thinking about that night and the green eyes that flared in the darkness, she jumped up off the porch. *Travis!*

Stumbling over her own feet, she took off running as fast as she could, her open-toed sandals slipping on the gravel. She glanced up at the fading daylight. Maybe she'd get lucky and someone she knew would stop and give her a ride. She slowed to a jog when she came to the gravel road, but being out in the middle of nowhere, and alone at night, she wasn't like Megan. She continued down the highway, seeing the stoplight in the distance, and using it to guide her. With a stitch in her side, tears rolled down her face. *Another brilliant idea.*

Too many thoughts cluttered her mind. She wondered why her friends never told her they were wolves. And why was her dad sitting in the middle of them at the council meeting? Had he known the whole time? Wiping her eyes, she crossed Main Street and headed for the cafe.

Streetlights flickered overhead as the remaining daylight faded. "Jesse?" She looked up and her dad waved from beside his truck. "I've been looking everywhere for you."

Jesse ran towards him, the strap of her sandal breaking and causing her to stumble before she fell into his arms. "I'm sorry. I didn't know." She bawled into his shirt.

"I know. We'll talk about it when we get home. Your grandmother is worried sick about you."

It was dark by the time Jesse and her dad walked in the back door. Following her grandmother into the living room, she sat down on the sofa and stared out the front window as thoughts of Tucker replayed through her mind.

Uncovering the town secret sounded simple enough, but as time went on, things got out of hand. With proof of wolves in the area, she never thought they were real werewolves until the night she was attacked by Travis. By threatening her, he started a war that she had no intention of losing. She made it personal, even when Brian and Megan tried to talk her out of it, but the night of her attack sealed their fate. Jesse was determined to stand up to them, no matter the cost, even though it turned out to be so much greater than she expected. When Tucker walked out the door, everything changed. She changed. Tucker, Jack, Whitney, Mason, Tracy, the Cabin Crew, all of them were wolves, and her friends. "I sure made a mess of things," Jesse said, wiping her face with her sleeve.

"You're not alone. It was as much me as you. But what's done is done, and now we move on," Gramma said, handing her a cup of coffee.

"Jesse, why didn't you tell me you knew about the wolves? All of this could have been avoided," Dr. Williams said, walking over to the front door and flipping on the porch light.

"I thought I was protecting you," she said as she pushed her trembling hands between her knees. She was only trying to help, not to harm anyone, or at least, that's what she told herself. "I didn't mean to embarrass you, but someone had to stand up for the elderly residents here."

"You can't blame it all on her, son. I played a role in it as well. I've carried that secret around with me for years, afraid that if anyone found out, I would be killed. Then, when Jesse came and told me what she wanted to do, it made sense. So I'm just as much at fault here as she is," Gramma said, looking him in the eye.

"So you basically lied about... you should have told me you were attacked. That would have been the perfect opportunity for us to discuss the wolves," he said, sitting down in the chair across from Jesse. "I would have told you everything if you had just told the truth." He exhaled a long breath.

"So you're saying you knew about the werewolves?" Jesse asked.

"Yes, of course I knew."

"Then you should've confronted me at the hospital. Because I didn't answer the question the way you wanted me to, you kept that information to yourself. You should've told me you knew it was a wolf attack, and I assume you did know. I assume you know a lot more about them than you're willing to tell me right now. I mean, really, Dad, are the elderly supposed to live in fear because of the poor wolves? Maybe the wolves shouldn't have tried to control the people with fear. They were nothing more than a pack of bullies; and bullies can be stopped if people are willing to confront them. Sure, I should have done a lot of things differently. I'm a teenager for Pete's sake! I'm allowed to make mistakes. But honestly, it wasn't my place to do anything. This should have been taken care of years ago before I was ever put on this earth," Jesse said, her anger getting the better of her.

"Do you know the name of the wolf that attacked you?" her dad asked.

"The female that was with him called him Travis," she

said, pissed that he caused her to lose her temper.

"Then he was the same wolf that attacked Megan. Did you know that?"

"Megan was attacked?"

"Yes, by the same wolf. He was trying to command the pack, and used you to do it. What do you think would have happened if our alpha took the pack and left? And a werewolf like Travis took over?"

"That's harsh, don't you think?" Gramma said as she walked around the sofa and gently squeezed Jesse's shoulder.

"No, Mom, I don't. He was dangerous... and what in the world were you doing out in the backyard with him, anyway, Jesse?"

"I didn't know he was there. The girl called me outside. She said she had information I could use to expose the wolves." Jesse thought about that night. It wasn't clear if his intent was to harm her or not, but she suspected he only wanted to scare her enough to stop her from going forward with the information. "What will they do when they find him?"

"He's already been found. Wolves are different. They live by a different set of rules. He attacked a pack member and then exposed his true identity to you intentionally. He would have been put to death, but instead, he was killed in a fight."

Jesse shivered. "I wish you had just told me about them in the beginning."

"I thought it would frighten you, and make you not want to live here." He looked down at his lap.

"I'm sorry but you should have told me. I'm not a child. I could have handled it," Jesse said.

"Well, the pack is fully exposed, and I'm not sure what the residents will do. Only time will tell," Dr. Williams said. He walked over and opened the door as Sonya walked across the porch. Pulling her into a hug when she stepped inside the door, he held her for a minute longer before leading her into the living room. "Jesse, I'd like you to meet Sonya."

Jesse looked at their laced fingers, and then up at her dad's face. Sonya was the lady from the bookstore, his old girlfriend. But why was he introducing her now?

"Sonya, dear, how are you?" Gramma asked while crossing the room.

"I'm fine, Emmalyn. I've missed you," Sonya said, hugging Gramma.

"Sonya is my mate. I left her years ago to keep her safe, but I won't give her up again," David said. "Nothing will ever come between us again."

"Why would you have to give her up?" Jesse didn't understand where he was going with his statement. It sounded so weird and was not something she expected coming from him.

"Jesse, Sonya is a member of the pack. She is my world and always has been. That's not saying I didn't love your mother. I did, very much. She is a wonderful person and if not for her, I wouldn't have you."

"Oh, dear me! I had no idea," Gramma gasped, sinking down on the sofa next to Jesse.

"It's all right," Sonya said as she kneeled down in front of Gramma. "I know this is hard for you; you've had to deal with a lot because of a pack that no longer exists. We had no idea the threats were continuing because most of that pack was killed off years ago. Alpha Cooper saved us, not just the pack, but also the residents here in Cloverly."

"I don't know what to say. I wasn't personally threatened, but I knew the secret," Gramma said. "I was afraid."

"Emmalyn, you had every right to be afraid. Please don't blame yourself. Protecting your family is the most important thing. It takes guts to do what you all did."

"But... you're really a wolf?" Jesse stared, unconvinced. "You're so beautiful; not at all like the pictures in my book."

"Yeah, books like that aren't always accurate. It's hard to write about something you've never encountered, so most stories come straight from the imagination of the writer." Sonya smiled.

"I'm sorry. I don't understand any of this and at the moment, my brain has flat-lined. All I know is: I had to protect Gramma," Jesse said. Stressed and exhausted, all she wanted to do now was go to bed and sleep for the next seven days, forgetting about all things wolf.

"I'm sorry also," her dad said. "If I had been paying more attention, I would have noticed you questioning things like the wolf book and the picture. I guess I'm as much at fault here as anyone else. I've been a little distracted."

Jesse giggled when Sonya blushed. She wasn't opposed to their relationship, although it wasn't something she could picture either. Sonya was a wolf. What the hell did that even mean? "I love you, Dad, and I didn't mean to embarrass you, but..."

"No buts," he said, "I love you too. And had you not exposed those mangy wolves, Sonya wouldn't be here with me right now."

"David!" Sonya scolded him with a grin.

He winked and pulled her to his side. "I didn't know how to tell you about her. I've wanted to since the day you showed me the picture."

"Oh, that reminds me," Sonya said, turning to face Dr. Williams. "There are roses on the porch that I assume are not for me."

Jesse jumped up and hurried across the room. "I'll be right back." She walked out on the porch and tears filled her eyes as she picked up the bundle of red roses. Before going back into the house, she drew in a deep breath.

"Is there something you want to tell me?" Dr. Williams asked, causing Jesse to blush.

"No, Dad," she said, hiding behind the roses.

"Red roses seem pretty serious if you ask me."

"I'm not asking." She went straight into the kitchen, ignoring the chuckles and snickers from the living room. She desperately wanted to see what was written on the card, but her dad was obviously enjoying her discomfort. Reaching down under the sink, she pulled out a mason jar and quickly filled it with water.

In her room, Jesse put the roses in the jar and untied the red ribbon. Her hands trembled as she looked through the stems. Retrieving the card, she stared at her name, already knowing they were from Tucker. The look on his face when he walked out of the meeting was sheer agony, and that's when everything fell into place. She felt a connection to Tucker every time he was around, but she was so wound up in the pissing match with Brian, and her mission to expose the wolves, she kept pushing him to the side.

She pressed the card against her chest and lay back on the bed, staring at the ceiling. He was the only one that noticed the ribbon in her hair; and when they were on Hunter's Ridge, he helped her through the panic attacks. A tear trickled down the side of her face. At the dance, he was concerned about her, yet her anger at Brian distorted what was happening right there in front of her face. She rolled over on the bed and stared at the card before finally opening it. "Passion rules the heart, but denial destroys the soul." She squeezed her eyes shut.

# Forty-Nine

*Jesse*

By the following week, things had settled down in
Cloverly, and although there were still a few whispers
from time to time, Jesse shrugged them off. Based on the
gossip she heard around town, the werewolf story was
actually a fake documentary staged by a group of
teenagers from the local high school. Where that notion
arose, she didn't know; but if it helped the citizens sleep
better at night, it was all good.

Jesse sat on the front porch swing, listening to birds
chirp as they fluttered through the trees, and she glanced
across the street. She hadn't seen Brian since he offered
her a ride home last week, and it was time to clear the air
between them. Thirty minutes later, she stood at his front
door with her hand raised and ready to knock. *Maybe it
was better to give him more time.* Or maybe she should

have assumed there was nothing left to salvage from their friendship and moved on. As she turned to walk away, the front door swung open.

Brian yawned into his fist as he leaned against the door frame. His hair was flying in all directions and a clear indicator that he just crawled out of bed. It wasn't often Jesse caught a glimpse of him without his shirt on, but as he stood in the doorway wearing only a pair of faded jeans, she looked down at his bare feet.

"I'm sorry. I should have listened," she said.

"No, I should be the one apologizing. You were right to stand up for your grandmother. I would have done the same," he said and a smile stretched across his face.

"Then you believe me?" Jesse asked, looking up.

"No, but I don't fault you for doing what you thought was right. Like I said, I would have done the same thing if I thought my grandmother was..." Brian ran his fingers through his hair and looked over at the woods.

Jesse was amazed that after everything that happened, he still refused to believe her. Lori was right. For a good-looking guy, he was a bonehead. She smiled. "So are we good now? Like... friends?"

"Yeah, we're good but only on one condition." Brian chuckled.

"And that would be?" Jesse bit her lip. He seemed nervous, and she braced herself for what would probably end up a lecture.

"Just promise me you won't go telling anymore silly town secrets."

Jesse groaned and shook her head. "Don't worry, my secret telling days are over. That I promise." She smiled at his smirk. "But I have a condition of my own."

"Okay," Brian said, motioning her into the house.

Jesse waited until he shut the door before nailing him with her suspicion. "I want you to tell me about Annie. You were with her that night, weren't you?"

Brian lowered his eyes and shifted nervously. "Annie stopped by the station to drop off some study materials for her dad, my boss. I didn't realize it, but she was waiting in the parking lot when I got off from work. She is an old girlfriend from high school, and now she wants to get back together. I'm not ready for a serious relationship, but she doesn't take rejection well." He glanced over at Jesse. "Right now, I just want to work on my career."

"I know exactly what you mean," Jesse said. "I also want to apologize about the flowers. If I had known you weren't the one sending them... I truly thought they were from you."

"Yeah, Megan told me you were pretty upset. You deserved the flowers. I just wish I'd sent them." He smiled. "Did you ever figure out who they came from?"

"No," Jesse lied, tucking a strand of hair behind her ear. She knew who sent the flowers, but since she promised not to tell anymore secrets, she wouldn't. The moment Tucker walked out of the council meeting was the moment she realized her mistake. Thinking about him made her stomach hurt and her heart ache. She cleared her throat. "Did you ever check the cameras?" She knew it was a longshot, and when she looked up and saw Brian's frown, she expected the worst.

"I pulled the cards, but I never got around to looking at the pictures. They're in the kitchen if you want to check them," Brian said.

"If you don't mind, I mean, I am curious as to what left those tracks," Jesse said as she followed him into the kitchen.

"Well, don't get your hopes up, because I don't think you're going to find what you're looking for. If anything, you might see a dog or deer." Brian shuffled a few things around on the desk. "Have a seat."

Jesse sat down in front of the computer as Brian leaned over her shoulder and inserted the first camera card. Scrolling over the menu, he clicked open the file. Within a few seconds, thumbnails popped up across the screen and Brian clicked on the first picture, then the second. "There's nothing there," Jesse said as he continued clicking the pictures.

"It was probably the wind blowing through the trees that activated the cameras," Brian said before deleting the pictures from the card. Handing Jesse the two remaining cards, he looked up at the clock on the wall. "I have to be at work in twenty minutes, and I still need to get in the shower."

"I can leave and come back another time," Jesse suggested as she looked down at the small black cards in her hand.

"No, you're fine. Just delete the pictures when you're done," he said before walking out of the room.

"You don't want to see them?" she yelled out, and he stopped at the stairs.

"Not really," Brian yelled back.

Jesse turned back to the computer as footsteps traveled overhead. She stared down at the camera cards, but did she really want to see what was on them? To say no was a lie, and not knowing... She took a deep breath and inserted the first card, but as Brian predicted, she saw nothing but trees. She deleted the pictures and removed the card as the upstairs shower came on.

Inserting the last card, she scrolled over the menu and clicked open the file. As the thumbnails popped up, she looked up at the ceiling before clicking on the first picture and then the second. Her heart raced when she stared at the three large wolves. Quietly studying the photo, she wasn't sure if she believed what she was seeing. She chewed her lip and scrolled through the remaining pictures. Seeing her friends and then the wolves verified everything her dad told her about the Cabin Crew.

She scanned back through the pictures until she found the one with Tucker standing near the boulders. His shirtless figure caused her face to heat up; he was sheer perfection. Butterflies danced in her belly and she giggled softly. *If only.* Clicking on the next picture, her breath hitched as she stared into the warm brown eyes that she knew could only belong to Tucker. The large, brown wolf, staring across the clearing, was so perfect and she could imagine hanging the photo on a wall.

She reached over and turned on the printer while listening to the upstairs shower. Once the menu popped up on the screen, she clicked on the print button. "*Come on.*" She murmured as if it would make the slow moving printer print faster. *Finally,* she thought, blowing out a breath.

Taking the two prints, she tucked them under her shirt and glanced up when the shower shut off. She considered showing Brian the pictures so she could say *told you so* because that would have been the mature thing to do. She rolled her eyes. Looking back at the screen, she quickly deleted the pictures and pulled out the card, then reached over and turned off the printer.

Placing the cards on top of the computer, she hurried

through the house and went out the front door. There was no reason for her to wait until Brian came downstairs because she knew if he asked about the pictures, she would lie.

She ran across the street, hoping she would make it inside before Brian noticed she was gone. As she opened the screen door, she yelled, "It's just me, Gramma," and raced up the steps, taking them two at a time. Pulling the pictures from beneath her shirt, she closed the bedroom door and stared down at the wolf. Her chest tightened. Everything that happened was her fault, and the thought of never seeing Tucker again practically crushed her spirit. It was hard to breathe when she thought about the big lug because, whether she admitted it or not, she truly felt a connection to him.

It wasn't necessary to hide the pictures under her mattress, but to her, very important. It was her way of protecting him, even if it were just his image. As tears filled her eyes, she looked at the wilted red roses. The thought of throwing them out was unbearable so she opted to keep them for a little longer, maybe another week or so. Wiping her eyes, she opened the door and with one last glance around the room, headed down the stairs.

"I'll be back later," Jesse yelled, walking out the front door. The shelter was just a few blocks on the other side of Main Street and she hoped the brisk walk would clear her head.

For obvious reasons, she was glad she went to Brian's before going to the shelter. They had started their relationship on the fast track and she was ready to put on the brakes and just be friends. Her future plans of opening a shop with Megan remained at the top of her to-do list, not worrying over a failed relationship. Plus, not knowing where she stood with Brian sucked, and she swore she would never make that mistake again.

Doing her best to make her grandmother feel safe was her top priority and after talking with her dad and Sonya, her grandmother realized she was no longer in danger. Jesse noticed the change in her grandmother immediately. She was spending more time sitting on the porch, watching the sun rise and even adding a new flowerbed in the front yard. Sonya volunteered to help her plant the flowers and actually brought a few of the pack members over to till the ground ahead of time. They were all on their best behavior and seemed really nice.

The day was a complete turnaround compared to a week ago, but all of that could have been avoided. Starting over in Cloverly, she and her dad were distracted by everyday life and the communication between them had failed. *All things happen for a reason,* she thought, but she wasn't sure what that reason could be. One thing she did know: she and Megan would be touring the bookstore later that afternoon. Sonya was ready to sell it but since Megan was a member of the pack, and Jesse was practically her stepdaughter, she agreed to rent the building to them, with an option to buy at a later date. Jesse smiled, knowing it was just what they were looking for and hopefully within six months, they could open for business.

As for the pictures, she didn't need to prove anything to anyone, which was why she chose to delete them instead of showing them to Brian. Tucker's picture became a reminder. *Never deny that which is in your heart, for it too shall walk away.*

Thirty minutes later, Jesse stood outside the cinderblock building, debating on whether to go inside or run home and hide in her room. She loved volunteering at the animal shelter and giving snuggles and huggies to all the little animals that didn't have homes. Their bright eyes begged for attention, and she was willing to assist whenever needed.

Moose was a shelter cat, and she still remembered the day she rescued him. He was abandoned in a cardboard box and left on the sidewalk in front of the Indy Animal Shelter. Curled up in a corner, a fluffy, gray furball, so sweet and cuddly, he was instantly precious to her. Over the years, he grew up to become a grumpy, ol' stud muffin, and that's why she loved him. He was magnificent.

Taking a deep breath to steady her nerves, she pulled open the door and walked into the reception area. It had been a week since she dared show her face but she was glad to be back. Still feeling a little uncertain, she gathered her courage as the veterinarian walked into the room. "Hello, Dr. Stevens," she said and smiled. It was time to face the music and after exposing the pack, she could understand if he sent her away, but that didn't mean she wouldn't bawl her eyes out.

"How are you?" he said, motioning her over. "I'm glad you came back. This place has gone to the dogs without you," he joked. And just like that, the awkwardness evaporated. She grinned at his welcoming smile. He and his wife were good to her and the thought of never working at the shelter again sucked big time.

"Well, you know me. I love animals," she said, visibly relieved.

"I'm glad to hear that because I could use a good assistant. It's not always full-time hours, but if you're interested, it is a paying job."

"You want me to be your paid assistant?" Jesse narrowed her eyes as she looked around the room. "But I thought your wife was your assistant."

"She was, but with the baby due in three months, she highly recommended you." Dr. Stevens held out a key.

"Well, in that case, I'll take it. Thank you so much." Shoving the key into her pocket, she hurried to the kennel area, grabbing a smock off the coat rack on the way.

Scooping poop and bleaching cages wasn't a glamorous job, but she wasn't a glamor girl. Okay, that wasn't true. She loved to dress up and go dancing, which meant wearing beautiful gowns and heels. Then she thought about the best dance partner she'd ever had and her shoulders slumped as her mind drifted back.

Three days after Tucker walked out of her life, she ran into Seth at the cafe. As soon as she walked through the door, he pulled her into a hug. At first, she didn't know how to respond to the wolfman but Seth was a good friend, both he and Mallory, and she fell into his arms. Tears welled in her eyes and she wiped them away with the napkin Mallory stuffed into her hand. By the time she left the cafe, her heart was heavy knowing Tucker had returned to Tennessee and she would never see him again. She shook her head. Nothing good could come from dwelling on past mistakes.

After emptying the last of the litterboxes, Jesse hauled the trash bags out the back door and set them on the ground while she removed the cinderblocks from the tops of the trash totes. Raccoons were notorious for digging through the garbage and the heavy blocks kept them away. As she picked up the last bag, she noticed a scruffy, brown stray watching her from across the field. The shelter was located at the end of the road with farmland to the right and an empty field on the left, which was where they held the county fair each year. She glanced down at the bag and then back to the dog. It was probably a herding dog, belonging to one of the local farmers and running between fields. Still, it looked pitiful and mud-caked, or maybe its fur was matted. *It could be a wolf.* The thought crossed her mind, but the dog was nowhere near as large as Tucker's wolf. Plus, Megan said their wolves rarely ran during daylight hours, for safety reasons, so she was confident it wasn't one.

Jesse called to the dog as she searched through the bag, digging for scraps she could use as bait. It was hesitant, but eventually inched closer, pausing from time to time as it bravely continued toward her. She cooed and stooped down, pushing her hand out, offering the dog the food. "You like that smell, don't you?" Her voice, soft and soothing, caused the dog's ears to flick up and down. After placing the food on the ground, she slowly offered her hand, and it sniffed her. "Good doggie." She encouraged as it scarfed down the crunchy kibble.

Moving slowly, she dug into the bag and brought out more scraps as the dog continued to eat. The canine didn't seem skittish, and once it let its guard down, she reached out and rubbed its ears with the tips of her fingers. But when she withdrew her hand, the dog quickly snapped. The bite was unexpected, and she jerked her hand back, shaking it as if that could stop the sizzling pain that spread beneath her skin. She screeched a swear word as the dog snarled and then darted across the field. "I wasn't going to hurt you!" she yelled, looking down at the trail of blood between her thumb and index finger. *Stupid dog.*

Tossing the trash bag in the can, she replaced the concrete blocks and headed back inside. *Brilliant*, she thought as she removed her smock and threw it into the dirty clothes bin along with the dirty towels she pulled from the cat cages. As she passed through the kennel area on her way into the exam room, she looked down at her throbbing hand. Hearing Dr. Stevens talking at the front desk, she opted for the restroom instead.

She ducked into the bathroom and locked the door, scowling at her image in the mirror. Her bun hung at the side of her head and her face was a red, blotchy mess. Turning on the faucet, she pumped the lemon-scented soap into her hand and quickly worked up a thick, pink lather as the sudsy water swirled down the drain.

It was foolish to think she could catch the dog, and judging by the way it accepted the food, she didn't expect it would bite. But as with everything else in her life, it seemed the more she tried to help, the more harm she caused. She sighed. Telling Dr. Stevens would only pile more humiliation onto her plate and at the moment, she wasn't that hungry. She pulled several paper towels from the dispenser and dabbed her hands dry.

The thought of rabies entered her mind, but when she lifted her left hand, she saw nothing. No puncture wound, no scratch, no broken skin. Rubbing over the area, it felt bruised and tender, but only to the touch. Apparently, the dog merely pinched her with its teeth, but that didn't explain the blood. Telling herself the dog probably bit its tongue was believable in her mind. And there wasn't anything more she could do unless the dog came back, which wasn't likely to happen. She finished cleaning herself up and adjusted her bun and walked out of the room.

"I'm finished for the day. Is there anything else you need done?" Jesse asked from the doorway of Dr. Stevens' office.

"No. Today's been slow and there's nothing on the schedule for this afternoon, so you can take the rest of the day off if you like."

"Well, then, I'll see you tomorrow," Jesse said as she turned to leave. "Oh, be careful when taking out the trash. I saw a stray dog running across the back field."

"It was probably someone's pet. We rarely find strays in Cloverly, but I'm sure I don't have to tell you why. They can sense us, so they usually go the other way. That's not saying we don't ever get dogs here. It's just not very often. Cats, on the other hand, well, they just want to put us in our place."

"Yeah, you gotta love the temperamental furballs." She laughed.

It was odd hearing Dr. Stevens speak so openly about wolves. Sure she discussed it with her dad and Sonya, but Dr. Stevens? It was just weird. Jesse smiled as she closed the door behind her. She was excited to get home and tell her grandmother about her job, plus, the extra money would come in handy for the store. She walked down the sidewalk as the sun beamed hot, typical weather for an August afternoon. Mindlessly rubbing her hand to relieve the itch, she could feel the sting beneath her skin. She lifted her hand to the sunlight, but the only sign of the scuffle was a faint bruise the size of a pencil eraser. *Stupid dog.*

"Are you ready?" Megan asked.

Jesse squealed and ran over to the car and threw open the door. Slipping into the passenger seat, "I can't believe we're actually doing this." She closed the door as a blast of mutual excitement surged between them and Megan pulled away from the curb. After everything they had been through, it was the perfect ending to an almost perfect day.

# Acknowledgements

To my family: Thanks for listening to my incessant droning over the past four years.

Thank you, Teri at editingfairy.com. I look forward to working with you again.

To my beta readers: The diva girls, D. Herzog and J. Kulhanek. Thank you for reading my first draft and still encouraging me to go forward. And my first reader, C. Leslie, thanks for kick-starting my flat-lined brain.

But more importantly, I want to thank you, the reader, for reading my first novel.

# About the Author

B. S. Todd lives in a small western Kentucky town with her husband, son, two dogs and a ferocious feline. A nature enthusiast, she has always drawn her greatest inspiration from the natural world around her. Her hobbies include reading, writing, and on certain nights throughout the calendar year, she can be found watching meteor showers or lunar eclipses conveniently from her backyard.

Facebook: B. S. Todd
Keep an eye out for Paisley Wolf, the next installment in the Cloverly Wolf Series.